COMPLETELY SATISFIED

A NOVEL

DANETTE MARONEY – DAVOREN

ENVISAGE PUBLISHING

QUEENS, NEW YORK

ATLANTA, GEORGIA

Envisage Publishing
Copyright© 2002, 2012 Danette Maroney

First printing 2003

Second printing 2010

ISBN 978-0-9729042-0-9

Editing: Chandra Sparks-Taylor

ATTENTION CORPORATIONS, UNIVERSITIES, COLLEGES, AND PROFESSIONAL ORGANIZATIONS: Quantity discounts are available on bulk purchases of this book. For information, please contact ENVISAGE Publishing, (678) 362-4158 or envisagepub1@gmail.com.

Danette Maroney

Acknowledgements

First and foremost, I would like to thank the man that first breathe the breath of word into my lungs and then gave me the vision of story, my lord and savior, Jesus Christ.

My son, Rahsaun, the love of my life - thank you for blessing me with your love and light. Your youthful joy brightens my darkest days and keeps me on my toes.

Grandmothers - Barbara and Carmen who took the time to teach me the ways of the world and help me to develop the skin, my armor, to make it through.

My mother and stepfather for accepting any and everything I choose to do and being there for support and encouragement.

My father for being my best friend and confidant and his wife, Bettie (welcome to the family).

Aunt Eleanore, wow! What do I say about the woman who says everything? You always knew what to say and when to say it. I needed that. (Princess)

My brothers and sister, Bobby, Monique and Eddie – I love you.

Jasmine, Jason, Minevia, Michael and the rest of the cousin clan (Brundage, Rivera, Maroney, Rivera – you know!) – For all the laughs we shared and will continue to have.

Robert and Norene Davoren, my in-laws, thanks for believing in me.

Amber, Janessa, Leteria and Aunt Lillian – thanks for accepting me into your home and your family.

Tammy and Hartley Baker – congratulations and many blessings.

Completely Satisfied

To my brother and sisters-in-law, Brandon, Brittany, Elizabeth, Ebony – nieces, Aqueya & Aquasia – little cousins, Sabrina and Chris – love you much. Mwah!!

Bernadette H. – thanks for always having my back. Love You.

Andrea Martin – my friend and favorite song writer. (Girl, you helped me through this) My extended family – 155 Wortman Avenue, East New York – thanks for growing with me. (Kiki, Kareemah, Stephanie, Shemeka and the crew.)

My peoples in D.O.C – Tomiko, Rebecca D., Samantha, Sonnett, Deborah, Keesha, Shynelle, Eddie M., Sam, Mike, Tyrone and the list goes on. Chandra Sparks-Taylor, my editor. Lydell Jackson, my cover designer and good friend. Barrie Dail Photography, Vincent Tyler (Rose Petal Publishing), Blessings the Poet (Minds Evolving Publishing), Deborah Maisonet (Webfully Yours), Gloria Mallette and Hope Clark – thank you for helping me and guiding me on the literary path.

If I missed your name, please don't be upset. There are just so many of you. I love you all. Thanks. MWAHH!

Danette Maroney

This book is dedicated to my uncle Jose' Antonio Rivera.

Although you were not here physically to witness my accomplishments, I know you were with me every step of the way.

Completely Satisfied

Quinton

Imani wiped away the tears that had begun to flow down her cheeks. She always looked her best but something was different. Her radiant smile and cinnamon complexion enhanced her glow. The dress complemented her supple curves, and her breasts presented themselves atop the plunging neckline, giving just enough to notice, but not enough to be tasteless. Perfect . . . The stars shone brightly; soft and gentle breezes blew mixing the sweet scents of perfumes and flowers. Smooth sounds from the shores played a relaxing song as I contemplated what was about to happen. The sidewalks were filled with people waiting for that precise moment . . . Where could she be?

Imani

The day turned to night as we continued to absorb the island's delights. The kids played and played until they were too exhausted to move. I watched Quinton as he moved about the room. He wore tan Ralph Lauren slacks with a matching black Ralph Lauren short-sleeved shirt; a simple selection but he made it look rich as he dressed it with his favorite Rolex and Ferragamos. The silklike material clung to his body and displayed subtle hints of muscle. He looked sexy in almost anything but I saw him in another light. Still, I couldn't shake this feeling. Something was not right. I struggled to gather my emotions as pictures of my life passed by. Then visions of Quinton flooded my thoughts. I thought the many trials and tribulations we had to endure . . . Was this really the end?

Completely Satisfied

"Throughout life's highways and byways, you're never ready for the unexpected…"

- Michelle 'Nana' Wright

CHAPTER 1
REMINISCE

Imani

"Please, don't leave me, Nana," I cried to my dying grandmother as she lay sick in her bed.

Her gray, wrinkled hands held tightly to mine while I cried out. As I lay my head on her bed, she placed a gentle hand on my shoulder. It was her wish not to be admitted to the hospital. She wanted her final days to be at home with us, her family.

"Chile, listen. I ain't going nowhere. Everything's going to be fine. Now hush and give Nana sugar."

I gave her the kiss she wanted. In my heart, I knew this was the last time I would ever hear her loving voice. The morning came and she was gone. I knew Nana was going to die; I just wished it wouldn't have been so soon. She had been fighting with breast cancer for several years. My siblings and I were surprised she made it as long as she did. I just wasn't ready. None of us were. She was all we had.

Growing up on the rough side of Brooklyn with three brothers and one sister, I thought we'd been through it all. We struggled every day to survive, barely making ends meet, until our grandmother took us into her home. Mama Wright, which was what the neighborhood kids called her, but we called her Nana. Nana, Michelle Wright, was Nadine's biological mother. She tried hard to keep us together after Nadine or should I say Mom disappeared and Daddy died. Nana told us our mother went to get help for herself and would be back so we could be a family again. That never happened. Nadine continued to chase the pipe and Nana kept us as her own.

Nana made my siblings and me promise to always be there for one another. She always said, "Family is all you have."

The promise never made it past Nana's death.

I was only twelve when Nana died and I was placed in the custody of my oldest brother, John. My grandmother took care of me all twelve years of my life; Nadine left as soon as I was born. I was lost without Nana. My father had died five years earlier leaving Nana to care for my other siblings, John, Justin and the twins, Jada and Jordan. Not once did my mother call or show her face—if she did, I didn't know. I never saw her.

Everyone said I resembled my father, mainly because of my reddish-
brown hair. The others had wavy brunette hair; Jada's being the darkest. We all were slim and fairly tall, something else people say we inherited from Daddy. John and I were the darkest two of the five kids, sharing the same creamy caramel complexion as Nana. Jada and Jordan had this mellow yellow complexion and Justin was just in between—not too light but a shade from tan. I couldn't tell you who looked like Nadine; like I said, I don't know what she looked like.

Being that John was oldest of the crew, everyone felt it was best for me to stay with him. Jordan and Jada were off to college and couldn't raise me with their part-time college jobs—they barely could raise themselves. John would have to send money for either books or food, and it was beginning to put a strain on his household. He was barely making enough to keep food on our table. If it wasn't for my monthly Social Security check, we might have been hungry plenty of nights. I don't think anybody really cared to be bothered. I was a preteen on the brink of puberty, which meant rebellion, tantrums, and trouble to many. Didn't matter much where I lived because I had no intention on staying there long. In six years, I'd be an independent woman, and I planned to go away and leave this life behind. Start all over.

John was twenty-five with a wife and two boys of his own. He took me in although he didn't have room for another mouth. He and his wife, Mia, lived in a small two-bedroom in the Bedford Stuyvesant—better known as Bed-Stuy—section of Brooklyn. Mia tried hard to make the best of their limited space. She bought an aluminum rack to hang my clothes and a couple of plastic containers for my underwear and socks. Can you imagine living out of boxes and bags for as long as I did?

The apartment was packed from wall to wall with stuff they had accumulated over the years—nothing bearing any sentimental value, just junk they thought might come in handy in the near future. I couldn't imagine how useful an old eight-track player could be or how handy a broken Hoover might become. The walls were painted an ugly peachy color throughout the entire apartment since the projects only supplied that or a dull hospital white. There were little cracks in the ceilings along the corners caused by leaks from the neighbor's. When John and Mia finally moved, I was in high school. It seemed liked forever before I got my own room. Three years, too long.

At the time, John had two sons. Matthew was nine and Steve had just turned seven. Me, being a girl, made it harder on my brother. All the little things a girl my age needed such as sanitary napkins, deodorant, and bras threw John for a loop. He wasn't mentally prepared for what it took to raise a young woman. The clothes I owned were hand-me-downs from Jada. The pullout bed that was set in the living room for me to sleep on wasn't fit for a guest. And for Christmas, John would buy me things like oversized jeans and hooded sweaters. John and Mia tried hard to include me as one of their own but I didn't want their sympathy.

Not too long after, Justin, my other brother ran off with some drug addicts, just like his mama. No one has heard from or seen him. At times, I heard John and Mia talk about how bad Justin looked before he left, and they wondered if he was still alive. Justin was on a warpath. That was his way of venting about the whole Nadine thing. I didn't think about Nadine and her nonsense much. Jordan and Jada, the twins, were eighteen when Nana died and were free to do what they pleased. They moved to Maryland where they attended Coppin State College. Years passed before I heard from them again. Jada called to let us know she was engaged but that was about it. John stayed in contact with them. Jada and Jordan never cared to visit me or just call and say hi. They just faded out. So, as far as I was concerned, they were better off forgotten.

Years passed and I grew distant. Mia tried to talk to me about things young women growing up should know, but it was nothing like a mother- daughter talk. All I wanted to know was where I could find my mother. I had questions of my own that needed answers. I wondered how could a mother leave her daughter to raise herself? Did she even remember she had a family? Was I the reason she left? I had heard so many different stories as to why she just up and left, but none made any sense to me.

In school, I would isolate myself. Making friends was not on my agenda, which wasn't so hard since no one noticed me anyway. I had nappy hair; big, thick glasses; and dressed like a boy. But I knew I was going to change. I had to. There was no way I was going to start high school like the ugly duckling. Besides, high school was like a fashion show. To be among the best, you had to dress the part. Everybody had the latest name-brand sneakers and clothes. I was still rocking a pair of British Knights that Nana had bought me three years before. Mia and John couldn't afford to buy us those new Air Max or those Girbaud and Guess jeans that everybody else was wearing, so I decided to find a job.

By the age of fifteen, I began to make my grand transformation. I received my working papers that year and got a little after-school job at the supermarket. When I cashed my first paycheck, I asked Mia to take me to downtown Brooklyn to shop. We bought a little of everything—summer dresses with shoes to match, jeans, shirts and a jean jacket. You'd be amazed what you could get from a ten-dollar store. Just when Mia thought we were done, I rushed into a jewelry store. There was no way I was leaving Fulton Street without a pair of bangle earrings. Mia chipped in a little since I couldn't afford all that yet. Finally, we went for manicures and pedicures and when we got home, Mia relaxed and styled my hair.

Before I went to bed, I laid out one of my new outfits for the next day and the new me.

September of 1990, I, Imani Wright, started my sophomore year at Irving High School in Manhattan. The building was eleven stories

13

high and had forty-plus classrooms per floor. Needless to say, I was scared to death. So many new faces, a borough with what I wasn't familiar, and a new appearance was reason enough, but to top it off, handsome men of all shapes and shades surrounded me. As the day progressed, things started looking up. I couldn't believe how many friends I had made.

By second period, I made several acquaintances, mostly boys. (Probably had to do with the fact that every time I climbed the stairs they got a sneak peek.) The first person I met was Rahsaun Tyler, a cutie. He had a smooth honey complexion with sexy grayish green eyes from his Native American background. I couldn't begin to tell you what drew me to him more, his looks or his personality. Rahsaun was a gentleman with a sense of humor, two things Mia had told me to look for in a man. Rahsaun and I had most of the same classes together so we talked a lot. He tried to tell me who to look out for and who not to associate with. Even though he was just a freshman he knew about most of the guys because they grew up in the same neighborhood, Brownsville.

There was a name that he mentioned on the list of "no-nos" that I already had my sights set on. Quinton Banks. Quinton, better known to the ladies as "Q" or the "ladies' man", was the cutest brother in not only the sophomore class but the entire school. He was six feet two inches dipped in chocolate—not too dark, just enough to make your mouth water. He was fine and I wanted him, but so did all the girls. Every time I passed him, my stomach would drop. I never thought I had a chance.

Rahsaun would meet me on the Utica Avenue platform where we would catch the 4 train to Fourteenth Street—Union Square, two blocks from our school. Every morning I would ask a ton of questions. Today was no different.

"Rahsaun, are you jealous of Quinton?" I asked as I checked my lip-gloss in the mini compact mirror inside my wallet.

"Mani, please. I look way better than Q. I get just as much play as he does or maybe more," Rahsaun replied, sucking his teeth.

Rahsaun was a major player too. If the girls weren't talking about Q, they were talking about Rahsaun. He also knew his way with the ladies.

"So, what's the problem? You'd rather hook me up with your ugly-ass friend George and be the talk of the school."

Why not try to hook me up with Q? I thought. I stopped walking and placed my hand on my hip.

Rahsaun turned around, grabbed my hand, and pulled me, causing me to stumble forward.

"Don't talk about my boy George like that. He's mad nice and treats all his women with respect unlike your boo, Q," Rahsaun whispered as we entered the school.

George Mack was sitting in the first seat by the door, grinning like nobody's business. I paused and composed a fake smile. George gave Rahsaun five, and we went to our seats in the back of the classroom.

"He ain't my boo yet. Plus, who have you ever seen him diss?" I asked.

"Didn't he spit in Stacy's face yesterday or did you miss that?" Rahsaun whispered as Ms. Vasquez began her class.

"She probably deserved it. She ain't no good for him anyways. All she do is sleep around."

"Is this conversation something you might like to share with the rest of the class, Miss Wright?" Ms. Vasquez said, obviously annoyed with our private conversation.

"No, Ms. Vasquez. Sorry 'bout that," I said, giving Rahsaun the evil eye as he laughed at me.

As soon as she turned her back to continue her lesson, we picked up our conversation.

"See what you did, asshole? Then you gonna laugh about it right? Stupid! " I was upset. Why was I the only one being scolded?

"You're an ass, Imani. Don't ever say no stupid shit like that around me again," he said as he mocked me. "She probably deserved it." Then he blew out an exasperated breath. Rahsaun was obviously tired of me defending Quinton.

I didn't pay Rahsaun any attention. I still wanted Quinton. Q was right!

Quinton

"Ma, get off my back! You wasn't worrying about me then, don't start now. I'm damn near a grown-ass man," I said, storming through the apartment.

"Quinton, as long as you're in my house, I'm going to watch over your every move. I'll worry about you until you're old enough to take care of yourself. Then you can get the hell out of my house," my mother shot back.

For the past seven years, I had been taking care of myself. But, since I had a little money, my mother wanted to be a mother. She wasn't there for me when I needed her, so why start?

My father was my mentor—or so I thought. He was the one who taught me all the things to say and ways to treat a lady, things he said I would need to get by in life. "Always tell her how nice she looks. Treat her with respect. Remember a lady always deserves the best," and the good ole, "A real man never hits a woman." Too bad. He wasn't a man of his word.

My mother and father fought from sunrise till sunset. Every day my mother wore a new black eye. At first, I thought she deserved it because Mama had a way of getting on your last nerve. She always seemed to want to argue when you were already upset. But as I got older, the more I realized that my father was nothing more than a liar, cheater, deceiver, heartbreaker . . . shall I continue? He had a different woman with every passing wind. And he didn't hide his affairs. All he did was wake up, eat, and sleep in our house. I can't remember ever having a father-son day. He would delegate a couple of rules, pat me on the head, hit my mother, and was back out the door. But my mother stood strong. She never shed a tear in front of me.

I guess things began to be too much for my mother so she took to the bottle as a refuge. She would drink herself into comas.

16

Sometimes she wouldn't come home because she was drunk and stayed over at a friend's house. She didn't care about the house or anything in it—and that included me. In the mornings, I had to make my own breakfast and make sure I got to school on time. Most nights for dinner, I ate peanut butter sandwiches and chips that I bought on my way home from school.

Being that my mother and father were never home, I had to start fending for myself. Quinton Banks would never have to want for anything, ever! That was the promise I made to myself and was determined to keep. There weren't any jobs available for a twelve-year-old so I sold drugs. I was making money hand over fist. I always had the latest sneakers and clothes. And did I have girls. On some of them, I flashed some cash. The others I used for what they could give me. Sex, sex and more sex!

In high school, I was instantly popular among the ladies. They saw me and saw dollar signs. Didn't bother me though because I made sure I was getting what I paid for—in the bathroom, back staircases, empty classrooms . . . you know what I'm saying? My mother was disgusted with the man I had become. Ultimately, she threw my father out and tried to make our house a home, but she never gave up on her favorite men, Johnnie Walker and Jack Daniels. Since she wasn't willing to change, neither was I. I continued doing the things I was doing. Money and women became my main focus—my only focus.

During my junior year of high school, I began to slow down. The fast life wasn't going for me. Besides, I was becoming old news. Freshmen were coming in holding more weight than my fellow classmen. By this point, I had been dating only one girl, Stacy, seriously for about six months. It wasn't that I couldn't get as many girls as I wanted; I only wanted Stacy who was a year younger than me. She made me happy and kept me cool when my home front got shitty. Stacy and I were slowly developing a teenage love. Finally, I thought I found somebody who wanted me for me—until my boy, Rodney showed me different.

I walked in the lunchroom, still in my basketball warm-up suit from practice. The jersey hung loosely over my semi-broad chest while my premature muscles glistened with moisture. Normally, I would have changed before the next class but I had planned to leave early. Stacy and I were going to Coney Island.

All eyes were on me as soon as I stepped foot through the door. Most of the fellas turned back when they realized it was just me but not the girls. Their eyes fixed on my chocolate skin and as one girl called them, my kissable lips. Some waved while the others just watched. I took my towel off my head and ran my hands over my clean Caesar haircut. After looking around for a couple of seconds, I walked over to Rodney.

"What's up, Q? Mr. Casanova," Rodney said as I walked into what he called his territory, which wasn't nothing more than a spot in the corner.

"Nuthin' much. What you up to?" I wasn't really interested in what he had to say. I spoke without looking into his face, too busy looking for Stacy.

"Chillin', waitin' for class to begin. Lookin' for your girl?" His tone was devious. Either he had something up his sleeve or knew something I didn't.

"Yeah, you seen her?" I asked.

"Yep," he replied with a smack of his lips. I waited for an answer but that was all he volunteered.

"Where she at?" It felt like I was pulling teeth, but I knew why he didn't want to answer me. Rodney never really liked Stacy. Probably because she dissed him back when he was trying to get with her.

Rodney didn't get too much attention from the girls. He was rude and his looks were off but he was my boy. At the time, Rodney was trying to grow in his hair so he could get dreads but he never combed it so either it was matted or just extremely nappy. He had the clothes and the money but didn't know how to step to a girl. Rodney would say stupid shit like, "Yo, ho, can I talk to you for a second. What's up wit' me hittin' that?" and then grab her ass. I never said

18

much because it sent the girls right into my direction—right into my bed.

"Q, man, leave that ho alone. There are too many shorties in here tryin' to get wit' you for you to mess with that triflin' skank. Look at shorty over there," he said, pointing to this fair-skinned chic who was steadily staring in our direction.

"I don't know what her problem is. She be staring at me in our English class too. Some girls turn away when you make eye contact with them but not her. It's like she's a premature stalker or something," I said, chuckling.

"You stupid, Q. Yo, on the real though, your girl Stacy ain't actin' right. You need to let that whore loose," Rodney said, clapping out each syllable.

"I heard some shit the other day. But you know how these girls are

with their rumors and their jealousy, trying to break us up, so I just dismissed it," I said, still looking around the cafeteria.

"Well, don't dismiss it all yet," he said as he rose from his seat. "Q, walk with me to Ms. West's class."

"For what? Didn't you have that class last period?"

"Come on, man. I want to pick up something I left in my locker then go smoke a cigarette."

"A'ight."

I got my gym bag off the floor, put it over my shoulder and followed Rodney out of the cafeteria. We bumped into a couple of our boys from around the way and talked for a quick minute. Most of them were on their way to a cut party in the Bronx on Kelly Street. I would have left, too, but I was still looking for Stacy. After we broke up the crowd, we continued walking to Ms. West's room.

We picked up Rodney's stash from one of his lockers and walked to the boys' bathroom on the west wing. That was where all the guys went for a smoke or brought a girl they wanted to bone. Inside the bathroom, guys and girls stood around talking and smoking like we were at a social club instead of school. Rodney and I squeezed through the crowd trying to find a less crowded spot. Upon reaching an empty corner, moans of pleasure came from a nearby stall. Normally, I wouldn't have paid it any attention but the sound was familiar. Filled with anger and disgust, I kicked in the door to find Stacy bent over the toilet. Some freshman brother continued hitting it from the back as I stood and watched.

"Ain't this some shit? I've been looking for your ass all day. And here it is."

Stacy jumped at the sound of my voice almost taking homeboy's genitals with her. I gave the young boy a pat on the back as I grabbed Stacy by her hair. I wanted to bash her face against the dirty tiled walls. I imagined slapping the teeth out of her mouth. She squirmed trying to get loose but it was useless.

"Let me go, Q. I'm sorry. It didn't mean anything. You know I love you. Please let me go," Stacy cried. Her plea didn't affect me at all. I dragged her half-naked body out of the stall to the middle of the floor.

"Fuck you. You don't love me. You tried to hurt me, you scandalous ho. But I was a step ahead of you. I got a girl. You meant nothing more than sex to me and obviously everybody else." I was lying. I didn't have a girl but I needed to redeem myself in front of all those people.

"Q, I'll make it up to you. Let me suck your dick right here in front of everybody. If I didn't love you, I wouldn't be trying so hard to get back with you," she whined.

How could I refuse an offer like that? I let her loose, and she immediately went down on her knees—right there in front of everybody. Guys cheered her on as she bobbed back and forth. All the girls either left or turned away. But it didn't bother me. It wasn't going to be long before I finished. It felt too good. When she came up off the floor she asked, "So, you forgive me? You still love me?"

"Hell no! But I do want to thank you, and here—" I reached in my pocket and drew out ten dollars—"you deserve it."

Rodney was bent over laughing. In some ways, I felt bad for Stacy. She stood against the graffiti covered wall for several seconds after I walked away with her hands over her face. I quickly got over my sorrow when Tya, my homegirl from around the way, came over and grabbed my hand.

"Damn, Q. Was it that serious?" she asked, watching Stacy as she walked past us to exit the bathroom.

"You know how I do. What's up with you? I was beginning to miss you." I was amazed at how Tya's sixteen-year-old body filled out the shiny black cat suit she was wearing with a short jean jacket. Her golden- streaked hair highlighted her smooth tanned skin. I had a Jones for Tya but she had a man.

"Well, I was mad sick last month. My sister didn't tell you." The strawberry scent of her candy filled my nostrils as she spoke.

"Nah, I haven't been home to see her."

"Yeah, I was also trying to get over that fool Keith. He gon' break up with me on my birthday because he couldn't afford to buy me anything."

"That's messed up." Yes… No more Keith meant space for me to slide up in there.

"So, what's up? Let me make it up to you for him. We can do whatever you want to do," I said, ignoring the silly faces Rodney was making behind her back. He was trying to spell out gold digger but I already knew this. Tya was no different than any of the other girls we knew except she was more of a challenge. I had been trying to get with her since junior high.

"Whatever, Q. Call me when you get home so I can come through," she said as she pushed her finger into my forehead. She turned to walk out and caught Rodney making faces. Rodney and I laughed for a few seconds and then walked out behind her.

"Q, I'm beginning to think you like being used. You and I both know Tya ain't going to give you no booty. All you can do for her is buy her a new pair of Reeboks, some bangle earrings and be on your way. Get her all dipped for her next man." Rodney was a hater. Nobody was good enough for me if they didn't give him any play first. If he thought there was a chance in hell for him to get with Tya, he'd be there with gasoline drawers on.

"She ain't like that. Tya got her own dough. When her moms passed away, she and her sister had fifty G's to split between them. I'm trying to get her to trick on me. You know what I'm sayin'?"

We continued bouncing down the stairs when the bell rang. Rahsaun Tyler and his psycho stalker friend came walking up the stairs. I backed up against the wall giving them enough space to pass because the last time I could swear she tried to cop a feel. She eyed me all the way up the stairs; not paying attention to what was in front of her, until she tripped on the last step. Rodney burst out laughing as she collected her books and ran up the stairs. I tried to hide my smile with my hand as I watched her scurry away. As soon as I thought she was out of ear range, I bent over in tears from stifling my laughter.

CHAPTER 2
TEENAGE LOVE

Imani

"Rahsaun, how many times do I have to tell you? I am not sprung for Q," I tried to explain to my best friend. But he had been my friend for so long that he knew when I was lying.

"You'll see what I'm sayin'. Your head is too damn hard. Leave him alone! I understand you're looking for love but you're barking up the wrong tree," Rahsaun said. "You done embarrassed yourself enough already."

Of course I didn't listen. With each passing day, I tried harder and harder to get Quinton to notice me.

Sophomore and junior year had passed. I had one or two boyfriends, but I still wanted Q who was held back a year due to his poor attendance. I still had one more year to try to get with him. We took the same classes but still he never looked my way. Rahsaun grew jealous of my crush and occasionally stopped speaking to me but not more than two days would pass before he was chasing me down to tell me the latest gossip and sneak a kiss in here and there.

Although Rahsaun and I were the best of friends, it did stop us from testing the strength of our friendship as we made several attempts to become intimate. Neither one of us was experienced at the sex game but that did not stop us from experimenting. We had had plenty of narrow escapes but we never got too far. Either his mother would come home early or I was on punishment for not doing my chores. It was best that we didn't get involved. I couldn't deal with his insecurity. Rahsaun always thought someone was out to hurt him.

With each semester, Quinton grew more gorgeous and more popular. Every day he wore a new girl on his arm. At times, I found myself trying to wear my hair or talk like the girls he found interest in, hoping this would catch his attention, but it didn't. It was almost as if he was purposely avoiding me.

By May 1993, we were rehearsing for the annual Fashion/Talent Showcase. My body began to blossom. The sunlight caused my hair to turn a copper-like shade, which complemented my sun-kissed complexion and brown eyes. The weather became hotter and my clothes became shorter. My brother John was pissed, said I was dressing like a whore and guys wouldn't respect me. I didn't care much about what John thought. After all, he wasn't my father.

While in the auditorium practicing the march, Q and his ex-girlfriend were having an argument. I tried to read their lips but I wasn't so good at it. All I knew was Stacy had cheated on Quinton with this fine light- skinned brother from the basketball team a couple of years back and she had been begging for Q's forgiveness since. He shouldn't have been mad since the word was all over the school anyway. I found out Stacy was playing him through hallway gossip a week before he caught her in the bathroom. He chose to play stupid and in turned he got played.

See, when you were dating someone with status like Q, everybody was watching your every move. Every girl in the school was seeking the opportunity of advancement. Stacy thought she had Q wrapped around her finger. I had to admit, she did. Q would jump at her every word and that was highly unlike him. It must have been the nookie.

For a moment, Q glanced around until he noticed me staring his way. I shyly looked away trying not to make eye contact. After years of getting shot down, I was losing my bold edge. Soon, he began to walk in my direction. As he walked, the sunlight from the small windows of the auditorium shone on his baldhead giving him a heavenly glow. When he stopped right in front of me, licking those big sexy lips, I began to feel heat rising from my privacy. He looked so good! Quinton finally sat next to me. I didn't know whether to feel insulted or honored. I mean he did choose me on the rebound but, on the other hand, out of all the girls in the auditorium, he chose me. It took a while before I realized that Q was really sitting next to me. I thought I was Miss Thang.

"Hey, I noticed you were looking my way. Did you see something you liked?"

"I don't know. You came to me. Do you like what you see?"

Normally, I would play the shy type but not then. Not with Quinton. Thorough research had proven that he liked a woman who spoke her mind. She must also have something to say. He couldn't respect a girl who had no brain. He liked a woman who knew what to say and how to say it. I should know. I had been taking notes.

"Definitely! Anyways, what's your name? I've seen you around but never really caught your name."

"That's probably because you never really cared," I replied as I rolled my eyes.

"Oh man, don't be so cold. Give a brother a break. Look, let's start over." He stuck out his hand as he introduced himself. "My name is Quinton . . . Banks. And you are?"

"Imani Wright," I said as I shook his hand.

Seconds later words just began to flow. We were talking like old friends. He wasn't as stuck up as I thought. We discovered we had a lot in common. We liked the same movies, read the same books and shared the same background. Our fathers were of Hispanic descent while our mothers were African-American. He told me how his father hadn't been around for most of his life and although he lived with his mother, she wasn't there either. He said that since his father disappeared his mother never paid him much attention. My heart instantly went out to him because I, too, knew that pain.

No matter how much I tried to push my mother, Nadine, to the back of my mind, little things kept her around. Everything that had ever happened to me, I blamed solely on her. I wondered if she ever loved me. Did she know how much I had wanted to see her again? If I saw her again, what would I say? I just wanted closure. Maybe I hoped to form that bond, that special bond with Quinton and replace the hole Nadine left.

Quinton

Imani was different from all the other girls I had dated and after years of avoiding her I figured it was time to get to know the girl who stalked me for four years. At first, I really didn't care to know her because I thought she was dating Rahsaun. But then, when I found out they were just friends I began to look at her differently. And after all the bullshit I'd been through with these girls, Imani was definitely an invited change. She was smart and innocently pretty. She had a baby face and her shy yet sexy ways made her even more attractive. She knew how to position her body, cross her legs—everything was smooth and sensual, like a lady should be. To top it all, she was actually interested in knowing about me. She listened as I told her things from my childhood I had never told anyone. No one else ever cared to ask. She knew what it felt like to need someone.

I really didn't have a female in my life who wanted me for me, only what I had to offer. My mother never had the time of day for me. She shunned me the moment my father walked out of the door. He never thought twice about us. For the first couple of years I would ask about him and if he would come home, but by my thirteenth birthday, I had stopped wondering and never spoke of him again.

Imani told me about her life, coming up without her mother and all. Knowing that we could relate to each other made talking to her a whole lot easier. At first when I sat beside her I had no intentions of going out, being intimate. The girlfriend thing had never entered my mind until she leaned on her elbow, placing her hand on her face. She was too cute to let slip away. Plus her body was . . . she was gorgeous.

She played with the bangle bracelets she wore on her left arm as we talked and talked and talked.

"Do you have any brothers or sisters?" she asked, continuing to smile. "None that I know about. I haven't heard from my father in almost four years. Who knows what he's been doing?"

"Lucky you. I have three brothers and one sister. And, I don't like any of them. My brother thinks he's my father and his wife tries to be my mother." Suddenly her smile faded for the first time since I sat beside her.

"Aww, don't be like that, shorty. You know he's only trying to take care of you. He knows he ain't your father. It's his job to be protective of you."

26

"Try overprotective. I can't do nothing. He won't let me go to the store on my own, won't let me hang out. That's why I don't have any friends. I'm too embarrassed," she said as she giggled.

"It's cool though. At least you ain't giving it up all over the place like these other girls," I said as I glanced over at Stacy.

"Guess so," Imani answered coyly. She began to fidget in her seat. I hoped I wasn't making her uncomfortable. The more she moved, the more her skirt rose. I continued watching, waiting to see how far it would go. She noticed me looking and went to pull down her skirt but I caught her hand.

Her eyes bugged out of her head as she snatched her hand from beneath mine. It was best that she did because I don't know how much longer I was going to be able to contain myself. I felt the bulge building up in my pants, and it was becoming hard to hide. I put my book bag on my lap and continued our conversation. I was genuinely interested in getting to know more about her.

Imani

Our conversation changed from the regular chitchat to intimate flirting. Quinton began talking about sex and all the things he would do to me, given the opportunity. Obviously, sex was always on his mind. Only if he knew how badly I wanted him too. Q held my hand between his and began to massage . . . softly. He complimented my pretty smile and my new GAP top with the low neckline that allowed a sneak peek at my newly formed cleavage.

He and I shared a brief moment of laughter. We didn't say anything funny; we just felt like laughing. Before long, Stacy had caught wind of what was going on and began storming to our end of the auditorium. Just at that precise moment he leaned over and kissed me . . . gently. I was shocked and completely caught off guard. What startled me most was that it didn't feel awkward. It felt like it was meant to be. I guess my kissing sessions with Rahsaun paid off.

After Stacy walked passed and called me a bitch, Q and I returned to our conversation like nothing had happened. But I made a mental note to check Stacy on her comment. Out of curiosity, I decided to ask Q where he lived. His reply was cynical as he said, "I can't tell you. You have to come and find out."

That wasn't a problem; it would be my pleasure.

For the rest of the week, Quinton and I shared dreams of our futures and whatever else came to mind over chocolate milks in the cafeteria. We made plans to go out that weekend so that we could spend more than a lunch hour together. Quinton suggested that we meet at Broadway Junction and from there we would go to the movies and maybe grab something to eat. The only problem was my brother John. He was not as cool as Mia when it came to dating. The only male friend he allowed me to have was Rahsaun. Even when Rahsaun and I wanted to hang out I had to drag along one of my nephews. So how was I going to go? A million lies ran through my head. By Saturday, I should come up with something good, I thought.

Q waited for me after school every day so that we could ride home together. Rahsaun had moved to Queens and transferred schools so Q picked up in his place but my mornings were still lonely. Q lived in Brooklyn, not too far from where my family had recently moved to in East New York. He would hold my hand all the way there on the train. I wasn't one for the public affection but I didn't make a fuss as he kissed my neck and held me close when we stood on the bus. Broadway Junction seemed to come too quick. Quinton would continue on the L train while I transferred for a bus. As soon as I got home, with the exception of the days I had laundry I sped to my room and breezed through my homework so I could call Quinton and talk until I went to bed.

The weekend didn't quite work out for us. John and Mia decided that we were going to take a family trip to Maryland to visit Jada and Jordan. As upset as I was to have to give up my date with Quinton, I was excited to visit my sister and brother. Over the past couple of months I'd been developing a phone relationship with Jada and realized I really missed her.

I guess growing up took away a lot of the pain and anger we had toward each other, which should have been directed toward Nadine.

Quinton and I made alternative plans to hang out at his place for a while after school. I figured it was cool since he didn't live too far and I wouldn't get home too late. Quinton was waiting under the tree in front of the school, our regular meeting spot. When I approached him, he placed his arm around my shoulder and kissed my cheek.

"Ready to go, shorty?" he asked.

Briefly, I wondered if I was doing the right thing. I mean I waited four long years for this and I didn't want to cheapen it by giving up the booty so fast but my feelings immediately changed when I saw Stacy staring in our direction. She was waiting for the opportunity but I was going to give her the pleasure.

"Yeah, boo. I'm ready," I replied and walked off with a big smile.

When we finally reached his building, I began to feel nervous. Everyone outside was staring at me. The old women on the bench whispered to their hen friends as Q and I walked by holding hands. He led me to the elevator then quickly changed his mind and started up the stairs. Q stopped between the second and third floor and pinned me against the gray concrete wall. He licked up and down my neck and began kissing and caressing my 34Bs as I read the names of lovers written on the walls. The names Blacky and Sweetz were encased in a lopsided heart with an arrow drawn through it. In my mind I replaced the names with Mani and Quinton and giggled at my own silliness.

After about two minutes, I began to feel Q's nature rise. He unzipped his pants and put my hand inside of his boxers. At first, I only played in his pubic hair, not exactly sure of what I was supposed to be doing. Then, he guided my hand down until I finally reached the head. I began to massage him, amazed at how long it was. How is all that supposed to fit in me? I wondered. It was thick too. My fingertips briefly brushed the opening of his head, discovering a sticky substance. Immediately, he pulled me up the stairs and into his apartment.

I stood in the living room while he ran to the back.

The mint-colored walls were covered with pictures of Q. Trophies, medals and awards flooded the wall unit across from the pictures. It was like a shrine. Quinton took pride in all of his accomplishments and put them on display to show his mother what he had done without her. The sofa and love seat were still covered with plastic. The apartment was spotless. Directly across from the living room was the kitchen. The walls were painted white with mint-green borders. Pictures of fruits and flowers hung in wood frames. I was not sure if they were paintings or photos. But I was sure one thing—they were ugly.

Quinton

When I took Imani inside, I was nervous. I didn't want to mess up whatever we had going. No girl had ever made me feel comfortable and appreciated. I would take them to a friend's house or an empty hallway but never to my own crib. I felt like I needed to somehow impress Imani. I didn't want to disgust her in any way. I darted into my room and began to shove clothes under my bed in an effort to straighten up. I lit baby powder incense that I had picked up the day before, turned on the radio and unbuttoned my shirt.

Finally, the mood was right. I shook away my insecurities and re-entered the front area where my sexy woman was waiting.

"Do you want something to drink?" I asked, trying to be polite. "No, I'm fine," she answered.

"Do you want to go to my room and watch TV?"

"Whatever you want to do. This is your house."

Imani was a little too timid for my taste, but I could work with it. She stood in the corner of the living room with her arms folded. Her shyness began to turn me on. I walked over to her and planted several kisses along her neckline as I began to lead her to my bedroom. We stopped halfway up the hall due to my impatience. She had no idea what was going on as I lifted her and wrapped her legs around me. With my hand on her hips, I rocked her back and forth across my throbbing manhood, anxiously anticipating penetration. Her body began to shudder in delight as I fiddled around in her panties. Nearing eruption, I backed away and dragged her to the room.

Imani

Quinton took my hand and led me into the bedroom after some heated foreplay on the hallway wall. He locked the bedroom door and pulled me closer to him. Our kisses were more passionate than before. All the while I was thinking, am I really going to do this? He took off my shirt and unsnapped my bra. I wasn't ready. He took off his pants and revealed his red silk boxers. I wasn't ready. When he finally laid me on the bed placing, kisses from my lips to my navel, and using his finger to tease my kitty, I knew I wasn't ready. But I didn't stop him . . . it felt too good. Q continued to take off my clothes and stood back to admire me while I lay on his bed. I felt so embarrassed. My panties and bra didn't match, and I didn't know how to tell him I was still a virgin.

Quinton took off his final piece of clothing, and all I could do was gasp. My heart began skipping beats. His sculptured six-pack was followed by a rigid eight inches—or more—of flesh. I wanted him but not just yet. It was too soon. I wanted him to get to know me. I didn't want to disappoint him though; I was afraid he wasn't going to want me if I did.

Quinton

Imani shivered beneath me as I continued to fondle her curvaceous body. Her skin was silky smooth as I stroked her back, gently trying to make her feel comfortable. She didn't have to tell me what was already evident. This was her first time, and I was determined to make it memorable.

"Are you okay?" I asked.

"Yeah. Are you?" she replied nervously. "Do you want to stop?"

"No," she answered breathlessly.

I continued to caress her soft skin and kiss her perfect lips. Her inexperience showed as she lay stiff beneath me. I tried to slide my hand between her legs but she clenched them tightly closed.

"Imani, am I making you uncomfortable?" I asked, again confused by her actions.

"Unh-unh. It tickles down there. Sensitive," she said, trying to fix her hair as I parted her legs.

"Do you want me to kiss it? Make it feel better?"

She shrugged. I wasted no time going to work. I sucked and licked and tugged, making sure she was pleased. She used a pillow to muffle her groans as she wrapped her legs around my neck. She began to twist, and just as she came close to climax, I rolled my tongue on her clit, adding to her pleasure. Ultimately, she cried out in ecstasy.

Imani

As Quinton climbed on top of me, sucking on my breasts and tickling my cat, I flinched. He asked if I was uncomfortable and I was honest. I told him it was my first time and surprisingly he understood. My head was still spinning from the rush of euphoria I had experienced. At first, the thought of a guy going down had disgusted me. The thought of kissing him afterward nauseated me, but after that performance, I had to reward him with at least a peck.

Q suggested that we lie together and enjoy each other's company. I knew he wanted to finish what we had started but I was still too scared. He turned on the TV and passed me the remote control. I flipped through the channels for a little while, snug in his embrace. Within ten minutes, we were knocked out.

A loud slam woke us up about two hours later. A man, I later found out was Q's uncle, yelled to let Q know he was home. I wanted to get dressed but Q wouldn't let me. We began foreplay again but this time I was soaking wet. I was ready. Q reached out to his nightstand and picked up a condom. After I heard the sound of the tearing wrapper my heart pumped with fear. Immediately, I jumped up and sat to the far edge of the bed.

"What's wrong?" he asked.

"Q, this is just going a little too fast for me. I mean, I want to be with you and all but I'm not ready to . . . you know."

His disappointment was evident but he tried to play it off. Quinton handed me my clothes before he went to the bathroom. When he returned, I was fully dressed.

"You going home?" he asked.

I was confused. By the way he passed me my clothes, I thought he wanted me to leave.

"Do you want me to leave?" I replied.

"Nah. I can understand you weren't ready, and I ain't mad at you. You're just the first girl that ever told me no. I respect that. Just chill with me for a while. I don't want you to rush home," he said.

"Cool," I replied.

He then turned on his Nintendo and we played a couple of rounds of

Duck Hunt. After getting beat a couple of times, I was ready to go home. "So am I going to see you again?" he asked as he stroked my highlighted locks.

"I didn't think you did second dates," I answered. Honestly, I wished he didn't treat me like his other girlfriends but I didn't want to question him so early.

"Only if I really like her, and I really like you," he said as he nibbled on my earlobe.

"Are you sure or are you just saying that to make me feel better about not letting you get a piece?" I was shocked at what I said. I placed my hand over my mouth and turned back toward the screen.

"Nah, Imani. I'm really feeling you. I need a girl like you in my life," he said. I couldn't believe he hit me with one of those corny lines, but it worked.

Q called a cab to take me home. On my way out the door, he called me back.

"Imani," he paused as if he wanted to say more and placed a soft kiss on my forehead.

Is this what love feels like? I thought as I walked to the elevator.

Quinton

While Imani walked away, I caught myself wanting to tell her how I felt for her. I cared for her and wanted her to know, but I thought the relationship was still too new to show feelings. Especially since the feelings were new to me. After Imani left, I went back into my room and lay on my bed, just imagining Imani and me as a couple. Looking up at the ceiling, I imagined walking hand in hand with her, kissing in the park, going to the prom together and so many other thoughts that ran rampant through my mind. For the first time, I was whipped but not from sex. Her words, her voice, her face, everything about Imani made me want her more than any of the other girls I had been with. She made the hairs on my body stand at the thought of touching her, smelling her hair—so soft and so sweet.

My telephone rang and the images of my girl faded. Disappointed, I turned off the ringer, put my arms behind my head and tried to pick up where I left off.

I dozed off and about an hour into my nap, a loud crashing noise startled me and caused my heart to jump. I immediately walked over to my bedroom door to see what was going on. By the time I reached the hallway, my uncle was already helping my mother off the floor. Again, she managed to drag her drunken ass home. As long as we had been living in this apartment, you'd think she'd know where everything was. Nope, she always found something new to break, knock down or trip over. That day her object of choice: a shopping cart.

That had to hurt. I didn't even bother to help. Instead, I walked over her to get to the kitchen and fixed a sandwich. I was starving. She'd be all right. If not she'd be there the next day.

CHAPTER 3
TELL ME

Imani

All the way home, I nervously bit on my nails, worried about how John was going to react to me walking in the house so late at night. I knew my ass was grass if I didn't come up with a good story. See, if I had a girlfriend I could have said I was over at her house talking and had lost track of time. But, my only real friend was Rahsaun, and if I knew him like I think I do, he had called my house more than twenty times already, looking for me.

What the hell? John couldn't possible think I was with a boy. Last he knew no one even looked my way.

"Why are you just walking in the house? It's after ten o'clock. We've been looking everywhere for you," John hollered as I walked in the door.

"I was at a friend's house. We were studying for a test and . . ."

Slap. Before I was able to continue the lie I had been practicing, John had smacked me so hard I almost fell to my knees. One of those Ike the pimp smacks.

"What friend, Imani? You have friends we don't know about? Rahsaun called a couple of hours ago looking for you and that girl whose been calling you for homework left a message about five minutes ago. Now, do you have something you would like to tell me?"

John flipped. I should have known that lie wasn't going to work, especially since John knew I didn't mess with any of the girls in my school. All the arguments I got into, please. Mia would always say that those girls were jealous of my beauty but I doubted that. They just needed a punk but I was the wrong one.

I had no choice but to sit there and shut up. John began to chew my ear off about running around with those boys from the projects. Like we weren't from the hood. My nephew Steve had told his father

I was at a boy's house. He said he saw me leave school with Quinton. That was exactly why I didn't want Steve to come to my school. But no . . . Steve needed to go somewhere where he knew somebody, Mia and John said. That little snitch!

John forbade me ever to see Quinton again. I was to come straight home from school or work every day. Phone privileges, gone. Company, yeah right! He took away everything. I was furious! Mia chased after me as I ran off into my room crying and holding the side of my face. She held me and tried to console me. John came into my room searching my bags and pockets until he found Q's number. He tore it up and left the room. From that moment on, I hated him. Mia tried to make me understand John's reasoning but I wasn't listening.

"Baby girl, you got to understand. Your brother's not ready for you to be dating yet."

I ignored her. I couldn't care less what John was ready for.

"I hate him, Mia! I . . . hate . . . him," I said as I burst into tears. John had just made his first enemy.

I hoped that Q was at school the next day so I could tell him what happened. I wanted him to hurt Steve.

Finding your first love is supposed to be the best time of your life. But Lord, had I known how much trouble came along with it, I might have joined a convent.

That Friday there were no signs of Q anywhere. He didn't come to school, and I had no way of getting in contact with him. I wanted to go visit him but John wouldn't let me go out. I wanted the weekend to end. Monday morning, Q would be at school and I could explain why I didn't call him.

The weekend seemed to drag on and on. I didn't see or hear from Q, and it was killing me. When Monday finally came, I couldn't wait to get to school. With Q in mind, I wore a brown miniskirt with a tan Guess top, tied on the side allowing my midriff to show. Neutral colors always seemed to bring out the natural golden hue in my skin. I was definitely feeling fly. But John didn't think so. He hit the ceiling as he hollered, "Hos live on the street."

I couldn't take much more of that whore shit. I swore that as soon as I saved enough money, I was moving out.

When I got to school, Q was standing outside talking to some young girl. My feelings were hurt but I managed to be cool. I walked right passed him like I didn't even notice him. By the time my foot hit the first step leading inside the building, I felt a hand on my shoulder. I turned around and there was Quinton.

"Who's that girl you were talking to?" I questioned.

"Who, her?" He laughed as he pointed. He thought it was cute that I was jealous. "She's just some girl I grew up with. It's nothing more than friendship."

But the way she looked at me told a different story.

"Why didn't you call me yesterday? I waited for you to call me," he said.

I didn't believe he honestly waited for my call but I let him have that one.

"My brother heard I was with you and had a natural-born fit. Then he went through my stuff until he found your number and tore it up," I said. "I ain't mean to get you in trouble. Sorry," he apologized.

"That ain't the worst of it. He called me a whore and all this other foul shit."

Quinton expressed his sympathy with a hug and said, "You ain't no ho. You my boo. I'll take care of you."

See, I was destined to be his boo.

Quinton

The hurt on Mani's face burned deep into my heart. I couldn't stand to see her pained in any way. That was when I realized that she had me open. I didn't want to do anything to hurt her. It would tear her apart and away from me. I wasn't ready for her to leave me.

"Imani, what you want to do tonight?" I asked, trying to block my thoughts.

"I'on't know. Why? You got plans for us?" she asked as she smiled innocently.

"Yeah, but it's a surprise. Can you meet me at Junior's, downtown Brooklyn? Wear something nice."

"About what time? John won't let me out after seven. Once the street lights come on I have to come inside."

Imani looked up into my eyes, and I began to feel my insides flipping. I had never felt this way for any of my other girlfriends. Something about her was special.

"Okay, be there at six. Bring a bag of clothes with you. We're going to be out late." I did not intend to let her go home.

That night we went to the city. She said she had never been to Times Square. I took her to some of my hangouts and favorite stores and I let her get whatever she wanted. It was her night. Afterward, we decided to stay the night out in Manhattan. I took her to a hotel on the West Side called The Inn that I had heard about from some of my boys. The room had a Jacuzzi and waterbed. We made sure we used both. Repeatedly. Imani still wasn't ready to have sex but would do everything else. She knew how to bring me to the brink over and over and over only using her tongue.

Over the following weeks, Imani and I became close. Together. Everyday. We would cut classes just to be in the halls talking, kissing and holding each other. Imani listened to me when I needed someone to talk to and that meant a lot to me. Not to mention the fact that, she knew how to turn me on. She would lick my earlobe softly and instantly an electric shock would shoot down my spine, and I'd almost buckle at the knees. Vice versa, Imani was a sucker for long, passionate kisses. I would always tease her by sucking on her bottom lip and kissing her chin. Making her wait. Finally, she would grab my ears and pull me to her. Mmmm, she was delicious too.

During the summer, Imani spent a lot of time at my house. She had as many clothes there as she did at her brother's house. Whatever she didn't have, I bought. She was so good to me. The nights I worked, she cooked, and the nights she worked, I cooked and kept house. Imani and I had breakfast together every morning and had long conversations every night about anything. Imani was a sucker for gossip so on most nights I listened and learned about everyone and their drama.

At the tender age of eighteen, I had the responsibilities of a man. I kept my woman happy and maintained a home. Yeah, there were times when I thought that I was too young to be in a serious relationship but as my mother once told me during one of those I'm-trying-to-be-a-parent talks "love knows no age." Imani's brother, John, finally got upset and fed up. He came to my house with the rest of her stuff. He told her never to think about coming back to his house, and I really didn't want her to.

In the beginning, Imani was hurt; once again, her own family had turned their back on her. After some time had passed, I managed to convince her that it was in our favor. We didn't need anybody to approve or validate our relationship. What we had was real and binding.

I didn't mind her moving in but my mother was a different story. My mother would say slick shit out the side of her mouth. Her favorite was "there ain't going to be two women of this house." I would tell Imani not to pay her any mind. She was drunk. As long as I paid the bills, Imani was welcomed to stay. Plus, a real woman would keep a clean house and food in the fridge. So, as far as I was concerned Imani was the woman of the house. After about a month of complaining, my mother began to ease off when she realized the housework was lifted from her shoulders and she was free to come and go as she pleased, without having to be concerned with keeping house.

April 1995 was bringing in the spring and closing in on our first year anniversary. Things were going fine. Imani and I had begun City College in the fall, and life was really looking up. Imani and I were closer than ever. She was comfortable with our relationship, and I began to notice subtle changes in her. Imani would never disrobe in front of me. It was like she had a problem with letting me see her naked. But lately she'd been a lot more open and free. Even in bed she seemed to want to go further than our occasional foreplay.

Completely Satisfied

I tried to respect her wishes by waiting until our anniversary to have sex but she was making it hard for me.

One night after we finished organizing our room, we relaxed on the bed and began watching Beverly Hills Cops III on HBO. I thought it was kind of funny that we were watching the same movie we watched on our first date. Of course, Imani found it romantic. Halfway into the movie we were engaged in a heavy kissing session. My patience was beginning to run thin. I wanted—no, I needed to be—inside of her.

"Imani, Baby. You know I'm not going anywhere, right?" I asked. "Yeah," she replied.

"So, why are you making me wait? I need you, Mani." I begged. She waited before she responded.

"I'm scared things are going to change."

"Baby, ain't nothing going to change. I - I'm stuck to you." I wanted to say I love you, but choked.

"Please don't hurt me," she pleaded with fear-filled eyes.

"I would never do anything to hurt you," I said.

Imani rolled over on top of me and took off her shirt. I continued to lay back, motionless, waiting. We had been down this road before, and I wasn't in the mood to get shut down.

Imani bent down and whispered, "Q, be gentle."

I was excited. I pushed her to the side and jumped off the door to go lock the door. Quickly, I shed my clothes and retrieved a condom from the dresser. Imani's look of insecurity changed instantly to one of lust as I began kissing her most sensitive areas. She removed her sweatpants, and to my surprise she wasn't wearing any panties. I climbed into the bed and pulled her into my embrace trying to do things nice and slow but she had others plans.

Imani placed her warm hands on my face and looked directly into my eyes. "I want you, Q. I'm ready."

After I put on the condom, I gently tried to slide in but she was so tight. I tried to assure her that it wouldn't hurt if she relaxed. She relaxed and I tried again. Her nails dug into my back. It must have hurt like hell! Finally, after numerous attempts, I managed to get in. All she could do was cry out in pain. I tried to muffle the noise by kissing her. She clutched the sheets as tight as she could. We moved and rocked for what seemed like forever before she began to shudder and groan in pleasure. The sensation to go deeper inside of her was overbearing. I tried to control the feeling but as I came close to my own climax, I lost the battle as my thrusts became harder and faster. Ultimately, Imani began to claw at my chest as she cried, "It hurts, Quinton." Within in seconds it was over.

I wiped the tears away from Imani's cheek. "You know you're my heart, right?" I asked.

She just nodded in response and motioned for me to lie beside her. During our second year of college, we decided to get our own place since it was beginning to get crowded at home—you know the saying, two is company and three is a crowd? Well that was exactly what happened. Uncle Terry and Mama, I could deal with but another man, no way. My mother went and found herself a companion, as she called him. I didn't like James Hutch and never tried to hide it. Then again, I never really gave him a chance either. James wasn't a bad man. After all, he got Mom to enroll in an alcohol abuse program. Just something about him . . . he was phony.

Imani and I found us a decent place on 138th Street and Amsterdam Avenue. It was all we could afford, and the neighborhood wasn't any worse than what we were accustomed to. Our apartment was set in one of the oldest building still standing in Harlem. The hardwood floors complemented the apartment's antique design and décor. It was old- fashioned but it was just what we needed, a place of our own. We didn't need much to make the apartment feel like home. Imani and I only took what we could carry on one trip and made do with just that. It was a new beginning for both of, us, and therefore, we needed to start fresh.

We were a family—Imani and me. I had my woman, my own spacious one-bedroom apartment in uptown Manhattan and was I happy. What more could I ask for?

A position for a supervisor in a food court at school opened up. I wasn't very happy about Imani applying for it but I let her be. I felt I brought home more than enough working as a representative's assistant with the ATC real estate company, but that was it; we were making just enough—no room for luxury. She griped about never having the opportunity to have the finer things in life. Imani began to fall deeper into the name-brand frenzy that engulfed most of the young women around her age. Everything she owned either had to be Anne Klein or Liz Claiborne. Her shoes and bags began to overcrowd our hall closet as she collected the newest articles from Nine West, Dooney-Burke, and whatever other leather bag manufacturers that cost an arm and a leg. Her materialistic needs were beyond our already tight budget so she felt the need to get a job solely to support her habit.

Although I bitched and moaned about her not being home, her extra income was greatly welcomed.

Our time together became rare due to our conflicting work and school schedules. It began to put a strain on our relationship. On top of that, I didn't like any of the friends Imani had made at the food court. Not that I was jealous, just careful. I found a way to get rid of all of her friends except for Charisse Nettles.

Imani

Quinton felt threatened by my friendship with Reese. He felt that somehow Charisse had the power to alter my decisions and cause me to do things out of the norm. Quinton failed to understand that I was nineteen years old and capable of making my own decisions. No one could ever make me change who I was. I am and always will be Imani Nicole Wright, a survivor, an independent woman.

Charisse "Reese" Nettles was a little different than everybody else, which is what she prided herself on. She was new to the neighborhood and wanted somebody to show her around. I showed her all the usual hangouts and we hung out together every weekend. Of course, Q didn't like that. He would try to accuse me of picking up guys with Reese. But she wasn't like that. She wanted to see Q and me together; he just never gave her a chance. "Q, why are you acting like this?" I said one day as I crawled on the floor looking under the bed and dresser for my other shoe.

"Because I don't know why you have to go out every weekend. When are you going to make time for us? Or, don't I matter anymore?" His husky voice filled the room as he followed me around. His pity parties were becoming aggravating.

"Baby, look, why don't you come with us? I'm sure Reese wouldn't mind." I was putting on my favorite thin hoop earrings just when he wrapped his strong black arms around me. Quinton had developed a little muscle over the past year as his body began to fill out. At six feet two and two hundred twenty-five pounds, he wore the weight well.

"Why don't you and I go somewhere? Just the two of us. We haven't done that in a long time. Tell Reese y'all will hang out tomorrow or next week or something. Give me tonight, Mani." He rotated his hips becoming aroused each time his penis rubbed passed my behind. I couldn't ignore the hard-on pressing through his slacks.

I turned to face him and ran my hands over his hairy, muscular chest. He looked at me with seductive eyes. We kissed slowly and passionately. He wanted to make love to me, and I wanted him also. He began to lead me back toward the bedroom. Just as we reached the bed, there was a knock at the door. Q acted as if he didn't hear it but the constant banging echoed throughout the apartment.

"I gotta go. That's Reese. I'm sorry, Baby. I picked up my black leather Fendi pocketbook and walked out the door. He slammed the door behind me and put on all the locks. Didn't matter, I had all the keys.

After months and months of verbal attacks, Q finally asked me to quit my job. He figured he'd kill two birds with one stone. Easier said than done. Although I was beginning to feel weak from all the pressure of school and work anyway, I didn't want to quit and let him think I did it because he told me to. I had too much pride. Instead, I began to use my sick days as an attempt to ease some of the tension in the house. I thought that if I let him think I was taking days off to spend more time at home with him, he would stop giving me so much grief. And, eventually, when I had exhausted all my days, I would quit like I had planned.

I took a day off from work to redecorate the house with the little bit of money I had saved solely for that purpose. I loved our place but it was boring. We didn't have any pictures on our walls except for the black-and- white antique we took at Great Adventure the year before, the sofa was dull and the kitchen was straight ugly. After hitting all the stores necessary for my home improvement project, I decided to rest because I was feeling a little faint. Q wanted to help so he'd taken off to stay home with me. We didn't realize how much we missed each other until we got this time to relax and talk. I massaged his shoulders as he told me about his hard times at work. He turned on his back while I straddled him. I could feel the pressure of his penis rising beneath me. Lord knows I missed it.

Quinton

Almost three years had passed, and my feelings for Imani began to intensify. She was the only woman who had ever loved me and did anything to please me. I felt it was time for me to tell her how much I loved her. I wanted to spend the rest of my life with her. I wanted to satisfy her in every sense of the word. One night, I ran my hands through her hair and looked deeply into her eyes trying to read her heart. I wanted to know and experience everything she was feeling. The connection between us was real. Her big brown eyes looked at me passionately. As I inhaled her sweet-smelling perfume, I reflected upon the first time we met and how she stood beside me through all the rumors and scandal about Stacy and me sleeping together after Imani and I got involved that had circulated the school. Not once did she question my affection or fidelity. She knew, hands down, that I loved her, which was why this conversation was long overdue.

I turned the stereo system on and the sounds of Lenny Williams poured through the speakers filling the room as he belted out those words "'Cause I Love You." The moment was right; the mood was set. It was time.

"Imani, do you know how special you are to me?" I asked, peering into her eyes for an answer.

44

"I can imagine," she said. "You told me once before I believe, or was I dreaming?"

"Seriously, I don't know how to express with words the feelings I have for you. I promise, Imani, I will do everything within my means to keep you happy."

"Q, you've already made me happy. You were there for me when my family wasn't. That's more than enough."

"Same here, and I want to thank you. I never knew what it meant to have someone devoted toward making your life pure bliss. But you have done that and, I love you for it." The sincerity in my tone was strange to my own ears. It was as if I was sitting outside my body watching my heart talk to Imani. Anything I felt was being exposed and for once, it actually felt good.

Imani

Quinton ran his hand down the side of my face and began to stare in my eyes. I had never seen this look on his face. Before I could ask him what was wrong, he told me he loved me. We had been together almost three years and this was the first time he actually said, I love you. I had loved Q since I was a freshman in high school. I wanted to tell him I loved him, too, but all I could do was cry.

Q pulled me to him. He held me tight while rubbing my back. As he placed soft kisses along the side of my neck, I felt myself wanting him in the worst way. This time I was in charge. I unbuttoned his shirt, kissing from his chin down his neck to his belly button. Slowly, I licked around his nipples while he unsnapped my bra and began massaging my breasts.

I began to give him a strip show. Standing at the foot of the bed, I let my bra fall to the floor. I moved, demonstrating what I was going to do to him. As I began to take off my panties, I turned around so he could get full view of what he owned. This body belonged to him—mind and soul.

Q could no longer restrain himself. He jumped up from the bed and tackled me, again, professing his love for me, this time I replied, "I love you too."

Quinton and I lay entwined in each other's embrace following our lovemaking. Any insecurities I had had been flushed out of my heart as his love flooded in. I took the next several minutes just to reflect on how much I wished I could have had this same feeling of security within my own family. Although I was content with my present situation, I still felt that void, that incomplete feeling from missing something or someone.

My head began to spin from what I thought was the overwhelming feeling of love. But as my stomach began to knot up and my mouth began to water, I knew something was wrong. Rapidly, I hopped off the bed and ran across the room to the garbage pail. I thought I was going to die. My body began to go limp. Q rushed over to help me.

After tossing up all my organs, Q ran a warm bath and made me some chamomile tea.

Quinton

The next morning Imani was worse than the day before. She looked pale and felt like she was running a fever.

"Imani, let's go to the doctor. You look like the walking dead."

"Quinton, I'm fine," she replied weakly. "I just need to rest."

"Come on I'll call Dr. Bess. He's in today. Don't sit around here dying on me."

"You're overreacting. Baby, I'll be fine."

She placed her cold, clammy palm on my face. I didn't feel like waiting around for her to get better. I let her sleep some more while I called the doctor to tell him what was going on. He suggested I bring her in if she developed a fever. An hour later, she complained she was dizzy and fainted. I quickly dressed Imani, carried her to the car and rushed her to our doctor. While approaching the office, I thought of a million diagnoses. I was convinced it was stress related. I told her that school and work were too much to carry.

The nurse asked Mani to fill out a form and wait for her name to be called, the standard. On the form, it asked for her last menstrual period. I couldn't remember. I normally would remind her. Neither one of us could remember. Out of all the possibilities, pregnancy never occurred to me. Needless to say, the doctor confirmed our suspicions. Imani was indeed pregnant. That was when I became adamant about Imani quitting her job. I felt it was time to be the man my father wasn't. My mother had to work throughout her pregnancy to keep food in the house and a roof over our heads. My father never cared how my life ended up. He let my mother suffer and struggle. She was stressed, which was the reason I believe she rejected me. I wanted more for Mani and our baby. I wanted us to be a family. I wanted her to stay home and be a mother while I worked to pay the bills and give them everything they desired. I wanted to be there.

Imani

Well, I was going to be a mother. I wasn't even a wife, and I was going to be somebody's mother. I talked to Q about getting married but he kept giving me shady answers and excuses. Quinton acted as if something was holding him back from me. I was beginning to suspect someone. The more I questioned it, the more he would flare up. Yet, he couldn't account for his late nights and the hang-up telephone calls. I tried to trust him but he never gave me a reason to.

"Q, where were you for the past five hours?" I barked one day as he walked through the door. He tossed his briefcase and suit jacket on a chair in the kitchen.

"Where the hell else would I be? I was at work, Mani. Can a nigga get in the door good before he's interrogated?" He loosened his tie and unfastened the first two buttons of his shirt as he walked over to greet me. As he bent down to kiss me, I inhaled deeply, trying to find any traces of perfumes. But there weren't any. "What's wrong with you, Imani?"

"I don't know. You tell me. You're the one out all night long and can't tell me where you've been."

"It's not that I can't tell you. It's that I won't tell you. Imani, I'm a grown-ass man, and I don't need to explain myself to anyone nor do I have to ask for permission to hang out with my boys."

"Your boys my ass. You ain't with no fuckin' boys. Your boys call here all damn day looking for your trifling ass. Now, who's the stupid one? Stupid! "

"Fuck you, Imani. You're being paranoid for nothing. I am not cheating on you, if that's what you want to know! Leave me the hell alone." He hung his jacket in the hall closet then locked himself in the bathroom for an hour.

I wasn't paranoid, nor was I blind. I could tell when he was lying. I was determined to find out—hopefully sooner rather than later.

CHAPTER 4
DIFFERENCES

Quinton

"Did you feel that? He's happy to see me too," I said as I placed my hand on Imani's belly.

"Does every man wish for a boy? I keep telling you that he is a she," Imani said as she took my jacket.

"Whatever. No girl kicks like that. That's the strength of a man." I picked up the pieces of mail that were on the table.

"Don't get your hopes up, Daddy," she said as she carefully sat down. Daddy. I hadn't heard that name in a while. I wished for one minute I could see him and ask mine why he never came back for me. I wanted him to see the man I turned out to be without him.

Time flew by as my love for Imani grew with every kick. The baby would give a swift blow to Imani's abdomen every time we attempted to make love. Instead of growing frustrated, we drew closer, sharing more and more intimate moments. It felt good being a man, a family man.

During Imani's fifth month, I decided it was time. I was going to propose. Rodney, my homeboy from childhood, convinced me it was the right thing to do. He and I searched several malls looking for the perfect engagement ring. It had to be perfect; Imani was perfect and deserved the best.

"Just think, this is the same girl that use to stalk you in high school," Rodney said as I studied the diamond rings in the glass casing.

"You remember that." I laughed. "She was persistent but she got what she wanted."

"I can't believe you're about to be a father, man. You and Imani have really come a long way," Rodney said as he patted me on the back. "Did you ever get to talk to her about you-know-who."

49

"Nope, I didn't feel like it was any of her business. What she don't know won't kill her," I replied.

"A'ight. Don't say I didn't warn you. That bitch is psycho," he said, concerned about a situation that occurred not too long ago.

"It's okay. I handled that. Mani is the only girl for me. Shit, she about to have my baby."

I bought the biggest rock that I could afford. I promised myself I would upgrade as soon as our financial situation got better. I knew this was right. It felt too good not to be.

When I got home, Imani was working out alongside a tape for pregnant women. She moved and stretched like the extra baggage didn't bother her. Her features began to change with the pregnancy, which only enhanced her natural beauty. Her nose began to spread across her face and her skin had gotten darker but she was still beautiful. Her hair hung loosely at her shoulders as she stood in front of the television with my Bucks jersey and a pair of black Speedo shorts.

I walked up behind her and placed my hands on her round belly. The baby kicked at my touch. Imani turned around to greet me with her everyday peck on the lips.

"Dinner is ready. Are you hungry?" she asked.

"Not really. Me and Rodney grabbed a bite at the mall."

"Oh, okay. What did you get?" she asked as she bent over to turn off the tape.

When she turned around, I was down on bended knee. With the ring in hand, I asked her to be my wife. She gladly accepted.

Imani

Not long after Q and I announced our pregnancy to our families and friends, we were announcing our engagement. It only took five months of begging for him to finally give in. Reese was ecstatic. She cried at the thought of Q and me being an actual family. Reese had been my friend for over a year and she knew more about me than anyone else, except for Q. She had been my shoulder to cry on, and she understood when I needed to vent. She was like the sister I never had. It was only right for me to ask her to be the godmother of my child.

A lot had changed over the past three years. Quinton had been more loving and attentive especially since we found out we were having a baby. Quinton mother, Mama J, and Quinton have been trying to bond and work on healing old wounds. Quinton is so happy to have his mother back that he had even agreed to hang out with her boyfriend James and try to get to know him better, for Mama J's sake. I guess the saying "time heals old wounds" is true.

My sister-in-law Mia was as excited as a mother would be but John didn't feel the same. He wanted to kill Q. Mia calmed him down and assured him that everything would be fine. John had eventually come to his senses. Whenever Q and I stopped by to visit, John tried to be civil but sometimes he'd slip in an insult or two. Jada, Jordan and I had put all grudges behind us. Our families were getting tighter at a time when we would need them most.

I don't think it fully registered that I was having a baby. My main question was, Are we ready to have a baby?

Q had started to work overtime and began buying little things here and there for the baby. I stayed home and took care of the bills, the meals and whatever household chores were left because Quinton didn't allow me to do anything strenuous. Before I could get use to being spoiled, things began to change. Just like all good things, our perfect life was coming to an end. Our money started looking funny and Q was coming home later and later claiming he was working overtime. Yet, I didn't see the fruits of the labor. Either he was stashing money or lying, but I never once complained, fussed or whined. I got smart and started putting a little away for myself, you know, in case of a rainy day.

"Q, we need to talk," I said one night as I sat in front of the TV with a bucket of chicken.

"What?" he snapped in anger.

"That's exactly what. Your funky attitude! I'm tired of you taking out your attitudes on me," I said as I slowly rose from my seat.

"What attitude? You're the one walking around here like Jekyll and Hyde. One minute you're bouncing around, the next you're throwing shit. I can't deal with this mood swinging shit," he said as he got up to load the washing machine.

"Well, it comes along with the pregnancy. Take it or leave it."

"I don't know sometimes," he said, exhaling.

"Excuse me. I didn't understand you. What don't you know?" I said. With my hand on my hip and finger waving in the air, the Brooklyn in me was definitely showing.

The only thing that stood between Quinton and me was my stomach or else he might have gotten slapped for his comment.

"Don't worry about it. Why don't you go wobble your fat ass back to the couch?"

That was it.

"I don't know what whore pissed you off last night but you better respect me . . ." I shouted.

The sound of my voice filled the room as we argued. Well, I argued. He ignored me. The best thing to do was ignore me. There was no way out.

Distance grew between us over the months. He stayed out later and later after work. Some nights he was so drunk Rodney had to carry him in. Q began following in his mama's footsteps. And when he was home, we barely spoke.

Rodney was a good friend to Q. Always there to pick up Q's slack and watch his back. He and Q never went anywhere without each other. I hoped Rodney would be around when I put Quinton's ass out. I was so tired of trying to keep up with him. I could never find him when I needed him. If I called him at work, he'd tell the receptionist to tell me he was out showing a house. I was ready to let him know that his time was up.

One morning, Quinton was putting on his gray silk tie as he stood in front of the mirror. He was fine as hell wearing a black button down shirt and gray slacks. Everything was fitting just right. The material brought out the broadness of his shoulders and almost made me forget how upset I was. I threw my feet over the side of the bed and took a deep breath before I attempted to stand. Everything I did would take so much out of me. As my feet touched the floor, a pain shot through my abdomen.

"Ooh, that shit hurt," I exclaimed as I rose from the bed.

"Stubbed your toe again? I can't wait for you to have that baby so you can see your feet again."

"Looks like you're about to get your wish."

Quinton was nervous enough for the both of us. He hurried to the telephone to call the doctor and let him know we were on our way to the hospital. While he packed my bag and called his office, I showered. Q wanted to carry me to the car but I convinced him it was okay for me to walk. The baby wasn't going to just fall out.

He sped all the way to the hospital almost causing an accident. I laughed on the inside. At the hospital, he held tight to my hand as I was checked to see how far along I was. Once Quinton left the room, I called his mother to come calm him down. He was starting to get on my last nerve. Mama J came as quick as she could. She took Q outside as Mia walked through the door. I was so happy to see her.

Of course John didn't come.

Mia began to massage my hands and feet, trying to keep me calm. Quinton was the one who needed help because he was bugging. He must have walked the tiles thin, pacing. The nurse thought he was going to faint when she asked him to help hold my legs. I was so busy worried about Quinton I couldn't concentrate on my breathing. I laughed when he finally broke down and let his mama take his place.

The summer of '97 came and so did our beautiful baby girl, Kai Aja Simone Banks. She weighed all of eight pounds and stretched twenty-one inches long. Her head was full of thick curly light brown hair similar to Q's as a child. She had her father's chinky eyes and long fingers but everything else was mine—my nose, my lips, my caramel color. She was my little angel. Quinton cried when he saw his little girl. He promised her a world free of heartache and loneliness. I just sat watching him as he kissed and hugged his first-born.

"Morning," I whispered the next day, letting know that I was awake. "Hey, Baby. How do you feel?"

Quinton was still in his work clothes from the day before. Tie undone and shirt unbuttoned, he was still pleasant to the eyes.

Quinton

"Okay. How are you?" she spoke softly, her voice still raspy.

"I'm fine. Better than that," I said, smiling. "I'm proud of you, Mani." Imani had given me the most precious gift that any woman could give. She gave me my little girl. Kai Aja Simone was beautiful. When I first held her in my arms, I felt complete. Kai was my angel. She had given me a reason to love again. I felt the urge to make sure she and her mother had everything they could ever want. They were my world. I couldn't explain how it felt when Kai's warm body found comfort in my gentle embrace. Imani and Kai they were able to fill the gaping wound left by my mother. I no longer searched for that love and attention.

Imani motioned for us to sit beside her as she cleared a space on the bed. It was funny how even at her worst she was still beautiful. Her hair was pulled back into a loose ponytail Mia had done that morning during her visit. Imani's lips were pale white and her eyes were swollen, but still her beauty shone through. I wanted her to know how much I appreciated her and what she had done for me. Softly, I ran my hand over her tear- streaked face as I recited the words to my favorite poem, "Love's a Lesson". Something short, sweet and to the point, just enough to let her know how much I loved her and always would.

Gently placing Kai in her arms, I began to feel a sense of guilt. I had really done some terrible things in the past behind Imani's back, and all the while she'd done nothing but stand beside me and bare my child. Although she hadn't known of my indiscretions, I felt the need to apologize and make it right. But how did I do that without incriminating myself?

When I brought Kai and Imani home from the hospital the house was full of flowers and family. Her sister Jada had come down with her four- year-old daughter Diamond. John, Mia and their kids—or should I say young men—were there; Jada's twin, Jordan, and his pregnant wife Tashii came from Maryland as well. Mama and James, her beau, had been there from early that morning cooking and cleaning, making sure everything was just right. Mama had been gloating for the past two days about her grandbaby "Nothing is too good for her," she said when I pressed on her about the heavy cleaning.

Imani's good friend Charisse and one of Charisse's younger sisters, Taniqua, also dropped by to welcome Imani and the baby. Rodney had been in and out all day running errands for Mama but at least he was there.

Imani was overwhelmed by the fuss everyone had gone through to make this a special day. It was too much for her to handle, and she began to cry. Her emotions were still all jumbled, and she was highly sensitive since having the baby. She went straight to the room and locked the door, and Charisse and I followed.

"Imani, what are you crying for?" I asked through the door.

"She's probably suffering from that postpartum depression shit," Charisse said.

Imani opened the door and replied, "I'm just happy, that's all."

Charisse rubbed Imani's head and assured her that was how she was supposed to feel. I pulled Mani into my arms and laughed while I lead her toward the living room.

Imani

Everyone had chipped in a little around the house to help me adjust to this new role as a mother. Mia came over every day to help me keep house and wash clothes, and Jada helped me stay sane. I thought I was going to lose my mind the first time Kai slept through the night. I called John's house several times to ask Jada if this was normal until finally Jada came over and stayed the night. Mia was too occupied with her hardheaded young men. Thank God, Jada came down for the weekend.

Quinton was the perfect daddy. When Kai cried he picked her up, changed her diaper and fed her. He made the first couple of nights very easy. After the newness wore off, Quinton returned to his regular routine. He did right by Kai. She had everything he could afford. He bought her earrings for each day of the week and a bracelet for each month of her first year. She had a wardrobe and bank account larger than mine. But that didn't make up for the time he spent away from home. I missed him very much. I needed to feel him next to me, smell his naturally fresh masculine scent, taste his sweet lips and touch his silk mahogany skin. Had his mama and Mia not kept me company, I would have broken down a long time ago.

When he did come home, we could never get together without arguing. Rumors of him and other women had begun to filter through the neighborhood. Whenever I went to Brooklyn to visit his mother, it seemed as if all the women would give me attitude. I got all kinds of dirty looks when Quinton and I were together and more than my share of accidental bumps as they would pass me on the street. And, of course, when I confronted him, either I was lying or paranoid. But, I knew I wasn't imagining the sore shoulders.

Quinton

Talking about arguing . . . Mani and I began to have our little differences. I told her I needed time to be myself; our arrangement was beginning to be too much pressure on me. The bills, the baby's stuff and then I had to try to keep up with my own life. I was so busy trying to be the man of the house I forgot about Quinton. Plus, all that love shit had a nigga feeling like Donnell Jones. I was hardly that, I was still a player. But my intentions were never to leave them. Then I'd be just like Michael, my father, letting real life run me out of my family's life. I couldn't do that to them. They needed me.

As fate would have it, I quit trying. Imani took me to that point. She complained, bitched and moaned every time I stepped in and out the door. It got to where I barely came home. All I wanted to do was hang with my boys, have a little fun. I never complained when she stepped out with Charisse, nor did I complain when she had company over, yet she insisted on stressing me about my social life. She would constantly accuse me of seeing other women—always sniffing my collars and checking my drawers. Mani was so naïve. Brothers didn't just slide up in some coochie and go straight home anymore. We made it our business to have another set of clothes somewhere else. Not saying that I would have known anything about that. Just common sense, you know.

Some of the women from Mama's building would tell me about Imani coming by asking questions about who I was seeing, where I was staying and all kinds of other bullshit. Tya, my friend from high school, had let me stay at an apartment she had on Kelly Street in the Bronx whenever I wanted to get away. She said she understood how it felt to be locked down. Sometimes she would spend the night; other times I would bring someone over. Imani began to ease up on the fighting. She had ceased the constant questioning and accepted what was going on between us. There was no love lost but it was not the same. When I did come home, she would act as if she hadn't noticed I was gone for days or weeks at a time. We still carried on as a couple. Everything was cool.

Imani

Quinton never left us, but he was never there. Within the six months following Kai's first birthday, Q had lost his job and started hanging out with his friends on the corner, drinking and smoking. The Quinton I knew was gone. I was struggling all over again; trying to pay second and third bill notices. I had to find two jobs—one to pay for school and the other for Kai's Pampers. The situation was getting out of control.

As Quinton and I grew farther and farther apart, the more focused I became. I was determined to be successful and not have to depend on Quinton and his sometimey self. I had received my bachelor's degree in accounting and immediately began working for the same firm where I did my internship the summer before. I waited until after graduation to move from our apartment into a furnished room, leaving Quinton and his bullshit behind.

I had my move planned to a T. I knew that Quinton never stayed home on weekends. So one Friday morning, I made Quinton breakfast in bed, ironed his clothes and ran most of his errands. He hadn't even noticed that some of our stuff had been moved around. When he left that night for his weekend rendezvous, I called Charisse, Mia, Jada and Craig, Jada's husband, over to help me pack all of our furniture onto a U-Haul. All the locks were changed, so Quinton wouldn't have access to whatever I had left behind. Kai and I stayed at Jada's house until we were able to find a place of our own. Most of our belongings were in storage. I left Q with nothing. Both of us were going to have to start over.

Quinton

"Imani, are you sure this is what you want to do?" I repeated as she carried the last of her belongings to the car she rented.

She called Mama's house and left a message for me to pick up the rest of my stuff. I couldn't believe what was going on. Imani had gone from the sweet woman I had known to some ruthless, cold-hearted bitch I didn't want to know. She had disappeared for almost two weeks without a word. No one knew where I could find her. All she left me with were the clothes on my back. Luckily, I had some outfits at Tya and Mama's house. Finally, she called and said she would meet me at the apartment to finish clearing out the boxes. I thought she was joking.

"Q, don't you think I've taken enough of your nonsense for one lifetime?"

"Mani, but you got to give me a chance. I'm tryin' to do right. Let me show you . . ."

"Show me what! Huh, what can you show me that will make me forget the drama you have put me through?"

"What drama? What have I done to deserve this? I was there for you!

" I said sternly as I pointed a finger in her face.

"Get ya finga out of my face, you low-life . . .b-bastard. You were home long enough to change your drawers. Does an eviction notice warrant a separation? Yeah, I think so! "

"You got your little bit of schooling and now you too good for a nigga! I made you. If it wasn't for me you would have nothing! "

"You made me? I made my damn self. You didn't do for me any more than I could have done for myself."

She backed into the driver side seat of the car and slammed the door almost catching my fingers. I banged on the window motioning for her to roll it down. She ignored my relentless knocking and started her car.

My baby girl looked at me with the saddest eyes as they drove away.

Imani had finally decided she had taken enough of my shit. After she left, I felt like my chest was torn open and my heart had been stolen. Our separation was the best for the both of us, and I knew it, but for some reason, it didn't feel proper. I missed Imani and Kai for the first couple of days and even thought of looking for them but something held me back. My mother would ask me repeatedly where they were, if I was keeping in contact and all those other questions that made me dread the decision of moving back home.

Truthfully, I had no idea where they were. I tried to call Mani at her job but never caught up with her. She had her cell phone disconnected and asking her brother was not happening. It was almost as if she disappeared without a trace. Finding her would be next to impossible.

CHAPTER 5
HEALING

Imani

"No, John. He didn't hit me," I said as I cradled the phone between my neck and ear as I brushed Kai's hair.

John was getting all excited over nothing. He swore I wasn't telling him the truth about why I left Quinton. I was just tired of Q's bullshit. John and I had been arguing this same point for two years.

"John, listen. Why would I lie to you? I just wanted out. I needed to breathe and be Imani for a little while. Kai and I are going to be fine," I said and then hung up.

There were times where I would rethink my decision to leave Quinton but it was too late. What's done is done.

It had been two years since I had seen Q. Quinton was a thing of the past, never to be revisited. Kai and I had to fend for us. One of the first things we did was rent a room in Flushing, Queens. A long way from the East New York section of Brooklyn but we could manage. We lived there all of two years until I had enough money saved up—with a little help from the bank—to buy a home in Rosedale. This house was for my little girl. She had her own backyard with a mini-playground, her own room decorated with Hello Kitty dolls and enough space to run around and be herself. I didn't take my stuff out of storage. We didn't need any memories of Q.

Charisse came over almost every day to help me decorate. Jada would bring her daughter, Diamond, over to spend time with Kai while we rearranged some stuff. With the two extra hands, it didn't take too long before my house became a home.

My four-bedroom home was too big for us but we would learn to make use of the space. I envisioned a playroom for Kai and an office for myself. Our lilac-colored kitchen was small but that was cool, because it was only two of us—no need for any heavy cooking. The living room and dining area were separated by a sliding door, which would eventually be removed. One of the bedrooms was on the first level. I had decided that would be my office. The other three bedrooms were upstairs. They were very spacious. The master bedroom had its own bathroom that we painted a soft shell and decorated with warm earth tones that matched the russet and beige scheme of my bedroom.

In my bedroom were the furnishings I had always dreamed about.

One of my favorites was the king-size canopy bed that occupied half of the room's space, which was my own idea. I draped the bed with taupe- colored lace with gold trim. The trim accentuated the gold paws attached to the end of each post. The hardwood floor gave the room an antique look. My mirrored closet stretched the span of the entire wall opposite the terrace, whose door and windows were covered with a paisley print curtain that incorporated all the colors of the room. This room was fit for a king— or in my case a queen.

My king was dethroned. Dismissed. Expelled.

After three months of hard work and long hours, Kai and I finally ended up with a home. The environment was pleasantly warm and inviting. African violets used in the bay window of the living room gave a burst of color to the different shades of green used for furniture and drapery. An Oriental rug covered the center of the dining room floor. The chandelier tenderly illuminated the space, setting a peaceful mood. The smoke-glass table surrounded by black, high-back metal chairs was set for four. Gold- trimmed ivory plates and cups accented by gold handled silverware decorated the table. Ivory napkins were placed in gold-and-silver napkin rings. The dining room was never used; Kai and I always ate in the kitchen. Its sole purpose was decoration.

Kai had a ball picking out decorations for her room. She chose a soft pink for the walls with a Hello Kitty border. Her twin-sized bed was decorated with a white-and-pink sheet set with a matching pink Barbie comforter that Charisse bought. Teddy bears were used around her room as an addition to the décor. Kai's room was the kind of room all five-year-old's dream of. I know I did.

Charisse and Jada suggested that we have a housewarming to celebrate the move. Not that I was totally against it but I wanted to enjoy my own space for a little while before having company over. Shortly after the house was completed, we sent out invitations for friends and family to partake in some food, folks and fun. On the day of the party, everyone was there except Quinton and his trifling ass, to bless our new home. Charisse invited him against my wishes, and he didn't even have the decency to call to wish us well.

"I'm sorry, Mani. He's always talking about wanting to see y'all so bad. I thought he might show up." Charisse shrugged.

"He doesn't care about us. That's why I left his sorry ass in the beginning."

"I'm going to go talk to Kai. Meanwhile, go walk off some of that steam," Charisse said.

I was fuming. It was one thing to disappoint me but when you disappoint my child, you have gone too far. He knew Kai was looking for him. I wish Reese wouldn't have told Kai. No good bastard!

John was happy when he found out I was through with Q. You know his famous saying; "I told you he was no good." I didn't even argue. He was right.

Quinton

Years after Imani moved I had gotten a call from Charisse. She had invited me over to Imani's housewarming but I turned down the invitation. If Imani wanted me there, she would have invited me personally. She hadn't cared to see me over the past years, why now? Yeah, I missed her. But mostly, I missed Kai. I hadn't seen her since the last time she was at John's house. That was the only way I got to see her. When Imani went away on her business trips, she would leave Kai with Mia or Charisse. Both Mia and Charisse would call me and arrange for me to see Kai but we never really spent any time together. Mia didn't want me around when John came home so our visits were always short.

That was a year and two school photos ago. Mama had been sending copies of the pictures Imani had given her of Kai since Imani found it too strenuous to send them directly to me. I wasn't mad at Imani though. My life was really out of my hands, and Kai didn't need to be a part of it. Maybe when she was older I'd be able to explain to her and her mom why I made the decisions I had. Meanwhile, I had my own situations to deal with. Tya had been going around telling everyone in the neighborhood we were engaged and that was far from the truth. We barely had a relationship. I was a player. Women flocked to me when they heard I was back on the market. And, I made it my business to take them up on their invitations.

Tya had begged me to stop messing around. In all actuality, she had proposed to me. I never accepted nor did I decline. She came to her own assumption that we were going to be married. She even went as far as buying her own ring. Desperate, don't you think? Truth was I still had some feelings lingering inside for Imani. Stewing in my own misery, I began to see how I did her wrong and how I wished I could hold her one more time. Quite a few times I caught myself calling out her name when Tya and I were in bed. I even went as far as to buy Tya things that Imani would wear.

Finally, Tya was upset and fed up. When she found out she was pregnant, she wanted a real commitment. But when I told her I didn't love her, she lost her temper. She ran out the house and never turned around. Three days later, her brother came knocking on the door. I knew what this meant so I packed as much stuff as I could in my duffel bag and left, down the fire escape. For the weeks that followed, I hid out in different houses ending up at an ex-girlfriend's house. Trina was my last resort. We had issues that needed to be dealt with as well. It was like my life had taken a downward spiral. I was trying to survive.

Imani

After the affair, Mama J, Q's mother had been over every moment that she could to spend time with her first granddaughter.

Kai enjoyed spending time with her as well. This gave me time to relax, unwind and think—thoughts like, Why did he leave me? Is he ever going to see his child again? Did he even care? Isn't it pitiful? The brother had been gone for more than two years and he still invaded my mind. Quinton may have been gone but not forgotten. There was still a place in my heart that held a special kind of love for him. I didn't understand nor did I question it.

Mama J and I would talk about it and she would tell me not to think about it. "Everything happens for a reason, chile. You'll see." Q had my number and my address and never used them. There was supposed to be some logical reason for that? Please. Mama J told me she was going to make sure Q visited Kai the next day.

Sure enough, he was ringing my doorbell at eight o'clock in the morning.

He had gained some weight but it was all toned up and he had a goatee that made him look like a model. At least he's been taking care of himself, I thought. Nervously, I gave myself a look-over in the hanging mirror beside the door. I inhaled and exhaled repeatedly trying to calm down. It was crazy how after all those years he still had that effect on me. I wiped my sweaty palms against my pajamas and took one last glance out the peephole, reassuring myself that he was indeed real.

Quinton

It seemed like forever before Imani opened the door. Coming was against my better judgment but my mother insisted that I go and visit. I stood at the door with my hands in my pockets trying to be calm but my nerves wouldn't settle down. The peephole darkened one more time before the door slowly opened.

Imani stood behind the door as I walked in. The smell of fresh coffee filled my senses as I stepped inside. Behind me, I could hear Imani locking the door. I drew in several deep breaths before I built up the courage to turn around and finally confront her after almost three years.

Her beauty blew me away. Seeing her again was like looking at her for the first time. She looked new to me. Her hips had filled out a little, and her breasts looked a whole lot bigger. She stood with her arms clutching her body as if she was trying to shield herself from the cold or hide her body from a stranger. As I thought of Imani considering me as a stranger, I felt a pang in my heart.

French vanilla filled the air as the coffee brewed and smooth sounds of Kenny G's saxophone played, setting a tranquil tone.

We stared at each other for a second before she invited me into the living room. She took my jacket, hung it in the closet and took me for a tour around the lower level of her house. I picked up a picture that sat on a table near the couch. Inside the wooden frame was a portrait taken of us when we first came home with Kai. I gazed at the photo for a few seconds, trying to figure out where we went wrong then placed it back on the table.

"Nice place. You did all the decorating yourself?"

"Not really. I had a lot of help from Jada and Charisse." Her answer was curt. I began to feel as though my visit was a bother.

We chatted briefly over a cup of coffee. Upon completing my cup, I asked to see my daughter.

We ascended the lengthy stairway leading upstairs to the bedrooms. Imani darted to her bedroom and quickly pulled the door closed.

"Did I come at a bad time?" I asked, hoping she would say no.

Instead she cut her eyes and continued walking.

She took me to Kai's room to wake her. I just stood there for a minute and peered over my little girl. Then I turned to Imani and apologized. I tried to explain to her how I wasn't sure she would let me in if I came over and that I wasn't sure how she felt about me. I touched her face, my eyes asking for her forgiveness. I knew she wanted to forgive me but couldn't— too much time had passed.

Imani jerked away from me as if she was repulsed by my touch. What could I say besides I'm sorry? I never meant to hurt her. She was all I had then and I suddenly realized all I wanted in my future.

Kai turned over toward the sound of our voices and screamed. She didn't know who I was. I had become a stranger to my own daughter.

Imani sat on the end of her bed running her hand over Kai's head, trying to explain that her daddy had finally come to see her after two and a half years. Imani hadn't known of my visits with Kai when Imani was out of town. It had actually only been a year since I last saw Kai, but evidently, a year was still too long. She peered deeply into my eyes as I stood before her, waiting for her acceptance. I reached out for her but she refused to come to me. The sound of my heart breaking filled the hushed air.

"Kai, sweetheart, it's Daddy. Remember me?" I said, hoping she would recognize my voice.

"Q, it's been a long time. Give her a little while." Imani tried to make me feel better but instead her comment stung.

"What do you mean give her some time? This is your fault, Imani.

Had you not tried to take her from me, she would know who I am." I tried to keep a respectful tone.

"No, Quinton. This is your doing. You were given more than enough opportunities to see our daughter."

Imani carried Kai from her bed to a chair in the corner. Kai rested against her mother's breast. Kai sniffled and wiped her eyes as Imani rocked back and forth comforting our baby girl.

"What am I supposed to do, Imani?"

"Try spending some time with her. She's been here waiting for you. Come around sometime."

"Do you mind if I hang around for a while? Maybe we can have breakfast together. I'll cook." I know I was reaching but at that point, but I had to. I needed them to forgive me. More importantly, I needed them.

"I don't see why not. I guess it's a start. "

Imani was so calm while she held Kai but I could see the pain in her eyes.

After that episode, I visited as much as possible. I wanted to form a bond between Kai and me. On one of the visits, Mani and I took Kai for lunch and then a movie. Once we returned to the house, we sat in the living room and recapped the day's events over a cup of cocoa. I made a promise to be there for them from that day forth. I begged Mani to take me back. I wanted to be a family again. But her response was shaded with indecisiveness.

"Where are we going from here?" Imani was silent. I ran my fingers through her highlighted tresses and waited for her response. But there wasn't one.

"Kai, go get the cordless phone out of the kitchen for Mommy, please?" she said, diverting her stare.

"Imani, stop ignoring me! I'm asking you one simple question with a yes-or-no answer." I turned her face toward my own.

Her eyes were cloudy, sympathetic. I couldn't tell if she was protecting her pain or trying to protect my own.

"It's not that simple, Q. I don't even know you. The Quinton I knew would have never walked out on his family. The Quinton I knew understood what it meant to have a mother and father. Any decision I make will not only affect my life but my daughter's life too."

Kai came back with the telephone and immediately returned to her toys on the floor. Once or twice, she turned our way, only to take a quick glance, reassuring herself that we were still there. Imani was so beautiful I couldn't stop looking at her. She wore a black one-piece halter dress. Her perfectly toned legs peeked from underneath. I couldn't help but get aroused at the way she played with her earlobe as she pondered our relationship.

"Damn," I said as I placed my head in my hands. "Shit wasn't supposed to be this way. We were supposed to be married, probably out- of-state somewhere in our home. Not here, two or three years later trying to determine the state of our relationship."

She placed her warm hand on my leg and exhaled softly. "Then you know what you have to do to get back where we belong."

With those words, a huge weight was lifted off my shoulder. Knowing that I had the power to change our destiny gave hope to a possible future with Imani and Kai. But, Imani couldn't trust me. Imani offered a thirty- day trial period stipulating that the minute I stepped out of line, my black ass was out of there. I accepted and promised to make things better. Then we kissed. It was different than all the others. This kiss was trying to make up for lost time . . . rushed yet intense.

After we put Kai to bed, we sat up and talked about what I was feeling. I repeatedly said I was sorry—for more than what she thought I was apologizing for. When we went to bed together, it felt awkward. But when I began to massage her feet and kiss up her leg, it felt so right. Without missing a beat, I kissed and caressed every inch of her body. I wanted to do the things to Imani that would make her feel like the woman she was. I massaged her back with hot oils and placed butterfly kisses from her fingers, up her arms to her neck. That night was going to be different than the other times.

I slowly, passionately made love to Imani, providing pleasure in ways that were unmentionable. Following our lovemaking, we laid in each other's embrace. As she drifted off to sleep, I whispered, "I love you, Imani."

The next morning was different for us but it felt good. It was our first time waking up together in almost three years. I called repeatedly to check up on Kai and Imani. Every time I called, I would tell them how much they meant to me and how special they were. Of course, Imani questioned herself, wondering whether she did the right thing by allowing me back in their lives. But when she saw the smile on Kai's face as I walked through the door, all apprehension faded.

"Hey, baby girl. Who is Daddy's angel?" I said as I greeted my daughter.

"Me," she replied. Her smiled spread across her face as she opened her arms to be picked up.

"That's right. Look what I got for my girl. Do you like Barbie?" I pulled a box out of the plastic Toys R Us bag.

"Thank you, Daddy! " she screamed as she ran off with her new doll. "You're the best."

Imani

Over the next months, Quinton tried very hard to make us a family. The three of us took a vacation just to spend some quality time together. And he definitely took care of business in the bedroom.

Q bought a brand-new cream-colored leather sofa set, two flat-screen TVs—one for the living room and one for the bedroom, brand-new carpet for the entire house and kept the mortgage paid. As any decent woman would, I became curious as to where he was getting the money. He said he'd been saving up but he didn't have a job.

Trust, it wasn't long before he confessed he was dealing. I was so disappointed. Quinton was so much smarter than that. We're talking about a brother who graduated high school top honors and received nothing less than an A throughout college. Q had been offered scholarships from colleges from all around the country to continue his studies. What was he doing? We needed to talk.

"Baby, you're wasting your time with this petty drug dealing. You are too smart for this. Is the money really worth it?"

He hesitated for a little while. "Ask yourself. Is the money worth it? I don't hear you complaining when you go on shopping sprees or when your house was redecorated. Plus, it's not long-term. Just till I get my feet on the ground," he said as he scratched his head.

Until he got his feet on the ground. Yeah, right!

One year, two cars and some diamonds later Q became the H.N.I.C.— head nigga in charge. Quinton had raised the bar on the statistics graph. Another brother had fallen to the life of fast money. I couldn't make him get out of the game so I insisted he keep his business away from home and he did—he hadn't been home to stay since. I began to wish I hadn't let him back in my heart and our lives. I should've learned my lesson the first time around. Nana always said, "A leopard never changes his spots." But first loves are so hard to let go.

Quinton stopped by, hit me off, spent a couple of minutes showering Kai and me with gifts, stayed one or two nights and then he was back on the streets. I shouldn't care much, my bills were paid,

I had the newest ride and was living in the lap of luxury but I didn't have Q, at least not the way I wanted him.

CHAPTER 6
LOVE WAS HERE

Quinton

Things started to hit the fan out in Brooklyn. Real ugly shit. Trina Knight began a psychotic rampage. I didn't want to involve Mani and didn't know if she would have been able to understand what I was going through so I felt it best to keep my distance. When things did die down, I went home and spent some time with Imani and Kai, but it wasn't long before the streets were calling. I never intended for things to turn out that way but the circumstances were beyond my control.

Mani spent a lot of time out of town on business with the new firm she was working for so I didn't worry much about my dirt catching up to her. And I doubt if anyone was stupid enough to mess with my child.

Kai and I had the relationship I longed to have with my mother. We were the best of friends. And I liked that. We hung out all the time. Everywhere I went Kai went with me. Well almost everywhere. Mani trusted me enough to leave Kai when she was away on trips. Even though I had no idea of how to take care of a little girl, I wasn't scared to learn, and try to be the parent that neither my mother nor father was for me.

Imani

"Hello." I was making my checking-in call. Normally, I wouldn't call so late but I missed my afternoon check-in due to a last-minute meeting.

"Yeah, what's up?" Quinton's soft, raspy whisper made my stomach do flip-flops. I missed him so much.

"Hey, Baby. How was your day?"

"Everything was quiet. What happened to you earlier? Kai was waiting for your call," he said right before clearing his throat.

"I know. I was so busy I couldn't call until right now. I'm just getting back to my room."

"Damn, girl. It's three in the morning. You're letting them work you too hard."

As I began to crawl out of my clothes, I thought about the real reason I was late and felt bad. I hated lying to him but I knew he wouldn't understand.

"I know, Baby. But a sistah's got to do what a sistah's got to do," I said as I combed my hair in a wrap, preparing for bed. "I love you, baby girl."

"I love you too, Q. Good night."

Since the beginning of 2002, I have been out of town a lot for P.G Johnson Inc., an accounting company I was working for since college. At the age of twenty-seven, I had finally made it to the executive board. So you know, a sistah was doing her thing. The position included a corner office with plush carpeting and all the other perks, including a secretary who brought me coffee. It had been a long road but the reward was worth the travel.

But, above it all, I missed my baby so much. It seemed as if we barely got to spend any time together. Kai was in school during the day and between her homework and my overdue projects at work, we never got to enjoy our nights together. Quinton had been taking care of Kai while I was away on the weekends. He tried his best to do her hair clothes but he didn't do such a good job. Most of the time he took Kai to Jada's house and she would fix her up.

Q and I were still struggling to be a couple but my business trips were giving me the opportunity to think of all my other possibilities.

One weekend, I took a trip to an Expo in Maryland, which was where my drama began. For years, I had done nothing but love Quinton and yearn to be together and every day I thought of my life under different circumstances. You know the usual, What if I would have just . . . maybe, I should've done . . . and the infamous If I could do it over again.... However, when I thought about it, I realized I had plenty of time and chances to change my life but chose the same dead end. I owed it to myself to take a break and broaden my horizons. To be me!

Mr. Omar Smalls, business consultant was a man in all aspects of the word and maybe the man to change my life. He knew how to treat a woman, knew what to say and how to say it, besides that, he was simply gorgeous. He had fair-colored skin, hazel eyes and his Adonis-like body caused my mouth to water. He was very clean cut and financially stable, legally. When he looked at me it almost felt sinful and when he touched me with his soft, manicured hands it sent tremors throughout my body.

We first hooked up after the Expo, Saturday night. He invited me to the 70's Soul Jam concert, which included bands such as The Delfonics, The Persuaders and The Chi-lites. We sat quietly through the first half as we enjoyed the crooning of The Intruders. During intermission we had a drink at the bar and talked. The drinks lightened our spirits as we clapped, sang, and danced to the upbeat tempos that took me back to when John would blast his music when company was over. We swayed to the Stylistics as they sang "Betcha, by Golly Wow." We held hands as I reminisced on the times of yesteryear. When John and Mia were dating and they used to have parties in Nana's basement while I sat quietly on the stairs learning the dances. Although I was only twenty-seven, I knew how to enjoy and appreciate good music. After the show, we found a small café in town.

Omar and I talked for hours, sharing each other's life stories over a few cups of coffee. We laughed at each other's jokes and offered suggestions regarding our current relationships. I guess I should mention he is married.

By the end of the night, we had exchanged numbers. After he took mine, he kissed my hand with such gentleness yet it was so deep. I was so engulfed in our date that I forgot to call Quinton. I couldn't wait to get home though and tell my girl Reese about Mr. Omar.

Knowing Reese, she would probably try to hook us up. Since Q stood Kai and me up at the housewarming, Reese lost all respect for him. They argued and fussed and fought every time they saw each other. They actually hated each other. When I allowed him to come back Reese didn't like it but was cool if it made me happy. She never said I told you so after he left again. She was always there for me. Those late nights Q walked out on me, Reese was there. She was like the sister I should've had in Jada. Since Jada and Craig moved to New York, she isolated herself from the family. Craig provided Jada with all the luxuries of the rich, and it all went to her head. She felt everyone was beneath her, especially me. She made it her business to take a shot at Quinton whenever we spoke while putting Craig on a pedestal. And no matter how right she may have been about Quinton, she didn't have the right to talk about him.

I was walking through the front door to my house as my telephone rang. I didn't catch the call and the caller didn't leave a message. I hated when people did that. Flashbacks of the women who would call for Quinton abruptly came to mind. I had my share of hang-ups for a lifetime.

After I put my bags in the living room, I picked up the telephone and dialed Charisse.

"Hello?" she answered, unsure of who was calling at nine o'clock in the morning.

"Hey, girl! I'm back," I hollered into the telephone.

"Hey, Mani. What's up! " She perked up. "How was your trip?"

"Girl, I met a cutie! "

"For real? Give me the scoop."

"His name is Omar. He's thirty-three and he's a business consultant for some company, I don't remember."

"Well . . . what happened? Did y'all hook up? Did you get some?

What? You all hyped up and shit. Something happened."

"You know I don't get down like that. Nothin' happened. We went to a concert, talked, got to know each other better . . . exchanged numbers. He says he wants to hook up again and continue where we left off but I'm not ready for all that yet." I took my shoes off as I listened to my best friend huff into the telephone.

"Oh yeah, I forgot I'm talking to Imani, Q's girl—I mean baby's mother. It would be too much for you to enjoy yourself."

"I did enjoy myself, thank you very much. Omar convinced me that chivalry is not dead, yet. He's so sweet, sincere, married and fine! "

Charisse and I shared a brief moment of laughter before she caught on.

"Married! Oh, you know how to pick 'em. What's up with him and his wife?"

"He's says they're separated and waiting on their divorce." I began to unpack my bags.

"So, are you trying to indulge yourself in that kind of relationship?"

"Girl, I don't know. He seemed like he was really feeling me but what about Q?" I said as I looked over at a picture of Q as he and Kai played in the sand at Manhattan Beach. I didn't know where we went wrong. It was like we weren't meant to be.

"Imani, what about Q? You need to kick him to the curb. That's all I see. You're miserable with him and I don't like the shit he does to you. It pisses me off to think that you don't feel you deserve better. Don't think I'm not saying that a married man is any better."

I knew Charisse was telling the truth but I felt like I owed Q. He took me in and took care of me when no one else did.

"Mani, are you listening? Quinton doesn't even have a real job. He ain't worth shit." Charisse was beginning to get an attitude. "Girl, how many times are you going to let him play you? You know he was with that bitch this weekend! " She paused. "Imani, I love you and wouldn't say this to hurt you. You need to face the truth. You are a twenty-seven-year-old single mother of a five-year-old girl who does not need to see her mother catering to no man. Not even her father. You and Quinton are not in high school anymore, and he needs to realize that you have your own life to lead." I could hear the suppressed anger in her voice.

"I know, Reese, but every now and again he tries to do the family thing, and Kai needs that." I sounded so pathetic. "And if I ask him about that chick, he'll lie about it—"

"Look, you need to be pushing up on Omar. He wouldn't have asked to see you again if he wasn't feeling you."

Charisse cut me off to get her point across. I couldn't argue because I knew she was right but I also knew Q loved me. Plus, Omar seemed like one of those too-good-to be-true type of guys. He did everything so right—massaged my toes, nibbled on my ear and said what I wanted to hear.

"I know, I know. I need time to think. Look, I have to go get Kai from her grandmother's house. I'm taking her school shopping at Green Acres mall. You want to meet us there?"

"A'ight." Reese had cynicism in her tone. "Whatever, I still feel you're going to settle for less, again."

"Bye, Charisse," I said, trying not to engage in that argument. "Later, Imani—punk."

Upstairs in my room, I began to iron a pair of Calvin Klein jeans to wear with the blue halter I had bought that weekend. Meanwhile, my tub was running. The grape fragrance from the bubble bath I purchased at Bath & Body Works filled the house. As I lowered my tired body into the porcelain tub, my telephone rang. I was hesitant to answer it, wanting to enjoy the peaceful moment. The recording picked up . . .

"Hi, you have reached Imani and Kai. Sorry, we are unavailable at the moment. Please leave your name and number at the sound of the beep, and we'll be sure to get back to you."

"Imani, I know you're there, pick up. Come on, Mani."

I hate to hear a damn near thirty-year-old man whine.

"What's up, Q?" I said flatly although I was happy to hear his voice. "Listen, Baby. What time are you picking up Kai? I'm about to step out and my moms is at the doctor."

Q makes me sick with that bullshit lying. The minute I returned from my trip he was always trying to get rid of Kai, like she was cramping his style or something.

"Well, Quinton, Baby. I'll be there when I get there. Until then act like she's your daughter." Without waiting for a reply, I placed the telephone back on its cradle and continued to try to relax.

I ran my finger over my kitty as it began to throb at the thought of seeing Quinton. Up and down, round and round, in and out, I played in an attempt to provide myself with the pleasure I had imagined receiving from Q. The soft bubbles brushed against my nipples. My back arched as the feeling intensified, my mind running rampant. "Q," I called out as my body came closer to climax. I shuddered in spasmodic jolts as I reached a full-fledged orgasm. Wheww. I fell limp with exhaustion as my hormones calmed down.

Quinton

"Imani! " I huffed into the telephone shocked by her attitude. "I can't believe she hung up on me."

She had been coming out her face lately. I didn't know what her problem was but she had better calm down. That Charisse bitch was probably filling her head with that lesbian bullshit, like always. The she- man men hater.

"Daddy, where's Mommy? Is she coming?" Kai's voice broke my train of thought.

As I looked over at my little girl, all I saw was Miss Imani Nicole Wright. They share the same golden complexion, pretty little lips, rusty brown hair and massive attitude. My baby girl had grown to be her mama's twin over the last six years.

"She's on her way. Get your stuff together."

I wanted her to be ready just in case Mani wanted to start that petty arguing shit again. She's unpredictable. One day she showered me with hugs and kisses and then she'd turn around screaming, "I hate you."

We began packing toys and clothes that were scattered throughout the apartment and placed them in either the black plastic hamper or a Little Tikes toy box. Both were in a corner in the living room. Kai's room was a mess but that would have to wait for another day. The sound of the telephone broke through our laughter as we played basketball with the laundry.

"Hello, who's this?" I knew who it was. Who else? Trina was really becoming a pain in the ass.

"What do you mean, who this!" Trina had too many attitudes too. "What's taking you so long? I'm getting tired of waiting! "

"Hey, yo, I'll be over there as soon as Kai gets picked up."

I couldn't wait to get over there to tell that psycho bitch "It's fucking over." She needed to leave me the hell alone.

"That bitch—oh, my bad, Imani—coming over?"

You could hear the jealousy breaking through. This had to end and I was going to do just that. I hung up.

I wished I had never gotten involved with Trina. I knew she was trouble in high school but that's what happens when you let the wrong head do all the thinking.

Cleaning had exhausted Kai so we laid on the couch to watch her favorite movie Friday. She only watched it because she loved Chris Tucker. Mani would have a fit if she caught Kai watching an R-rated movie. It's not like Kai was unfamiliar with the language. Kai heard Mani and me argue all the time. That definitely warranted an R rating. Within the first half an hour of the movie, I dozed off. When I finally awoke, I found Kai sprawled out across the floor, drooling. The fight scene with Deebo and Craig let me know the movie was almost over. Seemed as if cleaning took a lot out of us.

Where the hell is...the sound of the intercom interrupted my thoughts.

"Yeah," I hollered into the box on the wall. "It's Mani. Let me up! "

It was about time. I was beginning to get upset.

"Kai, let's go! Your mom is here! " I said as I tapped her leg in an attempt to wake her.

Imani

"Hey, Imani. Whatcha doing round here?" Tya asked as she exited the building.

78

"I came to pick up Kai. What you doing over here? Q said you moved to Long Island," I said as I looked her up and down.

"Yeah, well. I gave my sister my old apartment and she ain't been paying the rent. You know how that goes," Tya said as she checked her watch.

"Do I? Sound like something Nadine would do," I said, referring to my mother. Tya knew my mother better than I did. When my father died, gossip had it that Nadine started dealing with Tya's father.

"Girl, don't start," she said jokingly. "I gotta go. Call me."

"Okay, girl. Talk to you," I said as I waved.

Please. I was not calling that ho. She and Quinton called themselves having a thing going on while we were together. And the only reason I found out was because Kai told me that her daddy was having a baby after she heard them arguing in the hallway. But Tya had suffered a miscarriage three months later.

As I entered the building and headed to the stairs, the stench of urine brought tears to my eyes. Making my way up the stairs with my hand covering my nose, I tried not to inhale the fumes as I began to giggle. The hallway had a lot of old memories. Q and I shared many almost intimate moments there. Our names were still embedded in the concrete walls. That was seven years and many heartaches ago.

Finally, I had reached the third floor. The seven flights of stairs had left me breathless. The extra weight I had picked up didn't make matters any better. I lifted the square knocker and knocked three times before I attempted to turn the knob. I didn't want to walk in on Quinton and any of his female friends. Things didn't change much. We still loved each other and had occasional sex but he was still a player.

I entered the apartment quietly and tried to sneak up on him but Kai was at the door waiting for me.

"Mommy," Kai shrieked as she jumped into my arms.

She must have heard me at the door over the loud music blaring from the Gemini speakers that were positioned in opposite corners of the room.

"Hey, sweetie! How's Mommy's angel?"

Quinton was too busy gathering Kai's stuff to acknowledge me. "So, how have you been, Mr. Banks?"

He didn't respond. "Hello, I asked you—"

"Oh, I'm sorry, Baby. I was trying to get the baby's bags together and uh . . . "

Quinton

I hope she doesn't wanna . . . Damn! I thought. I hadn't seen Mani in a couple of weeks. Obviously, she had been doing real well for herself. Shit, she was fine. She had a new look; she cut her hair allowing her long, beautiful neck to show, lost a little weight and had a little tan going on.

"Baby, I wanted her stuff ready . . . y—you know how you be rushing and shit." Her beauty had me stuttering. And that smell . . . the mixture of fruits was driving me crazy. It must be some kind of aphrodisiac.

"See, why are you so fast? I was planning on spending some time with you."

Imani only wanted me when she was lonely. If she couldn't get Charisse to hang out or Jada to spend some time with her, then she was looking for me. This act normally happened like every two weeks. Otherwise, she was in and out the door so fast she'd left smoke behind. Didn't even give me a second thought.

She began to sashay her big ass over in my direction while I stood on the area rug in the living room with my mouth hanging open. I couldn't take my eyes off her sexy self. Her eyes finally fixed on mine. Both saying 'I want you'.

I pulled Imani near so she could feel what I was feeling. Her body fit into mine, curve for curve. Everything immediately connected, feeling right. I began to kiss her forehead, down to her nose, then her lips. I placed my hands on her hips slowly making my way to her butt. Oh, she was so . . .

Imani

Sexy! My five-foot, five-inch frame was no match for Q's six-foot- five, sculpted one. His mustache and beard were neatly groomed. His clothes hung loosely from his body but I was still able to see his form. The way he licked those sexy lips... Q was doing everything so right. I flinched but didn't fuss as I felt his masculinity rising to a full erection. My blood began to boil as the heat rose between us. My breaths become heavier as my mind slipped in and out of erotica, imagining what I would like to do to him. His thumbs ran over my nipples, as they stand to full attention. No other man could ever make me feel that way.

"So, what are your plans for tonight?" I tried to speak without my voice cracking but all I could manage was a whisper.

"I want to be inside of you." His words shot through me, straight to my center of passion as he released small groans of pleasure. My hands were working double time on the bulge that stood in between us.

"Hmmm . . . first I got to . . . um . . . run out for a few," he said as he pressed his body against mine.

Excuses. Why couldn't he just say, "I'm busy" or "not tonight"? Instant turnoff.

"Mommy, Auntie Reese is on the phone. She said what time are we going shopping."

"Tell her I'll call her back."

The sound of Kai's voice put an end to our intimate reunion. Quinton grabbed me from the back and began to hug me with his strong arms. It was where I wanted to be.

"Do you want me to come over?" he whispered in my ear. "That sounds good," I replied as my insides purred.

He looked over at our little girl with her smile reaching from ear to ear. Her smile, short a couple of pearly whites, filled the room with happiness. Quinton smiled in return, obviously content with our togetherness.

"Kai, let's go get Aunt Reese to go shopping. Then Daddy can come over. We'll order pizza—" I abruptly interrupted my suggestion, trying to control myself. Q was hitting my spot.

"Then we can get some movies like . . . " Shivers ran up and down my spine.

"Oooh, oooh can…can we get Spy Kids and Shrek! " Kai got so excited when we had our family nights.

Quinton

"Yes, Mama. Whatever you want," I answered my little girl, trying to resist Imani's tempting-to-touch apple ass.

I loved spending time with my girls. When they were happy, I was happy. If it wasn't for that crazy bitch making her bullshit threats, I would have still been home. I was about to end that episode with Trina though. She was just going to have to try to hurt me or stalk me or whatever the hell it was. I wanted my girls back—they didn't deserve to be alone. Imani didn't do anything but be there for me. I was ready to tell her the truth and hoped she forgave me. I didn't want anything to do with Trina; I loved Mani.

"Mani, can you wear this?" I handed her the gift box. I had picked it up for her upcoming birthday, but it wasn't a problem to get her something else, something better.

As she bent over to get the bags, I knew why I needed to make it over there. I missed her badly.

"I'll open this when you get there, okay?" she said as I watched her every move. "By the way, Q, do these clothes need washing?" She picked up Kai's pink Barbie overnight bag and began to look through it.

"Baby, you know my moms wouldn't send her stuff back dirty."

"All right then. Can you be home by eight?"

"That's cool. Can I have my key?" I shouldn't have had to beg to get the key. I paid the bills in the house.

"It'll be under the rock. Can we have some money to go shopping?" she asked as she turned with her palm out.

"Like, how much?" Here she goes, I thought. "Like, four hundred. Kai needs school clothes."

"All right, here," I said as I peeled off four crisp one-hundred-dollar bills. "Now, Imani, when are you going to stop taking my key?"

I had to readjust my pants. It was becoming a little uncomfortable. "Heh . . ." she said, giggling, " . . . when I stop going away?"

I didn't find that as amusing as she did. She laughed heartily at her comment. You would have sworn I wasn't in the room.

"See, that's that foul shit . . ." She ignored me and kept on walking. "Bye, Daddy," Kai said as she followed her mother out the door.

I watched out the window waiting for Imani to exit the building. Kai ran out with Imani following after. Imani turned off the alarm to her car and they got in.

All right, Imani was gone. All that was left was to call that heffah Trina and let her know I was on my way. "I'm coming through now."

I really couldn't stand her; the sound of her voice irritated me. "Well, don't forget the money for Jahlek."

She slammed the telephone in my ear. Rude ass. No respect. Fuck her. If it weren't for my son, I'd be out with Mani and Kai.

Although Imani had the tendency to stir up an argument, they were never as bad as those I had with Trina. There had been times where Trina and I had physical fights. I had never laid my hands on a woman and never wanted to. Trina brought me to that level. She wouldn't let me just walk away and calm down. She thought she could keep me by fighting. Imani had never let an argument lead to a fight. Either she'd walk away or I'd leave. After a couple of hours, we'd forget the whole thing with no desire of bringing it up again. I could see myself going to jail if I continued to see Trina. She wasn't worth the trouble.

I picked up my car keys and headed out the door. On my way down the stairs, I ran into my neighbor. She winked as she motioned for me to follow her back to her apartment. Any other time I might have followed her big ass but not that day. I was a man on a mission. I waved her off without looking back and continued down the stairs.

Dawn you dong be

CHAPTER 7
MIND-BLOWING DECISIONS

Imani

Kai and I had made several stops before we started for home. I had thought back on my brief encounter with Q and how it didn't take much for him to get me hot and bothered. I wanted him, and the night seemed too far away. No matter how bad times had gotten between Q and me, he knew I'd always want some of his good loving.

It didn't make any sense to punish myself and go on a strike. I had needs too. I reflected on Quinton's weak-ass plea to move back in. Could he have his key? Hah. He must've been crazy if he thought I was going to leave my house to him. How could he possibly believe I would let him and his bum friends in my place? I had put a lot of money into my house; I couldn't afford to let him mess it up. Q had just started putting money into the house but the first two years I did it, alone.

"Kai, take your hand off the railing. Hold Mommy's hand," I said as we exited the subway.

Could you imagine how many of those nasty bastards spat and pissed on the staircase? Whoo, the smell of urine was strong; it lingered in your nose. It was time to catch up on my Essence and Ebony magazines and the subway was the only place I could always find the newest publications. I would have gotten a subscription but I need to skim through and see if the article were interesting enough to buy the whole magazine.

"Kai, pass Mommy her phone, please." Kai reached reaches into my bag and searches for my cell phone.

I had to do her hair and change her clothes. Q didn't know how to take care of my baby.

"Yeah, Reese, what's up?"

"Nothing much. What's by you? Did you pick up my child yet?" Charisse sound like she was waking up or trying to get some sleep.

"Yeah, I just left Q's mama's house, 'bout to go home and change Kai. She looks like nobody's child. You promised your godchild you were going to take her out."

Charisse began to laugh. "Mmm, I did, didn't I? I guess I'll take her

to lunch while we're shopping. Listen, I've got to go . . ." She must have company.

"What time you got to work tonight?"

"I think eleven to seven. I'm not exactly sure. I've got plenty of time." She began to rush off the telephone.

"Are we taking your car or mine?" I was only asking questions to keep her on the telephone. "Nah, I'll drive since you've got to work tonight. Remember you're not as young as you used to be," I said as I began to laugh at my twenty-nine-year-old best friend.

"Imani, I . . . really have to go. I'll meet you at your house in an hour.

Please be ready, Mani. You're one slow bitch."

"All right, I'll try. Tell your friend I said hi."

Charisse had a different partner for each day of the week. I don't think she'd ever take any of them seriously. The worst part was they bent over backward for her—paying her bills, giving her cash and buying her all kinds of expensive shit.

Before I could put my telephone down, it began to ring again. Who could be calling me now? Who do I know with a 201 area code?

"Hello?"

"Hey, how are you doing, sexy?"

The deep voice sounded very familiar. Oh God, it was Omar.

"Hi, Omar. I didn't think you'd call so soon." This was shocking. I was almost convinced it was just a weekend fling.

"So, why didn't you call me when you got home? I thought we were cool."

His voice was sultry. Images of our night together came to mind as I listened to him speak.

"I've been busy. Today wasn't a good day. Anyway, what's up? How's your wife?" Uhh, wrong question. Was I nervous? I was too old for that.

"Ha, she's fine, I guess. I haven't seen her yet. But never mind her. How do you feel about us seeing each other again? When are you going to be available?"

Omar didn't seem like the hasty type. We had just seen each other.

"I-I don't know. Can I call you? I need time to think, you know."

My decision was made, no, I don't want a relationship with Omar. But I didn't want to be cold. For some reason, it didn't seem right.

"Certainly, sweetheart. I'll be waiting. I'm at work right now so I gotta go. Bye, love."

Quinton caused me to forget about Omar and his fine ass. I'd worry about it later. No need for immediate attention. Omar would be there tomorrow.

"Come on, Kai. Bring your doll," I said as I reached my house.

When I looked up, I noticed there was a bouquet of flowers on my porch swing.

"Mommy, look! You have pretty flowers."

Where did these flowers come from? Where's the card? I thought as I picked up the beautiful arrangement.

> ***Imani,***
> ***Just to let you know I was thinking about you.***
> ***Omar***

This man was funny. Flowers! One day went by and he missed me like that! Q could have learned a few things from that man. Yeah, right. I couldn't teach that old dog new tricks.

Opening the front door to let Kai through, the stupid telephone began to ring. Did it ever stop?

"Kai, get the phone. My hands are full, Baby."

I brought in Kai's suitcase and arranged the multicolored flowers in a crystal vase on the dining room table. Omar is a trip. How did he know where I lived? I must have given him the wrong business card. My personal cards must have mixed in with the ones from work.

"Kai, who is it?" I asked, remembering the telephone call.

"It's Uncle John, Mommy." She passed me the cordless phone. "John, what happened?"

The only time he called me was to baby-sit their three-year-old baby girl, Amber, or to borrow my car.

"Nothing. Justin just came from rehab and he wants to see you."

My brother Justin hasn't been home for sixteen years and all of a sudden he wanted to see me. Not happening!

"When?" I questioned with no enthusiasm whatsoever.

"Tonight, if possible. Mia is cooking a big dinner. Q can come too." That was a first, especially since John couldn't stand Q—never did and probably never would.

"We have plans. Tonight is family night."

"Well, if Mr. Make and Break strikes again, just come over. Our door will be open."

It was funny how all of a sudden John wanted to let me in his house. I remember when he told me to never come back.

"John, he's trying. Just chill," I pleaded with my brother, hoping he wouldn't go into one of his fuck Quinton speeches. My brother was more like my father. He's the only father I know, and although we did not get along, I valued his concern.

"Imani, I love you and only want what's good for you and K-Jay." After six years he still insists on calling Kai, K-Jay, no matter how much I detested the name. "I don't like how that asshole keeps walking in and out your life like his shit is sweet. You're better than that. Y'all deserve to be happy." There was compassion in his tone. Normally, he would preach on and on, reminding me of all the things Q might have done in the past and all the rumors circulating in the neighborhood about the things he had been up to. But not this time. He let me off the hook. Thank God for small miracles.

"We're going to be all right. We can take care of ourselves."

Shit, I had been taking care of myself. Q and I have taken care of each other. When we had no one else, we had each other. I bet John wouldn't bring up the positive qualities Quinton had. Although he wasn't shit in a relationship, there was no end to the things he would do for Kai and me.

"Okay, then I'll talk to you soon. Take care of yourself, baby girl."

"John, I love you too." He didn't have to say it. I knew what he meant.

I wondered if I should I go to John's and see Justin. It really wasn't the time to be thinking. Justin was my brother and he needed his family. But, where was he when I needed a family?

"Kai, take off your clothes and get in the shower. And I'm going to wash your hair so don't try jumping in and out. Leave the door open so I can see you."

My baby looked horrible. Her hair was still in the same three ponytails that I had put it in on Thursday. The sides were nappy and matted. She needed a serious conditioner and press. There was no way I could have combed through that forest.

"Daddy gave me a shower already." She stood in front of me waving her hand up and down about to have a fit. There wasn't anything I hated more than whining, especially from a little girl, over a bath.

"Kai, don't work me, please! You want to be nasty? Huh? Remember when we were on the train and that stinking person was on there? Remember how bad she smelled? That's how you're gonna smell if you don't get upstairs and wash. You're a lady, Kai. Ladies have to always keep their bodies clean and their kitty cleaner." I pointed to the spot between her legs. She knew my stand on hygiene and that there was no way out.

She went stomping off like I was supposed to be scared.

After I pulled out Kai clothes, I washed her hair. I checked the cabinets and made a mental note of the toiletries that needed to be added to my shopping list.

"Your clothes will be on my bed. Come straight to my room, I don't have time for your foolishness, okay?" I said as I left her in the shower.

Like she was really going to answer me. That little girl had one nasty- ass attitude. She got it from her father. He wasn't the easiest person to deal with either but I love me some him.

The gift Quinton had given me was calling as I took the long, gold gift box out of my bag. I wanted to wait but I couldn't. The temptation was hard to resist. I tore through the wrapping like a child on Christmas morning. As I opened the box, I prepared myself for what would be inside. It was a diamond tennis bracelet. Quinton had outdone himself yet again. I had gotten some decent gifts in the past—cars, furs, island getaways—all of which I loved but this had to be the best. Looked like six carats, probably better. Q was funny; you never knew what to expect from him.

Attached to the box was a note.

> *Imani,*
> *I know I did you wrong. I sit back and think about it every day. This is just a small token to apologize for all the things that I've done. Let me make it up to you. It may take some time but I promise you, you won't regret it.*
> *Love,*
> *Quinton*

We've been through so much already and were still young. Who knew how much more I would have to endure before he could make it right? I cared for Quinton, and I was sure he knew it but to give myself to him whole-heartedly again, I didn't think so. I was becoming comfortable with our relationship just the way it was. No hassle and no strings attached. Either one of us was free to walk away at any given time. No doubt I'd be hurt but taking it slow was the best decisions we made so far. And it would have to benefit Kai.

I placed the diamond bracelet on my wrist. As I glanced over the shiny stones, I wondered whether it was a gift of love or an apology. Either way, I love it. The bracelet fit as it were made just for me. The

Peridot stones, my birthstone, surrounded each diamond, forming clusters between each link. If Quinton didn't know how to do anything else, he knew how to make me happy.

Kai called me several times before I decided to answer. I was so into my own thoughts. Finally, I responded and began to climb the steps to the bathroom.

After Kai came out of the shower, she hurried into my room to lotion her bony body. She liked to use my scented lotions and oils on her soft tanned skin. I rubbed some scented baby powder on her neck and wrists and watched her face light up with joy. I never knew such happiness as a child, and it filled me up knowing I could provide so much love and joy for my baby—moments I couldn't imagine living without. I missed not having a mother to share those times with.

As Kai slid into her Pocahontas T-shirt and panties, I went downstairs to plug in the straightening comb. I began to prep my little area with hair grease, hair pins, barrettes, combs and brushes. Kai entered the kitchen wearing the yellow jeans I had laid out with a multi-colored ribbed turtleneck.

"Kai, where's your towel? I thought I asked you to bring it down with you," I said calmly with a hand on my hip.

"I forgot it. I have to go back and get it?" She looked at me like you got to be kidding me.

This little girl had too many attitudes for a six-year-old. When I was growing up, talking back to Nana was never a thought. You said "yes, ma'am" and went about your business. And you didn't forget anything either. Nana said things once, and that was it. You did it or suffered the consequences. Kai wouldn't have survived in Nana's house.

"Who else is going to get it? If you weren't so busy playing with these dolls—" I snatched the Barbie out of her hand—"you might have heard me the first time. Now go get the towel so I can do your hair."

She immediately about-faced and headed up the stairs. Her thick, wild, wet hair dripped down her back and onto the floor. If I were as mean as she thought, I'd make her mop the floor. Instead, I picked up a piece of paper towel and placed it over the wet area.

As I finished pressing Kai's hair, Charisse rolled up. You would swear she was rich. Every time I turned around, she was in a different ride. They weren't any busted ones either, straight top of the line—Benz, BMW, Jaguar, you name it. She dealt with some high-class broads.

Charisse stepped out of her car with some tight-ass D&G jeans, a skin-tight tank top that was cut just above her midriff to display her newly pierced navel, her infamous Chloe shades and Italian leather boots. Her hair was permed straight and streaked with brown and blond highlights. She looked like she stepped out of a magazine. She reminded me of those models you see in the ads with a flawless mahogany complexion who used hardly any makeup.

My neighbor watched her walk to my door. Charisse paid him absolutely no attention. Only if he knew, she didn't flow that way.

"Imani, you ready? Where are you?" She used her key to get into the house, screaming like we were in the projects.

"I'm in the kitchen, coming right now!"

I quickly tried to style Kai's hair. "Whose car you got?"

"Oh. It's my friend Myra's car. She's chillin' at my house for a while. She said I could use it." Charisse giggled. She finally entered the kitchen and set her keys on the counter. "Bitch, where are your clothes?

"I took my shirt off to do Kai's hair. What? I'm not your type?" I said playfully as I covered Kai's ears.

"Stop playing with me, Imani. You know we don't get down like that." Charisse pointed to Kai as she crunched her lips tightly together.

Although I may have been just playing, there were times I questioned why she never found me attractive or why she didn't try to get with me. I was hardly into that lesbian lifestyle but it was just one of those things that made you say hmmm . . .

I grabbed my shirt off the dining room chair and slipped it over my head. I tried to hurry and finish Kai's hair as I watched Reese become restless.

"You sure that's not going to cramp your style, having someone at your house," I said, trying to buy time.

"No, actually, she likes it better when I have a friend or two over."

"You are one freaky chic, Reese."

"Mani, you should know by now, the more the merrier."

We both shared a brief minute of laughter. I walked out of the kitchen, through the dining room and into the living room to get our jackets. Kai wasn't far behind.

"Can we go now? I got a new card I want to use," she said as she flashed an American Express platinum card.

"Kai, get my pocketbook off the dining room table, please."

I turned to face Charisse. "Girl, look at this bracelet." I turned my wrist to give her a full view. "Q gave it to me when I picked up Kai."

"What's that? His get-out-of-jail-free card?"

"There you go with this 'Q ain't shit' attitude."

"Did you get it appraised?" she asked as she peered closely at each diamond.

"Has Q ever half stepped on any of his gifts? He may not be the best man on earth but at least he has good taste. Reese, he's trying to be a better man."

"When? When he's not with his other chick? Why don't you ask him about these girls? Do they know he has a fiancée and child? And, how much longer are you going to pretend to be engaged?"

Charisse never let Q get a chance. I hated when she started with all the questions. I felt like I was in front of a firing squad instead of my best friend. I would try not to get upset. But the truth hurt. Worst of all, I felt stupid. After all those years, I was still wearing a meaningless engagement ring.

"I'm going to ask him tonight about his so-called girlfriends. But, if he tells me there is no one else, you have to just leave it at that. Eventually, the truth will come out, and if he's seeing someone else then I'll cut him off completely."

"Whatever," she said as she flagged for Kai. "Kai, you ready to go?" She took my daughter's hand and led her out the door.

Sometimes, I wondered if the rumors were true. Quinton and I hadn't been having the best relationship but at least we were there for each other. I prayed for the day Q would prove Charisse wrong. As I dimmed the lights and activated the answering machine, Charisse honked her horn.

On the way to the mall, we began to have our regular girlfriend chitchat. Charisse continued on and on as I stared blankly out the window. The soothing scent of vanilla mixed with the sweet smell of cherries as the air fresheners swung back and forth.

"What's up, Mani? You look like something's on your mind." Charisse asked after noticing my silence.

"Justin is back and John wants the family to get together at his house," I said.

"So, what are you going to do?"

"Q, Kai and I made plans to have a family night tonight." Charisse pushed her lips to one side, a sign of disbelief.

"Well, this is your brother. You should at least see how's he doing," Charisse said.

"He never cared to see how I was doing," I said, trying to stifle my sobs.

"Imani, you really need to let that go. That was years ago, and your brother needed help. Now he needs his family, and the least you can do is see him."

Charisse knew about my brother running off and being addicted to drugs but I had yet to tell her that he was HIV positive. That was what I was ashamed of. I didn't mind that Justin was an ex-crackhead but I thought being sick should be kept as family business.

"If Q doesn't mind spinning by there for a quick minute then fine, I'll go. Otherwise, Justin's going to have to catch me at a better time."

Quinton

Isn't it funny how life takes its course? After all I had been through, you'd think I would know how to treat a good woman, knowing how my mother felt when my father walked out the door, leaving us alone, broke and on the verge of being homeless. I had

94

vowed to be a better man than my father was but it seemed like failure was inevitable. Instead of learning from his mistakes, I was repeating them. But I would be damned if I would lose Imani.

I pulled up to the gas station on the corner of Linden Boulevard and Pennsylvania Avenue after realizing my tank was on empty. As usual, I pulled up in the full service lane to avoid pumping my own gas. One of the employees approached my window and asked, "What kind of gas?"

"Super. Fill it up," I replied as I handed him a fifty-dollar bill.

He then put the pump into the gas tank and began to wash the rear window.

I looked at my watch to make sure I was on schedule. I wanted to be on time to show Mani I meant business. After I concluded my meeting with Trina, I'd go run by Blockbuster to pick up the movies for Kai. Hopefully, they would keep her occupied while I took care of Imani. I had been waiting for another chance with her for a long, long time. There were days when I found myself losing control just thinking about making wild, passionate love to her. Although, I had many lovers, no one held a candle to Imani. Her first concern was to please me. Moments like those were so far and in between for us. We could go almost six months before touching or spending time with each other. We saw each other regularly but mostly in passing. But after tonight, things were going to be different.

My pager vibrated on my hip. I picked up the small black box and pressed the button to reveal the number. It was Trina again. She could wait. Just as I began to turn the ignition, Rodney sped in front of me, his cranberry Navigator blocking the exit. I took the key out of the ignition and opened my door to get out of the car. I straightened the wrinkles in my jeans and stomped my tan Timberlands to make sure my jeans fell right. My blue-and-white Hilfiger shirt was unbuttoned and blew with the wind, displaying my rippled abdomen. Not to sound conceited but a nigga looked good.

Rodney exited his Navigator and limped over. Two young girls passed by and gawked our way as we greeted each other with a hand dap and a hug. I winked playfully at one of the girls just to get a rise out of her. She giggled and looked away. As she and her friend continued to walk by, I couldn't help but notice how big her ass was. Those young girls were a lot healthier than the ones were when I was growing up.

"Damn, kid. A nigga going to wind up going to jail for shorty," I said as I took my hand towel from my back pocket and wiped my forehead.

"Put your eyes back in your head," Rodney said. "Imagine if that was your daughter. Would you want some young nigga staring at her like that?" He patted my back firmly.

"It be like that sometimes. When Kai gets older, she'll know better. She ain't going to be wearin' no skin-tight shit showing all her ass. Mani won't have that," I replied looking over into his jeep.

"Yeah, whatever. Just know her godfather got a double barrel loaded and ready for any motherfucka that plays himself," Rodney said.

"No doubt, my nigga." I gave him another hand dap. I knew Rodney would never let anything happen to Kai nor Imani. Shit, most of the time he covered my back for Imani's sake. He couldn't stand to see her hurt. Repeatedly, he would threaten to tell Imani everything if I didn't discontinue my numerous affairs but I knew he was bullshitting. Although, I couldn't front, sometimes I really wasn't sure.

I looked inside the passenger side window, checking out his company. He was rolling with a couple of brothers from around the way. "Where you heading to?" I asked curiously.

"Over to Brownsville to pick up some shorties. You wanna roll?" he asked. As we spoke a black Escalade pulled up behind my Lexus and began honking the horn.

"Is there a problem?" I asked, annoyed with the driver. Rodney shot the driver an evil eye as the driver stuck his head out of the window. "You're blocking the fuckin' exit! " a West Indian man shouted.

"Find another way out. We're busy," I said as I turned around to answer Rodney. "Nah, I can't roll with you right now. I'm going that way though. Follow me out there and then I'll follow you over to wherever you're going." I was still ignoring the horn honking behind me.

A police car pulled up into the gas station and stopped where we were standing. Rodney couldn't afford to get into confrontation with the officer so he casually walked back over to his car. He had a warrant out for a robbery and had been laying low since. Slowly, I got into my car, turned on the ignition and pulled away.

When I reached the corner of the next block, I called Rodney on his cell.

"Yo, are you going to follow me over to Trina's house for a hot second or what?" I screamed over the bass that pumped from my sound system. My car was equipped with the latest state-of-the-art Alpine entertainment system. I figured it didn't make any sense to have money and not have anything to show for it.

Rodney agreed to follow me, and we immediately made illegal U- turns and raced down Linden Boulevard.

Imani

As we pulled up to the mall, Charisse stared at me with a weird look. "Don't you want your family back?"

"I'll never have my family back. Nadine left me, and the only mother I knew died. Jordan's barely around and Jada is too busy being an asshole. The only time I see her is when she needs a baby-sitter or has an argument with her husband and needs a place to stay. John also has a family of his own. It's just me and mine. The only family I'll ever have is right here, right now."

Tears began to well up in my eyes so I turned away, looked out the window and said, "And that's fine with me."

"Sorry, Mani. I want you to be happy. You say you're cool with how your family's acting but I know it bothers you because all you talk about is wanting to spend time together."

"Charisse, let's leave it be. It's not going to get any better than this.

Our father died when I was two. You know about Nadine. My siblings and I have no real family structure. This is it! " I became angry as I thought about my situation. Just when things started to come together for my family, something always tore us apart. I needed my sister and brothers. They were the only family I had.

Charisse hugged me and said; "It's all right, girl. I'll always be there for you."

"Thanks."

CHAPTER 8
DO WHAT I GOTTA DO

Quinton

Rodney decided to make his runs first so he could drop off his boys. We hung out a little longer than I had anticipated. Instead of rushing to Trina's house, I went to several different block parties and picked up a couple of numbers on the way out. Some things took precedence over bullshit baby mama drama.

"No, no, no. Trina, are you deaf? I'm not staying. I'm coming to see Jahlek, drop off the stuff and that's it," I said as I drove through the blocks.

I had called to let her know I was on my way and to listen for the bell but Trina, being herself, had to make an argument out of everything.

"This ain't got shit to do with Imani. Look. Follow the bouncing ball, okay. I . . . don't . . . want . . . to . . . " Before I got to finish my sentence she hung up.

The time had come for me to start doing what was right for mine and me. My life had been wasting away like I didn't have the credentials to excel. I graduated college with a 3.8 grade point average and received a bachelor's in political science so there was no reason for me to be living this way. Dealing drugs ain't even my style.

To top it all off, I couldn't do right by Imani. And if I didn't start doing right, I'd lose her forever. I couldn't let her go again. She filled the void left by mother that yearned to be loved. But the pressure of family life was too much for me to deal with. I didn't have anything to offer Kai and Imani. They didn't deserve to have someone who would mess up their lives. I wanted to do right. Shit, I loved my girls, but I wasn't ready to settle down. So many temptations on the streets kept me away from my responsibilities.

My number one distraction was Trina who needed to know that there would never, ever be an "us." The bitch already tricked me into getting her pregnant. "I'm on the pill. Use this condom." Should have never even started messing with that chick. She would call my mom's house and come by my place trying to find me or should I say, catch me out there as if my life was any of her business.

Back when I first started seeing Trina, I knew it was going to be a real fucked-up situation. From day one she had built up animosity toward Mani. I didn't want to be with Trina but I wasn't ready to settle down with Imani.

Being a player was a part of my repertoire. But Mani was so sweet and innocent, which was what I was looking for. At least that's what I thought.

I was feeling all kinds of pressure from my boys about being strung out and needing to explore my options and have fun. That was how I met Trina Knight.

My boys took me to some strip joint in the city. Trina's stage name was Chocolate Delight. She was all of five feet and had a booty to die for. The more she shook that thang, the more I wanted her. She was attracted to me too; she didn't leave my lap all night. We exchanged phone numbers and hung out a couple of times but it was nothing serious.

Not too long after we moved, Mani and I started having little arguments here and there—mostly because of her jealousy—and that was the first sign that stuff was a little too serious. The more we argued the more Trina comforted me, making me feel like a man again. Her comfort was never enough to make me leave Imani or be faithful to Trina. There was still Tya's emotional ass. When Imani took my daughter and Tya finally decided to leave me, Trina took me in. That was when I signed my life over to the devil.

Trina was the freak Imani wasn't. She kept me coming back for more. We became so enveloped in our sexual attractions I had totally forgotten about Imani and our family, even tossed the possibility that Tya might be having my baby.

Trina soon found out that Mani and I shared a child and she wanted one too. I tried every excuse in the book for her not to have this child without trying to hurt her feelings. This was not the kind of woman I wanted to mother my child. She already had a kid with big-time hustler. Plus, I already had one I barely ever saw and another one on the way. About three months later, I found out Trina was pregnant and Tya was not. I offered Trina thousands to get rid of the baby but she wouldn't. Instead she left town and came back when Jahlek turned one. For months, I tried contacting her but it was to no avail. When I finally saw Jahlek, I fell in love with him. This was my son; he looked like me when I was young with my mahogany skin, curly hair, chinky eyes and small ears. Although it was unfair for him to be born into that kind of relationship, I couldn't turn my back on him.

Seeing Jahlek made me think about Kai, my baby girl. Noticing how much they looked alike broke my heart. That's when I realized the mistake I made by leaving Imani. That's when I went back—the first time. After being gone for three years, she still took me back. I wanted to be a better man for Mani but Trina kept threatening me, telling me she would drop Jahlek at our doorstep with a note detailing everything. Trina was serious too. There were some nights I caught her driving past Imani's house, peeping to see if my car was gone. So, to avoid causing Mani any more pain, I left again. I visited occasionally but never stayed more than a night.

I was ready to tell Imani everything and hoped I could make things right for us. First, I had to deal with Trina's crazy ass. I stood there in front of Trina's building, preparing myself for what was ahead.

"Who?" a voice said through the intercom over the static.

"Yo, open the damn door."

The door began to buzz. I walked all the way down the dim hallway to Trina's apartment and used the key she gave me to open the heavy brown metal door.

"Trina! We need to talk," I called out as I looked around for her.

She came out wearing purple two-piece lingerie that barely fit. Incense filled the air.

"Hey, Baby. What's up?"

"Check it, I ain't with doing this anymore. I'm going to be with my heart. This shit right here is not working out," I said as I unwrapped her arms from around my waist.

I couldn't stop looking her up and down. She had a body like whoa! Her nipples stood at full attention, peeping through the lacy lingerie as she twirled her finger through her shoulder-length jet-black weave.

"So, whatcha sayin'? You're going to forget about your son and me?

Whether you like it or not, you're stuck with me for life."

"No, I'm not. I'm going to tell Mani all about our little affair and about Jahlek. Hopefully, try to work things out. I will still hit you off for Jahlek and shit. You know, I'll come get him and let him spend time with his sister—"

Trina cut me off immediately. "Jahlek ain't got no fuckin' sista, and he ain't going to some bitch's house. Oh yeah, and as far as I am concerned he won't have a father either. When you walk out that door, you walk out on us both."

"Bitch, don't tell me I can't see my fuckin' son! I should take his ass. You ain't shit. Everything up in here I bought, you broke-ass ho! When I walk out this door, I'm walking out on you. I'm still going to be here for my son. Here, take this." I handed her the last two hundred in my pocket. "I hope you find a job or else you'll be living on the street next month."

"A'ight, you black bastard. I wanna see you come and take my son from me. It will be some smoke in the city. As far as this apartment, fuck it. I'll move in with my other baby father. That way Jahlek and his brother can *spend more time together*. So, take whatever you want. I'll sell the rest."

"You're not bringing my son to Bryan's house."

I grabbed her by her throat. "That nigga runs hos and drugs out his spot. If you let something happen to my son, I'll kill you."

Letting her go I began walking to the door then suddenly turned and said, "I'll be by this weekend to pick up my stuff and my son. Have him packed! "

"Fuck you, Q."

Without a reply, I walked out the door. Taking my first steps as a free man into the hallway, I decided to call Mama and tell her to ride with me to pick out a new ring for my new life with Imani. Just as I pulled out my phone, I heard a door creak open. Two shots were fired; I went down. The shots rang through the empty apartment building. I tried to call for Rodney but my vocal cords felt restricted. No sound escaped. The warmth of blood oozing from the wounds coated my flesh. One bullet ripped through my shoulder exiting the other side; the other plunged into my thigh. The fear of death rose inside my chest. Panic froze my body while tears burned my eyes.

I picked up my cell and hit the talk button, which dialed the last number I had called. Rodney answered his phone but I was unable to reply. Immediately he rushed inside after my number came up on his Caller ID.

"Yo, man. Shit. You gonna be all right," Rodney said as he placed his jacket underneath my head. He reached for his waist and I knew that meant problems. I shook my head.

"What you mean no? Man, fuck that bitch."

"My son is in there. Just get me to a hospital. This shit is starting to burn like hell," I managed to say through a strained whisper.

"A'ight, kid. I told you a long time ago to leave that crazy bitch alone." He laughed. Although this was no time for jokes, he was right and it was funny. I wanted to laugh but the pain shot through my body.

"Ahhh, shit. Man, Rodney get me the fuck outta here," I said as the pain became unbearable.

"I'm gonna call an ambulance. I don't wanna move you." Rodney's voice was full of concern.

"Call Mama too."

"A'ight, just relax. Everything's gonna be all right. Trust me, I should know," he said as he pointed to his shoulder.

About two years ago, Tya's older brother, Rick, had walked up to us on Lott Avenue. Tension began to build up between Rick and me. Shoves were exchanged then from out of nowhere her other brother, Li'l Dee, whipped around the corner and let off several shots. Rodney took one to the shoulder and by the grace of God, I managed to walk away untouched.

"Thanks, Rod."

"Ain't nothing, bro," he said.

Imani

"I can't wait until Q sees me in this. What do you think?" I playfully elbowed Charisse to show her the piece I had been holding up. The soft pink sheer negligee would look good against my lightly toasted skin. I picked up a lace thong to wear underneath. This night was going to be special.

"Yeah, that shit is cute. My girl got one like this," Charisse said.

Charisse and I had decided to see what was new in Victoria's Secret. We had finished whatever shopping we were going to do for Kai. It was our turn. Victoria's was our final destination. My feet were sore from following Reese in and out of every store. I had picked up a couple of things for myself at New York and Company and the GAP. But that was not good enough for Reese. She spent her time in the fashion-filled aisles of Macy's and all the other high-priced stores. That stuff was well beyond my means and most of it didn't look like me, at all. Give me some jeans and a couple of nice blouses or sweaters and I was fine. My trend frenzy had long escaped. Since having Kai, I had to learn how to count my pennies, despite the high-class position I held with the firm. Rainy days were never too far away.

The fruity scents of lotion and perfumes began to irritate my nose, causing me to sneeze. As I reached for my pocketbook to get some tissue, Kai began pulling on my arm.

"Mommy, that man over there keeps staring at you. He's scaring me."

Kai grabbed hold of my hand and moved between Charisse and me. "Who's that, Mani?" Charisse asked with a puzzled look on her face. I wasn't sure who it was but the face looked familiar.

"Excuse me. Is there a reason you keep staring over here?" I asked from across a rack of clothes.

"Oh, excuse me, miss. I didn't mean to startle your daughter. I was trying to remember where I know you from," the light skin man replied with a puzzled look. His green eyes were so friendly and warm. The way he smiled sparked a brief memory but I still couldn't place the face. Normally, I would never forget a name or a face but this time I had no clue.

"What school did you go to?" I asked, hoping to get an idea.

"I graduated from Jackson after I transferred from Irving."

"Rahsaun? Rahsaun Tyler, right?" I asked, realizing he was my best friend from high school.

"Yes, that's my name but who are you?" This was getting embarrassing.

"It's me fool, Imani. Imani Wright."

He began to laugh at his own embarrassment. After seconds of laughter, he walked over and wrapped his arms around me.

"How are you doing?" I said as I hugged him back.

"I'm fine. How've you been? This is crazy. I would never have thought we'd see each other again. Who's this little lady?" He looked over to Kai who was clutching onto my jeans.

"This is my daughter, Kai Aja Simone Banks. Yes, Quinton's daughter," I answered before he asked.

"Y'all still together? Damn! That's my wife, Yuvette, over there. We don't have any kids yet. She's too busy with school and work; we barely got time to—" he smiled at Kai before finishing his sentence—"you know."

"Hmm. Yeah, I know. Rahsaun, I want you to meet my best friend, Charisse."

He took her hand and placed a gentle kiss on it. He was such a gentleman. Charisse began to smile. She thought it was funny.

"Nice to meet you," he said to Charisse before returning his attention to me.

"Imani, we have to keep in touch. I can't imagine not seeing you again. I've missed you."

"That's funny. You never called. We've always waited until we saw each other in school the next day to talk or gossip—that was until you left. You just totally forgot about me."

"I tried to call and tell you I was moving but John said he didn't know who you were."

Charisse began to laugh. "That must have been when he kicked you out." She continued laughing after I pinched her arm.

"Not funny." Everybody thought her little comment was cute but me.

"Rahsaun, your wife's not going to have a problem with us keeping in touch?"

"No I'll tell her you're my cousin or something. If I told her you were an old friend, she'd have a million and one questions before having a jealous fit. Sis, give me a pen and paper."

Charisse handed him a piece of paper and a pen so that he could give me his number.

After handing it to me, he said, "You sure Q won't have a problem with you calling."

"That's if he's home when she calls you," Charisse said, trying to be funny.

As I put my finger up to respond, my cell phone rang. It was Q's number on my Caller ID.

"What's up, Q?" I answered flatly, assuming he was calling to cancel.

"This ain't Q. It's Rodney. Q's been shot. He's at Kings County Hospital." He sounded mad.

"Where . . . who shot him?" Panic had instantly taken over as Rodney continued to deliver his message.

"I don't know if I should go into all that. Just calling to let you know." Then the line went dead.

Mechanically, I put my cell in my bag and instantly grabbed Kai's hand. Without uttering a word, I had started for the door when Charisse grabbed my bag to catch my attention.

"Wait! Imani! Where are you going?"

I could hear Charisse but I couldn't respond. "Imani! What the hell happened?"

"Q's . . . Q's been shot." Tears flowed from my eyes and trickled off my cheeks.

"Listen, Rahsaun, we have to go. Try calling later tonight and I'll let you know how she's doing," Charisse told him as she hurried behind me.

We jumped into Charisse's car and rushed to Brooklyn. I tried to stop crying for my little girl's sake but the thought of losing Q was too much for me to handle. I dealt with him leaving me, I dealt with him coming over whenever he felt like it but I couldn't deal with Q dying. We needed him . . . I needed him. We were supposed to be together.

Questions flooded my mind. I hoped he was going to be okay. I told him the street life was not for him. I told him it was dangerous.

"Why didn't he listen to me?"

"It's going to be all right, Imani. Be strong. Kai is watching you," Charisse whispered as she held my hand.

Kai was sad but she didn't cry. She almost never cried. Like her father, Kai was strong.

When we reached the hospital, I went directly to the emergency room while Charisse and Kai sat in the waiting area. The receptionist looked for Q's name and told me he was still in the operating room. She told me he had been shot in the back of his right leg and his right shoulder. "Thank you" was all I could manage to say as I looked up to heaven.

I went back to tell Charisse what was going on. Although she did not like Q, she was relieved. Charisse thought we should call Mama J and ask if she knew any more than what Rodney had offered over the phone.

On the way to Mama J's house, Charisse called and told her friend she would be home late. Mama J was sitting outside with a couple of her friends when we reached the building. She looked like she had been crying; she must have gotten the news.

"Mama, are you okay?" I asked as I hugged her.

"Yeah, chile. I'm fine now. Come, Kai. Give Nana a hug," she said as she motioned for Kai to come over to her.

"He's in the operating room now. They say Q is not severely wounded. He got shot in the right shoulder and in the back of his right leg. Do they know who shot him?" I asked.

"Imani, I already know. I went with him to the hospital but I couldn't stay. I was a nervous wreck. One of the nurses recommended I relax before my pressure went sky high so James and I just came on back home," she said as calmly as possible. Mama's face let me know something was wrong. "We need to talk. Let's go inside," she said.

This didn't sound good.

Inside the apartment, Mama J began to tell me what happened. Q had told his mother that he wanted to make everything right between us. He had a secret he wanted to reveal. Q felt this secret was the reason why our relationship went wrong.

Mama told me about some girl named Trina. Over the years, some of the women from Mama's neighborhood would tell me things about the women Quinton was keeping but Trina's name was never mentioned. Mama said Trina was giving Q a hard time. Mama J had explained that Quinton never loved her; she was there and one thing led to another. Before long they had a son. I could not believe what I was hearing.

I turned to Charisse to see if she had heard the same thing. She said, "I tried to tell you."

Heat rose up my back and neck. Rage had taken over. At any moment I knew I would snap. Reese's stupid-ass smirk didn't make matters any better. If she wasn't my best friend, she might have been a victim of my wrath.

Mama J said that the only reason Q didn't tell me about Trina was because he thought I wouldn't want to be with him. He was right because I felt like hurting him.

"He went over there to tell her it was over and that he wanted to be with you. She threatened him and told him he would never see his child again. In return Q told her he would kill her if he couldn't see his son. While he was walking down the hall to leave the building she shot him. Rodney was with him. He contacted me after calling 911 and told me the story as we rode to the hospital," she explained.

"So where is this bitch now! " I was ready for war. Quinton may have been cheating on me but nobody fucked with my man.

"The police came with the ambulance and arrested her," Mama said as she wringing her hands.

"So, where's the little boy?" I asked, not really caring.

"He's sleeping in the back room. I have him for right now," she said. The walls seemed to close in on me as I began to absorb the information. This was too much for me. Quinton had a family somewhere else. Why didn't he tell me he had a son? He must have loved her. She must have been the one who kept him away from home. All those nights I couldn't find him. He was with her. What kind of man was he? He wasn't a real man. A real man would have confessed a long time ago, realizing he made a mistake. Not saying that I would have felt any better about it. But for him to keep this whole thing a secret was like saying he still had feelings for her. How could he do this? I thought as I tried to regain my composure. I guess what we had wasn't good enough. Or, was it that his sexual urges had taken over his better senses?

I didn't know. Maybe I was just making excuses to disguise the fact that he was a sorry-ass excuse for a man, like his father.

"Mama, I got to go. I need some time to think," I said absently. I had no idea where I was going.

"Imani, you want me to take you home?" Charisse asked as she gave me a consoling hug. She looked like she wanted to cry for me.

"Yeah, I got to umm . . . yeah, let's go," I replied.

I picked Kai up off the couch where she was sleeping and told Mama I'd call her later. Charisse carried Kai to the car while I called Jada and asked her if she would watch Kai for me. I needed some time to vent and get some of this hurt of my chest. Mostly, I needed to think of what my next move was going to be.

On the way to Jada's, Charisse tried to make jokes and cheer me up. It was no use; I was too deep in thought to digest her weak comedy. At a red light, she waved her hand in front of my face to get my attention.

"Mani, are you there?" she asked.

I didn't know where I was.

Quinton

As the anesthesia wore off, I began to open my eyes. Mama sat there holding my hand. James stood behind her watching the news. She smiled when I finally focused on her face, completely opening my eyes.

"Hey, Baby. You're going to be just fine," she said softly.

"Ma—" I cleared my throat—"where's Mani? Is she here?" I asked as I looked around.

Mama glanced at me with a scared look. I don't know what happened but I had a feeling it was nothing good.

"Son, Mani was here but she went home to calm down," James said as he massaged my mother's shoulders.

"She knows about Trina and Jahlek. I had to tell her. She was hysterical." Mama kept wringing her hands.

"What? How could you...?" I tried to sit up but the pain was excruciating.

"Q, calm down. She'll be all right. She just needs to chill out," James said as he motioned for me to lie down.

"What the fuck are you talking about? She doesn't take everything as calmly as y'all think. Her exterior may be tough but inside she's baby. I need to speak to her." I spoke with a raspy voice, weak from medication.

I tried to reach for the phone but my arm was full of IV needles.

Mama passed the phone and dialed the number. I listened, waiting for the phone to ring. Instead I got a busy tone. Mama hung up and dialed again, and again, and again but it stayed busy.

"Shit, I don't believe this. I need to see her. I need to explain. Ma . . ."
I ranted.

"Q, she needs some time. She'll come around. You need to rest," Mama said as she ran her hand over my head.

"I can't. You messed up everything. You should've stayed out of it.

Left it up to me," I said through tightly pressed lips.

110

"Your mother was trying to do the right thing. You should have done that a long time ago. You can't blame nobody but yourself," James said as he wiped the tears out of Mama's eyes.

"Leave . . . me . . . alone. Leave! I don't want to see you right now. Neither one of you." I turned my head and looked out the window, waiting to hear the door close.

After Mama and James left, I felt like someone had knocked the air out of me. Imani was never going to forgive me. Mama should have minded her own business. I closed my eyes and tried to suppress the tears that had begun to build up. Anger and hurt had taken control of my body as I began to hate myself more and more for what I had done. I didn't have to see Imani to feel her pain. I lay there, staring at the ceiling, searching for answers.

CHAPTER 9
HOW COULD YOU FORGET?

Imani

After Charisse and I dropped Kai off, I went home and sat in the dark for a while. To my left, a picture of Q and me at Jada's housewarming stood in a metal frame. We were so happy then, posing for this picture while we were dancing. He was my friend when I needed someone to talk to and my lover when I needed someone to love. Quinton was everything to me. How could I replace that and move on?

My heart felt like it was tearing apart. I held the frame close and tried to recapture the love we shared that day. Anger filled me. The thought of him loving Trina the same way he loved me. Filled with rage, I flung the frame across the living room as I curled up like a baby and wept. Who could I turn to? I spent my whole life living a lie with this man. There was no one left for me to turn to. No one who would console me and care for me the way I wanted to be.

Suddenly Omar flashed across my mind. I did promise I would call him when I had time. He said if I ever needed a friend, not to hesitate to call. Now was as good a time as any.

"Hello?" a voice answered the person cleared his throat.

"Hello. May I speak to Mr. Smalls, please?" This didn't feel right.

"Mr. Smalls speaking. Who's calling?"

"This is Imani. What's up?"

The words rolled off my tongue as if we were old friends. Still, I was a little nervous. We started talking about what had been going on since we had been back. He told me that his wife was still out of town and hadn't even called to say she was okay. I was hearing his words but my mind drifted from the conversation. He noticed the vagueness in my responses and asked what was wrong. All I could do was cry. I bottled up the pain for as long as I could.

Through my sobs I was able to give him an edited version of the story. No details, just the basics—Q has a family with another woman.

Omar tried to soothe my pain with comforting words. But that was not what I needed to hear. I needed to hear Quinton's voice, waking me, telling me this was all a dream.

"Imani, do you want to meet in the city?"

"When?"

"Tonight. That way you don't have to be alone. This is not a time to be by yourself."

"I guess. Where do you want to meet?"

"At the café in the Marriott on Broadway? I can be there in about an hour."

"Not a problem. I'll be there. Bye."

Omar was sweet. At least he cared enough to travel from his home in Jersey. Q probably would have been too busy to even care what I had to say. Most nights, I couldn't even find Q. Now I knew why. I still couldn't believe he did this to me. Not only did he cheat; he had another kid and never told me. Those phony-ass I love yous. I wondered if he had bought her a bracelet too. I wondered if he'd paid her bills, bought her a car and hit her off with hush money.

The more I thought about it, the more it hurt.

As I drove into the city, I thought of all the good times Q and I had together and all the shit I did for him. We always managed to find our way back together throughout everything that had happened. No matter what, our love was never at question. There had to be a reason why he was with her. But, what? From what I had heard, she was a ho.

The sounds of the rain beat against the window as I thought back and tried to find the moment that destiny chose to tear us apart. For so long, I had tried to fool myself into believing that we were meant to be. Silly of me, huh? What hurt most was that Trina wasn't even a woman of my stature. She was nothing like me. Not saying it would have hurt any less if she were.

113

I remembered Charisse telling me she knew Trina. While we drove back to my house from the hospital, she went into detail of how she and Trina met.

Trina was stripping at some bar Reese went to. That was how Charisse knew what was going on, which explained why she hated Q. Reese said one night while she was picking up her girlfriend, she saw Quinton and Trina leaving together. Q and Charisse made eye contact but he acted as if he didn't know her. Since then they had built up hatred toward each other. I didn't blame her for hating him. The way I was feeling wasn't too far from hate.

A single tear rolled down my left cheek as I turned on Forty-third Street. I vowed that would be the last tear I shed for Quinton Banks.

Omar and I pulled up to the Marriott about the same time. I can't begin to explain how happy I was to see him. He was fine as hell rolling in a burgundy 2002, Hyundai Sonata complete with cream leather interior and moon roof, which was rolled back allowing the cool night air in. Omar wore a mustard-colored fitted shirt that clung to his muscular chest with some khakis and brown sandals. His hair was shorter than when I last saw him. His mustache was trimmed perfectly framing his gorgeous smile. This man knew how to take care of himself. Stuff like that turned me on.

Quinton was the same way. His hair was always cut low but when he let it grow, it was naturally curly from his Hispanic roots. Q's goatee was always neatly groomed and his body filled out his shirts better than Omar's. Quinton's boyish smile would melt my insides. Quinton had begun to build up a little muscle over the past couple of years giving his abdomen that rippled appearance. Quinton's flawless mahogany-colored skin and diamond-shaped dimples made him hard to resist. Q was my version of Morris Chestnut, simply gorgeous. Then again, he probably was Trina's too.

When Omar realized who I was, he put his car in park and handed his keys to the valet. I followed. After he tipped both valets, he came over to greet me. The touch of his warm hands made me think twice about our encounter. This might not be a good idea. His scent drove my body wild.

114

He wore a soft sensuous oil; the scent intrigued my senses. I was turned on in the worst way. This was not good news.

"Hey, girl. You lookin' real good." He walked around me to get the full effect.

"Thanks." I shouldn't be here, I thought as he placed a soft kiss on my hand. Omar's full lips against my skin were intoxicating. I felt drunk. Needless to say, I was blown away.

"Let's go upstairs and grab a bite or something," he said.

Omar took my hand and led me into the hotel. We rode the elevator up to the seventh floor where all the shops and restaurants were located. He picked up one dozen long-stemmed roses from a florist, as a sympathy gift. I accepted them. They suited the occasion. I felt like the Quinton I thought I knew died.

When we reached the café, we sat at a table in the corner, away from everyone else. The dim lighting made me feel safe. I didn't want anyone to see me there with another man. Even though Quinton had done his dirt, I would never stoop to his level. I was too much of a lady for that. If Mia hadn't taught me anything else, she taught me how to conduct myself as a lady at all times, even under the most hectic of situations.

The waitress walked over to take our orders. I ordered coffee; I didn't have much of an appetite. Omar asked for white wine. He stroked my hand while he tried to make sense of the situation. He looked into my eyes, and it felt like he was invading my soul, searching realms that he was not given permission to explore. Omar was looking for something. For what, I had no idea.

"Omar, how do you handle finding out the one you love is cheating on you?"

I had to know how someone else would act in this same predicament. Maybe the voice of an outsider could be the voice of reason.

His tone was flat as he replied, "We were having problems for a while. It wasn't really a surprise when she told me. I wanted to work it out and she shot me down. The only reason why we're still together is because her little boyfriend left her when he found out she was married."

"What should I do? Q shouldn't be allowed to hurt anyone like this and get away with it. But I love him too much to stop now. Sometimes I feel like there is no way I can live without him."

"You need to weigh it out. Does he fulfill your every need? Outside of the sex? Is he there for you mentally and emotionally? Is he a prominent figure in your life?"

"Q hasn't been there every time I needed him. When I wanted someone to hold, he couldn't even be found. That was what I wanted. Instead, he came around every now and again to see us. Never long enough for us to bond."

"Did you ever tell him how you felt?" he asked, after taking a sip of his wine.

"I tried but he would always have something to do and said we would talk about it when he got back, at least that was the plan. Two days later, it was no longer an issue." Carefully, I sipped a small amount of the black coffee.

"Not true. There was always an issue. We were too angry to talk about it." He placed his hand over mine. "Sometimes we need to stop dwelling on the past and appreciate what we have at the moment. We could get more accomplished that way. If you weren't so busy worrying about where he was at times, you would have been able to pick up on conversations from where they left off."

This guy had to be kidding; you couldn't just shut your emotions on and off to accommodate someone else. Besides, I was not one for swallowing my grudges.

"Listen, Imani. I wouldn't tell you something unless I experienced it firsthand. I had to suck it up to enjoy my wife's company. Trust! "

I let out a small giggle. "So, what are you saying? You think Q and I should talk about it?"

Talking about him with another woman, that's not a topic where I would be able to suck it up.

"I think if you really love him, you would give him that much."

He smiled to let me know my feelings were okay. All this time I thought Omar might have tried to take advantage of me at my most vulnerable hour. Most men think women fall for the lights and

116

romance of the city. This wasn't his intention at all; he genuinely cared about my well- being.

As we brought the night to a close, he offered to walk me to my car. Throughout the evening Omar proved to be chivalrous. Opening doors, pushing in my chair and kissing my hand deemed him to be a true gentleman. I guess chivalry hadn't died after all. At my car, I thanked him for being there for me and lending a shoulder. I wanted to hug him and place a friendly kiss on his cheek. Instead I accidentally kissed him, smack on his lips. Although, I wasn't too sure it was an accident.

"Imani, did you mean that?" Omar asked.

"What I want is a man who doesn't question my actions."

His eyes widened up in shock. "Is that all?"

"I'm not sure. Let me see. No, I need someone who's into romance, someone who has no problem doing what needs to be done to please me, someone who doesn't expect anything in return. You know," I said before moving closer to him. I paused to check my lip-gloss.

He nodded in agreement. "I completely understand. No strings attached. But what about his needs?"

"I always aim to please my man. Pure, sweet, one hundred percent satisfaction but I have to be completely satisfied first," I said seductively as I moved closer.

"Selfish, hmmm. I can get with that. You deserve it all, sweetheart," he said before leaning back into me.

I kissed him again. Only this time he was into it. He placed his hands on my shoulders and began to run them down my back. In midstroke, he pulled away from me.

"I don't think this is a good idea. I mean, you're sexy as hell and Lord knows I want you but you're upset right now. If you still feel this way after you and Q talk it out, call me. But right now is not a good time."

His respect turned me on even more. Everything was sexy about Omar. This man looked like Denzel Washington and had the voice of Blair Underwood, soft and sexy. I had to go. I might not have liked myself in the morning if I had stayed a moment longer.

"Thank you. I'll call you," I said as I stepped into my car. He closed my door and waved good-bye but I knew we'd see each other again. After I pulled off, I tried to think of Q. Indeed, Quinton may have been my world but I saw Omar being my future.

Quinton

"Imani," I said as I grabbed the nurse's hand.

The pain medication caused me to sleep all day and night. I had the same recurring dream, every time I closed my eyes. There was Imani and Kai, packed up in my car. Kai was waving good-bye while tears streamed down Imani's face. I would be standing outside, banging on the windows, begging for Imani to forgive me. She never spoke in the dream, just stared blankly as she shook her head.

Several days had passed. For the first few, I stayed in my bed. No lights, no television and if it wasn't for the pain, I might not have eaten. I wanted to see Imani but I wasn't ready to face her. She would be full of questions and for the first time, I wouldn't have any answers. Rodney came over to check on me and give me the updates on Imani. He was checking on her to make sure she was all right. I acted as if she were suicidal. Rodney had to remind me, black women don't get suicidal, they get revenge.

Imani had just called to let me know she was on her way to get me from the hospital. They were releasing me since there weren't any complications. During our brief phone call, she told me that she would be bringing me back home with her, and I didn't argue. I felt horrible but it wasn't because of the wounds to my flesh but the pain I knew I put Imani through. As I looked into the mirrored walls of the hospital lobby, I admired my features. I hadn't shaved in ten days, but through the roughness I still looked good.

Our ride back to the house was quiet. Ironically, the sounds of Surface sprayed through our ears as they sang "Shower Me with Your Love." The same song I had hoped she'd walk down the aisle to. Another dream flushed down the toilet.

Neither of us knew what to say. There wasn't much to say. Mama told me she had told Mani the whole story. I was wrong and I knew it. I just had to sit and wait for my punishment.

Mani spoke first to break the ice.

"Q, what's wrong?" she asked.

"Mani, you act like nothing happened. I want to say I'm sorry but sorry doesn't seem like enough. What can I do to make it up to you?" I asked. I was upset that she was taking it so lightly yet I wanted to express my apologies.

"Q, you could start by being honest with me. Do you love her?" she asked.

On the outside she appeared civil, but on the inside I could tell she was erupting.

"Never! Mani, I only loved you. She wouldn't let us be together. She wanted to hurt you. I only went over there so she wouldn't come to your house. There were nights when she would pass by the house to see if you were home alone. So, instead of jeopardizing your life I gave her what she wanted, me," I explained as best as I could.

"Why didn't you tell me? Q, you've been hiding this for three years. You have a son. This is stuff you should've been able to come and talk to me about. Let me know something. You just don't up and leave. If she wanted me, she could have gotten me. Now instead of her hurting me, you did! " she said as tears streamed down her cheeks. As a tear fell on her blouse, my heart fell.

"I didn't want to hurt you any more than I already have. I know I haven't been the man I used to be or could be but I try. Still want to try, if it's not too late," I pleaded.

"What if I said it was too late? What if we turned the tables and I cheated on you? Would you forgive me? Would we be able to move on and continue to grow as a family? Did you think of any of this?" Her anguish became more and more apparent as her tone began to rise. I stood stunned by her remark but realization brought me back.

"Yes, every day and I still don't know how I would react. Mani, I could understand if you hated me; I could even understand if you never wanted to see me again but you're taking me home. That means something. We need to move on from here. I love you and want us to be a family, again," I said.

"You have a son now! How are we going to be a family? You have a family with another woman! " Imani's voice cracked.

She was on the verge of crying but she held it back. She was determined to be strong.

Her accusations added insult to the existing injury. Trina was not the type of woman I would want to make a family with. Imani could never understand the nature of my relationship with Trina, not in a million years.

"We were never a family. Only when I'm with you and Kai, I feel like

I'm home. I want us to be able to have Jahlek and raise him as a part of the family, our family—Kai, you and me. I can't get rid of him, Mani. He's mine," I said, trying to somehow make her see my dilemma. I wanted to be with Imani but if it meant losing my son, I didn't think I would be able to make that sacrifice. No way!

"You were able to walk out on me and Kai," she blurted out.

That was a low blow. I never imagined Imani being so callous. Immediately, I turned from her view and faced the window, watching the road. I couldn't respond.

"I'm sorry . . . that didn't come out right. It wouldn't be fair for you to disown him. I just don't know if I'm ready to let another woman in my house." She wiped a trickling tear from her cheek.

"He's a child. He didn't have anything to do with this. It's unfair to him for me to exclude him from my life. By saying he can't come into your house, you're saying I can't be there either." Her words choked me. I felt as if I were gasping for air.

"Q, I love you. But this is going to need some thought and a hell of a lot of time."

She looked at the pained expression I wore and knew I was hurt, not from the cuts to my skin but the hurt in my heart, wounds I had inflicted.

We pulled into our shaded driveway on the side of our beige brick house. My car was in the garage with the rest of my belongings. The day before Rodney helped Imani bring whatever he could out of Trina's apartment before the sheriff could put the padlocks on.

Imani helped me inside the house and cleared a space on the sofa. She sat beside me, leaned over and kissed me gently. She looked into my eyes as a tear dropped. Yeah, I truly missed her. Yet I wasn't sure if she felt the same.

She took off her jacket and placed it over the back of the couch as she gathered pillows to make me comfortable. I studied her every moved as she swayed back and forth through the living room. Her lilac pants fit her small waist snugly as her hips stretched wide. She rolled her sleeves and loosened the top buttons on her pink blouse. Finally, she sat beside me to take off her heeled sandals, massaging her feet as she closed her eyes.

Imani

"Mani, I do love you. I want us to be together but I can't deny my son." He gently grabbed my hands and softly kissed my fingers. "Please ... please don't make me choose."

Quinton cried as he pleaded for me to make a decision that would obviously change our lives. My body felt as if it were about to explode. So many mixed emotions burrowed their way to the surface. I wanted to say yes but would I be happy? That was when I heard Omar saying, "you were too busy being upset . . . you couldn't appreciate what you had."

"Q, I'm sorry baby. I don't know what came over me. I would never ask you to deny your own child. We can try and work something out for Kai's sake. We'll pick Kai up from Jada's house, first. That way we can explain what's going to be happening. Afterward, we'll get your son. Let them get to know each other," I said as I thought, *You're going to regret this, Mani.*

"I'm home, Baby. This time for good." He kept kissing me and hugged me so tight, I knew this was the real thing. Not an artificial take- me-back hug.

"Well, all your shit is already here. But as far as you and me, that's going to take some time. This is too much right now for us to fix," I said, trying to take charge.

"I don't want to fuck up again and have you and Kai hate me."

I stopped him.

"Kai will never hate you. She looks up to you," I said.

Q cleared his voice, obviously choked up with emotion. "What do I have to offer? Kai has nothing to look up to, Mani."

Quinton obviously didn't know how much Kai loved him.

"Kai has your strength and attitude, both of which will take her a long way in life. She's smart and willing to learn. All the same things I found in you, Q," I whispered as I looked into his eyes. This is the man I fell in love with, I reflected. "Let's not discuss this anymore tonight. Let's let nature take its course."

Then I gently kissed his stubble-filled cheek. He needed to shave in the worst way. Gently, I rubbed his broad chest as I looked him in the eyes. Q was really sorry. It was all over his face.

"I need to get away and reevaluate the state of our relationship. You having another woman in your life will be hard enough to get over without the meddling of my family," I said.

"Where do you want me to go on such short notice?" he asked.

I wasn't exactly sure if I wanted him to go. The point of going away was to be alone, to be able to concentrate on my decisions.

"Anywhere. I don't want to be around when John starts up with his tantrums. Besides, you owe me," I said as I rolled my eyes and sucked my teeth.

"We can go to Jersey, use our time-share, take the kids and let them get to know each other while we work out our own kinks." Although I didn't like the idea of his son tagging along, I agreed. Another topic to be discussed.

"I have to go to mom's house to get some money. Hopefully Jahlek has some clothes there too," he said.

"Talking about money, are you going to stop this dealing?" I questioned.

"Mani, can we talk about this some other time?" he asked.

"I guess that's my answer, huh?" I said.

"Didn't you just say we got a lot to talk about? Add that to the list," he said as he winked, still trying to find a way out.

"Okay . . ." I said reluctantly.

I wanted to continue but Q began to nod off. The doctor did say that his pain medication would put him to sleep.

I got a pillow and blanket when my phone began to ring. Never can have a quiet moment to myself.

"Hello," *I can't have any down time*, I thought as I waited for a response.

"Hi, sweetie. How you hanging in there?" Jada was acting concerned only because I hadn't called her about my child over the past couple of days.

"Oh, hi Jada. I'm fine. We're coming to get Kai tonight. Q is sleeping right now. He's not feeling so well," I said as I looked over at him lying on the sofa.

"Imani, I know it's none of my business but when are you going to put your foot down?"

Jada didn't need to talk about putting feet down as much as she let her man rule her. Craig would slap the taste out of her mouth if he thought she was about to say something that was disrespectful. He literally had to give her permission to speak. And Jada loved to sugar coat the shit—"he didn't mean it", or her favorite, "he was stressed." I was so glad he was on a business trip. At least she has some time to relax.

I couldn't stand the way he treated her or understand why she liked to be treated as if she were a child.

"Okay, you're right. It is none of your business," I snapped.

"You are letting him walk all over you! Q is going to continue his bullshit until you make a change. Every time he fucks up, you forgive him. I know you love him but he's not the only man in the world."

"Jada, I really don't want to talk about this," I whispered into the phone as tears began to well in my eyes. I looked into the living room at Q lying on the couch.

"Baby girl, you have to start thinking about you first. Are you happy? Now you're stuck with a son you didn't even have. You may have his firstborn but that's his son and I guarantee you, if Trina comes around again he'll leave again to be with his son."

"Wrong. He was leaving her and taking his son, anyway. Jada, I told him I needed time to review our situation, now I'm telling you. Give me some credit."

I hated the fact that in my time of weakness I called Jada for comfort and understanding. I knew it was a matter of time before she threw it back in my face.

"Look, John is furious. I told him what happened and he's coming over to your house—"she mumbled.

"What do you mean over here? Jada, you have a big mouth. You know he never liked Quinton the fuck-up! " I hollered.

That was how John would say Q's name whenever he got upset. He said it so much you'd think it was Q's birth name.

"Well, he has reason. You can't seem to see the real man in Q. You're blinded by this façade he has created." She spoke softly as if she was trying to be careful not to say the wrong thing.

"I'll call you later. I was in the middle of cleaning and I want to finish while Quinton is asleep," I lied. I had to. She was making me upset.

"Liar. That's cool . . . whatever. I'll let you find out for yourself. Girl, I'm telling you from experience. Don't be stupid! "

"Thank you. Bye, bye," I sang and hung up.

Jada picked the most inopportune time to be a sister. Any other time she couldn't care less.

After I put the cordless phone on its cradle, I looked over to Q. He looked so at peace. Still, I knew I had to make a decision that will benefit me. He might be lying again but I would have to find that out myself. Why did love have to hurt so badly?

While putting the pillow under his head, he whispered my name.

"What? You okay?" I questioned.

"Mani, lay with me," he whispered.

Q needed me, and that was all that mattered. Our relationship was everything, anyone else had to wait. I had to take care of my man, my friend.

CHAPTER 10
GET IT TOGETHER

Quinton

As the sweet melody of Luther Vandross' "If This World Were Mine" flowed through my ears, I thought of Imani. If this world were mine, I would give her everything. There were so many reasons why I would give my last for Imani yet none were necessary. She loved me and that was more than enough to deserve the world. She didn't have to give me another chance, but she did. All the times I hurt, deceived and deserted her; yet she stood by my side when I needed her.

Then look at the way she took to Jahlek, my son from another woman. Allowing him to go with us on our family trip was enough to make me realize that Imani was too good to be true. I didn't know what I could do to make up for all the wrong I'd done. It didn't matter because whatever she asked for from this day forward would be hers without any question. That's why I chose to propose again. I bought another ring, bigger and better than before. This time was for real. The ring symbolized my growth as a man and my evolution as a husband.

"Imani, let's go out to eat tonight," I said as I kissed her on her forehead.

I felt like doing something special, celebrating.

"I don't know. I was thinking more on the line of going to sleep. Look at the kids."

Never thought I'd see the day both my kids were together. They looked so cute sleeping next to each other.

"Mani, Baby, did you book the suite?" I put my arm around her and guided her head to my chest.

"Yes, that's what you asked me to do, didn't you?" she snapped.

Imani's attitude was nasty when she was tired.

"So . . . we can lock the kids out of the room and do our thing," I said.

"You are something else . . ." she scuffed. "That's all you can think about, sex. Well, let me tell you—" she turned so that we were face-to- face.

She got so close her lips touched my chin and sternly said— "I can't wait to put these kids to bed so I can climb all over you."

She laughed quietly. Times like those I missed the most. Mani and I always had fun with each other. I kissed her forehead again and rested the side of my face on the top of her head. Imani relaxed the rest of the trip while I drove in silence.

Once we reached our room, Mani put the kids in their pajamas.

While she was in the other room, I began to set the mood. I lit candles and poured the wine I bought at the store before we got on the road. I change into my red silk boxers with black hearts she bought for me during her last business trip. Looking around the room for a place to hide the ring, I decided to place it under the pillow until I felt that the time was right.

Still humming the sounds of Mr. Vandross, I lay rose petals across the bed. Being that I couldn't walk that well, setting the mood was taking a little longer than I had anticipated. Just as I dimmed the lights, my angel walked through the door. Her eyes lit up like a child on Christmas morning. She wasn't expecting this at all.

"Is this to your liking, Miss Wright?" I asked her as I posed in the shadow of the candle glow.

In all my life, I had never felt so good. Tears trickled down her face as she walked my way. I took my beautiful lady in my arms and we began to sway, dancing without music, only the sounds of the clock keeping us in step. Looking into my lady's eyes, I began to sing one of my favorites for her.

Imani

As Quinton belted out the words of Luther Vandross' "A House is Not a Home," I broke out in tears. I couldn't believe he was

126

actually doing this and was doing a damn good job. He continued to amaze me as he kept his acapella tune. His strong voice ran chills up and down my spine, as I stood mesmerized by his song.

Although I loved the song, I didn't understand its purpose. Quinton knew I loved him. We established our living situation. What else could he be asking for? Not wanting to spoil the moment, I closed my eyes and continued to soak in the sounds.

Quinton sang the words from his heart. His voice was filled with the same emotion he had displayed several days before when our relationship was undetermined. All the while I stood in his embrace treasuring this moment as one I would always remember. Captivated by his voice, I drifted off into a daydream of our future. I imagined us in a house almost three times the size of my home in Queens. Our children played around barefoot in the plush green grass. Steel drums played a Caribbean medley through the sound system as Quinton and I held hands, admiring our children in their youthful grace. Neither of us had a care in the world.

Lord, what could I do to have this dream become a reality? Just once, could I have life go the way I wished for it to be? Could we finally bathe in the essence of our happiness? The thought of such happiness overwhelmed me as I began to silently cry out for the life not promised. What else must I endure to be granted serenity?

Quinton

My baby began to shed tears as she continued to sway to the music. All the while I was thinking Luther was the motherfuckin' man!

Abruptly, I cut to my main reason of choosing this particular song as a proposal, hoping she'd catch on as I continued.

"Imani, please don't let this one mistake keep us apart. I'm sorry. . .so sorry, so very sorry. I know I did you wrong, Baby. But let me make it up to you, right now. Right here," I said through tears.

All of my heart had poured out and taken over. The words I had memorized disappeared. I wanted her to know how I was feeling, not

Luther. Even though he was a hell of an introduction. For the past twenty minutes, I had been holding back my tears. I had to let loose.

"Mani, do you understand what I'm saying? I'm saying I love you. No one else can take the place that you occupy in my heart. Sometimes when I think of living without you, I feel myself choking as if all the air has been sucked out of my body. I realize I am nothing without you. Without you I have nothing."

"Quinton, stop," she said while I continued to pour my heart out to her.

"Imani, please say you love me. No, not that you love me, tell me that you're still in love with me."

She mouthed the words I'm still in love with you. Taking her by the hand, I slowly lead her over to the bed and sat her down, gently. Sliding my hand under the pillow, I got down on my bended knee. Imani covered her face in disbelief.

"Baby, I told you I wanted to make everything right. I know I fucked up, big. But Mani, I'm nobody without you. I regret all the things I've done and wished more than a hundred times to be able to turn back the hands of time so you would never have shed tears for my stupidity. I'm sorry. I don't know what else to do but offer to be with you for the rest of your life, honoring and obeying your every command. This is all I have left, Baby. Please forgive me?" I begged.

Imani dropped her hands from her mouth as I wiped her tears away. She stood speechless for about a minute. Her silence was beginning to scare me. Was it possible that Imani wouldn't accept?

"Q . . . I . . . I don't know what to say. This is what I've been dreaming of but right now isn't the appropriate time. We haven't even talked about being together and how we're going to work our present situations. I love you, indeed, and would like nothing more than to be your wife but this doesn't solve our problems," she spoke through her tears.

"Mani, what do you want me to do? I can't erase what I've done. I'm human, I make mistakes . . ." I pleaded.

"I'm human, too, and not once did you think that I may have feelings. I can't keep turning my love on and off like a switch. I need time to forgive and forget," she said, breaking my heart with each syllable.

"Please don't do this to me. Living without you, that's something I can't do." My words almost stumbled over one another.

"Quinton, it shouldn't have taken some bullets and a surprise son to figure this out. I've felt the same about you for years. Everyone told me to give up when I put my all into our relationship, one that never existed in your world. And that hurt, every day! Not when we broke up or you walked out but every time I saw your face or heard your name." Imani inhaled deeply then continued, "Q, how am I supposed to get over that? You're asking for a commitment. That's serious! " She pointed her finger into my chest. "Are you ready for that?"

"Imani, I wouldn't have asked if I wasn't. I want you. You are the only woman I have ever loved and the only woman I ever want to love."

Tears began to well up in my eyes at the thought of my woman not taking me back. Imani was the reason I was still sane to this day. I couldn't imagine what I'd be doing without her. The thought of life without her had begun to vex me.

"Q," she whispered as I lifted my head, "can you understand where I'm coming from?"

I did understand but I didn't want things to turn out like this. I guess things weren't going to go my way.

"You're right. We have things that need to be worked out—" I began until she interrupted. She put her forefinger in the air as if she was about to make a declaration.

"But understand this. After we're married I want a little boy of my own." She smiled. "My own. A little mahogany replica of you, dimples and all. Are you with me?"

"So, you'll marry me?" I asked, not sure of her response.

"Of course. I've waited this long, why give up now?" she asked as she ran her finger down the slope of my nose. "So some other bitch can come and pick up what I've worked so hard on." She giggled to lighten up the mood.

In return, I hurried up from the floor and gave her the tightest hug I could muster with my bad shoulder and all. She pushed me off her and wiggled her finger. The ring totally slipped my mind; this girl had me going. As I slid the ring on her finger, I made a promise to be faithful and loyal from this day forth.

Slowly, I began to undress Imani, wanting to treasure every moment. This was to be the first step of our new life together. She was glowing with happiness. This was how it should have been. Unsnapping her bra while she ran her fingers up and down my back, I laid her gently on the bed of roses I had prepared. I kissed her all over starting with her fingers, up her arms to her neck, down her torso as I took her thong off on my way down. It was my turn to fill her with the same pleasure she had given me.

I parted her legs slowly, making sure to never lose eye contact as I kissed down her thighs before devouring her. As I nestled my face in her cavern of heat, she moaned in delight. She grabbed handfuls of roses as she clutched tight on to the sheets. Finally she reached an orgasm, I laid beside her wanting nothing more than to hold her. Imani ran her soft hands down the side of my face and looked deep into my eyes.

"What's the matter?" She seemed worried about something.

"What are we going to do about Jahlek when his mother comes out?" she asked.

"Let's worry about that later. Right now he's with us and he's happy," I answered.

She began planting mild kisses along my chest while I lay flat on my back and was turning me on more than ever before. Was this for real? She had to stop or else I wasn't going to be able to control myself. I pulled her on top of me and inserted myself into her coziness. This was going to be quick; it felt so good. Imani worked her show, riding like never before. The candlelight presented Imani in all her radiance. Before long, I cried out in satisfaction.

She left me breathless as she lay on top of me.

Gently she spread the sheet over us, and for the first time in a long while I felt complete. Her body snuggled into my curve, my arm wrapped around her. I kissed her ear as she found comfort in my embrace. This was the woman I desired. Within seconds, we were both asleep.

CHAPTER 11
THE SOONER, THE BETTER

Imani

Q and I wanted to take the kids out for breakfast and take the kids to the carnival afterward. We were like two high school kids, hugging and kissing at every red light and stop sign. The kids were so busy playing with each other they didn't pay us any attention. They adjusted to the situation rather quickly. I guess it was because they're kids and really didn't know there was anything wrong.

My ring glistened under the bright morning sun as I drove down the Monopoly named streets of Atlantic City. Q had come a long way. He would have never poured out as much emotion before; he would have said "fuck it" and moved on. My man cried for me, damn, he even sang for me. He had a good voice too. To think I almost didn't accept his proposal. My heart felt as if it was under restraint. The words yes and I accept formed in my mouth and almost choked me.

Up until last night, all I could think about was Omar. He had been on my mind ever since we met in the city that night. He was there for me when I needed him most and helped me to keep my sanity when I thought I would lose it. But Q had made an impression on me last night that forced me to put all thought of Omar on the back burner for a little while. Maybe Q and I could make it through after all. I hoped this wasn't another one of his please-take-me-back proposals and we never got married.

"Q, so when do you want to start putting our wedding together?" I asked, trying to determine his seriousness.

"As soon as possible. I ain't with waiting anymore. Tonight when we put the kids to bed, we can start thinking of dates and places," he said quickly.

His answer surprised me. I was waiting for something more along line of "later," "I don't know" or "whatever."

"Are you for real? What about money? You're not working and you've been out of the game for a week," I reminded him.

"Money is not an issue. The game works for me. Even when I'm not around my money rolls in. I got enough stashed away for a hundred rainy days. You could have everything you dreamed of in a wedding—the white doves, stretch limos, princess dress, anything your heart desires. Don't worry about the cost."

"Quinton, are you going to be dealing forever?" I asked, disgusted with the thought.

I needed to know; I didn't need to be running for the rest of my life. The money, power and respect were all he was accustomed to. Q's greed was beyond his control.

"Nah, Baby. I'm thinking about leaving it in Rodney's hands after I get this last bit. Hit him off with a little something and back away. My savings will suffice until I finish law school," he replied.

"Thank you!" I rejoiced. I was beginning to believe that Quinton's professional endeavors were abandoned by his new lifestyle. When Q and I talked about our future, he mentioned that he wanted to go back to school. Until now I thought he was talking nonsense again.

When we reached our hotel, we grabbed our bags from the shopping spree we had embarked on after breakfast. Kai took Jahlek's hand and carried her book-bag in the other. She enjoyed having a younger brother, and I liked seeing her happy.

"Mommy, can me and my brother get in the pool?" Kai asked.

"Q, you feel like watching them at the pool? I'm tired. I need to rest up for work next week."

"I don't think Jah has a bathing suit," he said.

"He could wear his underwear, Q. He's a baby."

"Aight, but I'm not going to be down there long."

"Thanks, sweetie. I have to call Charisse so she can help us with planning our wedding."

"Whatever. I hope she doesn't throw your bridal shower. She might hire a female stripper for herself," he jokingly remarked before walking out the door.

"Y'all really need to get over this petty arguing, for me at least," I said while taking the rubber bands out of Kai's hair so the water wouldn't tangle her hair around the elastic.

While Quinton got the kids dressed and grabbed some towels to go down to the pool, I decided to go to the newsstand and pick up one of those magazines about the modern bride. I thought to take my cell in case Q came back while I was out. My cell phone was blinking a green light indicating that I had messages. After I accessed my voice mail, I heard the voice of Mr. Smalls.

"Hi, Imani. Just wanted to make sure you're okay. I'm sorry about the other night. If you still want it, it's possible. I'm feeling you in the worst way. Q doesn't know what he's got or what he's missing. If you were mine you'd never feel alone. Call me."

Hearing Omar's voice made me realize how much I missed him. I couldn't stop wanting to be with Omar. Who was I fooling? Q had made the same promises before and broke them every time. But my love for Quinton and my belief that this time would be different made it easier for me to follow my heart. He had never been sincere. I mean never! Omar would be there in case of emergency. We'd keep in contact but I was giving Quinton the benefit of the doubt to see what he was about this time around. He might surprise me. But this was definitely the last time I was going to fall for his bullshit.

Shortly after I had returned from the newsstand, Q and the kids came upstairs. They were shivering with blue lips from the cold air blowing throughout the room. Kai's hair was all over the place. Immediately, I went to shut off the air conditioner.

"Did y'all have fun?" I asked the kids as Q undressed them.

"Yyyeeesss," Kai managed to answer through her chattering teeth.

I never realized how much Jahlek looked like Q until he held him up close. He couldn't deny his kids if he wanted to. Both of them look like their father; the same slanted eyes, narrow face, Jahlek had his mahogany- coated skin and Kai had his slinky limbs. Jahlek and

Kai were both rather tall for their age being that their father was also fairly tall. It was apparent both loved their father very much; they clung to him like bees to honey.

"Daddy, I'm hungry," Jahlek said as he looked my way.

"Mani, what are we doing for dinner tonight?"

Q didn't even look up at me while he spoke.

"Let the kids decide. It really doesn't matter to me," I said.

"What do you want?" Q asked his mini clones as they stood in front of him wrapped in towels. Jahlek just shrugged and looked toward Kai.

"Mommy, I want a burger with French fries," Kai said as she shook her wet hair.

"Do you want McDonald's or do you want me to cook it?"

Our suite was equipped with a kitchenette that included a small refrigerator and microwave but we always brought along our indoor grill. Quinton wasn't a big fan of restaurant dining. At home or on vacation, he always preferred a home-cooked meal.

Kai turned to whisper into her little brother's ear then turned to her father.

"Can you make it? Daddy likes how you make it better," she replied.

I looked over at Q with an evil eye. He shrugged. I shouldn't have been surprised though. Kai was his twin—of course they we in cahoots. The smile that stretched across Quinton's face changed my whole attitude. Seeing how content he was filled my heart with joy. It was rare that his face held so much happiness.

"Okay. We have to go to the supermarket. Go take a shower and then we'll go," I said to Kai as she looked up at me.

Quinton interjected, "Mani, pull out their clothes please? I'll give them a bath."

He was really enjoying having both his kids around. Quinton was a great father; I'll give him that. But he also had to take it easy. His wounds weren't fully healed.

"Okay, Baby. But I'm going to put out their pajamas because it's getting late," I said.

"Oh, I was thinking about taking them for a walk on the boardwalk after dinner," Quinton said.

"Whatever. Just hurry up. Remember we have some planning to do."

Q finally looked up at me and saw my expression. I was not happy.

"Oh, Baby," he said as he walked over to give me a hug, "I'm sorry for ignoring you, I'm . . . I don't know. This was what I dreamed of . . . us together."

I felt bad for being jealous of his kids. "Sorry. I'm not use to this yet.
Normally, when we go away, we're laid up underneath each other and I have your undivided attention."

He kissed and hugged me then whispered in my ear, "You'll have me after the kids are sleep."

We laughed briefly before he returned his attention to the kids. It could be worse. He could be with Trina.

Quinton

"Kai, Jahlek, don't run so far ahead. Stay where we can see you," Imani said as we walked along the boardwalk holding hands. We talked and laughed while the kids ran around in amazement, looking at the bright lights.

We were finally happy, together. Never thought we'd see the day.

Although it took a hospital visit, I'm glad we made it. People say things happen for a reason, I guess this was destined to be.

We talked about what we expected our wedding to be like and whom we would invite. I thought it would be a good idea to get married right away so we decided upon Imani's birthday, August 23. It seemed like a good idea for many reasons. For starters, it was a summer month, therefore, we could have it outside. Plus, it was a special date for her and it was next month. The sooner, the better.

We didn't want a big wedding, just our close friends and family, no more than a hundred people. We'll have it catered and arranged by Charisse's mother. Ms. Linda, Reese's mom, coordinated weddings and parties. She put together some of the most extravagant affairs in the New York area. There was this one event she organized for an up-and-coming singer in Brooklyn that was very beautiful and incomparable.

Just the dance area alone stood out in my memory. Candles were placed inside each floral arrangement to illuminate each table. The main dance floor was decorated with gold lace. The place sparkled under the soft lighting provided by a huge crystal chandelier that hung low in the center of the room. Her style was marked with class and elegance.

Kai would be the flower girl with a dress similar to Imani's. Jahlek being the ring bearer would wear a tuxedo identical to mine. Imani decided to ask Mia and Mama J to go with her to pick out her dress; they're the only mothers she had and she valued their opinion. Rodney, James and I would go to pick out the tuxes and limos. The planning was easier than I anticipated.

"Are you feeling any better?" she asked as I rested against the banister trying to fight the pain that shot through my leg.

"I'm fine, Baby. Don't worry about me." I grabbed her around the waist and pulled her closer to me. "How about you, Imani? Are you feeling any better?"

I wondered how she felt about Jahlek.

"I'm cool. Q, promise me that you're not just filling my head with all these ideas. This time you're for real, okay?"

"Imani, I want to be with you for the rest of my life. Seriously, I can't stand to lose you again. This time is for real." I wanted to put all Imani's worries to rest but I knew that would take more than a mere promise. My credibility was shot from previous promises I had not kept, so my word was worthless. But I knew this time I was for real.

The next morning, I woke the kids, got them dressed and started breakfast by the time Imani woke up. The kids were wearing matching short sets that we had bought the day before while we were shopping. Kai's hair was combed into two ponytails with matching orange bows and barrettes. I was amazed at how much I had done since the family man thing was still fairly new to me.

When Imani finally got out of the bed to go take a shower, I had already pulled out her clothes and pressed them. I was a very busy man that morning.

"Good morning, Baby," I said, standing behind her as she stretched her back.

"What time did you get up?" she asked, in awe of what I had done.

"I couldn't really sleep; I had a lot of stuff on my mind. Nothing to worry about, just some minor shit," I said.

I turned around and pick up a box from the love seat and passed it to her.

The long slim pink box was wrapped with a white bow. A little card read thank you. She looked at me with a question on her face.

"Just open it," I insisted.

I sat and watched as she slowly opened the box. Inside were six long stemmed pink roses.

"Thank me for what?" she asked.

"For being you and loving me even when I didn't deserve it," I said. "Oh, Baby. You didn't have to do this," she said.

"I did. Now go ahead and get in the shower. We've got a long day ahead of us," I said as I shoved her in the direction of the bathroom. "Mom said we could drop the kids by while we did what we had to do."

"All right. Undo Kai's hair so I can do it after I'm showered and dressed," she said.

"It's done. Don't worry about it. Hurry up," I said. I playfully slapped her butt as she walked into the bathroom.

As Imani closed the door to the bathroom, my pager went off. Who the . . .? Trina was home? Her other baby's father, Bryan, must've gotten tired of watching his son and bailed her ass out. I decided to call her back before Imani got out of the shower.

"What?" I snapped.

"Where's my fucking son?" she screamed through the phone.

Her attitude was unnecessary. She knew he was safe with me.

"He's with us," I said mildly, trying not to get upset.

"Who's us? You and Imani? Oh, y'all are trying to play the happy family. Well not with my son. You better bring his ass home now."

"He'll get there when he gets there. I'm not running for you. By the way, lose my number. I'll call you. You'll never have to call me," I said.

"It ain't over, Q. You wait," she said.

The phone line went silent.

There she was making those threats again. She just couldn't move on and leave me the hell alone. Mani and I never got to discuss what we were going to do regarding Jah. I needed to ask her how she felt about having full custody of him but I never found the right time. I guess now it was as good a time as any. Imani walked out of the bathroom as I placed the phone down. She must have sensed something was wrong because she immediately asked what just happened.

Here it goes, I thought. "Mani, Trina's home and she wants Jahlek." I waited for Imani to get upset but she surprised me.

"Did you tell her we'll bring him when we get back to New York?" she asked.

"No, I wanted to talk to you first." This was not going well. I could feel it already.

"About? There's nothing to talk about. That's her son," she said nonchalantly.

"He's my son too! If Trina gets Jahlek back, I'll never see him again. I wanted to know how you felt about full custody."

"It's maternal over paternal, sweetie. Mothers normally have a better chance in the courts than the fathers."

She sounded almost as if she was happy. I almost expected her to break out into a song and dance.

"And, there've been cases where fathers were given full custody," I said matter-of-factly.

"Not happening. You don't have proof of employment nor do you have proof of residence. Plus, they look to see where he would be better off and if there's nothing wrong with her, he stays," she said.

Imani was making the situation more complicated than it needed to be.

"First of all, the bitch shot me! And believe me, I'm pressing charges. She doesn't have a job or a place to stay after this month. At least we're getting married and we have a house," I said.

"Q, you can't take a woman's child because y'all are not together. You were spending time with him before, what's the problem?" she asked.

"Our relationship is the problem. I'm with you now. She doesn't want her son to become part of our family."

"Well, I don't know what to tell you, Baby. This is going to take some serious consideration. Anyway, if she goes to jail for the attempted murder charge, don't you get custody?"

"No. She didn't put my name on his records. Jahlek doesn't have my last name. He has her married name," meaning he had another man's name.

The part of my life that I shielded most was revealed. My son carried another man's name. Isn't that a bitch?

A few months after we graduated high school, Trina married Bryan in an attempt to make me jealous. Trina couldn't accept the fact that she was never someone I could settle down with. I continued to sleep with her but nothing amounted until Imani put me out.

"Not to be funny or anything. Is he even yours? Did you get blood work?" She scoffed. She smiled but I didn't find any humor in her comment.

"Yes, Mani. I'm not fuckin' stupid. You think I would've sat back and not questioned whether or not he was mine. You're buggin'," I barked.

"I'm not calling you stupid although you have made some fucked-up decisions," she said.

I was becoming angry. In the mirror, I could see that my anger was visible as my nostrils flared and eyebrows arched inward, resembling the devil.

"Look, what time is it?"

"A quarter after nine," I answered through tightly clenched teeth. She knew it was time to try and lighten the situation.

"Tell her to meet us at Mama's house at two. Then, you and Trina can sit together, talk about what's best for the kid and how to get this name changed," Imani suggested as she admired herself in the mirror.

"Trina said I couldn't change the name because I wasn't there when he was born."

I stood up from the chair in the corner of the room.

"That's bullshit. Craig wasn't there when Jada had Diamond and she got his last name. You believe anything, don't you?"

"You know what, Mani, you act like I'm supposed to know all this. Am I allowed to make mistakes? You act like you're perfect."

Even though I couldn't really put a finger on any of her flaws or mistakes.

"Honey, listen," she said as she held my face in her hands. "We'll work this out. Take it easy. I'm not getting on you about your mistakes. Okay?" Then she kissed my nose while I sat on the edge of the bed.

"Mani, this shit has got me stressed. I want my kids together with you and me. How many times do I have to tell you before you realize I'm serious?" I asked. I was becoming tired of this cat-and-mouse game.

"Q, it's going to be okay. We'll always be together," she said forcefully as she pointed her finger from her chest to my direction.

I pulled Imani close and rested my head on her stomach. She rubbed my back and continued telling me not to worry. There was too much at stake for me not to. Trina was capable of ruining my life. Shit she already tried to kill me, what next?

Kai and Jahlek walked into the room. Imani told them to go wait in the living room while she got dressed. Kai didn't move.

"Daddy, what's the matter? Are you sad?" Kai asked.

"No, baby girl. Daddy's fine. I'm not feeling well," I lied.

My girl was so sweet. She came over and put her little hands on my head to check my temperature.

141

After Imani urged her to go watch her brother, Kai kissed me and said, "Feel better, daddy."

I loved that girl so much. I couldn't bare being without her.

"Quinton, I love you and it's evident that your kids do too. Somehow we'll find a way to be together, all of us. Okay baby," she assured me. She walked toward the dresser and began to lotion her body. "Let me get ready so we can leave," she said.

I let her go but didn't take my eyes off her as she let her robe slide off her shoulders, down her body and on to the floor. Her body was screaming my name and mine was screaming hers. I continued to watch as she put her leg up on the chair while she rubbed lotion over her calf then up her thigh. Although, she had her back toward me I knew she knew that was turning me on.

As she slid into her pink thong and bra set, I pressed up behind her to show her how I felt. Imani continued to tease me as she ran her butt up and down over my hardness. Her sweet scent sent tingles throughout my body. I couldn't take any more. I turned her around and looked deep into her eyes. So much was said without a word spoken. She loved me unconditionally and would never turn her back on me, her stare said.

"I love you too." I began to kiss her neck and to suck her earlobes as I lifted her up and sat her on the dresser, placing my body between her legs.

"Q, if you . . . keep that up . . . we'll never, ooh, make it back," she said breathlessly.

I forcefully pulled myself away and went to the bathroom to try and relieve myself while she finished getting dressed.

Imani

Trina was working my last nerve. She was going to stop threatening my man. Fuck she thinks I am, I ain't no punk bitch. She is bringing the ghetto out of me. I hoped she was mature enough to sit and converse without arguing. The minute she disrespected my man or me I was kicking her ass. Enough was enough; she had her chance and blew it. She needed to get back with her husband and leave mine alone.

Awwwh, my husband. Imani Banks, that had a professional sound to it. I liked it.

Q checked out while I took the kids to the car. When I brought the car around, Q was walking out the hotel looking fine as hell. He wore a cream- colored short set with a cream Kangol hat to match. His shirt was open to show off his hairy chest. He walked with a slight limp due to his injury but others probably thought that was his style, you know the cane and all. I found it sexy as hell. I liked a little thug in my man.

The kids were buckling up in the back while I adjusted my mirrors.

As I looked through the rearview, I smiled at how cute they looked in their matching orange GAP shirts and white jean shorts. Quinton had put orange barrettes in Kai's hair to match her outfit, which shocked the hell out of me. Normally, he'd leave her hair standing all over her head. Jah had on a white visor that displayed his low fade and side burns. They both wore the white Nike Downtowns that Quinton insisted on buying. I don't believe children should own a pair of white sneakers. But who was I?

Q smiled getting into the car.

"What's up? Why are you smiling?" I asked.

He had one of the most gorgeous smiles that displayed all his pearly whites and deep dimples. It added to his sex appeal.

"We look good, don't we? That skirt is fitting you right. It's nice and tight and short, hmm," he said as he licked his sweet, thick lips.

"You would think this is cute. I can't drive comfortably with this skirt. If I open my legs the skirt will be around my hips. And this shirt neckline is so low . . ." I complained.

"Stop complaining, Baby, 'cause you're wearing it and you're wearing it well. At least you can pull the shit off. Besides you're with your man."

He leaned over and bit me on my neck. He's a fool, I thought, but Lord, do I love him! I strapped on my seat belt, put the car in drive and drove off. I couldn't help but feel some anxiety about our meeting with Trina.

Ready or not, here we go. Back to the land of mischief and mayhem.

CHAPTER 12
ENOUGH IS ENOUGH

Imani

"Quinton, why are you shaking your leg like that? You nervous?" Hastily he answered, "Impatient, not nervous."

"It'll be all right. If anyone should be nervous it should be me," I said calmly.

Truth be known, I was erupting on the inside. Finally, I was going to confront Q's baby mama. After seven years, I finally have the opportunity to meet my competition and find out what's been holding Q back. I should have set this straight from day one when the rumors first started circulating. Quinton obviously was uncomfortable about the situation but he was trying to play cool.

We dropped Kai at Charisse's house en route to Mama's. I didn't think it would be appropriate for her to be exposed to our situation. She had been around enough of our arguments to last a lifetime. That was why she acted so grown.

When we arrived at Mama's, she said Trina had called and said she would be a little late. I tried to assure Quinton that everything was all right and that I would remain calm but he had his own issues to deal with. And honestly, I didn't believe what I was saying myself. Calm had been erased from my vocabulary a long time ago.

About an hour later, Trina finally showed up with this big gorilla- looking guy as her bodyguard or something. She wore a skintight F.U.B.U. dress that was so short you saw the bottom of her cellulite-covered ass. Her blond weave was worn up in a ponytail and her big bangle earrings had gone out of style with Lee jeans. She smacked loudly on a piece of cinnamon gum as she placed her hand upon her hip.

I couldn't believe that was what he had left me for. Yuck! Like the saying goes, you can take the man out of the ghetto but you can never take the ghetto out of a man.

She held onto her other son, Bryan's hand while the other hand was

up in my face waving and pointing as she said, "What's this bitch doing here? Unh-unh, Q. You didn't tell me you was bringing this bitch with you."

"First of all you don't address me as 'this bitch,' it's Imani, get it right." As I pushed her hand away from me, she stumbled and posed as if she was getting in a fighting stance.

"Anyways Q, you didn't tell me you was bringing her with you! " She looked me up and down, cutting her eyes every time they met mine.

"So, why is your man in my mother's house? He's your protection. This was your threat, you gotta come better than that," Quinton said as he measured up the oversized dark skin brother at her side.

"Yo, I didn't come here for all this bullshit talking. Trina, go get the kid and let's go. I got some people waiting for me back at the house," Big Bryan said. His deep voice sent chills through my spine as it echoed in the hallway.

"Look, I already told Trina my son is not going to be in the same house with you and your bullshit, and I meant it. Jahlek is staying here until she can find her own place."

Quinton was adamant about keeping Jahlek. But, like I already told him, Trina had legal custody of him. If anything, Quinton could be charged with kidnapping since he wasn't listed as Jahlek's father. Thank God Trina wasn't smart enough to go that route.

"Whatever, dawg. I'm not trying to play daddy to the li'l brotha anyway. Just so happens that legally he's my son," Bryan said.

"All that is going to change. Q is taking Trina to court and he's going to get his son, trust! Shit, the whore going to jail anyway. You don't wanna be stuck with both of them! Barely taking care of the one you got!" I had to step in for my man.

"I know you ain't call me no ho. I will fuck your bitch ass up, Imani. Play yourself! " Trina's irritating, high-pitched voice creaked like an old door. She was heated but it's not like she was scaring me. No bitch who stood on two or four put fear in my heart. She would be another notch on my belt. I fought bigger coming up in Bed-Stuy.

The rank smell of alcohol filled the air as she huffed with attitude.

"Listen, why don't y'all sit and talk 'bout this like adults." Mama J rose up off the couch and entered the hallway where all the commotion was coming from. "Quinton, did you get blood test done for Jahlek?"

Q's mother wasn't the one for dealing with bullshit.

"Yes, Mama. We got the work done as soon as she came back from wherever she ran off to," he said as he lowered his tone. He didn't want the kids to hear what was going on.

Trina continued to stand behind Bryan with her hand on her hip. I caught her staring at me several times, and each time I rolled my eyes and waved her off. She was barely any competition.

"And why doesn't Jahlek have his last name again?" Mama addressed Trina.

Trina sucked her teeth then replied, "Because, he wasn't there to sign the papers." She twirled strands of her weave through her fingers and continued to mutilate her gum.

"I didn't know where the fuck you was! Then you come back married to your ex. Was that some kind of plan?" Q asked.

Quinton got up in Trina's face with a deranged look about him. She had bought him to the brink and there was no way to get him back.

"No, at the time me and Bryan was already planning on being together but after I saw you again, I wanted to be with you. Bryan said I was free to do what made me happy. At the time you made happy," Trina explained as she rolled her neck.

"Now here she is, nigga, back where she belongs. I don't know what she saw in your punk ass anyway—" Bryan began until Q punched him in the mouth. Blood flowed out the side of Bryan's mouth as Q pulled his fist back drawing in force to strike again.

Bryan approached Quinton and Trina turned to pull him away while Mama and I held Q back.

"You know what, Q, you can try to take my son from us but it's not happening. You better pray that you'll ever see your son again. Junior, Jah, let's go! " Trina shouted.

Bryan Jr. came out the room without Jahlek.

"Where's your brother?" she squealed as Bryan Jr. returned to the living room. The sound of her voice gave me goose bumps.

"He's in the room. He don't wanna go," the little boy said as he looked at his mother.

"Y'all turned my son against me. What did you do to my son, bitch?"

Was she talking to me? Did she refer to me as bitch again? I had to be the bigger woman; I didn't want to make the situation worse than it already was. Although I tasted slapping the shit out of her and showing her who she was dealing with, I simply replied, "Trina, I don't need to brainwash your son. He knows where he belongs."

There was no real need to escalate the matter. I'd see her on the streets.

Q went to check on Jahlek while Trina followed. I stood in the hallway with Bryan and Mama, although, it was tearing me up inside to know they were together alone.

Quinton

"Trina, why are you making shit so hard? Let me have my son."

Being that we were behind closed doors, I was sure I could change her attitude.

"No, we're supposed to be together. If I can't have you, you can't have him." She spoke calmly, leaving no trace of anger.

"You don't really want him nor do you take care of him. I will still give you money if that's the problem. How much do you want?" I turned to the closet to make a withdrawal from the stash I kept in old Nike and Timberland boxes.

"Five hundred thousand dollars, right here, right now," she said.

148

"Get the fuck outta here! I don't got half a million dollars right now." Even if I did there was no price for my kid.

"Then you don't want your son. What can I say?" She turned her back to start toward Jahlek. Suddenly she turned to face me and said, "Listen, how about this? Next weekend you can come and take him and if you have a hundred thousand you can keep him."

"That sounds like a plan. But first, tomorrow morning we'll go down to get his name changed."

I shouldn't have to buy my own son but if it got her out of my life, whatever.

"As long as Imani never hears about this," I whispered, making sure no one heard what was going on.

"Why do you want her over me?" She wrapped her arms around my neck as she spoke. Her breasts rubbed on my chest. The feeling of her erect nipples pressed my skin. Instantly, I became aroused.

"Do I really need to answer that? We never really had anything, Trina. I need someone to love."

The temptation to touch her was pressing through my pants but I had to restrain myself.

"But I love you. I'm not good enough for you?" She slowly slid down to her knees and untied the strings that tightened the waist of my shorts. The warmth of her hands on my flesh sent a sensation throughout my body. My eyes began to roll into the back of my head as she fondled my manhood. Just as she began to encase my penis with her soft, full lips, I remembered Jahlek was still in the room.

"No, you're not good enough for me," I replied. "What kind of woman would do this in front of her child?" I pulled her up against my will and began to fix my clothing. "Mani would never sell her kid or her ass. We were a mistake. Get over it."

Trina, infuriated by my statement, picked up Jahlek and stormed out of the room.

"Fuck you, Q! Don't try to look for us," she hollered.

"Trina, Trina! I'm going to get my son. I'm going to see my lawyer tomorrow. You won't keep him from me, bitch! "

Jahlek reached his little hand out to me but there was nothing I could do. She had me backed into a corner.

Imani came to console me after they left but I wanted to be alone. I pushed her away from me, headed out of the apartment and got in my car. I didn't know where to go but I had to get away and think. Suddenly, I found myself thinking about Tya Smith, remembering the way she took care of me the last time I was in that same situation. But things had changed. Tya was happily married with kids. Still the thought of smelling her sweet skin and touching her face, lingered in the back of my mind.

When I came out of my daydream, I realized I was on the Southern State Parkway. I guess the only way to escape that feeling was to see her one last time and let her tell me, "It's over."

Imani

I knew Q was upset so I didn't flip when he pushed me away or follow him when he walked out the door but I did cry. I felt helpless, like something I could have done could have prevented that whole ordeal. But in reality, there was nothing I could do. I wanted to do something but things were far gone out of control.

Mama gave me a strong hug and sat with me for a while.

"He just needs to vent. He'll be right back. Sit back and calm your nerves," she said as she rubbed my back.

I paged Quinton several times, hoping he would return. I was becoming worried. He couldn't drive that well with a bandaged arm and leg. Panic took over as I frantically flipped through the television channels and continued to wait. I stretched across the couch to try to make myself comfortable. Mama brought in a comforter and pillow for me. After changing into a pair of Quinton's sweats and a T-shirt that nearly swallowed me, I began to calm down. I must have been too comfortable because within minutes I had fallen asleep.

Two hours had passed and James had finally come home. Mama started to tell him what happened but I couldn't sit through the drama again so I decided to go home. I made an attempt to get in contact with Quinton one last time but still no luck.

On my way out of the building, I heard a faint ringing sound. Finally recognizing my phone, I searched through my bag hoping to reach my phone in time.

"Hello, Q. Baby, where are you?" I asked.

"No, Imani. It's not him. It's me, Omar." The voice startled me as I realized it was not the voice I had been hoping for.

"Oh, yeah . . . what's up?" I replied dryly. Not at all interested in entertaining a conversation with Omar, I tried to sound as unenthused as possible. "Whatcha doing?"

"You don't sound so happy to hear from me. Did I catch you at a bad time?" Omar's voice began to ease me into a comfort zone as I thought about the complete gentleman he had been on our last encounter.

"Yes, an extremely bad time," I said before I began to replay the events that took place only three hours ago. He listened as I whined and wailed about missing Q and wanting to be able to make things better for him. As I sat in the cab crying my heart out, I began to feel awkward. That same man who cared enough to listen to my dilemma was the same one who caused me so much confusion. There was no doubt that I loved Quinton but how did I really feel about Omar?

"Omar, I gotta go. I'm sorry for dumping my problems on you," I said, trying to escape that feeling.

"Imani, it's not a problem. Remember, I'm here for you. You—"

"I gotta go," I said before hanging up. I turned off my phone, not wanting to get blindsided again. I needed to find Q.

Quinton

I drove around for an hour cursing to myself, trying to ignore the pain in my leg and in my heart. I knew that was going to happen. I knew Trina was going to try and take Jahlek away from me. If I had just kept going the way I was I would never have been put in that predicament.

Tya was so comforting. She said all the things I needed to hear, like she always did. Knowing that she still cared about me, stirred up so many emotions.

Tya and I talked like old friends for about an hour before she began to reflect on the reasons that forced her to move to South Carolina. All led back to me. From cheating to lying to doubting her pregnancy, I was the reason she left. Inside my heart was swollen with regret. Knowing what I knew, Tya was a good woman. She didn't deserve half the shit I did to her. Especially, leaving her alone in one of her most desperate hours. Tya replayed the day she told me she was pregnant. She also replayed my reaction.

"But, I don't blame you for the miscarriage, Q. And I grew to understand what you were thinking. You weren't ready for the family you were running from much less to start a new one," she said as she bit on a cracker.

"It seems like I can't do right by the women who care most for me. I lost you to my stupidity and risk losing Imani now." I quickly filled my mouth with the ice-cold Corona that Tya had brought out of the kitchen.

"Imani . . . Yeah, I saw her a couple of weeks ago going to pick up Kai from your mother's house. She looks like she's doing fine for herself." Tya stirred her tea before taking a sip, never losing eye contact.

She had a thing with reading facial expressions.

"Did she say anything to you?"

"No, Quinton. Imani is not that kind of woman. Besides what happened between you and me was a long time ago." She looked away as she made her last comment obviously disturbed by it.

"If everything is squashed between us, why do you still get upset when you hear or speak her name? Come on, Tya. I need some clarity here." I was confused.

"Because I couldn't take you from her. You loved her then but didn't know how to express it. I tried my damnedest to be like her, hoping you would let her go. But she had a lock on your heart. In desperation, I got pregnant. I had no idea that it would push you farther away from me." The words raced out of her mouth without hesitation.

Tya was helping me understand my inner soul better than anyone else.

Imani was the one. No one even compared—as much as I hated to say it, not even Tya. Like she said, she was just a replacement, a temporary replacement holding the place for the real thing. Imani was the real thing. It was a damn shame that it took me several years to realize but, better late than never.

None of this drama would have happened if I had been there with Imani. No custody cases, no attempted murder, no rekindling old flames, none of it. All she wanted was a man to call her own, me. Selfishly, I denied her that. Although she had never made me feel as full as Tya, Tya had never made me as complete as Imani. There was no way I could get Tya out of my system but it would be a cold day in hell before I lost Imani again.

I was stuck between a rock and a hard place. To keep Imani I would lose my son and to keep my son I risked losing Imani. I wanted both. What the hell was going on? My thoughts had spun out of control. I couldn't think anymore.

Tya's oldest son, Jason came downstairs to wish his mother good night before he went to bed. Realizing I had overstayed my welcome, I decided to leave. Tya walked me to the door and advised me to find somewhere quiet and try straightening out my thoughts before making a drastic decision. I stood and listened to her for a couple seconds more. As the pain in my leg became unbearable, I hugged and thanked her for being a friend. I got in my car and headed home. At least there I could have two- thirds—Imani and Kai—of a whole.

I listened to the soothing sounds of Kenny G as I drove up Springfield Boulevard. "Havana" played softly, filling the car as I turned into the drive-thru of White Castle. My stomach had begun to talk to me as I thought about what I was going to do with my life. The sound of the static from the intercom broke my concentration. I looked over the menu board and decided on a combo meal. My stomach pained me even more knowing that in a few minutes I'd have my food.

I turned the music down as I approached the window. The young lady repeated my total as I handed her a twenty. Upon receiving my change, I noticed a small piece of paper mixed with the dollars. On it was a number and the name Angie. I smiled at the young lady and drove off. Before I got halfway down the block, I tossed the number out the window.

"That's how I got in this mess to begin with," I said aloud to myself.

Imani wasn't home when I got there. I called Rodney and told him what happened. Afterward I checked the answering machine, hoping Imani had called. I was becoming worried about why she had not been home yet. Several messages from Charisse played, a message from Mia, of course we got a hang-up call and then a male voice began to play.

"Hello, Imani. It's Omar. Just wanting to make sure everything is all right. Call me." The voice echoed through the spacious room.

Who the fuck was Omar? She never told me about any Omar. And that wasn't a business call. Shit, I couldn't trust anybody!

Imani

As the taxi pulled up to the driveway, I noticed Q's car parked out front. After paying the driver, I walked to the house. When I got inside, the lights were off and the recorder in my office was playing. Q was checking my messages. I walked into the living room where Q sat outside my office on a stool.

"What took you so long to come home?" he asked.

He never looked up at me.

"I was waiting for you at your mother's house," I replied.

There was a faint smell of smoke lingering.

"Q, were you smoking?"

"Yeah. I lit a joint to relax. Who's this Omar? Somebody I need to know about?" he asked calmly as I choked on my gum.

I cleared my throat to respond. "He's someone I met on my trip."

"You fucking him?" he blurted out.

Q had definitely lost his mind. He was starting to scare me.

"Excuse me." I couldn't believe what I was hearing. Nor, could I imagine Q disrespecting me like that.

Quinton started limping in my direction as he said, "What's up with you and this Omar? He must have left like ten messages over the weekend. That's your man."

"No, I thought you were my man." He got in my face as I began to slowly walk backward.

Several times I stumbled over toys and other articles that were on the floor but not once did I lose my balance.

"I thought I was too. It looks like you made other plans." Q grabbed my arms tightly and pulled me close as he yelled, "Who the fuck is Omar?"

"He's a friend. He's got his own problems with his marriage." I tried to wiggle my way out of his clutch but it didn't work.

"Q, why are you doing this to me?" Scared and confused, I tried to reason with Q.

He looked at me for about two minutes as if I was some stranger before he released me.

"Imani, do you want to be with me? I need you . . . " Q sat down and put his head in his hands.

He was hurting and I didn't know how to help him. I sat beside him and rubbed his back. I tried to ease his pain.

"What do you want me to do, Baby?" I asked as I walked over to where he was sitting.

He didn't respond. Quinton leaped off the couch and headed up the stairs to the bedroom. He picked up his robe and went into the bathroom. I followed him into the bathroom and watched him undress and get into the shower.

"Q, would you please talk to me?" I begged.

"Mani, I don't feel like talking right now. I'm sorry for grabbing you . . . but . . . you're not being honest with me. I got enough shit going on in my head." He continued walking away from me.

"Q, Omar and I have nothing going on. He's just a friend. Honestly . . . I thought we weren't going to make it. Omar wasn't my backup plan though. He's married, trying to work out his own thing," I explained.

My hands shook violently as I told the story, scared of what his reaction may be.

"I know I haven't been Mr. Perfect lately but I tried. I'm still trying to. . . " he said.

As he talked through the shower curtain, I undressed and stepped inside.

"And that's why I'm with you now. I want us to be able to work this out," I said from behind him.

He turned toward my voice. Suddenly, he pushed me against the wall and held my hands above my head. Fear briefly washed over until I was taken over by lust. I wrapped my legs around him and kissed him more passionately than ever before. We washed, massaged and caressed each other for what seemed like an eternity. Those were the moments I longed for—spontaneous, intense and emotional.

"I'm sorry for being insecure but things haven't been going my way. I need you to be there with me when all this shit goes down with Jahlek and his mother," he said as he ran his hands over my shoulders, my body shuddering at his touch.

"Why didn't you tell me about this Omar character? We should be able to talk about everything and be truthful to each other. If there was nothing going on, you should have been able to tell me. Trust me enough to be able to talk about this! " His words were piercing as he spoke through pressed lips.

"I didn't feel it was any of your business. We have been living separate lives for years, and I wasn't sure if I was ready to tell you everything. We're just getting back together." I ran my hands up and down his back as we held each other close. "Plus, we need time to mend our lives."

156

He nodded as he stepped out of the shower and slid into his bathrobe.

"Imani, you will never know how much you mean to me. Hearing about you and another man . . ." He clenched his teeth tightly then exhaled before continuing. "It hurts to think I was the reason you turned to him for comfort. I never want to make you feel that way again. I want us to forget about all of this and confide in each other. Hopefully we can move beyond this."

We looked into each other's eyes. The feeling was real. The electricity sent vibes to my heart.

"Can we start over?" I asked as he tied my bathrobe.

"We will, Mani. Don't worry." Quinton was sincere when he wanted to be. "Can you redo my dressings after we order dinner? I got the munchies."

He must have believed I was telling the truth. My version, anyway.

He just dropped the whole conversation.

"Not a problem." Nope, no problem at all. Anything to keep him happy.

CHAPTER 13
CHANGES

Imani

Quinton and I stayed up late every night the following week talking about our future together and planning for our wedding. We laughed and joked while making all kinds of plans. It felt good to finally spend time together without the stress of the outside world to interrupt us. We had been so wrapped up in each other that Kai's birthday almost slipped by.

We invited some of her camp friends and our family over for a last minute barbecue. We pulled out the old inflatable pool and bought a couple of games and toys from Toys R Us, hoping she wouldn't notice it was a rush job. The party went smoothly although Quinton had run out several times to get things we thought we had covered in our brief party planning. Quinton spent the rest of the night wishing Jahlek could have been there.

After all was done and over, we went right back into our wedding planning. We decided on an outdoor ceremony followed by an indoor reception at our house. Our colors were light blue and gray. He picked out a charcoal-colored Pierre Cardin tuxedo with a banded collar resembling the one worn by Prince Charming with a long jacket reaching his knees. His groomsmen would include my brother, Jordan and Rodney. Shockingly, he wanted his mother's boyfriend James of all people to be his best man. John, of course, was going to give me away.

Charisse, of course, was my maid of honor, Jada would be my matron and Jada's daughter, Diamond, would be a bridesmaid. Jahlek and Kai, of course, would be the flower girl and ring bearer.

On my way to work, I picked up some more wedding magazines trying to piece together the perfect dress. I didn't have much time; the wedding was three weeks away. Quinton was home with Charisse's mother making all the arrangements. Charisse's mother suggested someplace in Long Island where she had catered many affairs. Q called me at least a hundred times to discuss every little detail. Mia and Jada helped me pick out my dress and veil, Jada even knew where to go for the best prices. Everything was looking up and that began to worry me.

After work, Charisse, Jada and I went out to eat and had our monthly women's night out. We discussed the wedding and what to expect as far as gifts and service. Mama J and Mrs. Nettles, Charisse's mother were at my house discussing the decorations, menu options and any extras they thought were necessary.

"So, Mani, are you nervous yet?" Jada asked as she sipped her daiquiri.

"No . . . I don't know. All this time I wanted nothing more than to get married and now I feel like I'm doing something wrong."

"Do you love him?" Charisse had a sly grin on her face as if there was something I didn't know.

"What kind of stupid question is that? I have loved Q for the past eight years and that shit won't change."

"Then, what are you afraid of?" Charisse asked, confused.

"I'm not... Do you think he proposed because he loves me or because he feels guilty?"

That's what I was afraid of! Would Q have proposed if I hadn't found out about Jahlek and Trina?

Charisse took my hand, "Q doesn't have a conscience, and therefore, he can't feel guilty. He loves you. That's the bottom line, kid."

"Besides the fact that there ain't enough guilt in the world to make a brother jump into marriage. They try to stay clear of commitment. The only way a brother will commit is either he finally finds the one he wants to spend the rest of his life with after screwing every women possible or home girl got some good-ass pussy."

"Damn Imani. I know my shit is good but your nanee must be GRRREAT! " Charisse said, emulating Tony the Tiger.

Jada and Charisse slapped each other high-five while we laughed. I sat back buried in my thoughts. I hoped Quinton knew what he was doing. I wasn't in for the loop de loop this time around. There might not be a next time.

Quinton

"So, you're sure about this?" Rodney asked. Here, my best friend of twenty years was asking me something he should already know the answer to. But I guess his concern was more for Imani than for me. He genuinely liked her and would constantly remind me that she was a good woman.

Rodney was one of my bad influences though. He wanted Imani and me to work it out but as far as the drug dealing, Rodney brought me into the game. After Rodney went to jail, I took over his hustle. I was only planning to keep his shit correct until he came home. But I started developing a repertoire for myself and became the new big man on the block. Rodney knew that wasn't the life for me but he didn't trust anybody else. We were like brothers, and we always had each other's back. Dealing wasn't supposed to be a long-term thing. Rodney had tried to convince me over and over to go back to school and get off the streets but I wasn't listening. The thought of fast money and the things it could buy had clouded my better judgment.

Rodney wasn't a stranger to addiction either. Where my addiction focused on money, his became women. Women threw themselves at him but he wasn't that kind of guy. When women offered their bodies he would educate them on what kind of woman he was looking for—funny, respectful, open-minded, educated and responsible. An educated woman turns him on.

And after he was sure they understood what he was looking for, he would give them a brief moment to evaluate themselves before he'd sleep with them. Some women were fortunate to get a call back for a second night of thug romance as he called it.

Looks and race didn't mean a thing to him, although, he did seem to shy away from white girls.

"Yeah, I'm ready. This is something I should have done a long time ago," I said, trying to convince myself more so than Rodney.

Rodney possessed a look of uncertainty, "You don't look like you're ready," he said. "All day you've been acting distant, daydreaming and shit. What's that about?"

"Nah, Imani got some brother calling her, and the shit really got me bugging. I know I haven't been the cleanest brother but Mani has never had another man in her life. Never! "

That was one thing I could bet my life on. She said he was just a friend but the look on her face when I mentioned his name told me something else.

"Man, you know Imani ain't going anywhere. If she wanted to leave your ass, she would have done it a long time ago. It's them jitters. Man, it might even be your conscience catching up to you."

"No, it's something. She has never, ever been with another man. I was her first and intend to be her last."

"Brother, listen to yourself. You really believe Mani is seeing someone else! " He laughed but I didn't find anything funny.

"I'm giving her the benefit of the doubt by thinking she would never lie to me. That's about the only thing that's keeping me from getting angry."

Rodney couldn't see how that was tearing me up on the inside. I believed there wasn't anything going on but did Imani intend to have an affair? That was a different story. I didn't believe in hitting a woman but if Imani decided to cheat on me . . . I hoped it didn't come to that.

"Do you know anything about the cat? Where he lives? What kind of car he drives? Maybe we can check him out." Rodney's idea wasn't sounding half bad.

"Ain't no need for all that. Imani said there ain't shit going on. Let's leave it at that." I didn't want to let him think I didn't trust Imani because I did. It was just my ego. Plus, the guy hadn't called nor had she mentioned him. Maybe they were just friends, someone she met through business. I had to find a way to disguise my jealousy. Couldn't let nobody see me weak.

Completely Satisfied

Imani

All week the only thing that would enter my mind was the thought of Q trying to hurt me. He had never raised a hand to me. Trina probably got him smoking that shit; Q never smoked, not even a cigarette.

I needed to call Omar and tell him what was going on and that it might not be a good idea to see each other again. I had his number blocked from our home phone but I knew it wouldn't be long before he found a way to get in contact with me. The last thing I needed was for Q to flare up like that again. After I put Kai to bed, I decided to call Omar, that way there wouldn't be any distractions.

"Kai, are you finished yet?"

She was supposed to be brushing her teeth but I didn't hear any water running. She'll find a million and one things to do to avoid going to bed.

"Mommy—" there came an excuse as to why she didn't do what she was told to do—"I wanted to know could I call Jahlek and see if he's all right."

That was so special. My baby had such a good heart. She loved her brother and it would kill her if she couldn't see him again.

"I don't know their number, Baby. You have to get it in the morning from your father. I'm sorry."

"That's okay. Good night." She walked over to give me a good night kiss. I took an extra whiff to make sure I could smell toothpaste.

"Night, sweetheart. I'll come and turn off your light in a minute."

I had to find Omar's number before Q came home. It was stuck between two bills, somewhere Q never looked. Not once had he ever taken time to look at the bills. He gave me whatever I told him they were.

"Hello." Omar was wide awake. There was music blasting in the background and sounds of laughter filling the air.

"Hello, Omar. This is Imani. We need to talk."

"Wait a minute. Let me go into a different room." The music began to fade. "Yeah, hello, what's up?"

"Q and I have decided to get married." I tried not to sound excited; I didn't want to hurt his feelings.

"That's funny because my wife and I finalized our divorce." His voice was full of joy, which was odd because from the conversations we had, I thought he would have been devastated.

"And you're happy. I thought you would be all torn up."

"No, Baby. I am too happy to be a single man again. We need to celebrate."

The conversation wasn't going the way I had expected.

"I don't know if that's a good idea. Q heard your message and flipped. He thought you and I was together and couldn't handle it. That's why I'm calling. I wanted to tell you that we would have to stop speaking for a while, you know until it boils over."

"Well, we have to see each other one last time, Imani. Can we at least have that much? I finally got my freedom and you finally got what you wanted. We owe each other a celebration date."

He didn't know what kind of trouble he was playing with.

"This needs some thought. I know it wouldn't be fair to say no right off the bat. You were there for me when I needed you most, and I thank you. I thank you for not taking advantage of me; however, seeing each other won't be a good idea. Not right now."

"I would never take advantage. I'd rather wait for the real thing, from the heart."

"There won't be a real thing for us. Sorry if I led you on. Listen, I have to go, don't call me, I'll call you. Okay."

"Okay, beautiful. Don't let him hurt you," he said, as if he knew what had transpired a couple of weeks before. The thought brought tears to my eyes.

"Bye," I whispered before returning the phone to its cradle.

I quickly hung up the phone as I heard Q's keys rattling at the door. I popped up off the couch and began walking toward the stairs to go to Kai's room. Quinton entered the house but I didn't even turn around to acknowledge him. I wasn't sure if he was in one of his moods or not and I didn't really care to find out.

"Mani, what's up?" His voice was mellow, no hint of attitude. It was safe.

"Nothing much." I turned around "Q, I really feel bad about Trina and the whole custody thing but I would have never expected you to put your hands on me." I had to let him know what had been on my mind.

"Imani, I told you I didn't mean it. I don't know what came over me—"

"That damn weed! When did you start smoking, anyway?"

"A while back. I don't do it every day and don't want to. It was there and it was a temptation . . . you know."

"Well, we don't need any of that shit in our lives, and I hope that was the end of it."

Q walked closer to me, grabbed my hands and looked deep into my eyes as I gazed back into his warm brown ones.

"I promise, Baby. I'll never smoke again. But Mani, please promise me that this would be the last time we hear of an Omar or a Trina."

"I promise. There will be no more talk of Omar, but Trina is a different story. Kai was asking for her brother before she went to bed. What are you going to do?"

"What did she want?" he asked with inward arched eyebrows. A little smile began to form across his face. He loved the thought of Kai looking over her brother.

"She wanted to call him and find out how he's doing. I told her to get the number from you in the morning. You're keeping her with you tomorrow, right."

"I guess. I'm not going anywhere she can't go. Lay out her clothes and do her hair." He walked into the kitchen and opened the refrigerator door.

"Q, I'll have to wake her up real early to do her hair. Just brush it up into a ponytail and let the rest hang down." I went to the microwave and took out the plate I had prepared for him.

"Whatever. I'll take one of the new outfits in her closet too." He carried a bottle of Coke over to the cabinet from where he picked his favorite glass and sat at the table. Meanwhile, I rinsed a fork and knife and grabbed the A-1 steak sauce and salt—two things he must have or else he wouldn't eat steak. No matter how it was seasoned.

"No. I'll iron her clothes when I iron mine tonight."

There were only certain outfits I allowed her to romp around in. Quinton didn't care what she wore as long as he didn't have to iron it. If he wanted to take her to the park and had to choose between a church dress or wrinkled jeans, she'd be in her Sunday's best with sneakers and dress socks.

Quinton finished his dinner while I began to put Kai's clothes together. When he finished cleaning his plate, he walked into the living room. He put his arm around my neck, and I followed suit by placing my arm around his waist. We walked into our bedroom, and my eyes almost popped out of my head. The room was a mess— papers and clothes all over the place. Q pushed it all to the side. But by the look on my face he knew I was not happy.

"What?" he said. "I'll clean it tomorrow? Calm down."

He winked like that would make the room clean itself. I hated having a dirty house more than anything I could imagine. From when we were younger Nana taught Jada and me to keep our homes impeccably clean and to cook dinner every night. She said that was the only way to keep your man. Although I had followed Nana's rules that barely kept Quinton home. "Please make sure it's done before I come home. My sister and my aunt are coming over to help me with the rest of the arrangements for the wedding." Jada would crawl out her skin if she saw the house and she would make sure I never heard the end of it.

"Okay, okay, Mani. Baby, I'll do it." He fixed his face to reflect some sort of attitude. I couldn't care less; my house was a mess.

"Mani, do me a favor? Tomorrow go to the mall and pick up some socks, boxers and T-shirts. All the stuff that's here is too tight."

Goes to show how long it's been since he had actually been home. "What about the stuff in the garage? Did you go through any of that yet?"

"Yes, I did," he said with a little sarcasm. "And I still didn't find anything that feels right. There are too many bad memories in those boxes. Besides, I just need underwear."

"No problem. You're giving me money, right? I'm broke." What did I look like spending my money on any of his shit?

"You're lying! You stay broke but let you see an outfit, a pair of earrings or a bracelet you want, you'll find some money then, right."

I laughed because he was right but what's the use of having money if you didn't spend it. He claimed he had so much. Show me.

"All right, I'll get it on my lunch break. Anything else?"

"Your treat?" he asked, surprised by my response.

Probably thought I was playing with his head.

"Why not? You're paying for the whole wedding. I'll treat you to the minor shit," I said as I thought, because you're about to go all out for the wedding. I want it all!

"True, that sounds fair. I need . . ." Q winked as he wore a sly grin; he was up to no good.

Any other time I would have tried to find out what he was thinking. All I could think about was Omar. Why does he want to see me again? I tried to block the thought but it wasn't happening. So instead of staying up to talk, I decided to look for my nightgown and go straight to sleep.

As Q continued to make the bed, I slid into my pajamas and began to brush my hair back.

"Mani, pass me some shorts please." The sound of his voice startled me.

"What the hell are you jumping for?" he asked.

"You caught me off guard. I was thinking about some stuff." I opened his drawer and began searching through his night pants.

"Anything I need to know?" he asked.

"No, Baby. It's little things I've been forgetting to do."

"All right. If there's something you need me to do, let me know. Tomorrow I won't be that busy."

He turned on the radio and began searching through the channels to find CD 101. We always relaxed to jazz.

"No, nothing that I can think of. Thanks anyway."

I pulled a pair of his shorts out of the drawer and a Ziploc bag fell out. The bag was packed with weed. "Q, what's this doing in the house? I thought we had an understanding." I held the freezer bag up high for him to clearly see.

"Mani, Rodney gave it to me this morning so he didn't have to ride around with it. I forgot to give it back to him. I'll do it tomorrow."

"You sure this is not your personal stash?" I asked.

Quinton

"Hell no! I told you I wasn't going to smoke that stuff anymore." She threw my shorts at me with the bag wrapped inside.

"I want that shit out of my house now! " she hollered.

"And take it where? It's almost eleven o'clock, where the hell am I going to go?" I whispered, hoping she would lower her voice.

"Call Rodney and let him pick it up," she said.

I didn't know what was wrong with her. She was really overreacting.

"Mani, is there something on your mind? You're acting real funny right now."

"Like what? I told you before to keep this shit away from our house. You obviously don't mind putting our family at risk."

"How? How am I putting us at risk? Police aren't watching me. I'm not hot like that plus, I handed over the business to Rodney. This is not mine! So what the fuck is your problem?"

"You! You have no respect for my wishes. I asked you for only one thing. Then to top it off not only do you sell the shit you smoke it too."

"That was my last time smoking, and I said I was sorry. I am sorry! If I hurt you, it will never happen again. Damn, drop it."

"Quinton, I am hardly worried about you hurting me. You've already hurt me. But what if you had been smoking and Kai would have made you upset?"

"That would never happen. You are making up situations to avoid telling me what's really wrong."

"You wanna know! If Trina hadn't shot you, would you have still proposed? Was that your apology or your take-me-back plea, what? I need to know."

Tears began to form in Imani's eyes. She was hurting, and I had no idea what to say to make it any better. I had no clue she had all that hurt bottled up inside. I wanted to make her feel secure but I didn't know what to say to make her believe me.

"Mani, Baby, I was on my way to you when she shot me. I had already decided that I wanted to spend the rest of my life with you. She was jealous because she knew; she knew I only wanted to be with you. I'm sorry it took me so long to realize that we belonged together." I walked over to where she was stood as I apologized.

She placed her fingers gently on my lips.

"I'm sorry, Q. I don't know what's come over me. Maybe, it's the wedding. Lately, I've been a little insecure about the way you feel for me and Kai and where you want to be. I feel like I have to compete to keep you."

"Come lay down and relax. Girl, don't ever doubt my love or commitment to you and our family. This is where I wanna be."

As I pulled the blanket back for Mani, I tried to think of ways to make her feel better, less shaky. I lay next to my lady and cradled her warm, sensuous body in my arms as I kissed her earlobe softly.

"Talk to me, Baby. Tell me what you're thinking about. What else is on your mind?" I asked.

I understood what she was going through because just that morning I was having the same issues.

"A whole lot. Is Kai happy? Are you happy? Will we make it? How long will this last? Will you hurt me again? I don't know. Take your pick."

"Oh baby, you're worrying yourself about stuff that needs no answer. You know deep in your heart what's right. Mani, are you happy that we're together or do you have second thoughts?"

"I don't know. I've loved you all of my life. You are the only man I have ever known outside of my brothers and uncle. I can't say that I'm not happy we're together because that's all I prayed for. But I wonder should I have…" She paused.

"Do you want to see someone else?" I calmly asked, knowing any answer other than no was going to cause problems.

"No, I'm saying . . . I don't know what I'm saying. Shit, I really don't know."

"Damn! Do you want Omar? Is that what this is all about?"

I sat up and looked over to see her expression. It was blank, no remorse, no regrets, no feeling.

She looked at me and with her expression alone I knew the answer.

"Q, I love you but I can't answer that tonight. I need time to think."

"Like how much time? We're getting married in less than a month. What the hell are you going through?"

That was exactly what I was worried about but I tried to ignore it. It was so clear that morning, like a premonition. It was there; I chose not to see it. Her feelings for that man were clear.

I got out of the bed and started to get dressed. "Where are you going?" she asked.

"To my mother's. Call me when you've straightened your shit out. Hopefully, you'll come to your senses. Until then the wedding's off!"

On my way out of the room, I picked up my cane and car keys.

"Q..." she hollered as I placed my foot on the first step of the staircase.

I turned around to stare at her but the look on my face let Imani know I wasn't happy. I didn't say anything more, I just continued out the house.

I slammed the door with all my might. Almost took the door off its hinges. I wanted the neighborhood to know the hurt I was experiencing. I waited a couple of seconds more hoping Imani would run out looking for me before I drove off. Staring at the door long and hard, I imagined seeing the door opening until a falling branch hit the windshield, bringing me back to reality.

After turning on the car, I kept it in park and pressed the accelerator allowing the loud engine to roar. Maybe she didn't know I was still outside. Maybe she didn't care.

CHAPTER 14
MIND GAMES

Quinton

"I can't believe this shit," I said aloud to myself as the events replayed in my mind.

I had tried to push the incident with Imani to the furthest corner of my mind but the pain of losing the woman I loved had taken its toll. I couldn't eat or sleep when I was constantly thinking of Imani and her new beau.

Time and time again I tried to reconcile for nothing more than the sake of our child but all she wanted to do was argue, fuss and fight. I had tried to walk away but I couldn't back down because I loved her so much I hated her, if that made any sense. Plus, laying down my pride was something I couldn't do. But if I thought for one second that Imani would reconsider, I would.

Thoughts of being with Trina had entered my mind, and I tried to make sense of it. Me being with Trina would be the right thing but she wasn't who I wanted.

Kai had been waiting night and day for her mother to come back and be a family. Whenever the phone rang she would jump to answer anticipating hearing her mother's voice. With each passing hour of each passing day her sad expression deepened at the thought of her mother forgetting about her and never returning. It seemed as if nothing I did could make her happy. Kai didn't deserve that. I was the one who caused Imani's pain not the baby. I wondered if Imani realized what she was doing to Kai—or to me for that matter.

Imani

The last couple of weeks had been horrible. The month of August had come and gone. I spent my twenty-eighth birthday alone, replaying over and over the decision that caused my life to come to an immediate halt. Q and I had been arguing every time we saw each other. As much as we tried not to argue in front of Kai, it never worked. She was torn apart when she found out her father and I weren't together anymore. She stopped speaking to me for the first two days. When she finally spoke she said she wanted her father. And she had been with him since.

Mama J and my aunt Barbara, Daddy's baby sister, had been very understanding though. Mama said she thought we were rushing things a bit and we hadn't given each other time to heal. Although, Charisse tried to reassure me that I was doing the right thing, it never felt right.

Q had been in and out of court with Trina and the stress was had begun to take a toll on him. He started smoking weed and hanging on street corners again. I was losing all the respect I had for him, and he had lost all respect for me. He talked to me like I was one of his customers or hos. I was hoping things wouldn't have turned out that way. But I guess it was inevitable.

I started seeing Omar, and we agreed that we were ready to be with each other. We wanted to make sure that there were no rebounds to get over. Although I thought of Q night and day, I didn't see us making it as a couple anymore. I was sure he would have been a better man the next time around but I owed it to myself to explore other opportunities.

Omar wanted to spend the weekend with me as a belated birthday celebration. I had already agreed to but I felt I needed someone else's approval. I called Mia to ask her what she thought I should do.

"Imani, I can't tell you what to do. I can suggest for you to follow your heart. If you believe that you will be happier without Quinton then pursue that feeling but don't string him along."

"Mia, has John said anything to you about this?" I was almost too scared to ask.

"Yeah, he thinks that Q did something to you again. He said that he has a feeling that Q hurt you in."

"But he didn't. Recently, Quinton has done nothing but be the most loving and caring man any woman could wish for but I know it's only an plea for forgiveness. I can't let go of the past. When I think of us having a life together, I see more sad times, more lies." I never told her how close I came to getting a black eye that night.

"Did you tell him that you felt this way?" she replied.

"No. What else could he do outside of what he has already done? Plus, the thought of Omar being there for me outweighed the possibilities of Q and me. There's something special about Omar, something in the way he looks at me. With Q it feels as if he owes me or is somehow obligated to love and respect me. Omar is genuine," I said.

"Mani, I wish I could make the decision for you that would make your life so much clearer but I don't know the answer. Just be careful. Sometimes what you think may be a good thing might not be so good after all. Pray, and God will help you find your way."

"Okay. Thank you, Mia. I love you." Mia didn't know how much she meant to me.

"I love you too, baby girl. Stay strong," she said.

Strong, a word I haven't heard in a while. I had been weak-hearted and feeble-minded. Normally, people regarded me as being capable of making clear and rational decisions. Nana would roll over in her grave if she saw me.

Nobody could give me an answer. Charisse said to do what I felt was best. I felt it would be best to patch things up with Q. He wasn't doing well, and I sensed it was my fault. Mama said he had been lashing out on her and James for no reason. Little things would aggravate him. The only thing he had time for were the kids since he and Trina have come to an agreement about visitation. He was a patient father but a horribly miserable man. It hurt me to hear Mama talk about Q falling apart.

As I cleared off my desk, preparing my papers for the next workday, my phone began to ring.

"Hello," I said after pressing the button for speakerphone.

"Hey, Baby. Are we still on for tonight?" Omar's soothing voice put a brief end to my misery.

"I don't see why not. Kai is staying with her father, and I was able to finish all my paperwork here. My bags are packed and ready."

"Good. So, where do you want to meet?" His eager voice caused me to blush.

"I could meet you at your place. Let me go home and get my things. I should be there by nine."

"All right. Use your key. I'll be waiting."

I forgot about the key. Where did I put it? It should still be with the flowers he sent it with yesterday. This man had flowers for every occasion. Omar sent a beautiful bouquet of white roses with pink edges decorated with pink and lilac baby's breath. That was the best gift I got outside of the forced "happy birthday" I got from Kai. I missed the homemade birthday cards she and Q would have waiting for me when I came home from work.

Quinton called to ask for some clothes for Kai. The sound of his voice caused my stomach to drop. But his hastiness proved that he was not interested in carrying on conversation.

I missed my little girl but she didn't want to see me, and I couldn't blame her. I messed up big time and I had to find a way to make it up to her.

Quinton

"Kai, did your mom send any other clothes?" I asked as I went through the bag Imani dropped off.

"No. She said that's all I need. She gave me a hug and kiss and then she left. She didn't even pack my dolls."

Mani had really been falling off with Kai. How many days did she think four outfits would cover? Kai had been with me for a month and Imani only dropped off two more outfits. I couldn't take her outside in the same clothes day after day. Not after all that money I spent on clothes. If you want the job done right you have to do it yourself, that's how the saying goes. Going to the house for anything was a conflict. The clothes were a necessity, therefore I had no choice but I really hated going over there. The house was filled with too many painful memories. We made love in every inch of that house.

173

Lately I had had thoughts of that man sleeping in my bed, fucking on my sofa. I tried to believe Imani when she said "I'll never bring him to our house." But she also said she'd never leave me or let another man into her heart.

Kai was the one who was affected most. She didn't even want to see her mother, and I don't think Imani even cared. Imani didn't call or visit. You would think she would at least sit with Kai for a little while trying to bond when she came by. Then she had the nerve to talk about me. Sober or not I spent time with my kids, quality time.

I stood from the couch, fixed my pants, threw on my jacket and grabbed my keys off the glass end table.

"Ma, watch Kai and Jahlek while I go over to the house," I said as I gave myself a once-over in the huge mirror over the sofa.

"Why don't you take the chile to see her mother?" Mama shouted from her room.

"How long did Imani stay when she dropped off Kai's clothes? If she wanted to she could have spent time with Kai but she chose not to. Plus, Kai don't need to hear us. I have something I need to say to her. I hope she's not there when I got there."

I began walking to the corner store to get a Philly to roll my blunt when I bumped into Ro. She was the neighborhood trick; she would do anything for a hit. Ro was also the informer. If there was anything you wanted to know on the streets, she knew.

"Hey Q, have you heard?" she asked, struggling to keep her eyes open.

She was high; there was no doubt about it. Her eyes were cherry red and her breath told it all.

"Nah, heard what?" I asked, trying to avoid eye contact with her.

"Bryan's house got hit up and they took everybody down, including
Trina."

"Took everybody down? Police ran up in there?" I asked.

"Nah, some bangas from The Bronx. Killed everybody, took the stash and flew before po-po showed up."

"I picked up my son from there 'bout an hour ago. Trina wasn't even there. She took Junior to get his school clothes."

174

"Yo, kid. I'm trying to tell you. She's dead. Bryan's son was at the neighbors. He was in the bathroom while the shit was going down."

Damn! I hoped that shit wasn't true. Trina's dead. How was I supposed to explain that to Jahlek? My little man wouldn't have a mother. Even though I hated Trina, he still needed his mother. What about his brother? They couldn't be separated. Bryan was the closest person to him besides Trina and me. Bryan was his best friend.

After I picked up Kai's clothes, I would get the whole story, or at least parts of what happened. I wasn't going to let anybody separate the boys so the right thing was to check on Bryan Jr. I wondered what Imani would say. How would she react to Bryan hanging around? Even though we weren't together, her opinion was still important to me.

Imani

Everything was packed. I brought pink lace lingerie hoping I would have reason to wear it. Even if it was for only a couple of seconds. After the weekend, Omar and I should know where our relationship stood. I had been second-guessing myself though. Did I really want to jeopardize the friendship Omar and I had? Was I just sexually attracted to him? I hoped I wasn't making a mistake. If Omar and I didn't work out, what would that mean for Quinton and me? He wouldn't forgive me or take me back.

I took a look at my watch and realized the time. I slid my hands down my sides to smooth out my teal tank dress. I picked up a matching teal bag and headed for the door.

"I got to get moving or I'm going to be late," I said to myself, acknowledging the time.

Headlights illuminated my dining room as I headed for the door. Through the window, I saw a gold BMW with pitch-black tints. That was Q's new signature. What the hell was he doing here? Another shouting match was in the air. Some things were inevitable and Quinton staying quiet was definitely inevitable.

Q walked towards the door and stared at me with angry eyes as I stood in the doorway. Looking past his stare I glanced over his body. Not much had changed. He was still well built, chocolate, sexy. . . fine. As he walked past me and the aroma of his oil lingered in the air, my private began to thump. His baldhead glistened in the moonlight. Something about when he wore all black turned me on. The black silk shirt hung loosely over his body. As the gentle breeze blew the shirt against his chest, I caught hints of muscle. And, although he wore black khakis, the enormity of his penis still pressed through.

"Imani, you planning on going somewhere?" he asked as he stood in the door.

Q reeked of marijuana as he darkened the archway of the living room. Instantly my GQ image had vanished, bringing me back to reality.

"Yes. I'm taking a weekend trip. What are you doing here?" I asked, closing the door behind him.

"Well you know your daughter, Kai, needed some clothing. You dropped off two outfits like that was supposed to suffice. Besides the fact that I pay bills here." He paused, briefly looking away from me. He returned his gaze and asked, "When are you going to come visit her? Spend some time with her? Every girl needs her mother, you know."

If anybody understood what it was like not having a mother, it was me. He knew that. "Q, you know I haven't gotten my mind right and I don't want Kai to see me like this. I don't want to confuse her."

"Like how, chasing after a man other than her father?" he said sharply.

"I'm not chasing anybody! " I replied.

"Then, why didn't we get married? All the money I put into that wedding went to waste. Why? 'Cause you ain't got your head right?" he said, mocking my sorry excuse.

"I needed some time to be myself. Feel free from all the pressure of being with you. Shit wasn't exactly all that easy with you. You kept a sistah wondering when you'd be home. What bitch you were out with? How many other kids do you have out there? You know, shit like that," I said sarcastically nodding my head and thinking yeah that's about it.

"If that's how you felt, then why did you take me back in the first place? And what the fuck do you mean feel free? Oh, being loose! So you're his ho now?" he said as he began up the stairs.

"No, that's your other baby's mother," I shot back.

"Leave her out of this," he said as he turned around.

"Why? She's better than me now? Oh, I see y'all got a thing going on, huh." I stopped midway across the living room.

"First of all Trina has nothing to do with you. Secondly, if Trina and I were back together, it would be my business. I'm a free man now, remember?"

My heart almost came out of my chest. Extreme fury had taken over my body with each thought of him and Trina together.

I continued on my wild ranting. "That's what you wanted all along. You wanted to be with that nasty, stank-ass, crackhead, bad-weave-having ho anyway. She was more your type. Street rat! No class whatsoever…" I cut myself short, not wanting to bring myself to her level.

"Cut your shit, Imani. You're from the streets too. Trina had a rough life. Where you thought you had no family she actually had none. She's been in and out of foster care all of her life. She chose a different path than you but your backgrounds are the same."

"Don't compare me to your bitch, Q. You want me to pity her? Fuck her. That bitch deserves everything that has happened to her," I said.

"Imani, shut the fuck up!" he roared down the hall from Kai's room. "She's dead, Mani. You're saying she deserved to die? Jahlek deserved to lose his mother? Huh! "

His massive chest began to swell up as stepped closer to me. My heart skipped beats as fear took over. Quinton's reaction caused me to stop breathing. I choked, gasping for air. Trina was dead…damn!

"I'm . . . sorry. Q, I didn't mean it. Really, I'm so sorry to hear that." *Yeah, right.* "How did she die?"

"She died in some gang-related shit. I don't have the exact details yet." He continued packing Kai's clothes into her Barbie suitcase. Q had yet to look me in the face.

"Sorry to hear that. Are you okay?" I asked, pretending to care.

"I'm living. I'll get over it. But I have a question for you. If there was a chance that we could get back together . . ." Quinton had turned to face me for the first time since the conversation started and before he could finish I cut him off.

"Can't answer that! But, are you sure you're all right?" We didn't need to get any deeper than necessary.

"Yeah . . . well, don't let me hold you up any longer. You know you got things to see, people to do," he replied, continuing down the stairs.

"You know what, fuck you!" I picked up my bags and started for the door.

In mid-stride, Q called my name. His voice, full of love and frustration, caused my heart to swell with hurt and regret.

Without turning around, he said, "Don't let him use you, Mani."

On that note, I continued to walk to my car and load my bags onto the backseat.

I drove for hours, imagining what life would be like without Q.

Suddenly tears begun to well up in my eyes. "As long as it's the final good-bye, don't let him see you cry," I imagined Charisse saying as I wiped away tears. That was it. It was over.

In all the confusion, I managed to hurt my baby. My little girl was crying herself to sleep because of my selfishness. What kind of mother would forget her child? She hadn't seen or heard from me in two weeks before today. I felt as though I was freakishly becoming Nadine. She ran out on me when I young, close to the same age as Kai. To this day I hated her. I didn't want my baby girl to despise me. I loved her and wanted to be there to watch her grow and become the intelligent woman I had taught her to be. Unlike Nadine, I needed to be there for her but something was holding me back. Between work and depression, I totally forgot what mattered most, my baby.

Quinton

After Imani pulled off, I sat and replayed everything that happened, trying to find some sense in it all. Maybe, she wasn't coming back. She seemed to be happy. Imani couldn't be over me. I wasn't over her.

My intentions were to make her see what she was doing to our daughter and maybe change her mind about us but instead I let her beauty sidetrack me. I tried not to look at her, hoping I could muster up strength but the minute I caught a glance, I lost it. Her body was still tight. Her silky skin was still smooth and soft. Her mix of cocoa butter and Victoria's Secret Heavenly Angel was intoxicating. I wanted to tackle her and make her feel my pain. Give her all of me and take in all of her—her moans, her scent, her sweat—and her passion.

"Shit," I said aloud as I banged my fist against the wall, causing the mirror to shake. "I shouldn't have let her leave."

Running my hand over my head, I tried to think of the next best step. Should I follow her and risk getting my feelings hurt even more or should I go home and let time do its thing. Begging was hardly my style so I decided to go see what really happened with Trina. See what I could do.

CHAPTER 15
ENDLESS LOVE

Imani

After exiting the New Jersey Turnpike, I called Omar to let him know I was a couple of blocks away. When I pulled up in front of his house, he was waiting at the door with a black silk robe draped over his shoulders. He grabbed my bags and kissed my cheek. I didn't respond to his greeting as I normally would. He automatically sensed something was wrong.

"What happened? Are you okay?" He led me to the sofa and took off my sandals. Omar looked scrumptious in his T-shirt and boxers. He was the total opposite of Quinton. Omar was light skinned with a smaller frame. He wasn't as rough as Quinton was either. He was more refined.

I continued to admire his body as he began to massage my feet. His body may not have been as rigid as Quinton's nor were him muscles as defined but he still looked good.

"My baby hasn't seen me two weeks. I didn't even call her to see if she was okay." I started to cry.

"Baby, she knows you love her. When you get back, spend some quality time with her. Let her know that she didn't do anything."

"I want my life back. I have never felt this bad before. All the times Quinton and I had our disputes, I have never neglected my baby."

"Do you want to go back to Q? Would that make you happy?"

Comments like those were when I remembered what captured my heart most about Omar. He was authentically understanding and compassionate. No fronts.

"Can we change the subject?" I asked, feeling a lump build in my throat.

"Okay." He moved behind me and held me as I tried to calm down.

"How about I try to make you forget about your troubles for tonight? Let me give you your birthday present."

He slowly positioned his body on top of mine. Suddenly, I felt uncomfortable behind Q's use of the word ho.

This was what I had been waiting for. Omar had left me waiting and wanting for so long, always talking about waiting for the time to be right. Here it was. The time was right and I was ruining it. It was the worst birthday ever.

"Do you want me?" he asked in his deepest, sultriest voice.

"Yes, but . . . I just got here; I'm a little tired. Can I take a shower first?"

Sitting upright on the couch, I noticed a wedding picture. An older man was in the picture resembling Omar, so immediately I knew that was his father. But the lady in the picture stuck out like a sore thumb. Beside the fact that she looked much younger than his father she looked familiar. She was one of those women with a high yellow complexion. Her short, slim frame was extremely shapely. I'm talking about hips galore. She had jet-black hair and hazel eyes. Something about her eyes . . . Omar's voice took my mind away from the picture.

"That's my dad and his wife. Some low-life he met in Virginia," he said as he stared at the woman in the picture. If looks could kill, that woman would be dead.

"Oh, she was one of them gold-digging bitches whose prey is older men with money," I said.

Still staring at the woman in the picture, I realized there was no way I knew her. He said Virginia, and I hadn't done any business or taken any vacations in Virginia. He slammed the photo down on the table and turned his attention back to us.

"Would you like me to join you in the shower?" he whispered in my ear.

"Huh. No, I'll be all right by myself," I answered.

Searching through my bags to find my nightgown, I had a feeling something bad was going to happen. Quickly, I dismissed the feeling. While in the shower, I tried to shake off any bad feelings I had and tried to think of the good things to come but the woman from the picture kept entering my mind. Her slanted eyes and dark hair stuck out most. Outside of Jada, she was the only other person I ever saw with black hair. Maybe the resemblance she and Jada shared made her look so familiar. I thought to ask Omar her name; she was probably someone I met at a conference. You never know, it's a small world.

As I turned off the water, I heard another voice in the house. It was clearly the voice of a man. The stranger's presence didn't ride well with me; therefore, I waited and listened before I exited the bathroom. When I opened the door, the scent of cherries filled my nose. There were candles from the end of the stairs to the bedroom.

I walked into the bedroom only to catch Omar and the unidentified voice sniffing a white powder off the night table.

"What the hell…?" I hollered at the top of my lungs, startling the duo. I stood shocked at of what I was seeing.

"Oh, Baby. It's not what it looks like. This is just a stimulant, you know to get me started." He had a hollow look in his eyes.

"Omar, you done got us a pretty one tonight," said the other heavy, congested voice in the dark room.

"Hold on! Who the hell are you and what the fuck you mean us?" I said to the man as he stepped into the light.

The other man was tall and fat, wore a tired Jheri curl and too-tight sweats. I immediately named him Bubba.

"He didn't mean us, like that. He's kidding. Look why don't you go downstairs and make yourself comfortable on the couch until I finish," Omar said.

Yeah, Omar must be on something if he thinks I'm going to be nonchalant about that.

"All right, I'll be in the living room." *Yeah, right!*

Bubba grabbed my arm and squeezed my ass as I turned toward the staircase leading downstairs. Looking at Omar for his defense was useless. All he did was smile. Homeboy was bugging. Bubba pinned me up against the wall and began to slobber on my neck. Omar turned to look the other way and continued what he was doing. In the meantime, Bubba was grabbing my breasts and trying to put his hand in my panties.

Through my fear, I built up as much force as I could and kneed him right in the balls. The blow to his nuts caused him to let loose. When he turned around, I hauled tail down the stairs and picked up my bags. Omar and his friend darted down the stairs trying to catch up to me. While heading for my car, I reached down in my pocketbook and got my gun. Thank God, I forgot to take it out my bag. After I found the gun in one of Q's sneaker boxes, I put it in my bag so I wouldn't forget to give it to him when I saw him. Bubba stopped dead in his tracks and hollered to Omar, who was trailing but there was nothing he could do. I was gone.

On my way back to New York, I thought about calling Q and apologizing and begging him to take me back. I needed him so bad to comfort me. With my hand on my head, I replayed the night's events. Still in my nightgown, I sped down the highway trying to find a service station. At the next rest stop, I had to change into something; I got some jeans and a sweater I could throw on real quick. Meanwhile, I had to call Reese.

I knew it was too good to be true. Homeboy was too fine and too mannerly to be perfect.

Quinton

Everybody on the block gave me his version of what happened at Bryan's house. All the stories were from he say, she say so it was hard to tell the truth.

The main story was it was a drug-related shooting. Bryan obviously overstepped his boundaries when he tried to pump his shit in the Bronx. Queens didn't have a large clientele and Brooklyn was on lock-down. He made a deal with some brothers from the Bronx to form one team and take over Brooklyn. Bryan had made the same deal with some dealers in Brooklyn and Uptown. Word had spread to the brothers in the Bronx and Brooklyn.

Rodney, being one of the biggest dealers in Brooklyn, had planned to take Bryan down a long time ago on some personal shit but when word passed that it was Bryan who tried to cause another drug war, things went in to effect a lot sooner. In a matter of days Rodney and his boys had set up Bryan and his organization, taking away all his business, supplies and cash. The Bronx had their own agenda when Bryan's crib got shot up.

Police were barricading the area when I arrived at the house. Detectives were talking as police officers scurried to gather evidence. One police officer came toward me and instinctively I turned to walk away. Not that I had any dirt on me but I'd rather be safe than sorry. Any black face was a suspect. My involvement with Trina wouldn't have made it any better. The case would have been solved before they started—a jealous lover scorned. They would claim that as my motive and close the investigation.

Sandra, Trina's best friend, was among the many in the crowd. I tapped her lightly on her shoulder hoping to get some information on Bryan Jr.

"Hey, what's up, Q?" she said as she sniffled.

"Hey. How you holding up? Sorry to hear about your girl. Did you get to see her?"

"No. They took everybody out in body bags. Nobody survived but little Bryan. He's over at my mom's house now," she said.

"Is somebody coming to get him? Did you get in contact with Trina's mother?"

"Q, you know her mother couldn't care less and Bryan's old ass ain't got no surviving relatives."

Sandra became upset with the mention of Bryan's name.

"Are you going to try and get custody of Bryan or are you going to call Children Services?" I asked. Before I could complete my thought Sandra was cursing and carrying on.

"Take care of another one of his bastards. No thank you. I already got one at home and one on the way." She pointed to her small round belly.

"You was fucking Bryan too? How you going to do that to your girl? You and Trina was supposed to be like sisters." I was disgusted.

"Shit, Trina knew. My daughter Sharay is Bryan's oldest. Trina knew we were together but she didn't care. All she saw was them dollars. When she got pregnant with Bryan Jr., they decided to get

184

married and do shit right. Meanwhile, I was still living in the house and sleeping with Bryan every other night," she explained.

"Y'all bitches are a mess."

I couldn't help but appreciate Imani's little imperfections. Imani would never be that trifling.

"So, I can take Bryan then?"

"Yeah, I guess. You still have to report him to Children Services or it's considered kidnapping."

Sandra returned to her old flirtatious self. She grabbed hold of my Johnson and said, "This is what Trina was talking about, huh!"

I smacked her hand away. I had no interest in letting her find out.

The neighbors didn't ask any questions as to who I was when I arrived to get Bryan Jr. They looked like they were using drugs too. He carried his new clothes his mother had bought him earlier that day as the elderly man led him to the door.

"Are you all right, little man?" I asked as I opened the car door.

"Are they dead, Q?" he asked.

"Let's go to my house and get Kai and Jahlek."

The night had brought about so much drama. I couldn't wait to get home and finally rest. I knew Kai and Jahlek had to be in bed but Jahlek would pop right up when he saw his brother. As I thought of ways to make Bryan comfortable, my cell phone rang, startling me. Charisse's number showed up on my Caller ID.

"What?" I answer, annoyed with her timing. Charisse always managed to make a bad time worst.

"I think you need to go home tonight," she said.

"Why, what's up?" I became more concerned as I listened to the shakiness in her voice.

"Imani needs you. Please . . . go home." Her voice, on the verge of cracking, told me that it was urgent.

"Is she all right? Did she have an accident? Is she hurt?" The night wasn't getting any better.

"Listen, go home and ask all the questions you want when she gets there."

The line went dead. It was not my night and it wasn't over yet. Getting the kids out of bed and driving back to Queens was the last thing I wanted to do but Imani needed me.

"You ready to go for a ride, little man?" I said, looking at Bryan in the rearview mirror.

"Are you going to take care of me?" Tears fell from the child's eyes but his face was emotionless.

I turned to look Bryan in the face and said, "You got it. We're going to be best friends. All right?"

When I got home, Kai and Jahlek were on the couch on Mama's lap, asleep. I woke the kids and told Mama about the call. She got worried and insisted that I call when I got there. James was on the other couch and woke up from the commotion. Mama told him something happened to Mani and he asked if I wanted him to take care of it. He had the same idea I had. We both thought she and Omar got into it.

Before leaving, I assured him I was going to be all right. Mama asked me to leave the kids just in case but I thought it might be good for Mani to be with her family. I loaded my troop into the backseat and sped off down the block.

"Daddy, what happened to my mommy?" Kai asked as she gazed out of the window.

"Nothing. She doesn't feel good. We're going to take care of her. Okay?" I lied but I didn't know what else to say.

On the ride to the house, I thought of a hundred things that could have happened, and my heart quickly filled with rage. I picked up speed to make sure I was there when Imani got home.

Imani

Quinton's car was parked out front when I reached the house. I wondered if he'd left from earlier. I opened the front door slowly. I didn't want to make any noise in case he was sleeping. My bags were still in the car; I didn't have the strength to take them in. They'd be there in the morning.

To my surprise, Q and the kids were all laid out on the sofa bed.

"Imani, what happened?" The voice came from the dark living room.

Q rose up like the dead. I wasn't ready to deal with him. Why the hell did he come here? He probably got too tired to drive home after the Fair in Belmont Park. Q shouldn't have come here.

"Nothing, Q. I just have a headache."

Hopefully, he would leave me alone until morning when I was in a better state.

"Are you sure? I had this bad feeling about you going away so I came over, hoping to get in contact with you." His warm hands ran up and down my arms, and I almost lost it.

"I'm cool. Can we talk about this in the morning? My head is throbbing. Do you want me to put Kai in her bed?" I turned away from him, avoiding his stare.

"Imani, please. Please don't lie to me. I know something is not right. I
really don't want to have to ask piece by piece."

He begged for the truth but sometimes the truth hurt. Although it killed me to hold it in, I'd rather lie than hurt him again.

"Quinton, thank you for your concern but this has nothing to do with you nor is there anything you can do about it." I was adamant about keeping what happened a secret. "Really, I'm fine. Tired but fine."

"So why did you leave, Mani? I thought you were going to be with your man tonight. What did he do to you?"

Why couldn't he just go away? Q should know that his constant probing would only lead to hurt, more than he could ever imagine.

Quinton

"Nothing, I was uncomfortable." She looked away and said, "I guess I wasn't ready."

"Bullshit. Why were you crying then?"

"Because," the sobbing began, "I wanted to be with you! "

I knew that wasn't the reason but I'd let it slide for tonight. Tightly, I embraced her. I wanted her to know everything was going to be all right, but she pushed me away.

"I don't deserve this, Q. Why are you being so . . ."

"Shhh, you've been through a lot tonight. Why add to the fire? Come on. I'll run your bath and we can talk."

No matter how or what she did, I still had a soft spot for her. She'd always be my baby girl.

She looked at me with those big soft brown eyes, and I felt her pain. I rubbed her back with a sponge and let the water run over her beautiful golden skin.

"Mani, we have a lot of stuff to work out, you know, but can we at least try to be a couple without interference?"

She didn't answer. Imani stared at the walls with a blank expression. Her arms were clutched around her legs. She was balled up like an abused child.

"Mani, talk to me."

Still she was speechless. That couldn't be good at all. If I found out that he laid a finger on her . . .

"Q, take me to bed. I'm not feeling well." She spoke in middle of my mental rampage.

I wrapped an oversized towel around her and took her into the bedroom. Her pajamas were already laid on the bed.

"I'm going to put Kai in her bed and start some tea. Jahlek and Bryan will be fine down on the couch. Just try and relax. All right?" She nodded.

I peeped back in the room and softly said, "happy belated birthday." A single rose and card lay on top of the dresser. On the other side of the door, I held on to the knob for two seconds more trying to make my heart stop racing. I wanted to go back in that room and prove to Imani that I was the man she'd been looking for all the time. She should never doubt herself or our relationship again. Instead I let go and headed down the stairs.

CHAPTER 16
HOW DEEP IS YOUR LOVE?

Imani

The following days proved to be a test of our promise to each other. Q arranged the funeral for Trina, which kind of struck a nerve. But, it was his son's mother and her family couldn't afford it. We were unable to find any family for Bryan so being that there weren't any surviving members, Bryan was to be placed in foster care. I couldn't see them separating Jahlek from his brother; therefore, we decided to be his foster parents. We were in court every day trying to get custody of Bryan and also a name change for Jahlek. Money was definitely being stretched, and so was my patience.

Our wedding had been put on hold indefinitely. Not only because our
finances were starting to look funny but also because we didn't feel the need to rush anymore. Instead Q felt it was best to give Mama J and James all the arrangements for our wedding. They were already talking about getting married.

There was nobody in our paths that might have caused us to have any doubts but Q had never gotten over the whole Omar ordeal. And honestly, I hadn't gotten over his dead baby mama. Every day he had a snide remark regarding the kind of relationship Omar and I had, saying I was stupid for trusting a man I didn't even know. The feeling was mutual. I was kind of giving him a hard time too. My favorite comeback was, *"At least I don't have to adopt my own son."* Q would get mad as hell. Nine times out of ten that was how our feuds began.

As usual, Q wanted to hang out with his friends and leave me home with the kids, alone, again. Just like every Friday and Saturday night. My problem wasn't watching the kids; I had a problem with him going out with those friends. Every day, he was out on the corner, smoking and carrying on. He acted as if there wasn't anything wrong with it either. The more I asked him about a real job or rehab, the more he blew up in my face.

"When are we going to hang out together? The last time the kids and I actually saw you for more than ten minutes was Tuesday." *And here it is Saturday*, I thought.

"Well, I got to make that money. When I'm home during the day, you're at work and the kids are at school. By the time you get home with them, it's time for me to be on the move."

"So when are you going to pencil us into your busy schedule? What are you doing tomorrow?" I was being sarcastic but nothing was funny.

"I don't know. I have to see what's up."

"If you don't have anything to do then why don't you make it a point to be with us?"

"Because if Rodney comes through with something, I would have to leave, anyway."

"I thought we'd take the kids to Rye-Playland before it closes."

"Can't you ask Jada or Charisse? What's up with Matt and Steve? They're old enough to go with you."

Matt and Steve were John's sons. Matt was twenty and Steve was twenty-five. Steve was the little bastard who got me put out of John's house. Their little sister Amber was four. I thought Mia was crazy when I found out she was pregnant.

Stranger things had happened.

"Matt is at school already and Steve's got a newborn at home. Charisse's away on business and Jada, well you know the story with her and her husband."

"Ask Mom. She would love to have a day out with her grands. I'm not going to be able to do it, sweetie."

My blood began to boil. I hated when he talked to me like a child. He picked up his brand-new Hilfiger sweater I bought him last week. That was his sign to let me know he was leaving and the conversation was done. And just as he did every day, he kissed me on my left cheek, ran his finger down the opposite cheek and walked out the door.

Danette Maroney

The kids were in the kitchen finishing dinner. Bryan was a picky eater since he never really ate real food. His idea of a good dinner was a McDonald's Happy Meal. His plate looked like it was barely touched while Kai and Jahlek plates were nearly cleaned. Kai was no stranger to home-cooked meals. Fast food was foreign in our home.

"Bryan, you don't have to eat it if you don't like it but I'm not going to fix any sandwiches tonight."

"Okay. Throw it away?" He looked up at me with his plate in hand.

"Yes, sweetheart." My attention was diverted by the choking sounds coming from the table.

"Kai, a lady doesn't stuff her mouth. Chew what you have in your mouth and put your plate in the sink. Don't forget to put Jahlek's in the sink too."

Twenty-eight years old mother of three—an eight-year-old, a six- year-old and a five-year-old and already made up my mind to keep it at that. For a long time I wanted Q and me to have a boy of our own but three was enough. Bryan, Kai and Jahlek Banks, those were my kids and I loved them all the same. Bryan and Kai birthdays are three days apart. His was July 5 and hers July 8 so their parties would be together but my baby Jah's birthday was on March 12.

"Mommy," Kai whined, trying to get my attention.

"What? Stop tapping me. I don't like that."

She had a serious habit of tapping, which annoyed the hell out of me.

"Can we go to the park in the morning and ride our bikes?"

Q had bought all the kids new bikes with helmets and pads but didn't take them out. So, I was stuck with three bikes to lug in and out the house.

"You don't want to go to Rye-Playland?"

Jahlek was standing right beside Kai breaking his neck to keep up with the conversation.

"Is Daddy going tomorrow? He used to go with us, 'member?" Kai asked.

"Yes, I remember. Daddy has to work tomorrow, and he doesn't know if he can go."

She knew I was lying. Her face held disbelief.

"When is Daddy coming back?" Jahlek asked, tugging my finger.

"He'll be back in a little while but you'll be in bed by then. Let's go, Bryan. You and Jahlek are getting in the shower."

"Ms. Imani, can I sleep in your bed tonight?"

Bryan had slept in my bed ever since he came to us. I knew it was because he missed his mom. They were real close. I guess it was because he was Bryan's son and he came first.

"Why don't we all sleep on the sofa bed tonight? We can watch a movie, all right," I suggested as the kids helped clear the table.

"Yes, thank you," Bryan replied.

Bryan was a well-mannered child. Shocked the hell out of me considering who his mother was. Still, I enjoyed having him around.

"Come on let's get ready for bed, y'all."

They followed me up the stairs. At least I'd never be alone.

Quinton

"Yo, shorty." Rodney had changed, again. He hollered at any girl with short, tight clothes on. He gave up on the preaching role and strictly went for the, "can I bone you?"

"Rodney, she's like fifteen. Chill."

"Man, shut up. Shorty is too thick to be that young," he said as he passed the blunt.

I ignored him while he chatted with the little girl.

My family life was really stressing me out. I couldn't keep money in my pocket for shit. Jah needed new sneakers, tuition had to be paid, car notes and mortgage were draining my pockets. We couldn't even afford to go away on Labor Day like we normally would. Instead we went for dinner and exchanged cards for our anniversary. In Imani's card, I gave her some money to help her with her bills—credit cards, nails, hair, cable, phone and whatever else it was she was breaking about.

I missed spending time with my kids but money had to be made. I picked up my package from Rodney about two weeks ago and still haven't gotten it off. Police had been patrolling so much that we hadn't been making as many sells. The big weight had been slowing down too. Too many brothas were getting caught. At that rate we would never have any money. This Christmas I was planning on doing something nice and intimate but if business didn't pick up I'd have to cancel that too.

"Q, what time is it?" Rodney asked after he finished schooling the girl then taking her number.

"I don't know, man. I left my watch at the house trying to rush. As a matter of fact, I don't remember where I left it. I don't remember having it on." *Imani might know where I put it.*

I took out my phone and dialed the house.

"Hello, who's this?" Mani was sleeping. Her voice was soft and low.

"Sorry, honey. I didn't mean to wake you up but I can't find my watch."

"Which one? Be specific, Q. You've got like twenty of them."

"The new one—platinum, diamonds, you know what I'm talking about."

"Didn't you put it in the shop? Remember the clasp broke." She yawned. "You really need to lay off that weed."

You could hear the anger in her tone.

"Good night . . . "

She was right but I wasn't getting into that with her. I had been forgetting everything lately. But that could be from stress as well.

"Q, are you on your way home?" she asked.

"In a minute. Why? What's up?"

"Stop at Walgreen's and pick up some Tylenol or something. Bryan is running a fever."

"Anything else?"

"Not that I can think of… Oh, some ginger ale."

"Give me about an hour. I'm in Brooklyn." Really, I didn't know how long I was going to be there but in an hour she'd be asleep.

"Bye." She huffed.

She was doing a good job with those boys. Kai was becoming a little rough from being around them too. She played with the boys like she was one of 'em.

In some ways, I was glad we were back together but sometimes when I thought about Imani and Omar, I wanted to change my mind. He tried to call the house a couple of times and either the kids or I answered. Imani had blocked his home number but he found ways around that. She said he called on her cell phone and begged for her forgiveness. I asked her if she wanted me to handle it but she said no. She probably still had feelings for the man. She denied it; I didn't believe her.

Through it all, my love for her had never changed and probably never

would. One day when we got our lives together, we'd have the wedding we had talked about. Until then, we'd have to hold on to what we had—our family and our love.

Driving home, I thought about what my life would have been like had

I stayed with Trina. We were able to hang out together. With Imani I couldn't be myself. All we did was argue. Why couldn't she just accept the present? I was sure that was not how I was going to spend the rest of my life.

There was one thing I found in Imani though that I couldn't find in Trina, devotion. Imani was devoted to our family and our relationship. Trina didn't care which way our lives went.

I missed Trina though. She was there to comfort me when I felt lost and confused although it was purely sexual. Her loving took my mind off any problems I had. Somehow that wasn't enough for me when she was alive. I still needed the conversation and affection of my lady, Mani. There were just so many things that I loved about Imani. First and foremost, her femininity. She was a lady. She respected herself. You'd never catch Imani dressed down, her hair and nails were never undone, her work clothes were strictly designer suits and her tone was always calm. When she and her friends got together you'd never hear them laughing aloud with those high-pitched, ear piercing sounds. They never drew attention to themselves. They were ladies.

She kept an immaculate home and never condoned hanging out. She'd maybe consider a small family affair but as far as chillin', never. She was the lady I needed to help me level my life out. She might stress me but at least she was mine.

When I entered the house a neon yellow paper was posted on the closet door. Your dinner is in the refrigerator— top shelf. Good night.

The note was a sight for sore eyes because I was starving and Mani could throw down in the kitchen. Another thing Trina couldn't do.

Out the corner of my left eye, I saw a sudden movement. Kai was taking over the bed. Her arms were stretched out across her mother's face and Jahlek was wrapped in Kai's long, lanky legs. I went over to wake Imani when I heard something outside rustling in the bushes. At first I thought it might have been a cat but then I heard a groan. I grabbed my gun out of my waistband and went outside to see what or who was out there.

Outside was shadowy; you couldn't see your next step. Suddenly, a tall, slim shadow went running away from my dining room window. I began to chase him, pointing my gun in his direction. Hollering and running was causing me to run out of air, especially since my injuries. The bastard kept running toward the Conduit, I was too exhausted so I turned around and went home.

Back at the house, I checked to see if he had tried to open any of the windows or doors. Underneath the dining room window was a folded piece of paper. I picked it up and tried to read the moist torn note. All I could make out were three numbers and the letter W. The numbers were the first three numbers of our address and the W was for Wright, Imani Wright. Who the fuck was looking for Mani?

"Mani, Baby. Wake up. Listen Ma, wake up." I shook her vigorously trying to get her full attention.

"What, Q?" She barely opened her eyes.

"Somebody was snooping around outside. Some tall, skinny motherfucker, and he had your name and address on a piece of paper." I spoke directly in her face trying to make her comprehend what I was saying.

"Huh. Outside of our house?" she said, wiping her hair out of her face.

"Yeah, outside the dining room window. Who did you give the address to?" I yelled at her again trying to get her attention.

"All of our family and friends have our address, Q," she said.

"Duh. Did you give Omar your information too?" That put some pep in her step. Her eyes began to flicker open and close, trying to adjust to the lighting.

"No, I didn't think it was a good idea to give it to him. I didn't want him dropping by," she said as she sat up and rubbed her eyes.

"Was it one of your customers?" she asked.

Is that what they call displacement? Trying to place the blame somewhere other than on you.

"They don't know where I live or your last name," I said. But not just any answer. I wanted her to say it was Omar so I could have him taken care of. Rodney had found a little information that might come in handy.

"So what are we going to do?" Imani asked in mid-stretch.

"We are going to call your homeboy and you're going to ask him what the fuck he wants! " I stood from the sofa bed to get the phone.

"I can't. I lost his number a long time ago. He always called me so I never asked for his number again."

See, was that an excuse to cover the brother's ass or was she for real? How did I distinguish between the two?

"The next time he calls we're going to talk to him together. Oh, and the next time he comes around here, he's leaving in a body bag."

That should be good enough. If she was lying, he'd get the message.

Imani

196

Q was serious. The crazed look in his eyes let me know that Omar had crossed the line.

What kind of stupid shit was that? Why would he come here? And, how the hell did he get my address? It was one thing to mess with him one on one but Quinton didn't like the thought of anyone messing with his home. Q was going to be looking for Omar in the worst way. It was going to turn out to be very ugly in the end. Q had never fought fair, therefore, he had never lost.

"Mani, I want you to go down to the police department in the morning to get an order of protection for you and the kids against this fool. From now on, you're carry a gun."

He was pacing across the floor, cracking his knuckles, punching walls and dishing out all kind of demands. The first wall he broke, he was fixing. "Q, calm down. There's nothing we can do about this tonight. Let's put the kids in their beds and go to sleep. We'll set the alarm and put all the locks on. I'm scared but getting upset isn't making it any better." I tried to calm him down but it was useless.

"This is your fault. If you hadn't kicked it with this nigga, he wouldn't be coming through . . . "

Wait, hold up. "First of all, you don't even really know it's him," I said, letting my sistah-girl attitude surface. "And second, if you had been taking care of business at home I might not have reached out."

Damn. I didn't mean to say that. My head came to an immediate halt, realizing I had just fucked up.

"Reaching out . . . How about I reach out and slap your ass?"

Q had been getting real loose with that violent talk. But I wasn't going to let him punk me.

"You don't really think I'm going to let you slap me and get away with it."

Like I could really beat him. Once he was up in my face, my stomach sank. My mouth had gotten real dry and my knees wanted to buckle.

"I promised I would never hit you but keep testing me . . . just leave me the hell alone! " he said, pressing his finger into my forehead.

He took Bryan in his arms and stomped up the stairs like that was supposed to scare me. Only if he knew, I was already scared. For starters, there was someone outside my home and there was a stranger in my home.

Q had started back down the stairs. I didn't want to continue the battle so I walked into the dining room while he took Kai and Jahlek to their rooms. When he reached the top of the stairs I walked back into the living room to put the sofa bed away.

"Where did you put the remote?" His heavy voice echoed down the stairs.

What the hell is he hollering down the stairs like some asshole for? I thought. I just kept on doing what I was doing and acted like I didn't hear him.

"Imani! "

I knew ignoring him would piss him off even more but I didn't even care.

Every day he acted as if it was my job to jump to his every word. It was my turn to act an ass.

"Why don't you look for it? Lazy bastard! " I said with a lump in my throat. The words fumbled out of my mouth, my heart still pounding in fear.

After folding the last blanket, I made my way up to the room, scared as hell.

"Q, why do you keep treating me this way?" I asked, trying to rationalize his actions.

"Like what, Mani? Tell me how I'm supposed to treat the woman who left me after I proposed to her. Not only did you run out on me but you ran out on your family too. For some dick! "

"I didn't run out on my family for a piece! You're just mad because I beat you to the punch. How many times have you made promises and broken them, Q? How many times. . ." *No more tears, Mani . . . keep it together*, I thought.

"Well dammit if you felt this way, why did you accept? I opened my heart to you! That's something I've never done before. Now I'm trying to be the man you wanted but that's not enough." He spoke quietly but his words were filled with anger.

He used his hands to express himself—clapping, waving and pointing. "It's too late! Why couldn't you be that man two, three even four

years ago? I couldn't wait another seven years for a commitment."

Q sat up on the bed. He didn't have anything on but his boxers, and no matter how mad I got, I still wanted him. His mahogany skin spoke my name, calling me in. The dim lights made the atmosphere seem romantic although I was on hostile ground. I watched him as he ran his hand over his freshly cut hair in frustration. One lick of his lips made my whole attitude fade. I tried to stay upset but the imprint of his shaft turned me on in unimaginable ways.

Quinton

The more I tried not to look at her, the more it hurt. She was so . . . her thick thighs called my name through her pajamas. I could smell the soft scent of roses on her skin, and it caused my body to ache, yearning to touch . . . to taste. Her rust-colored hair hung loosely over her tanned shoulders. Imani's nipples poked through the nightgown, testifying that she wanted me too. I stood and walked closer to her.

Imani placed her finger over my lips before I spoke my first word.

She began pushing my boxers down. Moans rose from deep inside as she caressed my penis. That was what I had been missing. Her flesh touching mine sparked fires.

We kept eye contact as we touched each other. My hands cupped her breasts as I licked between them. She threw her hands up, surrendering to my loving. I couldn't take too much more. Eager to penetrate, I picked Imani up, her legs wrapped around my waist.

Imani's big, firm butt felt so good. She placed kisses around my face and gently nibbled on my ear, licking and tugging until I couldn't take any more. I let her go only for her to slide down on her knees. She had never done anything like that before. As the warmth of her mouth encased my penis, high-pitched whines and whimpers escaped from deep inside my body. Fascinated by the way she worked, I almost lost control.

Her look of lust was the picture I carried around with me in my mind every day. Yes, I wanted Miss Wright more than she'd ever know.

Quinton

I was pressed against the door. Q placed his hands above my head and looked down into my eyes.

Overwhelmed with the urge to sink in to his cradle of lust, I sashayed over to the bed as he watched. I spread my legs wide and sat up on my elbows as I invited him in.

"Imani, why do you do this to me?" He spoke in a deep, throaty tone.

He kept his bottom lip tucked in as he pressed his body against mine, giving me something I could feel.

"Do what?" I asked.

I almost couldn't get that out. My throat was blocked with the sobs I held back for so long. Our relationship had been an emotional roller coaster, and my heart couldn't take any more suspense.

"Q, I'm sorry. I never wanted us to turn out this way. You hating me, it's tearing me apart."

"Baby, I could never hate you. I'm sorry it took me so long to be the lover and friend you need. Let's . . . ."

Q kept me waiting while he looked me over. The same way he did when he took my virginity. I licked my top lip slowly and continued to keep his attention. He crawled on top of me with such carefulness. Finally when he pierced my body, I remembered how much I missed Q.

We tossed and turned, making sure we satisfied each other. I was his freak and was prepared for about anything. The headboard began to beat against the wall from Q's thrusts of passion.

As I came close to my climax, I called out his name.

Quinton

She knew how to turn me on more. Imani continued to moan and call my name. The loving was getting so good I didn't want it to end, and I couldn't stop. I grabbed hold of the bed as I gave my all, releasing all my love. Tears trickled down her face as she cried out in pleasure. When my body fell limp and my grip on the bed loosened, I wiped away the tears from her eyes, hoping they were tears of joy.

"Are you okay? Did I do something wrong? Imani . . ."

She cried as I held her in my arms. Her head stayed buried in my chest while I rubbed her back.

"Baby, don't cry. I love you, Mani. There's nothing to worry about. We're going to be all right."

Imani never answered me.

"From this day on, it's me and you. There will never be anyone else for me. I've loved you for ten long, hard years and there's nothing or no one who can take that away," she said, tears steadily streaming from her eyes.

I wiped away her tears and kissed each cheek.

While she drifted off to sleep, I prayed silently.

Lord, please make me the man to make this woman happy. Please give us the strength to continue to love each other and be the family we set out to be.

I placed two kisses upon her tender lips and went to sleep.

CHAPTER 17
HIDDEN TRUTHS

Imani

"Doesn't it feel good to wear a wedding dress?" Charisse asked as she placed a sparkling tiara upon my head.

Charisse and I were at the bridal shop in midtown Manhattan getting the alterations done to our bridesmaids' dresses. Mama J and James had finally decided to tie the knot. James had proposed to Mama on Labor Day but the family didn't make a big fuss about it because we thought he was just placing claim. But much to our surprise, he was actually going through with it.

Everything was already paid for from my called-off wedding to Q so
all they really had to do was buy her dress.

That was fucked up! My dreams were shattered. I had nothing left to hold on to. Our favors, our decorations, our theme was theirs, and there wasn't shit I could do about it but pout. That was exactly what I was afraid of. Everybody was getting married but me. My brothers were married; Jada was married; my nephew, Steve was married. Shit, even Charisse was engaged.

"Yeah, but it would feel a lot better if it was mine," I said, admiring the long white gown in the mirrors surrounding me.

Q and I were supposed to get married on my birthday instead Omar's crazy ass ruined my life. He had been trying to call me, come see me, apologize but I was not feeling him anymore. It was a phase. I was over him. I was soon to be over Q, too, if he didn't make it his business to make me happy.

Lately, all that seemed to matter was how much money he had and how happy the kids were together. The hell with how I felt. But that soon was about to change. He was about to either step up to be the husband he promised to be or ship out.

"Reese, we need to talk. I . . ."

I was about to confess to Charisse what I had been feeling but was interrupted. The seamstress brought out a royal-blue satin strapless dress full of safety pins marking the areas where it was to be taken in. Although the dress was beautiful, I was not happy to see it at all.

"Miss, try this on now," said the little Asian woman as she held the dress up to my face.

The thought of not being the bride weighed heavy on my heart. Charisse noticed my expression. I thought being a part of Mama's wedding wouldn't have bothered me that bad but it does. At night all I dream about was my wedding. Each dream had become more vivid than the one before. I could see all my friends and family, especially my kids dressed in their formal attire and Q standing, waiting to take me as his bride.

"Imani, are you cool?" she asked. "You'll have your day, sweetie. Q and my mom still talk about what your wedding will be like and what kind of things they want to see happen," she said as she held her dress up.

"Charisse, we haven't even set a date. He's not even sure if he still wants a wedding. We talk about being married but that's it. It's just talk. Q says there's no reason to rush."

I knew giving our wedding to his mother would be a reason for him to change his mind.

"You can't complain, girl. At least he's home every day now, taking care of the kids while you're at work. . . Girl, he even went and got himself a nine to five. You can't deny that he loves you. Plus, it's evident that he's taking care of business at home because it's all over your face."

Charisse and Q had become the best of friends since the whole Omar ordeal. She said she could respect a man who would be there for his woman, no matter what. She and Q had even hung out a couple of times. Every time we had a fight, he was on the phone with her, his new confidant. I didn't mind though because when he wasn't around she told me everything. Well, what she could.

"Take it easy. You can't expect miracles . . . your day will come." I only half listened to what she was saying because honestly, that was not what I wanted to hear.

I knew Charisse was telling the truth but it didn't make things any better. There was still the feeling that something was going to go wrong. I hoped it wasn't Q and me. We had come too far to break up.

The kids were so happy being together, and I enjoyed every moment I spent with them. But I wanted us to be an all-around family. Marriage would mean more to me than his testament of love. It would mean our love had finally crossed the border of uncertainty and taken us into eternity.

After Charisse zipped the dress, the seamstress came and checked to make sure everything was right. When she finished putting in the necessary pins I gave her the dress and deposit. Charisse's dress was paid off already by her fiancée.

The seamstress returned with the receipt and the small patch of the material to find my matching shoes. We said our good-byes and departed the mall.

"Charisse, I need to tell you something."

"What's up? Everything all right at home, right?" she asked with a raised eyebrow.

Her concern made me appreciate the value of our friendship.

"Yeah . . . well . . . Omar called my job yesterday and left a message apologizing for that night at his house. I decided to call back and ask if he was the one who was snooping around but of course he said no; he didn't even know where I lived. But I know that's not true because he sent me some flowers a while back."

"Did you tell your man? This is something you should have told him. Do you think Omar's the one?"

"I don't know what to think but I know something ain't right."

Inside I knew Omar was the one.

"Bitch, you better tell Q! Let him and his boys handle that. You're putting your family at risk by pretending you don't know, acting as if shit is sweet. You know Omar is not right in the head," she said as she gave me one of those "What the fuck are you thinking" looks. "How many times has Omar threatened to kill you?"

I didn't respond because it was something I wanted to forget. Quinton knew about Omar calling my cell and leaving messages but he never knew the content. That was a time in my life I didn't want to relive. I kept my mouth shut.

During the ride home, I thought of different ways to tell Q that I had lied. I did know Omar's number. He did have our address. And yes, it was Omar at our house that night. I didn't know for sure but my instincts told me what I had been already thinking. A revelation as big as this one could jeopardize our relationship. Maybe, I should keep this to myself a while longer. Until I'm positive that our relationship was on solid ground.

Quinton

Working a regular nine to five took a lot of getting use to. Providing low-cost legal aide wasn't my dream job but it was a step up from where I was. My new job entailed sitting at a desk all day, in and out of meetings, interviews and phone calls. The work didn't end when I left the office. I had work at home for neighborhood clients who needed help in running their businesses. I had finished a proposal for a day care center applying for their nonprofit status and needed to review other paper that had to be sent out with the proposal. That meant I wouldn't be getting to bed until about two in the morning.

I barely had any time for my kids or Imani. I was in the house long enough to wash, eat and sleep. It was worse than the street hustle, but it paid the bills.

My phone rang as I walked back into my office. I rushed over to answer it, hoping it was the call I had been expecting. Anxiously, I fumbled with the phone before answering.

"Quinton Banks, how may I help you?"

"Hey, Quinton. This is Natalie. I got that information you needed." The young woman from the investigation unit replied.

"That's great. What have you got for me?" I began to loosen my tie as I sat on the corner of my desk. I picked up the photo cube from the far corner and turned it, looking at the four most important people in my life— Imani, Kai, Jahlek and the newest addition, Bryan.

"Well, for starters, Mr. Omar Smalls has had several name changes," she began.

"Oh, really?" I responded.

"His birth name is Omar Allen; mother died in delivery; father, Robert Allen was the owner of a chain of fast food restaurants in New Jersey. Robert remarried several years ago to a Mrs. Watts, no children from this marriage. Ms. Watts-Allen now lives in Maryland. Omar has been in and out of jail since he was eighteen for almost everything, including armed robbery, attempted murder, forgery and unpaid child support."

"So, Omar has children?" I commented as I took notes. "Who runs his father's businesses?"

"It shows that everything has been under his wife's control since his death. Omar was left with the house and a fifty-thousand-dollar bank account, which he exhausted on gambling and drugs. He has one child who is living with his stepmother."

"Okay, can you print a copy of this information and leave it on my desk? I have to go. My fiancée is paging me."

"Sure thing. I hope everything is all right."

"Everything is fine. Just a change in shifts. It's my turn to watch the kids. She has a pottery class on Monday nights."

"Oh, all right, partner. Tomorrow nine a.m."

"Yeah, see you then."

Omar didn't know with whom he was dealing. He came to my home, stalked my wife. Thank God Charisse told me about the phone calls Imani had been getting at work. Imani didn't want to believe that Omar would actually hurt her. But I got his card; I just had to set it up just in case he decided to do something stupid. Before packing my briefcase I looked over at the photo cube. Emotion built up inside me. I couldn't let anyone take them away. Finally, I was complete, no gaps, no missing links, no voids.

Imani

Work always ran fairly smooth on Mondays. After completing several reports, I had time to run down to the salon and get a massage. During my aromatherapy, I was able to clear my mind and focus on my home. Quinton had been acting strange the past couple of days. Every night he asked the same question, "Have you heard from Omar?" I had no idea what his infatuation with Omar was about but I wanted it to stop. Whenever I started on the Trina issue he would be quick to remind me that we promised to never discuss Trina or Omar but every time his mind began to idle, out flew Omar's name. The only way for him to drop it would be for me to come clean. And that was what I was going to do.

I busied myself with cooking dinner and folding laundry that had been left in the dryer. As Quinton stepped through the door, I pondered whether I would be as bold as to tell him the secret I had been holding for so long. If I was going to tell him it had to be then, right that minute.

I walked over to him slowly as he hung his jacket in the closet. When he turned to see me in his path, he instantly smiled, which caused the guilt to bubble inside me, causing internal pain.

His lips warmed my cheek as he greeted me with a kiss.

"Are you in for the night?" I asked.

"Why? You got plans?" he asked as he walked into his office.

When he started his new job downtown he had the extra room renovated and arranged the office for us to share but it was filled with most of his junk.

"Yes. . . No, not really. I wanted to talk to you." I began to wring my hands.

"About? You're not pregnant, right?" He turned in my direction with an arched eyebrow.

"No! It's about Omar."

"What about Omar?" he said as he sat in his favorite chair.

He placed his briefcase on his desk and began riffling through the papers.

"Are you listening?" I asked, trying to prolong what was inevitable.

"You have my undivided attention, Imani," he said as he continued to look through his work.

"He called me. He's been calling me. I told him to stop. I told him that you were looking for him but he acts like he doesn't care. I asked if he was the one at our house that night but he denied it," I rambled.

"Uh-huh. And. . ." Q turned to face me but seemed unfazed by my information.

"And, I think he's lying. Once he sent some flowers to the house but it didn't strike me as odd until recently. I never gave him my address."

"Why did you wait so long to tell me this? I've asked you over and over about this man, trying to protect you and our family from him. You lied to me, Mani. You don't care about our family. He could have come back and got in while we were sleep or away. What were you thinking?" he reprimanded.

"I don't know. Q, I'm sorry. I wasn't trying to protect him. I don't know what I was thinking. I didn't think he was going to stalk me." I sat beside him on one of the kids' chairs. He looked down at me.

"Well, he did. You know what's more sorry than you lying to me?"

Silence filled the room as he waited for a response.

"I knew you were lying. I had a copy of your phone bills mailed to my office. After I found his number, I had some people from my company to help me find out all I needed to know about him. I've got his address, background, blood type, you name it."

Quinton

"How? Why? Q, Baby, I'm sorry. I didn't mean to lie to you. I have no feelings for the man and haven't had any desires to be with him. I just wanted to deal with him myself." She stood stunned by my discovery.

"Well, an order of protection has been placed against him. He is not to be within a thousand feet of the house, the kids or you. Some of the guys at the office felt his background looked a little flaky and are doing a thorough investigation."

"Q, aren't you mad at me?" she asked.

"I was but then I thought of how it felt for me to come to you about

Trina and remembered how awkward it was. I knew when the time was right you would tell the truth. I trusted you enough to know you weren't still seeing the man and that's all that matters right now." I wanted to slap her. She sat in my face for weeks acting like everything was okay. But what was having one of those violent rages and breaking shit around the house again going to solve?

I returned my attention to my computer and continued working. She started back toward the kitchen to check on dinner until I called her back. I wanted to tell her that I wasn't angry with her just a little disappointed. "Mani, let's try to forget about this. I don't ever want to hear his name come out your mouth again. Okay?"

She nodded. For the first time, she didn't have anything to say. "Now kiss me before I get upset," I said with puckered lips.

"Q, I am really sorry. I didn't want to lie to you. I'm just still . . ." I pressed my fingers on her lips and replied, "Don't sweat it, Mani. It's over."

CHAPTER 18
LOVE AND TENDERNESS

Imani

Since Quinton handed over our wedding to his mother, I had been a little bitter. When our wedding was on standby, knowing that our space was reserved and our arrangements were made gave me hope that one day we would get married. There was nothing to look forward to. Charisse had said I needed to stop putting so much pressure on Q. Obviously, he said something to her so I had to stop the constant interrogation.

The month of October brought about a cool fall breeze but not enough to ruin an outdoor wedding. Everyone was at our house getting ready to depart for the hall. The photographer snapped shots of the bride. Mama J made a dazzling transformation from housewife to princess.

Mama was a beautiful bride. She wore a traditional high-collar, long- sleeved wedding gown. Her train stretched at least four feet and spread six feet wide. Her arms were covered in lace with speckles of glitter running through that sparkled from the shining lights. Her hair was pinned up into a snug bun with drop curls. Her makeup made her skin shine vibrantly. She was radiant.

Charisse, Jada and I catered to Mama J's every need, even though our dresses made it a little difficult to move around. Mama J considered us the daughters she always prayed for and we did our best to be there for her. The strapless royal blue satin gown she picked for us reached down to our ankles.

We wore a sparkling sheer blue duster that covered our bare arms, shielding them from the cool air. Our shoes matched our dresses, royal blue satin sling backs with two-inch heels. We were divas in our own right. I felt good about my appearance knowing that the dress was fitting me right. My hair hung loosely over my shoulders adding to my beauty but my heart ached tremendously.

Q had barely paid me any attention the whole day. He fussed over the kids making sure they were behaving and didn't stain or wrinkle their outfits. They were very gorgeous. Kai wore a full-length light-blue silk gown with matching bag and shoes. She knew she was cute. Quinton took her to the hairdresser early that morning and had her hair pressed and curled while the boys were next door getting their hair cut. The boys wore matching tuxedos with duck tails and top hats. They were sharp! I was a very proud mommy.

Kai made sure that she was in every picture. She tried to drag Jahlek along but that wasn't his kind of thing. He was more of the shy type. Bryan's temperament changed every time the wind blew. One minute he would be bouncing around and the next he would as quiet as a church mouse.

After the photographer finished taking our family portrait in front of the house, my smile immediately turned into a frown. This was supposed to be my day. I watched as the bridal party gathered by the limo. Mama waved for me to join them in another set of pictures. My heart wasn't up for the festivities. I slowly strolled over to the sidewalk to join the party. I was in no rush. For what, it wasn't my day.

My attitude became more apparent when it was time for us to leave for the hall and I sluggishly trailed behind. Q pulled me back inside the house.

"What the hell is your problem? You have been moping around all day like somebody stole your best friend," he said as he released my arm.

"Quinton, you act like it doesn't bother you that this was our wedding! That was supposed to be us on our way to the chapel," I said as I pointed out the window to James and Mama getting in the limo. "Yes, I'm upset. What the hell did you expect?"

"I expect you to get over it. This is my mother's wedding day. If you're going to continue to destroy the mood then you should stay behind. But be aware that I won't stay around to attend your pity party."

No words were spoken for the next two minutes. Q took my silence as an end to our conversation and walked out the door. He rounded up the kids and loaded them into his car. He made eye contact with me one last time. I read the seriousness in his face and decided to adjust my attitude for peace's sake.

I turned to the hanging mirror by the front door and composed a phony smile. "This is for your mama. Mani, get a grip." Maybe I was overreacting a bit but that realization didn't make me feel any better about us not being married. I checked the mirror one last time, making sure my hair and makeup were okay, and picked up my clutch purse.

As I opened the front door, I thought, You ain't got nobody to blame but yourself so just scratch your ass and get glad.

My day would come with or without Q.

Shortly after all the guests were seated, the wedding began. Mama chose "Stairway to Heaven" for the processional march. The bridesmaids were all paired up with their handsome partners.

Q stood beside his stepfather as his best man. He smiled as I made my
way down the aisle and winked when we made eye contact. A single tear made its way down my cheek but it wasn't from happiness. I smiled back at him when he blew a kiss my way. With him being so handsome and acting so sweet, there was no way I could continue to be upset with him.

Mama finally graced the archway with her beauty. Everyone watched as she walked down the satin runner covered with roses left behind by the precious flower girl. She swayed to the sounds of Jesse Powell's "You."

James had me search all of the five boroughs to find that song.

When she reached the altar James smiled. It was the happiest day of his life.

We stood and watched as the pastor began the ceremony: "Dearly beloved, we are gathered here today in the face of God..."

Quinton

Imani and I were the last to leave the reception. We collected all of Mama's gifts and made sure that there wasn't anything left in the main office of the reception hall.

As we pulled up to our house, I smiled as I replayed the wedding in my mind. It was magical. Everyone enjoyed himself, especially the newlyweds.

Glasses clinked as they entered the reception being announced as Mr. and Mrs. Hutch." There wasn't a dry eye in the house as they shared their first dance. James was truly happy as he cried. There was no doubt that he loved Mama, and Mama loved him too. She said she owed him her life. Without him she would be still drinking herself into comas.

The floor was packed from start to finish with people dancing to everything from "The Electric Slide" to Mariah Carey's "Vision of Love." Imani and I had one quick dance before I was running around making sure everything went smoothly. And it did. I was impressed. I went out of my way to make sure my mother was happy. I just wished I could have done the same for Imani.

Once we got home, I undressed the boys while Imani tended to Kai. I stood at the door and watched for a moment. Kai was standing in front of her mother wearing her slip and stockings when she asked the question that had been on my mind all day.

"When are you and Daddy getting married?"

I walked into the boys' room to help them get undress and put on their pajamas. It was that kind of moment that involved a mother and her daughter, alone.

Imani

Kai played with her Brandy doll, never looking at my face to see my vague expression. I didn't have an answer nor did I have the strength to lie. Quinton's footsteps became lighter and lighter, as he got farther away from the room.

Kai was the same little girl that I had read Cinderella and Snow White to as bedtime stories. I had to sit there and try to make her understand that every story didn't end happily ever after.

"Kai, Mommy and Daddy have to wait a little while," I said as I took her slip and stockings and placed them on the chair.

"Why?" she asked.

I should have known that was coming.

Why? Because. . . Daddy can't let go of the past. I wanted to tell her so bad what had been on my mind but it didn't make any sense; she wouldn't understand anyway.

It killed me how he held a grudge because I made one little mistake in ten years but didn't think the shit he did warranted any grief.

"Mommy and Daddy are not ready yet, Baby." I sat her on my lap and began to brush her hair back into a ponytail. "We are really busy with our jobs and really don't have the time or the money."

What a pile of shit!

Kai slid into her favorite nightgown and grabbed her teddy bear. She followed me out of her room, and she was halfway down the stairs before she realized she didn't have anything on her feet. Kai knew this was a "no- no" and immediately turned around and headed back to her room.

The boys darted past me down the stairs wearing matching Spider- Man footed pajamas. We had this thing that the first one to the living room chose the movie, which was fair, as long as there wasn't any fighting.

Q came down a few moments later. As he reached my step, he twisted his body and slid past me, trying to avoid eye and body contact. He carried his jacket in one hand and his house keys in the other.

"Q, where are you going?"

Our minor disagreement from that morning couldn't still be bothering him.

"I'll be right back. Why? What's up?" he answered, avoiding answering my question.

"You're not going to watch the movie with us?"

Every Saturday after Kai's dance class and the boys' karate class we would come home, eat dinner together and watch a movie to relax. That had become our normal routine. Usually, Q was the first one down the stairs lying on the sofa bed with a bucket of popcorn.

"I said I'd be right back. I gotta go to the store. Damn! " His face squinted up with attitude.

I followed him to the front door, waiting for an apology for his rudeness but to no avail. He turned away from the front door, kissed me on my cheek and headed straight out the door.

I looked out of the side window to see which direction he was going.

There are only two stores open at his time of night and they were on the same block in the same direction. I watched as he walked past his car, which was surprising because Q never went anywhere without his car. He did walk toward Merrick Boulevard, so he might have been telling the truth.

After watching him out of the window, I returned to my kids and continued with our weekend ritual without him.

Q walked through the door, about two hours after he left. He obviously didn't know what right back meant. Then, he came back empty- handed. I acted as if I didn't notice him standing by the archway in the living room's entrance. He stood there for a couple of minutes before he spoke.

"Baby, we need to talk," he said solemnly.

Oh, now I'm your baby. The cool air must have brought him back to his senses. Jahlek turned to acknowledge his father's presence. Kai and Bryan didn't move. Their eyes were glued to the movie. I also kept my focus on the movie but my concentration was lost. I heard Q and saw the characters but neither had my attention.

"Mani, don't ignore me. That's childish."

Childish? Now, I was fucking childish? I got his childish. I held on to my nightgown as I slid off the bed. Slowly, I made my way over to him.

Lord, give me the strength, I prayed as I imagined another shouting
match.

Quinton

We walked over to the dining room. I pulled out a chair for Imani to sit. I sat directly across from her with my arms folded.

"What are we going to do? We can't go on like this. It's been weeks since we actually had a civil conversation outside of things concerning the kids. Today was the first time we touched each other in weeks."

I shrugged before I continued, "So, are we calling it quits or what?

Tell me something."

"I have been thinking about what to say to you. I need to know what you want to do," she replied.

At that point, I was basically ready for anything. Whether she wanted to be together or not, I was going to be all right. I just couldn't take any more bullshit. Our relationship had been in limbo for too long. It was time for a change.

"I want us to be a family again. I've been here every day trying to figure out a way to work out our problems. I stay off the streets, you complain. I take care of the kids while you work late, you complain. Shit, I even wash clothes and cook dinner, and you still fucking complain! Nothing I have done is good enough for you."

"I have recognized all you've done and appreciated it. It's just that you keep pressing on that Omar shit. That was months ago. When are you going to drop it?" she asked.

"I've tried but that shit hurts. You of all people hurt me. . ." I said in a low whisper.

"And what about all the times you dipped out on me? Huh?" Imani's eyes popped out of her head and her neck cocked to the side.

"I've apologized for that! " I shouted.

"And so have I! " she retorted.

The conversation was going nowhere—the same argument over and over. It was up to me to put it to rest. Time for me to be the bigger person.

"Imani, do you want me to be your man? Can we try to forget our past and move on? I want so bad to love you but you make it hard for me." I was shocked at my own forwardness but it had to be done. It had been weighing on my chest for way too long.

"Yes, I want you to be my man. I want to be your wife but I want you to be sure that this is what you want." She stood in front of me in all her beauty and poured out her heart and opened her soul.

"Now, Miss Wright, are you sure you want to be my wife?"

A brief moment of apprehension flushed my body. Yet, there was no reason for me to feel that way. She looked up at me with eyes full of tears.

"Baby, you know there's nothing else I'd rather do. I love you," she said as she wept.

She pulled me from my seat and held me in her gentle embrace. "They say the third time's a charm," I whispered in her ear.

Imani didn't know how bad I wanted to be her husband, her friend, her one and only lover.

CHAPTER 19
IMPERFECT TIME

Imani

Quinton held the camcorder while the kids and I made snow angels in what used to be green blades of grass.

"Hey, Baby, why don't you join us?" I said, shoving snow in Q's direction.

"Not right now. I don't want to miss any of this. Ouch. . ." Bryan had caught Quinton in the face with a snowball.

"All right, I got you," Quinton said as he passed the camcorder to my

niece Diamond, and joined our party.

"Daddy, can you make a snowman?" Kai asked, clutching tightly to

Q's hand.

"We can try. Can't we, Imani?"

"I guess so. Umm, what should we do first?" I had no idea how to make a snowman. We never did such things in the projects.

"Mommy, first we have to make a big snowball. A real big one, like this big," Bryan said as he stretched his arms as wide as he could.

Bryan had really adjusted well to his new family. I remember the day he asked me if he could call me Mommy. I cried. He thought he said something wrong and began apologizing. Q explained to him that I was just a big bucket of water who cried when I was happy. And I was extremely happy. For so long, I felt like a stranger to Bryan. He could never know how much it meant to me when he called me Mommy.

"Alright, everyone can start making the big snowball while I look for the stuff for his face. Okay?" I said.

"Okay," the four replied in unison.

Life never felt so good. Q was everything we could have asked for and more. The kids enjoy having their father back in their lives. He made their breakfast, packed lunches, took them to school—you name it. He was a whole lot better at taking care of Kai too. Whenever I was away on business for the weekend, he wouldn't go to Jada; instead, he took Kai to the beauty parlor. And she ate it up. She thought she was grown. The boys didn't mind having a girl around either. Although, she never acted like one when they were together.

So many things had change but all for the better. Life was good!

Quinton

It was Imani's first weekend home since my mother's wedding and I wanted to spend every waking moment with my family. She was doing a lot of career seminars and training programs at different colleges for interns at sister companies. Sometimes she was so busy she didn't have time to call and say hi. When she returned from the trips she would usually spend the rest of the week home. The days were unpaid but well worth it because we spent quality time with the kids.

Money wasn't even an issue. I was doing really well at the firm where I had been working. I changed my attire as well. Every morning I left for work in a freshly pressed designer suit (tie and all), carrying a leather attaché case and wearing cologne that hypnotized women for miles around. Even on dress-down Friday, I dressed to impress with knitted mock-neck sweaters and khakis. I knew I looked damn good. My body filled out suits in ways unmentionable. I thought, Too bad ladies, I'm taken.

Was I conceited? Nah, just convinced.

After work, I would stop by Rodney's house to see how he was doing. Rodney never pressured me about getting back into the business. But he did hit me off every weekend. Imani never complained. Shit, she would be a fool if she did. That extra money was building a nice nest egg for our kids' future.

Reese and Imani continued to have their shopping sprees whatever

Sundays Imani was home. Reese was ecstatic with the way our relationship was mended. Life wasn't so bad for her either. She was getting her own things together. Reese decided to take modeling on as a new career.

Monday night she model on her first runway, and she was beautiful. Her fiancée, Myra, was there to cheer her woman on.

That was another story in itself.

Mia and John came over every week for family bingo night. It would be Imani and me; Mia and John; Steve and his wife, Santita; Jada and her husband, Craig and Mama and James. We spent our Thursdays reminiscing and trading childhood stories, embarrassing moments and all.

From time to time Imani's brother, Justin stayed over with us. He was doing real well too. He had begun to gain weight and wasn't as sick as usual. Things were looking up. Imani needed the family around her. And I needed her around me.

Jordan, my brother-in-law, sent clothing from his new line for everyone last month along with pictures of his newborn. Matt, John's younger son, was up there with his uncle learning the ropes with the hopes of starting his own line. They promised to come down for Christmas with their families. Matt was a proud daddy of a baby boy. No wife, though.

Like Mama always said, "The more the merrier." Speaking of about Mama, she and James had been doing fine. They glowed whenever they were together. I really hoped to see Mani and me like that in the future. James's son, Shea decided to stay in New York for a little while and get acquainted with his new family.

Imani and I took Bryan to the cemetery to lay some flowers for Trina on her birthday. He handled everything very well. He made Imani and me both very proud. Bryan even took it upon himself to say a word or two to his father. We gave him his privacy with both his parents and later took him for some ice cream.

The kids were upstairs taking off their snow-filled clothes and putting on their robes while Imani and I made lunch. I was preparing my homemade chicken soup while she made turkey sandwiches. As I set the table, I thought how lucky I was to have a family. Brothers today have a dozen kids and a half-dozen women all claiming to be number one. Imani was exceptional, and I thanked God every day for her.

"Baby, did you hear from Jada today?" I asked as I stirred the contents inside of the large pot.

"Uh-huh. Why? She called again?"

"Yeah. She called yesterday. She sounded a bit depressed. I didn't think much of it though. I assumed it was something associated with the pregnancy."

"Probably so. I can't imagine why she would want to have another baby with that asshole."

Craig treated Jada like his servant. She had to work, cook, clean and wait on him while he sat back and watched. She said she could handle it, that as soon as she got her shit together, she and Diamond were leaving but Imani knew she was lying. Diamond was at our house every weekend just to get away from the constant bickering. Jada was not the easiest person to live with but nobody deserved to be mentally or physically abused like that. Jada could deny that Craig was beating her, but were able to see through her bullshit lies.

John had to step to Craig a couple of times to set shit straight. Mia told me one time Craig had cried. Talking about he was going to go for therapy. Fuck therapy, he needed somebody to beat his ass. I didn't condone men putting their hands on women. I relapse once and regret it every day. But if Jada was not willing to leave him, then the family should sit back and mind their own business.

"That's her husband, Mani. She loves him," I said as I ladled soup in the bowls.

"I don't know how she can love him after all the shit he's put her through. If Nana were still around, Jada wouldn't even be with that punk, Craig. She would have put an end to this shit a long time ago," she whispered since Diamond was in the next room.

"Mani, you have to remember, after Nana died Craig was all Jada had to depend on. He helped put her through school when she couldn't afford it. He put a roof over her head—"

She cut me off and began to raise her voice, "So what? She owes him now? You put a roof over my head but I'll be damn if that means you can beat me! She's his wife, not his child."

"Relax! Have I ever said you owe me? Have I ever beat you? Like Ike beat Tina. No, so don't flare up at me. I'm just saying how some men see it. Some feel as if they own their woman. He happens to be one of those men."

"I'm glad she decided to move back to New York. Who knows what would have happened if they were still in Maryland? Jordan said if she allowed it, she deserved it, so depending on him to watch over her was a dead issue." She waved her hand, dismissing the thought.

"He's right. She's a grown woman. She knows what's right and what's wrong. Obviously, she doesn't feel anything is wrong with her relationship. Stop stressing yourself about it."

"Whatever. That's my sister. I'm just concerned."

I walked over to where Imani was standing and stood in front of her. She didn't change her position. She stood with her arms folded and her lips poked out. Obviously, I pissed her off. I wasn't taking up for Craig, just making a point.

"Look at you. Getting upset for what? What's going to change by you being upset?" I plucked her bottom lip.

"Something's gonna change. Watch."

"Shut up, tough girl," I said as I pulled her into my arms. "They'll be all right."

"I hope so," she said as she put her arms around my neck.

Looking into her eyes, she suddenly seemed relieved. I would never let anything happen to anyone in our family or us for that matter.

She kissed me lightly saying, "Thank you for allowing me to vent. I'm not mad at you. I'm just mad at her situation."

"That's what I'm here for," I said, kissing her forehead.

We shared a brief moment of laughter before we were interrupted. Awhhh, isn't that cute?" Diamond said as she snapped a picture. Diamond had grown into such a precious young lady over the years.

Although she was only twelve she was quite mature for her age. She was very polite and refined. She was nothing like my sister-in-law, Jada. Diamond and her mother shared the same fair skin and small eyes. Diamond had Imani's rusty hair color and that pissed Craig off. She had none of Craig's features, which was probably why she was Imani's favorite.

"Girl, I'm going to break that camera if you snap another shot of me looking like this," I said as I took the apron from around my waist.

"This is going to look so nice in my scrapbook next to the picture of you sleeping with your mouth wide open," Diamond hollered as she ran away. I began swinging the apron at her.

The kids stood at the top of the stairs jumping and yelling, "Run, Diamond, run."

Imani took the camcorder from the dining room table and started recording the cat-and-mouse chase. It was too funny to miss.

"Watch my glass," she hollered as we passed the china cabinet.

Moments like those were priceless.

Imani

The kids settled down in front of the television as Diamond looked through the movies to find one she liked. Q and I laid on the sofa cuddled up enjoying the heat from the electric fireplace while watching the kids lay out a comforter and throw pillows. I don't know what it was about being in Q's embrace that made me feel comfortable and safe. I could have stayed there forever but that was easier said than done.

It seemed that every time our life steered us in the right direction, we suddenly jolted the other way. First Trina, then Omar and now what? I couldn't help but think the worst because I knew it was inevitable. Q and I were the magnets for misery and trouble. It seemed as if they were drawn into our paths. Hopefully, the New Year would be better for us. The trip we had planned to Puerto Rico would be the boost we needed to survive.

"Mani, what's up? You look lost."

"Just thinkin' how much I love you."

"Too much," he said, his boyish grin displaying his deep, gorgeous dimples.

"Never too much," I said.

"You got that right, Baby," he whispered in my ear as he nibbled on my lobe.

"Mani, I was thinkin' about setting up the wedding for Valentine's Day."

"Shhh, someone might hear you and think you're serious."

"I am serious. I thought you wanted to get married."

"I did . . . I do but every time we try, we fail. I don't take failure pleasantly."

Q looked at me, his eyebrows arched inward.

"That's because we don't try hard enough. We always let the most stupid things come between us. If we continue to focus on what's important to us and say fuck everybody else, especially those who may provoke us to give up, we should be able to make it." He was serious.

"Q, I don't know. Everything seems fine just the way it is. Why disrupt the peace?"

"So, you're telling me that you don't want to get married?"

"I think so...I..."

"That's bullshit," he exclaimed as he rose from the sofa.

This was about the most twisted shit I had ever seen. For the past several months I begged to get married and Q kept telling me "there's no rush . . . we're better off this way." When I finally gave up, he wanted to get married. We were comfortable. The kids were happy, he was happy and finally I was happy. Why mess up a good thing? This brother had issues. That was a perfect example of what people meant by "you can't win for losing." Shit!

"Baby," I called out, trying to find out where he disappeared.

"What?" he answered from the office.

I followed his voice to the back and watched from the doorway as he riffled through his paperwork.

"Q, come on. It's the weekend. That can wait, can't it?"

"Yeah, but why wait for tomorrow to do what could be done today."

"Today is our day. Let's finish it together," I said, trying to ease his anger.

"What's holding you back, Imani? Why are you scared to commit? I am trying to spend the rest of our lives together but you're putting up some kind of block. What's your problem?"

"I don't have a problem. I don't see why we should mess up a good thing."

"What's so good? What's going to get messed up? Tell me something."

"See, now that the tables have turned, you understand what I was going through. I wanted to get married so bad and you kept pushing it off."

"We were going through a lot then."

I stepped into the room and sat on his desk right in front of him. I parted my legs so he could be right between, taking his hands to pull him closer. At first he didn't move but after a few more tugs he gave in.

"Here it is, I'll plan to marry you on Valentine's Day but should anything come up between now and then causing us to call it off, it's off indefinitely. We'll accept our life the way that it is."

"Are you sure that's what you want?" he asked. "Positive! "

"It's your call," he said. "Now, Baby, please move, you're turning me on."

"Is that a problem for you, Mr. Banks?" I said as I put one leg over his shoulder.

He looked out the door to see if any of the kids were walking around. But I knew Jahlek and Kai were sleeping and Diamond wouldn't move until Love and Basketball was over. Bryan normally sat through the whole movie, too, so it was basically safe.

After he was sure the coast was clear, Q began unbuttoning my shirt. Slowly, he caressed my breast while kissing my navel. I began to rotate my pelvis, inviting him in. Q quickly pulled off my lounge pants and discovered I didn't have on any panties. I knew this would drive him crazy. He quickly unbuttoned his pants and pulled me on top of him. I worked him like never before. He tried hard to keep his composure. He buried his head in my chest to muffle his groans.

"Mani. . .baby, stop," he begged in a low whisper but I couldn't. I was getting close to my own orgasm.

The phone rang but we were too busy to answer it. Q held on to my waist, guiding me up and down as I leaned back on to the desk. He was about to burst, and I wasn't far behind. The answering machine picked up in the other room. I could hear John's voice but couldn't focus on what he was saying. One of the kids ran to the phone. Q reached over and slammed the door shut.

I spun around letting him beat it from behind. I wiggled about two seconds longer and it was a rap. I cooed out in pleasure as he jerked.

A knock on the door caused me to jump. I wasn't sure if it was locked or not so I stood and pulled my shirt closed. The shirt was long enough to cover my naked body, just in case one of the kids burst in.

Quinton

"Who is it?" I asked as Imani got dressed.

"Daddy, Uncle John is on the phone," Bryan yelled through the wood door.

"Okay. I'll pick it up in here. Hang up the phone."

I took the cordless phone off its base and answered. Looking over to Imani, I silently questioned why John was calling. She shrugged.

"Yeah. What's up?"

"Q, is Imani there?" John asked with a cracking voice.

"Hold on," I said.

I covered the mouthpiece and told Imani John was crying. She immediately grabbed the phone.

"Yeah, John, I'm here. What's the matter?"

Imani's eyebrows darted up in shock. She sat down on the window bench and placed her hand over her head. Slowly tears trickled down her face. I walked over to offer her support. She rested her head on my stomach as she cried.

When she hung up the phone, I asked her what was wrong. "Justin died. John said he died in his sleep."

"Oh, Baby, I'm sorry to hear that."

I held on to Imani. I wanted to be her strength because she was going to need it. She had was developing a bond with her brother. Life just didn't get any easier for her

"He was so young. Justin just turned thirty-six," she said through her sobs.

"I know, Baby. He went peacefully. Do you think he knew it was his time?"

"No. His health was getting better. His body was filling out. He was starting to look real good. My brother's gone, Q! It's not fair. I just got him back."

"Mani, be thankful that y'all were able to spend time together. Those were memories you can hold on to and reflect on when you want to remember all the good times y'all had."

"I just wish I could have told him how much I loved and missed him. Since he came home, I had yet to tell him how I felt about him."

"Baby, he knows. He loved you the same. You were his baby girl remember."

Imani didn't speak another word. She rested on my chest as I continued to hold her and be the support she needed so badly.

Imani was so young yet she lived the lives of a thousand women; her woes were the same as so many others. She had loved and lost over and over, never knowing the true sense of stability. It was no wonder she became the strong woman she was. But I was determined to be the one constant in her life, the one person she could always count on to be around. I loved her and wouldn't have it any other way.

CHAPTER 20
BREAKDOWN

Imani

I called Charisse early that morning to let her know the bad news but I didn't know how to tell her Justin had AIDS, so I didn't. She probably already knew and was waiting for me to tell her. I never wanted to believe that he was sick. Telling Reese would be acknowledging the truth, and I couldn't.

She said she'd fly home as soon as possible. She had just left for Atlanta with her fiancée to do a show for MoeBern, two new designers who were trying to hit the streets. She said the clothes were made to give all African-Americans an individual sense of style. No two items were made the same. Most of the clothing was made by special order only. One of the designers gave her a bunch of T-shirts to give her friends and family. Of course, she had two for Q.

If she wasn't a lesbian, I might have thought Reese and Q had a thing going on. Q liked a woman with meat on her bones. Not to diss, but my girl Reese was as thin as spaghetti. She could hide behind a light pole.

For two days, John had been calling as many family members as possible from both Nana and Daddy's side. We decided to have a private memorial at my house on Tuesday, for the family.

Mia and I had cooked up a feast for hundreds of people. Straight soul food. Nana wouldn't have it any other way. We had collard greens, string beans, catfish, fried chicken, corn bread, candied yams . . . you name it. Aunt Barbara brought over her famous sweet potato pie and Aunt Lillian brought her peach cobbler.

Justin had become very dear to so many people during his time back in New York. He made many new friends. Editors and publishers from magazines that had published some of his photography came to attend the memorial service. And women, whew! He was definitely a ladies' man.

His current girlfriend, Marilyn, decided to come by and show her face after being missing in action for a week. She brought along her two- month-old son whom she swore was Justin's. Truth be known, Justin had a vasectomy after he found out he was sick. But he did have one child who was in Texas last we heard.

Her name was Christine. She should be about thirteen now. Justin never saw her because she was born shortly after he disappeared. The girl he was dating back then was on drugs, too, and after Justin disappeared, she began using harder than before. When Christine was born she was immediately placed in foster care. John and Mia had temporary custody of the little girl until Lydia completed her rehab. Nana was still alive then but wasn't able to take care of a baby or else she might have taken her in as well. Christine needed special attention due to her premature addiction.

Lydia, Justin's ex-girlfriend came home right before Christine's first birthday, so Nana adopted Lydia as one of her own until she was able to support herself. Nana wished Nadine would have done the same thing. Lydia was Nana's second chance.

Memories of Nana came back as the constant flow of people poured through the door. Daddy's family and friends came out of the woodwork. Cousins, aunts, uncles, sisters, brothers, nephews and nieces—all of Daddy's relatives that I don't remember ever meeting were there. Even Granny came.

All of the Watts had the same light brown skin as John and me, but very few carried Spanish accents. Their natural, thick curls and hazel eyes were also traits John and I had inherited from their side of the family.

Granny Tina made it her business not to get involved with anything that had to do with us. She was ashamed of us because of our mother. She never liked Nadine. Granny put up with her as long as he was alive. The moment Daddy passed away, she simply cut all ties.

Auntie Barbara introduced us to the rest of the family. Everybody was surprised to see us. We were the infamous "John's kids" everyone heard about, but no one ever saw us.

It was a terrible thing for a death to have to bring a family together but at least we had a chance to see one another. Daddy's sisters and brothers were in awe of my resemblance to my father. Jada always said I looked like him but I never imagined being his twin. Nana had no pictures of our daddy, and Granny Tina had managed to take most of his pictures, trophies and medals he had won throughout high school. Pictures that Nadine had taken with Daddy were torn in half. Unfortunately we were left with Nadine's garbage.

It felt good to have our family together. Justin would have been so happy. Diamond had been taking pictures the whole night with Justin's camera.

Granny looked so evil posted up in the corner trying to avoid contact and conversation. I pulled on John's arm to ask why she was so bitter but he said leave it alone, and I did. Jada brought Granny over something to drink and sat to talk to her but Granny showed no interest.

"How are you holding up?" Q asked as he brought out more hors d'oeuvres.

"I'm all right. I wish Granny would talk to us. Whatever grudge she had against my mother should be with Nadine, not us. We all tried reaching out to her but she won't give us the time of day."

"Give her some time, Baby. She'll warm up," Q said sympathetically. "I hope so. She's making me uncomfortable in my own house."

I wanted to know what happened to make her hate us. Again, I tugged on John's shirt inquiring about Granny's attitude.

"Baby girl, it's a long story. Leave it alone."

"I can't! I tried. I need to know, dammit."

John excused himself from his conversation and dragged me into the kitchen.

"Listen, Mani. Nadine and Granny have had differences for as long as I could remember. Granny thinks Nadine trapped Daddy and destroyed his life."

"She might have. It sounds right up her alley."

"Ma wasn't always a bad person, Mani. Just like any couple she and Daddy had their ups and downs. Ma was a good woman and mother once upon a time. She loved her family and there was nothing she wouldn't do for us."

"So what happened?"

"Life, struggle. She got tired of being left behind when Daddy went on all those business trips, and she started hanging with the wrong people. Dad tried to stay around and help but she chased him away. After he left, she blamed us. It was our fault she didn't have a life, our fault her husband didn't want her." John paused.

I looked over at Quinton and Bryan as they continued to serve appetizers to our family and friends.

John continued, "She was still young. I don't know if you know but Nadine was only fourteen, I think, when she had me. Anyway, when Nana saw that she wasn't getting any better she took all four of us—Justin, Jordan, Jada and me. You weren't born yet."

"And why does Granny hate us?" I asked.

John continued on about Nadine and her drug abuse and her partying but beat around the fact.

"Did y'all ever see Daddy again?"

"Dad put Nadine in a rehabilitation center and took us from Nana. He did the best he could. Sometimes Aunt Barbara came around and helped out. When Mama came out of rehab she was wonderful. She was back to normal. Shortly after, Dad lost his job. We lived in our house until we couldn't afford it anymore then moved in with Granny. They fought every day. Nadine got fed up and left again. When she finally came back she was pregnant."

So, Granny swore that Nadine slept with someone else and I was somebody else's child, which explained why everyone was so obsessed with my resemblance to Dad who never believed it and raised me as his own. Nadine ran off once again to be with her friends and live her life.

After Daddy died she came around, filed for Social Security and ran off with the money. Nana took us in and had social services sign everything over to her. Nana changed our names from Watts to Wright after she adopted us. Hence explaining why we didn't have our father's name and that it wasn't us Granny despised just me. She didn't want to believe I was my father's daughter.

"How did they find out if I was Dad's baby?"

"Nana had you tested so you could be able to collect from Daddy's Social Security too. Granny took Nana to court so that you could be tested."

"That bitch! Why would she do something like that?"

"Dad was her only son so you've got to understand. I told you to leave it alone but you insisted that you know. Now you know! "

"I needed to know. Now I need to speak to Granny! " I said. I walked out of the kitchen through the crowd and didn't stop until I was toe to toe with the woman who neglected me.

She looked up at me with disgust. "What do you want?" she said as we made eye contact.

"I want to know what I can do to make you talk to me."

I sat down beside her as I awaited her response. She hesitated and answered me through tight lips.

"I don't see anything for us to talk about. I'm here to pay my respects to my grandson not to make friends."

"I am not a stranger. I'm your granddaughter, the same as Jada. I wish for you to treat me the same."

"My blood doesn't run through your veins, young lady. My son made a mistake marrying your mother and paid with his life for it. Wasn't that enough? What else do you want from us?"

"Your acknowledgement. Acknowledge me as one of your own, and I will leave you alone. Everyone else has welcomed me. Now it's time for you to face the facts. Nadine may have been many things but she was a faithful wife."

Just as the old witch was about to crack her whip, my baby girl walked over. Granny looked over at my little girl and hissed. That was about all I could stand. To disrespect me was one thing but disrespecting my child was another.

"Give Mommy one second, Baby. Go to Daddy until I finish talking and then I'll come get you," I said.

As soon as I thought Kai was far enough away, I let the old heffah have it. "Listen here. My fucking kids didn't do anything to deserve any of your bullshit attitude. If you feel that way about my family, you might want to leave my house."

She looked at me in disbelief.

"Furthermore, I'm glad you weren't around to mess up my life any more than Nadine did. I just wish I could have met my father."

I immediately turned around and walked away before she could respond. I wanted to cry but she would not get the satisfaction. Directly in front of me were my kids and their father. Just what I needed. Q stood from his seat and motioned for me to sit.

"Mommy, are you okay?" Bryan asked as he leaned on my shoulder.

"Yes, sweetie. A whole lot better now," I said as I kissed him on his forehead.

Jahlek climbed up on my lap. Kai continued to follow her father around. I sat back and watched as Granny held a conversation with John and Mia. Not having Granny accept me as her family hurt more than anything I could have ever imagined. Suddenly, Marilyn, Justin's girlfriend came to sit beside me.

"Imani, I'm so sorry. Justin was a good man. Everyone who knew him could only speak positively of him. Junior is going to miss his father."

"Junior? Please tell me you didn't name your baby after my brother! "

"It's Justin's son. His only son. So the name was appropriate. Look at how your grandmother looks at him."

"She doesn't know any better. You should be ashamed parading that boy around as Justin's son. Why don't you find someone else to be your sucker? The baby's still young."

"He is Justin's son, Imani! "

"You lying bitch! Justin couldn't have any kids! Ha, betcha didn't know that, huh! " I said as I pointed a finger.

The whole room went silent. Granny looked over at me with one of the meanest looks she could muster. I held on to Jahlek as I continued with my rage.

"Justin has a daughter that couldn't be here today but I'm sure if she could, she would have. This bitch is lyin'."

"Mani, shut up! " Q hollered from across the room.

"Why should I shut up now? Justin couldn't have any more kids, Granny! I thought you would be able to sniff out bullshit. You can't tell that your blood doesn't run through his veins."

"Baby girl, that's enough. You're bigger than that. I taught you better than that," Mia said as she walked over to me.

As I looked around, the room seemed to be closing in on me. I felt flushed with fever as everyone glared at me. Tears fell as I stood to face the crowd. Jordan came over and grabbed me as I began to ramble on. He and John dragged me upstairs and tried to calm me down while I continued to holler and fight. My kids stood around and watched as I suffered my first emotional breakdown.

Q came upstairs to console me as I released all the pain and hurt that had been was bottled up inside me for so long. Reality wasn't the same for me. All at once it seemed as if I lost it all.

Quinton

I had never seen Imani act this way. For the first time I didn't know what to do. I knew she was going to break eventually. She was been taking everything so calmly. Everyone knew she was on the verge of breaking down, but I didn't think it would be tonight. I gave Imani one of the sleeping pills that were prescribed for her after she began losing sleep over Omar's threats. I continued to sit beside her until I was sure she was asleep.

John and Mia had Jordan, Jada, Mom, James and Shea, James's son meet in my office.

"Is she all right?" Mia asked with tears in her eyes.

This was Mia's child. She raised Mani as her own and just as any mother she felt the pain her kids endured.

"She's asleep! What happened? I mean, damn. She just lost it," Shea said as he shook his head.

"It was too much. Granny, Justin, Nadine—it was too much for one day. I give it to her though. She's a hell of a lot stronger than most women to have held it back this long," Jada said as she rubbed her stomach.

John offered her a seat but she preferred to stand.

"What are we going to do now? I can't have the kids see Mani in this condition," I said as I pointed to Kai who was sitting on Diamond's lap.

"We're going to have to do what we can," John suggested.

"To keep some of the stress off her for a little while." He comforted his wife who was still in tears.

"James and I could keep the kids for a while, Q." Mama rubbed my back as I kept my head in my hands.

"I don't know. She flipped when John took Kai."

"Q, the kids won't react well to their mom being sick like this," James said.

"Pop, we'll just have to see what tomorrow brings. Let's see how she feels in the morning," I said.

I hugged my mother as I fought back tears.

I had seen Mani hurt but never to this extent. She was my backbone when I was going through some tough times. Every time I tried to help her, she pushed me away. She was always in control. This was traumatizing to everyone.

When Charisse came into the office, I sorrowfully began to tell her what happened, and the more I recalled the incident the more my heart sank. Tears welled up in my eyes as I thought of Imani pushing me away, not wanting me by her side.

Charisse asked if I would be okay before she ran upstairs to be with her friend.

The rest of the night was spent in our bedroom. When Imani finally awoke, Kai was snug at her side. Charisse was sitting in my rocking chair reading a magazine. I stood on the terrace thinking about what I should be doing. I looked over at the clock to see the time. It was seven-thirty in the morning.

"Where's Q?" Imani asked as she sat up in the bed.

"Good morning, Miss Fit. Quinton is over there on the terrace. Your brothers and sister are trying to figure out what the hell happened to you. To me it sounds like I missed a hell of a party."

"That ain't even funny, Reese. I messed up. Damn."

My heart went out to Imani as she went over the night's happenings with her best friend. I continued to act as if I wasn't aware that she was awake.

"You needed to vent, Mani. I wish I could have seen ole girl's face when you told her Justin couldn't have kids," Reese said jokingly.

"It was horrible. Everybody must be really upset with me. I tried to be civil. It seemed as if people wanted to see me break down. They just kept pressing my buttons," she said as she held on to her friend's hand.

"You want me to call Q? He's dying to see you. You have a good man, girl. He was so scared for you. You really freaked him out. The man shed tears for you."

"Yeah. Call him in. Can you take Kai to her bed please?"

"No problem. Miss Fit, you got to take it easy. We love you too much to lose you girl,"

Charisse waved for me as she ran her finger through Kai's hair. Kai's eyes were swollen from crying. Dried tears ran down her cheeks. Bryan ran in the room and jumped onto the bed into Imani's arms.

"Mani." I held her tightly. "Are you okay?"

"Yeah," she said through silent sobs. "I'm better now. How are you?"

"I'm living. You scared the shit out of me. All this could have been avoided had you just talked to me. Don't hold anything back. If you feel stressed or pissed, let me know. Stop trying to carry the world on your back. What the hell do you think I'm here for?"

Mani didn't look the same. Her skin was pale, and she had swollen eyes that made her look sick. Her hair was scattered all over her head. Her face showed no emotion and her eyes were empty when they used to be so full of life.

Charisse came to get Bryan to give us some time to rest.

"Bryan, Mommy's okay, Baby. I'll be in your room in a minute, okay?" Imani explained in an attempt to calm him down.

"Mommy," he called out. "I want to stay with my mother."

"It's okay, boo. Mommy's coming," she said as she blew a kiss in his direction.

He calmed down a little after she assured him that she was okay. He just needed to hear her voice. I laid next to her and placed my head on her lap. She ran her hand over my cheek and whispered "thank you" and "I love you."

"There's no need to thank me, Baby. I was doing my job."

I nestled my face into her neck and placed gentle kisses reassuring her that I was there for her.

"Mama's gonna take the kids and you're going to go to the spa. You need to unwind a little."

"That's okay. I'll be fine. Plus, the kids need me. Bryan and Kai would have a fit if you dragged them out of this house."

"Mani, please. Worry about yourself. Mama and James will worry about the kids. Shea said he would take them to the movies or something. Come on, relax. We can be there about noon and spend an hour or two."

"Thank you, Q," she said as she smiled "Can I at least make breakfast? We do have guests."

"Mia already did. Relax. We're here to help you, Baby. Let us work for you." I looked deeply into her eyes.

"All right. Let me talk to Bryan then," she said as she got off the bed. "You and I can talk to Bryan. Then we'll shower and dress the kids." My eyes followed her every move around the room. After she put on

her housecoat and brushed her hair, she came to stand beside where I lay on the bed.

She leaned over and whispered in my ear, "Q, you're the man. You know that, right?"

"For you," I replied. "Only for you."

CHAPTER 21
MAMA

Quinton

Imani's family decided to have a funeral service for Justin after all. At first, John just wanted to have the memorial service then the cremation but after Granny had her say, John was on the phone making arrangements. Of course, Imani had a lot to say but in the end, the rest of the family felt Justin should receive a proper burial.

Jordan and his wife, Tashii stared bleakly upon Justin's lifeless body. Tashii's supporting arm held tight to Jordan's waist as he ran his hand over Justin's cold, pale skin.

"I wish I could've been there for you, brother. So much time slipped through our hands, and I haven't had the chance to tell you I love you," Jordan said as a single tear trickled down his cheek.

"He knows, Jay. He loved you too." Tashii's soft voice floated through the church.

"He talked about y'all all the time, Jordan. He was so proud of you and what you did for yourself and your family," I said, trying to ease his pain. I would never know how it felt to lose a brother or sister being the only child. I could only imagine how I would feel had it been my mother.

Imani was obviously affected the most. The ushers escorted her outside after she fainted. I knew she wouldn't be able to handle this. After her emotional breakdown the week before at his memorial, she hadn't been the same.

On Thanksgiving Day, we had our immediate family over to discuss the specifics regarding Justin's funeral. Imani didn't attend the meeting. Instead she locked herself in her room and slept. The only thing she wanted to do was work and sleep.

I watched Imani through the church windows wondering what I could do to take the pain away. Busy in my own thoughts, I wasn't aware of John standing beside.

"Quinton, listen why don't you go outside with Imani and I'll take care of everybody else," John said from behind as he tapped me on my shoulder.

"Nah, she'll be all right. I can't reach her right now. She has been blocking me out for some reason," I replied as I looked out the windows at her.

We hadn't been talking much and I didn't know whether that was good or bad. Imani had been so withdrawn from everyone that I just assumed that it wasn't personal. I hoped that it was a period of healing.

"Q, go ahead. She needs you," Rodney said.

As I headed for the doors leading outside, in came this woman dressed in a red suit with long black hair, hollering at the top of her lungs.

"My baby... oh God... my baby," she shouted as she ran toward the casket.

A roar came over the crowd as they watched in amazement. John turned toward the woman to console her. He placed a hand on her shoulder as she continued to hold Justin's frigid body. I figured she must have been one of Justin's many acquaintances and shrugged it off.

"Miss, Miss," John said as he tried to get her attention.

"Why do you address me as Miss?" she asked as she wheeled around and glared at him.

As John focused on the woman, his face changed from sympathy to rage.

"How dare you come storming in here disrespecting my brother's peace?" John said as he grabbed the woman by the hair.

I rushed to the front to break up the rising altercation. While Mia and I pulled John from the woman's mane, Rodney took the mystery lady to a seat in the first pew.

"What the hell are you doing?" I asked John as I slammed the door to the pastor's office where we had taken him.

"I can't believe she's back," John said as he slammed his fist on the desk. He about faced and stormed out in to the sanctuary and screamed, "Nadine!"

This didn't sound good. Before I had the chance to ask any more questions, another commotion broke out in the sanctuary. I started towards the door to see what was going on and was immediately struck by Imani's high-pitched cry.

"No, no, no, no. You can't be here. Please leave. . .just please go. Please…" Imani cried as she broke into a hysterical plea.

"Imani. My baby. Just let me explain," the lady pleaded as Imani backed away.

"Ma, please leave her alone. She's been through enough. Today is not a good day for us," Jada said, holding on to her sister.

Nadine was back! Un-fuckin'-belivable. She had a lot of nerve to show up at Justin's funeral. I quickly grabbed Imani to take her back outside. Charisse held Nadine and made sure she didn't follow.

"Let me go, bitch. I have to talk to my daughter," Nadine spat out as Charisse and Rodney continued to hold her.

"Ain't no bitches here. If you wanted your daughter, you should have thought about that twenty-eight years ago. Now, leave her the hell alone! "

"Fuck you! Who the hell are you to be talking to me about my children?" Nadine replied, shoving Charisse aside.

Charisse said nothing more. She turned around and punched Nadine. The blow to the face caused Nadine to stumble. Reese may have been a small chic but she packed a hell of a punch.

I held Imani close as I watched the ongoing events.

"Imani, maybe we should leave. Nothing good is going to come out of this. John and the rest of them can follow to the cemetery. You should be taking it easy."

I tried to get through to Imani but as usual my words had fallen on deaf ears.

Just as I began to feel as if my relentless attempts were useless, she spoke. "Quinton, I need to face my ghost. If I don't do it now, the opportunity might never present itself again. For years I wanted to see her.

Here's my chance," she said, turning to head back to the front of the church.

"I'll be with you. If I feel things are getting out of hand, we're leaving," I said.

She gently squeezed my hands and whispered "thank you."

Quinton

With Quinton by my side, we headed to the front of the church. No one had to tell me who the mystery woman was. The resemblance she and Jada shared was uncanny. It was as if Jada had stood in front of a mirror— same cream-colored skin, dark hair, wide eyes and thin frame. After five kids the lady looked like she was a runway model.

Rodney was holding on to Nadine as she struggled to get away while John and Jordan stood in front of Justin's casket like bodyguards. I walked slowly over to where she stood.

"Are you sure this is what you want to do?" Charisse asked as she walked over to Q and me.

"Positive! " I said. "I can handle this." I took one last step, which brought me face to face with Nadine, my mother.

"Imani, you are so beautiful. Let me take a look at you," she said as she took my hand. "Turn around."

"What do you want, Nadine? You come up in here as if you were going to be welcomed with open arms. C'mon, what's the deal?" I said sharply, snatching my hand away from hers.

"I'm back, Baby. Jada called me about the funeral. I didn't realize how much I missed you until she began giving me an update of the last three years. She and Jordan had been keeping me posted up until then." She spoke softly but there was no hint of remorse in her tone. And there was no forgiveness in my heart.

"Jada and Jordan knew where you were all along?" I asked before turning to Jada. "Why didn't you tell me? Why would you keep something like this from me all these years?"

"It's not her fault, Imani," Nadine said. "I asked them not to tell anyone until I was sure my life was completely under control. I didn't want to bring any of my luggage into our family."

I stopped short of slapping Nadine across her lying face. The only reason I held back was for my brother's peace. Justin's skin felt cold underneath my hand as I touched his face. She did this to him. He would still be alive if she hadn't introduced him to heroin. She never kept her addiction a secret. Justin was her favorite—wherever she went, he went. She used and abused in front of him and anybody else in the room.

A memory of Justin shooting up in Nana's bathroom flashed across my mind. All of Nadine's needles and cooking equipment laid across the floor as Justin tied Nana's kerchief around his arm preparing to take a hit. I stood by the doorway, shocked in silence as I watched Justin inject the poison into his body. He looked over to see me standing there in total ignorance of what was going on. He belted out in a rage, "Go away," then kicked the door shut, catching my fingers. I remember hollering at the top of my lungs. John and Jada came running over to see what was going on while Nadine yelled from the living room in her drunken slur, "She should have been minding her on business."

The same hatred I had felt then engulfed me once more as I looked into her evil eyes. "For years I wondered if you were dead, assuming that was the only reason you never came back for me. But as I got older I began to hope you were dead. Now that you're here, in the flesh, I wish it were you lying in that casket."

Her mouth widened as I continued, "I almost feel elated that you weren't around to destroy my life like you did Daddy's or Justin's." A soft chuckle escaped me. "Thank God John and Mia were there to guide me or else I might have been following your footsteps. Hoing around, turning tricks for a hit."

She raised her hand in an attempt to strike me but Quinton blockedthe hit with his arm. John grabbed Nadine's other hand. She tried to shake loose but his grip only tightened.

"You don't know anything about me. Who are you to judge me? You think you're better than me? That's what it is! You think you're better than me. Hah," she retorted in a sinister tone.

"The truth hurts, doesn't it? I'm not going to waste any more of my time with you. If you don't mind, I need to say good-bye to my brother." With my heart feeling relief, I returned my attention to Justin.

"Imani, please just let me explain. I know you don't need me or even want me in your life but I want you in mine. All of you," she said as she turned to look at John, Jordan and Jada. "Let me try to make things right between us."

"You can't. Too much time has passed. Twenty-three years, that's a long, long time," John said before taking Mia's hand and returning to their seat in the first pew.

"Jay-bird, will you please help me here? Talk to them. Tell them I'm sorry," Nadine said to Jada.

"It's gonna take some time. You've been gone for too long, Ma. Give them some time," Jada said as she took Nadine's hand.

"Imani, John, Jordan, I do love and miss you. I am so sorry you don't want me to be a part of your lives but I can't change any of that. Jordan, I thought you understood. We talked about this," Nadine pleaded.

"I understood but I never forgave you. I spent more than half my life looking for you, trying to bring some closure to a chapter in my life that hurt me most. Our meeting was pure coincidence. You had no intentions of ever seeing us again." Jordan wiped away a tear.

"I think it's time for you to go," Quinton said. He looked over to see if it was all right that he had asked her to leave. I nodded, assuring him that it was time. He motioned for Rodney to assist him with escorting Nadine out of the church as I turned to look over at Jada who was obviously avoiding eye contact.

"Imani, can we just spend an hour together? Please let me make it up to you," Nadine pleaded.

"I don't know. I'll think about it. I'll have Jada get in contact with you." Again. I looked over at Jada, cutting my eyes.

Quinton

Imani was back to her old, upfront self. Finally, she broke out of her depression and took control. That's the woman I had been missing.

Rodney and I waited as Nadine flagged down a dollar van to take her to the Parsons Boulevard train station. She continued with her pleading, asking me to talk to Imani.

"Quinton, that's your name, right?" she asked as she pulled her fingers through her long hair.

"Yeah. How can I help you?" I replied, not really interested in hearing what she had to say.

"Listen, I know I caused Imani a lot of pain, but it's always going to be there if she doesn't give me a chance to mend the wounds. I can guarantee she still has some questions. She's just too stubborn to admit it." Nadine ran her hands down her sides, smoothing out the wrinkles in her jacket.

"I don't think this is any of my business. If Imani wants to see you again, she'll contact you. I don't think that will be likely though." I tried to sound as convincing as possible, hoping she would get the hint and go away.

Rodney walked over, cutting into over conversation, "Yo, Q. Let me drop her off at the train and you go back inside and finish up. Imani's gonna need you."

Nadine and Rodney stared at each other for a few seconds before anyone spoke. Her face was filled with anger as she agreed. "I guess I'll be seeing you around, Quinton. Take care of my baby."

I didn't respond. There was nothing left to say. This woman was determined to be a part of Imani's life. All that was left to do was stand by and wait for the fireworks. I took my place at Imani's side as Justin's casket was closed and the funeral proceedings began. Imani placed a hand on my upper thigh and gave a gentle squeeze. I looked over to see her expression. She was calm and appeared to be undisturbed by Nadine's unexpected entrance. Taking hold of her hand, I silently prayed that she was gonna be okay. I couldn't even imagine how I'd react to my father,

Michael, deciding to rear his sorry ass back into my life. Mani and I were better off without them. Shit, we made it this far.

The next week brought about a new Imani. She acted as if nothing had happened. As far as I was concerned, this was the first day of our new life.

"Quinton, can you pass me the yellow paint, please?" Imani said as she continued to paint little spring flowers on the base of a wall.

Imani had been watching a lot of home improvement shows and was implementing her new techniques throughout the house. Today her focus was Kai's room. She had been transforming each room in the house to reflect certain characteristics or moods. I really enjoyed having her back to the happy, fun-filled woman I loved for so long.

The kids were in the living room sorting out the Christmas decorations from last year. It was about that time of the year and we planned on having a very special Christmas, starting with an intimate family dinner for just the five of us on Christmas Eve, then a Christmas breakfast at Mama's house for the whole family and finally a family vacation to Puerto Rico. We planned to leave the kids behind at first but with all that had been going on we changed our minds and decided to take them.

As Imani leaned closer to the wall, examining a specific line, I gently lifted her loose strands of hair and blew gently behind her ear. In response she leaned back into my chest, laying her head on my shoulder. I kissed her cheek and began to massage her neck.

"Maybe you should rest. Plus, you still have that trip tomorrow," I said into her ear.

"I know but I really wanted to finish this tonight. I know the boys are getting tired of having Kai in their room." Imani placed the brush on the can of paint and stretched, loosening her tired legs from their cramped position.

"Let's go see what the kids managed to salvage and then relax for a while. What time is your flight tomorrow?"

"I don't know. I really don't feel like going. It seems like I'm working more than I'm home. Shit, I just got back yesterday from that college seminar. They didn't even give me time to mourn my brother. That really pissed me off."

The day after Justin's funeral one of Imani's coworkers quit right before a scheduled lecture. Unfortunately, Imani was asked to fill in. That was three days ago. Now they were asking her, on her day off, to fly out to Philly and recruit some interns for their sister company. The worst of it all, neither one of us had been home with the kids. The same day Imani left I was scheduled to attend a conference in Indiana. Our kids hadn't spent any real quality time with us in more than a week. And Mama, although she hadn't said anything, needed her rest too.

"Don't go! I told you to quit that job already. They don't appreciate shit you do. You've been passed up on promotions you know you deserved. You're just another expendable black face."

My words were sharp but true, and she knew it. For years Imani had done nothing but give that company a hundred and ten percent. Several years ago, when Imani first began working for the company, it was still brand new. And at the time her position was one of the top jobs. But as years passed management found ways and means for higher offices. Although it wasn't said, Imani had been demoted.

"Why don't you try staying home for a little while? Let me take care of you and the kids."

Her eyes widened, shocked at my suggestion. "I wouldn't know how to be a stay-at-home mom, Q. I have to keep busy or else I'd probably go crazy. Thanks, Baby, but no thanks. I'll just have to find a way to let the company know what they'd be missing if I left," she said as she rose from the floor.

I followed her, picking up any loose materials and putting away all the unused supplies. She took my hand as we headed down the stairs.

As we entered the living room, the sounds of giggles and muffled screams filled the air. The boys found amusement in decorating Kai as a Christmas tree. They wrapped her in blue-and-white garland, threw icicles over her head and hung threaded balls from the rows of garlands. Quickly, Imani covered her mouth as I walked over to remove a white garland from Kai's mouth. I turned to Imani to see if she was all right with their behavior or whether there should be a punishment. She let go of her stifled laughter and burst out in a cry of giggles. We all laughed heartily for the remainder of the evening as we continued sorting through old decorations.

Imani reminisced about the past Christmases as she unpacked an ornament for every year of Kai's life. Happiness filled her eyes as she recalled memories, ones I regretfully couldn't share. But that Christmas was going to be a very special one we would never forget.

The phone rang twice before I answered. I wasn't really in the mood to speak to anyone. Imani and I agreed to have a quiet family night at home but neither one of us remembered to turn off the phone. We looked at each other as I put the phone to my ear.

"Hello," I said into the receiver.

"Hi. May I speak with Imani please?" A woman's voice came through the phone but it wasn't a voice with which I was familiar.

"And, whom may I say is calling?" I shrugged to let Imani know I had no idea to whom I was speaking.

"It's her mother. But don't tell her it's me. Say it's an old friend from school or something," Nadine whispered.

"I'm not going to lie to Imani for you. If she wants to speak to you or not isn't any of my business," I responded.

She had a lot of nerve to call my home and then suggest that I lie to Imani to cover her ass.

"Imani, Nadine's on the phone. She wants to speak to you." I handed the phone to Imani and waited to see if she was going to be all right before leaving her alone.

She gestured for me to close the door.

Imani

After I was sure the kids were out of earshot, I barked into the phone, "What the hell do you want from me?"

"I want you to meet Jada and me for lunch tomorrow. We need to talk
and put the past behind us, Imani. Give me a chance to make it up to you."

I wanted to forgive her and take her back in my life but so much pain had built up inside and that hurt had turned to anger over the years. As more time went by, more pain had built up and hardened.

Heat began to rise from within; my body felt feverish.

247

"Look, Nadine. I believe that you mean well but we are much better off not speaking. I no longer need you. Mia has been my mother most of my life. You could never take her place." My tone was curt and my words were sharp. I wanted her to feel the way I did.

"I know I wasn't the mother she was for you but I want to try and at least be friends. Please?"

"Why is it so important to you? Is it a part of your twelve-step program or something? If you need me to forgive you to move on you can forget it. Why don't you keep acting like I don't exist?"

Instead of striking her, I hurt myself. Tears began to well up in my eyes. I didn't want to lose my mother again but my pride wouldn't let me welcome her into my life. And the thought of her not ever acknowledging me again was harder to swallow than I imagined.

"This isn't for a program. This is for me. I love you and miss all of you. Jada and I talk about you and John all the time. I'm so proud of y'all."

"We've missed you too. I always asked about you but John never answered. Up until a couple of years ago, I was still curious whether you were still alive. I wanted you back in my life. I needed you more than anything."

Quietly, I let my emotions free. Years of tears and heartache overwhelmed me as I thought back on all the times when a mother's expertise and advice were needed. All the times Quinton and I argued or when John scolded me and I couldn't understand why. Mia was there but knowing that she wasn't my biological mother always made me feel insecure and unsure.

Quinton entered the room. His almond-shaped eyes widened with concern. Immediately, he asked what was wrong. I didn't respond. I didn't know what to say. His jaw hardened as he snatched the phone in attempt to end my conversation, "Maybe you should speak to her some other time," he said.

"Wait! Q, give me two more minutes. I can handle this. I just needed to get some stuff off my chest. Kinda hit a sore spot on the way, but I'm fine, Baby." I put up two fingers asking for more time.

"Are you sure, Imani? You don't owe her shit."

"I know. I just want some closure. Okay?" He just nodded and passed back the phone. Slowly he walked out of the room without closing the door.

"Excuse him. He's a little overprotective. Anyway, where were we?" I said.

"I was about to apologize but first you need to understand what was going on and why I made the decisions I did. Imani, when you were born, you were a miracle baby. We didn't think you were going to survive. I was heavily into drugs, which forced me into early labor. Neither your lungs nor your brain were fully developed, your heart would race and then suddenly stop. We thought we were going to lose you." She spoke softly and calmly.

"I admit I was a terrible parent but what could anyone expect from a teenager? I was only thirteen when your father and I had John and by the time you were born I was already set in getting back all those years I lost trying to be a mother." She paused and let out a soft sigh.

"Your father was a good man but I wasn't ready for a family. I was in my early twenties and your father was at least fifteen years older when you were born. He was ready for the family role, not me."

I had no idea my father was that much older. I knew my parents married young but I thought he was near my mother's age. Still, she had no reason to leave. And I didn't want to hear her bullshit reasoning.

"Look, I heard all of this already. When you came back Nana gave you an ultimatum to get help or get out and you chose to leave. It was your choice, not hers."

"And I regretted it every day. You were your nana's heart. I couldn't take you away. She let me have John, Jordan, Justin and Jada every now and again but you, never. I wanted to be there for you but by the time I decided to take responsibility you were gone. John had gotten custody and moved away with no forwarding address" she concluded.

"Why didn't you get the information from Jada or Justin? You said you kept in contact with them," I said, interested in what excuse she would use to cover up the fact that she really didn't care.

"My life wasn't fully together and Jada was suspicious regarding my intentions. Justin didn't accept the fact that I was back nor did he want to believe that I was really sorry for all the pain I caused y'all. Jordan didn't want anything to do with me," she continued but I had stopped listening.

My mind wondered, recalling times Jada and John would argue about Nadine. I never knew exactly what they were arguing about, only that John was adamant about not mentioning Nadine in his house.

"Whatever! I really don't feel like going through another history lesson right now. I have a family to get back to so I'll think about the lunch thing and get back to you. Do you have a number I can reach you at?"

"You can call me at my house. I'm normally home after five." She continued rambling for all of five minutes before hanging up.

I tacked her number on the message board, shut off the lights and went to join my family in our newly renovated family room.

Nadine's voice ran through my mind all night. I examined her tone and her words, trying to detect any signs of sincerity. Quinton waved his hand in front of my eyes to catch my attention once he realized that I hadn't answered one of his questions.

"Imani, did you hear anything I just said? What the hell is on your mind? See, you let that woman get under your skin. I knew talking to her was a bad idea," he ranted.

"I'm not thinking about her," I lied. "I was thinking about my father, what he was like and what would it have been like, had he been around."

"Well for starters, if your father is anything like your older brother, we definitely would not have been together." He laughed before smacking me on my behind.

"I don't think my father would have been as bad as John. Everyone always talked about how kind and easy-going my father was. He probably would have been more hospitable than John."

Quinton took two glasses from the bar. He filled my glass with Remy Red and his with Jack Daniels. He walked over to the sofa and sat beside me, smelling of sweet cologne. The mixture of his cologne and the liquor had my hormones raging. I moved around in my seat, trying to keep my composure. I took two more sips in an attempt to calm down.

Quinton kissed me softly on my collarbone and ran his hand up and down my arm. We looked at each other with lust in our eyes. Tonight had a lot in store for the both of us.

After inhaling his drink, he said, "Maybe. Maybe not. You sure there is nothing more on your mind? Now's the time to talk about it."

"I miss her, Q. After all is said and done, she is my mother and I want her to be a part of my life. I keep trying to reason with myself that I don't need her, but my heart says I do." Quinton looked over at me. "I don't want to imagine how I would react if Kai never wanted to see me again."

"It's not about how Nadine feels. It's about you. Do you think you're ready to meet your monster face-to-face?" Quinton reached over to grab my hand. The strength promised security. "No matter what happens, I got your back, Imani."

With that I had decided to go along with the lunch date. Plus Nana always said, "don't let anything come between the family." And she also said, "never hold a grudge against anyone because eventually it will kill you." Even though Nadine had done what was unforgivable, she was still family and deserved a second chance.

As for my job, I decided that the people there could kiss my ass. My family came first. If they couldn't understand that I'm a mother first then fuck 'em. Plus, Quinton and I had some catching up to do. He must have been thinking the same thing when he whispered, "Let's put the kids to bed."

CHAPTER 22
FAMILY AFFAIR

Imani

Nadine had called several times to make sure our date was still set for two o'clock. Although I had some apprehensions about our meeting, I was glad to finally have the opportunity to meet with her. Jada agreed to meet with us when we first arranged the luncheon but, of course, Craig overruled her. In turn, I asked Mia to accompany me. Knowing that a familiar face would be in my corner set my nerves at ease. I picked Mia up from her house at one o'clock.

When Mia stepped into the car, I noticed she was dressed in a pair of black jeans and tan leather boots to match the tan leather coat Quinton and I had bought her for her birthday. She always wore her hair long and loose, which was why she had a fit when I cut my hair. She always said, "A woman's hair is her crown." It had taken me four years to get my hair to grow.

I started the car and made a U-turn to get back on the highway. We rode for the first ten minutes in complete silence.

"Kai has grown so fast," Mia said, trying to spark a conversation.

The whole ride had been quiet. Normally, when Mia and I were together we would talk, like we hadn't seen each other in years even if it was only a day.

I pulled the car into an empty space in the restaurant parking lot.

"Isn't she though? Looking more and more like Q every day. And Lord if they don't act alike." I smiled. Kai may have been Q's twin but she would always be my little girl.

"How are the boys? How did everything go with the adoption? You never really told me what happened."

We arrived at the restaurant, and I turned off the car and took off my seat belt; I knew this was going to be one of those long overdue mother- daughter talks.

"Everything went fine. Time flew by so fast. It seems like only yesterday we got the boys and now you can't even tell we haven't always been a family."

"It seems like only yesterday you were crying over Quinton. You worried so much about nothing. I told you it was going to be all right."

"Back then, that wasn't what I wanted to hear. I wanted Q right then and there in our lives. But as time passed and I was able to see all the bullshit Quinton brought with him, it wasn't worth it. It wasn't worth the tears and stress."

"Don't say that. It was worth it. You got your man. He just needed space to grow and become a man. Now look at him."

"Can you believe it? It almost took thirty years but he finally grew up and took responsibility for his life," I said, remembering the day he got that internship at the law office. That was when I knew he had finally changed his life.

"But how about you, baby girl? You don't look so happy. Tell me what's really going on," Mia said as she rubbed my shoulder.

"Nothing's going on. I'm fine. My life is looking up, Mia."

"Then why haven't you called me? You've been so distant lately; your brother and I are starting to worry. Is it Nadine? Is it the kids? It has to be a lot on you, Mani."

Tears began to build up in my eyes. "It is a lot. Almost too much to bear."

"You don't have to bear it alone. I am more than willing to help with anything. I told you before whenever you needed a break, call me."

"Sometimes I want to call and ask for help but then I feel like I'm less than a mother, less than a woman for not being able to handle my own responsibilities." I wanted to model myself after Mia. She was always so strong. She took care of her home no matter what else was going on in her life. She never had to call anyone for help.

"Imani, you are doing an excellent job. I am so proud of you. Only God knows how much you make me happy. But I also know that every now and again you need a break. Trust me, I've been there. The only difference is I had no one to turn to. But you, you have so many people who love you and want to help you. Jada, Charisse, Q's mother and I have all tried to extend a helping hand and will continue trying." She pressed two of her fingers against her lips and then put them on my cheek. "I love you, baby girl."

"I love you too. Thank you," I said.

"My pleasure, Baby." She held out her arms and pulled me into her embrace. Mia always had the warmth and love of a mother. And I would always love her like a mother.

We entered the diner a little after two. I looked around to see if I would recognize Nadine but, of course, I didn't. I looked around again this time remembering Nadine said she'd be wearing a dark blue pinstriped pantsuit. Over in a corner booth, Nadine stood waving, trying to catch our attention. I waved back to let her know we saw her. Mia walked in front of me to greet Nadine first. I trailed still unsure of this meeting.

"Hello, Nadine. I'm Mia, John's wife. I don't know if you remember me." Mia stuck out her hand.

Nadine looked at her hand awkwardly and said, "Mia, there's no reason to be formal. We're family." Then she reeled Mia in for a hug.

"Well, I guess you're right," Mia said. "Imani—" she pulled me in front of her—"say hello to your mother."

I turned to Mia and sternly whispered, "She's not my mother."

"Imani, where would you like to sit?" Nadine asked.

At that precise moment, I felt like a six-year-old child being called up to the front of the class.

"I can sit next to the window. Right here." I quickly pulled Mia to occupy the seat beside me.

Nadine sat across from us. She watched me as I looked over the menu; her stare was making me feel very uncomfortable. Mia being the initiator that she was, decided to start the conversation.

"So, Nadine, how long have you been in New York? Last I heard you were in Virginia," Mia said before sipping on her water.

"I only came to New York for Justin's funeral. But I've been living in Maryland for the past nine years. That's how I bumped into Jada and Jordan. Jordan moved into the complex I'm living in." She waved her hand and giggled as if she were about to tell a joke. "And, one year the block association decided to have a Family Day Picnic."

"We were there," Mia replied. "I don't remember anyone saying you were there. Jada had given birth that year. John had taken the kids down but I stayed up here with Imani. Remember you and Q—" Mia said.

"Yeah, yeah, yeah. I remember. Jada and Craig had a big fight in the middle of the courtyard. I heard the story," I said to cut Mia off.

"Well, Jordan had become the talk of the community shortly after that. Especially after Craig had gotten out of jail. How many Jada and Jordan Wrights could there be?"

"Excuse me, Nadine. Let's forget about all that right now. I want to know about your present situation. Are you married, working, still drugging?" I said, bored with her chance meeting with Jada and Jordan. At least we knew their reunion was completely coincidental.

"Imani! " Mia shouted.

"No, it's quite all right. No, I'm not using anymore. I have been clean for twelve years now. I did remarry but as my fate would have it, my husband past away about six years ago."

Figures, she probably killed him too. I rubbed my hands on my thighs, trying to calm down. I really didn't want to know the answer to my next question but I had to ask, "Did you have any more children?"

"When I married my husband, Bob had a nineteen-year-old son. Then a few years later I had a baby girl, Anissa. She's eight now. And she's kept me on my toes. You know I almost forgot what it was like to raise a little girl," she said.

"Humh, I can see how that can happen," I said sarcastically. Suddenly, I felt a pinch at my side, Mia's way of letting me know I was getting out of line.

"Don't we know? Right, Imani? Little girls can definitely be a handful," Mia said.

"Yeah. Kai has gotten to be a little busybody. She's always into something she knows she isn't supposed to be doing. So does Amber. When they get together, somebody's getting in trouble," I said, recalling the time they sprayed all of Quinton's shaving cream on Bryan while he was asleep.

"Like mother, like daughter. You were something else too. Jada would cry about you tearing up her stuff and hiding her toys. Boy, between you, Jada, John and Jordan, I don't know who fussed more," Nadine said.

"Why didn't you ask Nana? She would know." I didn't mean to snap back but before I realized it, it was too late.

"Imani, I thought we were here to catch up on lost time. All you've been doing is giving me gut punches every chance you get. Why don't you just get it off your chest? What do you want to say to me?" Nadine put up one finger signaling for the waitress to wait until she was finished speaking.

Nadine continued to wait for my response. I looked into her eyes then turned to waitress and began placing my order. "I'll have the grilled chicken with mozzarella cheese on garlic bread. Can I have the broccoli steamed with very little butter, please? What are you having, Mia?" Mia looked at me with disgust before she turned around to place her order. My attitude had reached a new level and Mia wasn't too happy. Nadine ordered her meal then excused herself from the table.

"What is the matter with you?" Mia asked.

"You know I almost forgot what it was like to raise a little girl," I said mocking Nadine's table talk. "She never raised a little girl."

"How are you going to get to know her if you keep on insulting her?

Give her today, Imani. Let her try to express to you what held her back from being the mother she was supposed to be for you. What did you come here for?"

"I don't know what I came here for. Maybe this was a bad idea after all. I really don't give two shits about what she has to say."

Mia's face turned beet red. She was fuming and wasted no time telling me so.

"You don't know how lucky you are to have a second chance. Some people don't get this. I would give my life to have my mother back, hell or high water. Do you understand me?" She paused. "Now she may not have been the mother you needed but dammit she's here now and I know, if anybody knows, that you want her here. So get off your high horse and act right."

Mia raised her hand and motioned for me not to say another word. She was right. I wanted Nadine to be here.

Nadine returned to the table, and from the look of her puffy red eyes, she'd been crying. I didn't mean to hurt her, I was just venting. I should have just let it go, but I couldn't.

"Nadine, I'm-I'm sorry. I have been acting childishly." I took hold of her hands and continued. "I wanted to come here and try to make amends and maybe try to form some kind of friendship between us. Instead of listening I was being mean, and that's not me."

Mia placed her hand on my back and rubbed in a circular motion. She mouthed the words, I'm proud of you.

Nadine gently squeezed my hands and replied, "You don't know how much it means to me to have you back in my life. All I did was talk of my doll baby. Although I wasn't there with you physically, I was there spiritually. For the past six years Jada has been keeping me updated on everything that has been happening in y'all lives and I have never been so proud to have a set of kids as bright and wonderful as you, John, Jada, Justin and Jordan."

"Thank you, that means a lot to me," I replied. "So now that we got all that out of the way, tell me more about my little sister."

Nadine, Mia and I talked and talked and talked for what seemed like hours. I was surprised to hear how much Nadine had remembered about us as kids. She showed us the pictures she kept in her wallet of my little sister and us. Some of the pictures were so old they were cracked or torn and taped together. In the back of her wallet in a secret compartment she kept a picture that she said she had been holding just for me. Nadine pulled out a professional-looking photograph of an older man surrounded by four children and in his arms was a tiny white baby.

"This is the last time I heard from your father. He sent this picture to Virginia about four months after you were born. Shortly after his death, I made a promise that if I ever saw you again, I would give you this picture right here to see the man that loved you more than life itself."

Immediately, I snatched the picture from her. I stared trying to spark a memory but there were none. I was so young when my father died. I was only two.

I was stunned to silence by his smile. He had a graying mustache with skin the color of milk, and we looked so much alike. It was my daddy, and he was gorgeous—the most gorgeous man I had ever seen. He and John shared the same broad smile and pointed chin. We all inherited the same hair texture, full and wavy.

This was the best gift anyone could have given me.

"This is beautiful. They look so happy. Look at Jada with her pigtails and missing teeth and look at Jordan trying to look like a Mack," I said, pointing out my brothers and sister.

"And there you are, in all white, just like an angel. You are an angel. Your father lives through you, Imani. And if he were here today, he'd be so, so, so proud of you," Nadine said, fighting back the tears.

"You were always beautiful, Imani. Look at my man," Mia said, pointing to the pre-puberty John. Over the years, John's looks changed dramatically. No one would ever guess he was the same person.

We chatted for a while longer before deciding to depart. Nadine didn't have a ride so I offered to take her back to her hotel. For the rest of the day, I smiled. I was happier than I had ever been. I'd finally met my father.

The following week, Nadine had invited me over to her hotel to meet my sister, Anissa. We shared life stories over wine and cheese while Anissa played on her Nintendo. I enjoyed listening to Nadine as she told me stories of my father. Nadine eyes still sparkled when she reminisced on the love she and my father had for each other. He stole her heart and in return she broke his.

"My intentions were never to hurt your father. I loved him to no end but I was young. Young people make mistakes." Nadine's eyes became misty.

"Quinton and I have had our share of ups and downs but we manage to work things out. We try to stick things through if not for ourselves, for Kai."

"Your father tried to keep the family together. I was the one who was selfish. I became jealous of the love he had for your brothers and sister. I wanted it all."

"Like you said, you were young. But you've been given the chance to start all over," I said as I looked over at Anissa.

"I know. She's my heart but she will never be able to replace the years I lost with you. Imani, I want you to know that even though I wasn't there for you, I always loved you."

Tears began to roll down my cheeks. "And I missed you."

Nadine and I let bygones be bygones and promised not to allow the past to interfere with our future. This was a new beginning for us both. And it was long overdue.

"Well, I told you everything I can remember. Do you have any questions or anything?" Nadine asked. And as a matter of fact, I did still have one question.

"I do want to ask you something. It's nothing major. Why doesn't my name begin with a J? I mean I know it might sound stupid but I was just wondering . . ."

"Nana named you. She said it was faith that you survive and named you accordingly. Imani means faith in an African language. Personally, I think Nana did it to piss off your Granny. Granny had her doubts about you, and Nana didn't help the situation any. Even after we got the results back from the tests, Nana still let your granny believe otherwise," Nadine explained.

"Did you . . . I mean, was there somebody else?" I asked.

"No. I was a lot of things but I wasn't a whore. I never sold my body for drugs. I've never been so high that I slept with someone or woke somewhere I wasn't familiar with."

"I never thought you were a whore. I just needed to know if there was a possibility that the test could have been wrong."

259

"There was no chance of that, Baby. Your daddy was the only man I had slept with. Trust me."

"Thank you."

I felt like my lungs had just received a fresh breath of air. My chest felt lighter and heart danced in joy. All my questions had been answered. My mind was free.

Anissa and I talked for the remainder of the visit. She told me of all her school friends back in Maryland and was excited when she learned she had nieces and nephews. Just as I was about to walk out the door, Nadine handed me an envelope.

"Inside are forms for savings bonds. If it's all right with you I would like to get some for my grandkids so they'll have a little nest egg of their own."

"I don't see any harm in it. Q and I have started savings accounts for the kids but you know extra is always welcomed."

We shared a brief laugh before I entered the elevator. My life was complete. I got my mother back.

Quinton

Since Imani met with her mother last week, they have been on the phone all day and night. Although I was kind of skeptical of their relationship, I never said anything. If Imani was happy, then I was too.

I had just finished putting together some contracts for one of my clients when Imani walked through the door. Sounds of laughter came from the front. I shut off my computer and went to see who decided to pay us a visit.

"Hey, Baby, you didn't tell me you were bringing home company. I would have taken something out for dinner," I said.

I looked over at the women in the living room and said hello. There was Charisse, Jada, Mia and I must have been seeing things because I could almost swear that was...

"Q, that's Nadine. Nadine, this is Quinton," Imani said.

"Hello, again," I said in my most cordial voice. "How is everyone?" The women all responded, "Fine."

"Where are the kids? I want Nadine to meet them," Imani said. She was full of smiles and giggles. I tried to feel comfortable but having Nadine around kind of made me uneasy.

"They're at Mama's. I didn't pick them up yet. I just got in from work," I replied.

"Oh, you think Mama would want to come over? Come hang with the women?"

"I don't see why not. Shea and Pop were coming over in a few anyway to watch the game. I'll just call back and tell Mama to come too."

"Thank you, Q." She kissed my cheek then whispered in my ear, "Is the basement clean?" I admired Imani from head to toe, taking in everything that made her a woman. From her full hips, which filled her black linen pants perfectly to her firm breasts, that stood up underneath her fitted V-neck knit sweater.

"It should be. The kids haven't been down there since Saturday night. It was your turn to clean Sunday. Did you clean it?" I asked.

"I cleaned up yesterday but I didn't know if you had done laundry."

"Nope. I was going to do everything tomorrow morning," I said.

"All right. Well I'm not going anywhere tomorrow, so I can help you out a little," she said as she leaned against the wall.

"Are you ever going back? I mean are you going to work from home or ditch your career altogether?"

"Can we talk about this later? We have company," she said.

I looked in the living room at the women as they all admired Jada's pregnant belly and tried to determine the sex of the baby. Imani walked back into the living room with her own opinion of what was going on inside Jada's body.

I went upstairs to our bedroom to get out of my work clothes and to call Mama. As I sat on the side of the bed, I loosened my tie and unlaced my shoes. Slowly, I stripped out of my business attire and walked around half naked looking for something comfortable to put on. I picked up the cordless phone from its cradle and waited for a dial tone. The messaging service beeped twice so I put in the password and waited. I found this voicemail system much better than the old answering machine.

Several solicitations played and on the last message a man's voice began.

"Imani, I know I'm not supposed to be calling you but I couldn't stop thinking about you. For the past couple of months I've tried to get over you but you're too special to forget. Can you find it in your heart to give me one more chance? Whatever I did to make you hate me, I'm sorry and I want to make it up to you. Call me. The number is still the same."

I couldn't believe what I was hearing. After all this time, this bastard decided to call. I didn't know what the hell he was up to but I wanted to find out.

Quickly, I pulled on my pajama pants and picked out a T-shirt from the dresser. I raced down the stairs to get Imani. When I realized she was no longer on the first level, I called down the basement stairs. The women were partying with the music blasting and the lights dimmed. I flicked the lights on and off to get her attention. Seconds later Imani appeared at the foot of the steps with a drink in her hand.

"Imani, come upstairs for a minute," I said.

She bounced up the stairs and closed the door behind her.

"What's up? You called Mama? What'd she say?" she asked, obviously on the way to being intoxicated.

"I was about to but I was checking the messages and came across one I thought you should hear."

I pulled her into the office and put the phone on speaker. I skipped over about five messages before his began to play. I let it play in its entirety before I looked over at her. Her face was whiter than rice, like she had seen a ghost. Her drink dropped to the floor and glass shattered everywhere. Imani's hands began to shake violently as she looked at me.

"Q, that's him. That's Omar," she said.

"I know who it is. What I don't know is why he's calling our house after two, three months."

"I don't know. How did he get our number?"

"Huh?" Now I was stumped.

"Remember, we had our number changed."

She was right. After he called and threatened to see her, we had our number changed. I couldn't imagine how he could have gotten the new one. Unless someone gave it to him. But, who would give him our number? Who did we know who knew him?

Imani began to cry. "How does he keep finding me, Q?"

I pulled her into my arms and assured her nothing would happen. "I'm going to get to the bottom of this, Mani. Don't worry." I turned her face up to mine. "Listen, I want you to go wash your face and go back to your company. I'll handle this. Okay?"

She nodded and left the room. I picked up the phone and called Mama and Pop to come on over. I asked Mama to put Shea on the phone briefly.

"I need to ask him something," I said.

"Is everything okay? You sound upset," Mama replied. "Everything is fine," I said through a tightened jaw.

She hollered for Shea to come answer the phone. "Yeah, 'sup," Shea answered.

"Yo, stay there. I'm coming to pick you up. We need to talk."

"We're about to walk out the door right now."

"Nah, just wait right there. I need to see Rodney too. Hit him up and tell him to meet me at your house."

"Everything cool?" he asked. "I hope so," I replied.

An hour later, Rodney and I were on the highway. Rodney had his hair pulled back into a braid, ready for confrontation. His jaws were tightly clenched as he listened to the information Shea had gathered. Shea had given us the information we needed to find that motherfucker Omar. Shea knew people in high places.

When I arrived at Mama's house, I told Shea the situation. He smiled when I said, "I want to find this nigga."

Within twenty minutes, Shea made three phone calls and was able to get me all the info I needed. He told me where I could find Omar this time of day and who he'd be with. I was impressed. Shit, he should have been working with me at the firm.

First, we rode by Omar's house to make sure he wasn't home. The lights were out and his car wasn't parked in front. We drove around his hood for a quick minute trying to make sure he wasn't around the way. Next, we swung by Houlihan's, where Shea said we'd find him.

We parked around the corner and walked down the block to the bar. Houlihans was packed. There were light-skinned niggas everywhere. Rodney and I kept our coats on as we bumped through the crowd. In the corner by the bathroom, we found who we were looking for. He was only with one other person. A big black greasy looking motherfucker stood right beside him as they bopped to the music. Rodney and I split up; we didn't want to look too obvious. I stood in front of Omar, toe to toe.

"Excuse, my man, can I talk to you for a minute?" I said as I unzipped my coat.

"What the . . . Do I know you, nigga?" he replied.

I became tense with anger. It took all I had to remain calm as I asked him again, "Can I talk to you?"

"Look, I ain't into that faggot bullshit. Take that homo-thug shit somewhere else."

He tried to walk around me but I stepped in front of him. "You about a bold fucker, aren't you?" he said.

Tired of the bullshit, I grabbed him by his throat and brought him into the men's room. His friend tried to grab me but Rodney already had a gun to his head.

"Where you going, big man? Step inside the bathroom," Rodney said.

I threw Omar up against the wall, pulled out my steel and shoved it into his throat.

"What the fuck is your problem?" Omar shouted. No one could hear us over the loud crowd and music.

"That's what I want to know. Do you know a woman named Imani?" I asked.

"Nah, motherfucker. I don't know no bitch named Imani," Omar replied.

I knew he was lying. There was no question that I had the right man. I had seen his records and all his pictures from juvenile detention to Rikers. I jabbed my gun into his ribs. As he knelt over in pain, I kneed him and busted his nose.

"Why are you lying to me? I'm not in a fuckin' playin' mood! " I didn't know how much longer I would be able to hold off my anger.

The next time I hit him, I'm gonna kill him, I thought. "Listen here, nigga, I don't want to have to come back out here. Leave Imani the fuck alone. You understand?"

"Ain't this the same greasy bastard who tried to rape Imani?" Rodney's eyes were filled with vengeance.

"Look like him," I said.

Rodney cocked his gun and put it to the gorilla's dick.

"You want to lose this, black man? Huh?" Rodney hollered. "Keep your monkey ass away from my fuckin' sister! "

"That goes for you too, black. The next time we bump heads you leaving in a bag. You done fucked with the wrong one," I said.

I had lost control of my emotions. I used the handle of the gun to bust Omar upside his head. When he fell to the floor, I stomped on his face repeatedly. The sounds of my Timberland boots against his face bounced off the bathroom walls. Rodney and the Goon had gotten into their own scuffle across the room. Feeling relieved of my anger, I gave Rodney the heads-up and we left. After making our way back through the crowd, we hauled ass down the block and hopped in Shea's black Escalade.

"Where the fuck did you get that gun from, Q?" Rodney shouted after we pulled off.

"Don't worry about it! Thanks for riding with me, Man," I said.

"Nah, fuck that, Q. Where the fuck did you get the gun from, nigga? You was supposed to let me handle everything. If we would have gotten caught, you could have lost your job." Rodney slapped the back of my head like a father would a son.

"Shit. Rodney, man. I had to do something. I can't let you always put your shit on the line for me. That's my woman, my family. I had to step to that nigga," I answered.

"You stupid. We fuckin' boys, nigga. Imani is my blood too. Your kids are my niece and nephews. You have to stay clean and out of jail for them, not for me."

He was right. I didn't know what I was thinking but I didn't regret a thing. If I had to do it all over again, I would. As long as Omar understood that I am not a nigga to be fucked with.

"Rodney, sorry man. Yo, let's just get back to the crib and finish watching what's left of the game," I said.

He looked at me sideways for a few seconds before responding, "Whatever. You still my nigga."

"For life," I replied.

CHAPTER 23
THAT'S WHAT FRIENDS ARE FOR

Quinton

I sat back in my office thinking about all the shit that went down the night before. The incident had been replaying in my mind. Work had been piling on my desk, a message on my computer screen flashed "incoming mail" and my phone had been ringing off the hook. My concentration had been lost. All my focus was on Omar.

In a few days my family and I were going to be enjoying the beautiful island breeze of Puerto Rico. We needed to get away from the city life for a little while. Especially me. I needed to lay low. When we returned from our trip, we planned to move to Pennsylvania. Imani had been talking about buying a house out there for the longest, so I spoke to some of my people and was able to make some arrangements. One of my coworkers was just thinking about putting his house up for sale. He said he lived in Allentown and it was only forty-five minutes from Philadelphia. The schooling out there was supposed to be excellent and there was lots of space for the kids to be kids.

When I called Imani and told her about the house she almost came through the phone. She didn't even ask to see it; she wanted to get as far away as possible right away.

A buzz came from my receptionist. "Mr. Banks, your brother is here to see you."

I pressed the little black button and spoke into the box. "Send him in." Shea came walking through the door seconds later. Something told me something wasn't right when I saw the way he was dressed. He was wearing an old gray sweat suit with his house shoes, like he was in a rush or something.

"What's going on, Shea? You all right?" I pulled out a chair and offered it to him

"Q, we got to go. Right now! " he said in a calm but excited tone.

"What's up? I can't just leave like that." I closed my door so no one could hear us. We had some nosy motherfuckers on the job.

"Imani got a phone call today from Omar. He told her that you should've minded your business. He also said that if he can't have Imani, he'd make sure you won't either."

"This nigga must be out of his mind. Did she call the police?"

"No. She packed up as much as she could and came to Mama's house. Call her. She's a mess."

I picked up the phone and hit memory three for my mother's house. Pop picked up the phone.

"Quinton, your mother and Imani are going crazy over here. Imani called a professional mover to take all y'all's stuff to storage and has Mia and Charisse packing everything else. What the hell is going on?" James hollered.

"I'll tell you when I get there. Let me speak to Imani."

Silence filled the phone briefly. Imani answered the phone in a low whisper.

"Q, Baby. Please come home. I'm scared."

"Imani, calm down. I'm going to call Rodney, and he'll watch the house until I get there. Don't worry, Omar isn't that crazy. Boo, you hear me?"

"Yeah," she paused, "I'm really sorry about this."

"It's okay. We'll just have to take our vacation a little earlier than expected. The kids are out of school in a couple of days so they'll just get an early start. I'm gonna take care of this. Don't sweat it. He's not going to touch you or the kids." I tried to reassure Imani that everything would be fine.

"Be careful. I love you," she responded. "I love you too."

I held on to the line until I heard her hang up.

I stood, grabbed my jacket and keys and ushered Shea out of the office. I began to loosen my tie as I reached the front desk and spoke with the receptionist.

"If anyone calls looking for me tell them I'm out of town on business. Leave a message for Mr. Riley. Tell him I had an emergency and had to leave early. I'll have his contracts ready when I return."

The busy midtown streets had me trapped. Shea managed to dip through traffic in Mani's new Civic. Of all days I chose to take the Jeep. I tried calling Imani to let her know I was stuck in traffic but the phone was busy. I tried her cell phone but it went straight to her voice mail, and she had her pager disconnected. Damn!

The winter's chill turned the slush to ice causing most drivers to reduce their speed, and although the outside temperature was in the low teens, beads of sweat formed on my forehead. I reached over to turn the heat down but it was already off. Damn what the hell's going on?

The sound of my cell phone ringing startled me. I quickly pressed the talk button and spoke, "Hello."

"Q, it's me. Where are you?" Imani said.

"I'm on my way to you. I'm just getting on the bridge. What's going on? Is everything's cool?" I asked.

"Yeah. I called Nadine and asked her if she could come over and sit with me and the kids while John and Mia finish over at the house. John is having a shit fit, Q."

"I can imagine. Why did you call Nadine over? Where's Mama?"

"Umm. Well, she's at the airport buying plane tickets to Puerto Rico.

Our trip isn't going to be so intimate after all. She and James are going too. She said she'll watch the kids for us while we relax."

"That's bullshit and you know it, right." I laughed, finally I was beginning to calm down.

"Yeah, I know but I didn't think the idea sounded so bad myself. Oh, while I'm still thinking about it, why do you still have Rodney sitting downstairs?"

"He's still there. Good. I wanted to make sure you were safe until I got there. How are the kids?"

"They're fine. They're in Shea's room playing one of his game systems. Charisse said to tell you hi. She and her fiancée left for Florida about twenty minutes ago. She had another show."

"Alright. Well, I'm going to have to call you back. I have an incoming call. Okay, Baby," I said as the incoming alert sounded in my ear.

"Alright. Love you."

"I love you too. Call me if anything changes." I pressed the talk button to answer the other line. "Hello."

"Yeah, where you at? I'm waiting for you at the end of the bridge over by Metrotech Plaza," She'a said.

"I'll be there in five minutes. I got stuck in traffic. Yo, just go ahead to the house with Imani. I don't trust her in the house alone with Nadine."

"Nadine's on the way to my house?" His voice was full with attitude.

"Yeah, Imani felt the need to call her mother," I said confused by the situation myself. "Aight, bye."

I made another phone call to Rodney and told him to keep an extra eye out now that Nadine was coming over. He agreed that he thought she was a bit suspect. We both felt she was hiding something but I was unable to bring up anything on her background. I told him I'd be there in about another twenty minutes and then ended the call.

Imani

Nadine showed up shortly after I got off the phone with Q. She had her eight-year-old daughter, Anissa with her. Anissa was a beautiful, bright-eyed girl. She looked nothing like Nadine, which only meant she must have taken her looks from her daddy. Anissa was extremely fair skinned with dusty blond hair and deep brown eyes. Nadine's husband must have been a handsome man.

I sat and admired my little sister for a little while before introducing her to the kids. It was strange being able to acknowledge her as a little sister yet not being able to do the same for Nadine as my mother. I called for Kai and Bryan to come into the living room. Jahlek was too young to understand. Although he and Kai were only a year apart, Kai was wise beyond her years.

270

Mia said that would happen if I continued to allow her to sit in adult business.

"Yeah, Mom. What's up?" Bryan said as he stood beside me.

"I want you to meet someone." I took Anissa by the hand and pulled her closer to me. "This is Anissa, my little sister. Your new aunt." The little girl smiled up at me after her introduction as my little sister.

"Your little what? I thought Auntie Jada was our only aunt," Bryan said as he looked Anissa up and down.

"How can she be my auntie if she's only a little girl? She's the same size as me," Kai exclaimed as she stood by Anissa. She was right, they were the same height but then Kai was tall for her age.

"That's true, Kai. But she's Mommy's sister and that makes her your auntie like Jada. Why don't you play with her in the back while Mommy talks to her friend? Okay?"

Kai looked at me and then huffed.

"Come on, Anissa. I hope you know how to play basketball," Kai said before walking away.

After we heard the door close, Nadine and I started a conversation of our own.

"So, when are you going back to Maryland?" I asked.

"We're supposed to be leaving tonight but I wanted to make sure everything was okay before I left. Why is this man stalking you and who the hell is he?"

Nadine looked very concerned and I appreciated that but I didn't feel this was any of her business. "No one important. Nothing to worry yourself about. Quinton will handle it."

"Are you sure? If you need me for anything, all you have to do is ask and it's yours. Do you and Quinton have enough to move? It is kind of a short notice."

"We're fine. We have more than enough money. Thanks but no thanks." Quinton still had money saved from his hustling days. "You sound like you're swimming in money. You must have a good job. Whatcha doing?"

"My husband left me a couple of dollars. I made a couple of good investments. It's enough to hold us over. You have a good job too, Miss Senior Exec."

"I quit that oh-so-good job. There are some things I've been wanting to do. Plus, I want to spend more time with my kids."

"That's great. How long are you going to be in Puerto Rico? Maybe when you come back, you can bring the kids and come visit me. It gets lonely in Maryland. Jordan doesn't visit much. My phone bill has gotten sky high from calling Jada. What's going on with her anyway?"

"It's a long story. I can't wait until she has this baby though. She has been in a lot of pain with this pregnancy. The doctors are talking about inducing her because the baby is so big."

I couldn't believe how comfortable I felt talking with Nadine. Just like girlfriends.

Quinton and Rodney came through the door. Quinton came over to me and kissed my forehead. His clothes were sweaty and undone. "Quinton, were you fighting?" I asked.

"No, I was rushing to get to you! You had me nervous as hell and here you are chillin'." He looked over at Nadine and then back at me.

"Well, we were talking and laughing so much that I had forgotten about Omar. Plus, he would never find me here," I said.

Nadine gasped and then began to cough. We turned to look her way. I thought she was having trouble breathing.

"Are you okay? Can you breathe? Are you choking on something?" Quinton asked as he ran to her side.

"I'm fine. Just horrified that someone is stalking my baby girl," Nadine said as she tried to catch her breath.

"Are you sure? You looked like you were having chest pains or something," Rodney said as he brought a glass of water from the kitchen.

"No, I'm okay," she said. "Imani, I don't think you should be going on this trip. You should stay here where John can watch over you." She was talking crazy.

"Nadine, what are you talking about? Quinton is going with me, and he can take care of us the same as he's been doing. John has his own family to take care of," I said, trying to reason with her.

"Well, I would feel a lot better if someone else was going with y'all. Someone to watch over you and the kids." She began searching through her bag.

"What are you looking for? What is wrong with you? You're starting to act crazy! " I exclaimed as I rose from my seat.

"I'm getting my phone. I'm calling the airlines to make reservations. We're going with you." Nadine took out her cell phone and wallet.

"Listen, Nadine, that's quite all right. My mother and father are going. My brothers are going down with us," Q said as he looked over to Rodney who stood in the corner, nodding. "We're going to relax and take a break from all this craziness. Your daughter will be fine."

"No, I insist. Besides, I will feel better knowing one of her family members will be with her." Nadine looked away from Quinton and began to speak to a representative over the phone.

"What the fuck you mean 'one of her family members'? We all are one big motherfuckin' family. When did you become the matriarch of our lives? I've been her fucking family from day one. Where the fuck was you?" Quinton ranted.

"Q, calm down, man. Chill. Come on, man. Go change your clothes and let Imani handle this," Rodney said as he pulled Quinton out of the living room.

"Nadine, look this is really not necessary. We have more than enough people to watch the kids," I pleaded.

She continued to ignore me as she made her travel arrangements. "Uh-huh. Yes, tomorrow at twelve will be fine. No, thank you." She closed her cell phone then turned her attention back to me. "Imani, I have to be going. We have some packing to do." She closed her purse then hollered, "Anissa! Come now. We're leaving! "

Anissa slowly walked to the front where Nadine stood waiting. "Ma, why are we leaving so soon? I was having fun."

"Don't worry. You'll get to have plenty of fun with the kids while we're on vacation. We're going to Puerto Rico with your sister."

Anissa looked up to me with those bright, youthful eyes. "For real! For real, Mommy? Thank you, Imani." She came and gave me a big hug. Suddenly the idea didn't sound so bad.

I walked Nadine over to the door. She looked at me and asked, "See you in Puerto Rico?"

"See you in Puerto Rico," I replied.

I smiled from ear to ear as I closed the door.

I reentered the living room as Quinton and Rodney came from the back. Rodney had managed to calm Q down. Quinton sat on the couch beside me and put his arm around my shoulders. "Did you straighten everything out?" he asked.

"She said she'd meet us in Puerto Rico. You know, Q, it really doesn't seem like a bad idea. I mean it'll give us time to hang out and do all kinds of mother and daughter things with our daughters. She'll have a chance to meet your mother and . . ."

"Damn, this ain't even a vacation anymore. It's a fucking family reunion! " He shifted to the other side of the couch. "You might as well invite the rest of your family down since I'm not good enough to take care of you."

"Quinton, she didn't mean it like that. She's just worried about me.

And, inviting Mia and them might work since we're not going to be back for Christmas," I said.

"Imani, I can't fucking believe this. What about us? When are we going to spend time together alone?"

"Yo, Q man. I'm out. I just got a hit on my hip. Mani, take care. Give my goddaughter a kiss," Rodney said before walking out of the door.

"Aight. Later. Yo, what time you leaving New York tomorrow?" Q asked.

"After six," Rodney replied.

Quinton walked over to the door and whispered something to Rodney. I tried to be nosy but by the time I got my radars up the conversation was over.

Quinton walked over adjusting his jeans. I looked away from him not wanting to continue our previous argument.

He put his hand on my head and said, "Call Mia and John and see if they can go. Did you pack our things for the trip?"

"The suitcases are still in my car. Where the hell is Shea with my car? He said he was going to get you and never came back."

"He was on his way upstairs when I pulled up then Mama called him on his cell and asked if he wanted her to pick up his ticket. Shea told her to get it and he would pay for it when she came home. Then he went to the bank but I forgot to tell you when I came in."

"Well how far is the bank?"

"He'll be here any minute. He probably went to take a spin through the hood." Q started to walk away. "Are the kids awake?"

"Yeah. Shit, it's time for them to eat. My mind is all foggy."

"Go ahead and make those phone calls and I'll make the kids something to eat."

He didn't need to say any more. My fingers were doing the walking as he spoke. Mia and John were just settling down when I called. She said they had managed to pack most of the stuff and send it to storage. She complained that we had too much stuff and should think about giving some to Goodwill.

Like Mia, I had let years of junk accumulate in the garage and closets. Stuff that had sentimental value. Kai's first ballet shoes, busted up and all, were neatly packed in a pink tin can with school paintings and projects. Little things like the wrapper of the first condom Quinton and I used were packed in a shoebox with all the birthday, Christmas, Valentine and anniversary cards he had given me over the years.

She agreed to take the trip with us but said she wouldn't be able to leave until Sunday. We called Jada on three-way and asked her to watch Amber while Mia and John were away. Jada talked and talked for the better half of an hour, just for company. Mia and I knew she was lonely, and it didn't bother us that she needed us. Diamond and

Craig were out picking up things for the baby. Everybody feared this baby was coming earlier than expected.

Quinton fixed sandwiches for the kids while Mia and I made travel arrangements over the phone. He looked over at me several times. I flashed him one of my million-dollar smiles. He returned my gesture and returned his attention to the kids.

Mama walked in waving three airplane tickets. Her smile spread from ear to ear.

"We're going to Puerto Rico! " she shouted as she broke into a terrible Salsa dance. The children all laughed as James joined her.

"We're not going alone," Quinton said as he walked over to greet his mother.

"Who all is going?" Mama asked as she took off her coat and gloves.

"Nadine, Anissa, Mia and John. I invited Mia and John after Nadine invited herself," I replied.

"Who's Anissa?" they all said in unison.

I gave a slight grin and answered, "My sister."

"I guess having the family around will do you some good. We're going to have so much fun. You know I like Mia. Nadine is going to take some getting used to but it will be fine," Mama said as she kissed my forehead.

"Come on. Leave the kids alone and let's start packing. Our flight leaves at three tomorrow afternoon. And you know how slow you are," James said.

Mama followed James into their bedroom. Quinton looked at me and was about to open his mouth to say something I knew I didn't want to hear. I covered my ears and walked out of the living room. Q followed me until I finally put down my hands.

"Why didn't you tell me you had another sister? You haven't really told me anything about Nadine. What's up? You holding back?"

"No. I didn't think it was that important. It's Nadine's life. Doesn't concern either one of us. If you really want to know, we can talk about it tomorrow while we walk hand in hand in the island sands." I ran my finger down his chest as I answered.

I continued to trail my finger down the hairline underneath his navel into his boxers. We looked around to make sure we were out of immediate view. He pulled me into the guest room and closed the door. My back pressed against the door as he fondled my breasts. This was how it all started. Same house, same position, different room. I licked behind his ear and blew slowly over the moistened area. Q wrapped my legs around his waist and began to unbuckle his pants.

"Your mother is in the next room," I whispered as he tried to push my underwear to the side. My skirt was around my waist and my bra was on the floor.

"We're grown, Mani. Shit she'll understand. You think she ain't fuckin'?" He continued to play inside my panties.

"But the kids are still awake. Let's wait until everyone is sleeping," I said breathlessly as my insides began to fire up.

"Come on, Baby. You know you want it. Secret sex is always the best."

He pulled his shirt over his head and pressed his hard, sweaty chest against mine. Quinton cupped my breasts as he slowly licked my nipples. He then went in for the kill, licking the most sensitive area on my neck. The sensation of skin touching skin sent sparks throughout my body. I was ready to give in.

"Mommy, Kai spilled her juice all over my clothes," Bryan screamed.

"No, I didn't. It fell by itself. Why you lying, Bryan?" Kai hollered.

Q slammed his fist against the door, frustrated. The kids stopped arguing immediately.

Mama hollered, "What the hell? Quinton, who's banging on my doors."

Q let me down and began redoing his clothing. As I reached for my bra, he squeezed my behind. "This is mine tonight."

"Just for tonight?" I joked.

"Go handle the kids. I have to go to the bathroom," he said before walking out of the room.

I walked into the kitchen waiting to find a mess. Bryan had already started to clean up the spill and Kai sat quietly, avoiding my stare. Jahlek looked over at me then pointed his little chubby finger at my shirt.

"Your shirt is backwards," he said.

"Thank you, Baby," I said, feeling embarrassed.

"Are you finished?"

"Yes," he said as he pushed his plate away.

"Mom, Kai threw the
juice at Bryan because he called her a cry baby."

"Unh-unh," they said. "Tattletale! "

"Kai and Bryan, get over here now! " Quinton demanded as he reentered the front area.

Solemnly the kids walked to their father. I took Jahlek into the back room to get ready for bed.

When I came back the kids were watching a movie. Mama had given me one of her sleepers for the night. It really didn't make any sense to go all the way downstairs and unpack everything for pajamas. Quinton had just gotten off the phone with the airline to confirm our flight change from Christmas to the next. Then he went down to the car to check the suitcases to make sure I hadn't forgotten anything.

While he was downstairs I had decided to do something with my hair, the little bit I had left. I used Mama's curlers to style it. The short do was cute but not manageable. I wasn't used to having short hair, having to remember which pieces belonged to the front to hang long and which pieces belonged to the back to be curled tight. I shouldn't have cut my hair but being home with nothing to do made me want to experiment. Mia hadn't spoken to me when she first saw my new style but unlike John she doesn't carry long-term grudges. Mia called me before the day was out.

After about a half-hour of fussing with my hair, someone knocked on the bathroom door. I assumed it was one of the kids but before I got to respond, Shea bust through the door started pissing. Right there, like I was invisible. I turned to look the other way. I waited for him to finish before I said a word.

"You could have asked me to leave," I stated.

He began washing his hands and replied, "You act like you never saw a dick before."

"Don't you think you're being a little disrespectful? If Q comes upstairs and sees you in here—"

He interrupted, "Damn sis, you got a nice ass. Mama never filled out those pajamas like that."

As he approached the smell of alcohol became heavy. "Shea, you're drunk. Leave me alone."

He came closer, disregarding my plea. He put out his hand to cop a feel and caught a blow to the nuts instead. As he crunched over in pain, I stepped over him.

"Good night, motherfucker. Oh, and expect to hear from my lawyer in the morning."

His face filled with horror as he pleaded, "I'm sorry. Please don't tell Q. I had too much to drink. You can't blame a brother for thinking you look good."

"Shea, stay the fuck away from me," I said through my tightly clenched teeth.

I walked back into the living room where I had set up the sofa bed for Q and me. I laid on the bed, pulled the covers all the way up to my neck and contemplated whether to tell Q who walked through the door with a Subway's sandwich bag and soda. I figured he took a little long downstairs.

"Any for me?" I asked.

"I didn't know if you were still awake. I saw the light out before I left," he said.

Q pulled out a tray table and sat down. "I bought a foot long. You want some?"

I got up from the bed and sat on the end nearest Q. "Whatcha got?"

"Roasted chicken."

"Yeah. I'll take a piece." I went to the kitchen for a plate and knife. Shea walked in behind me.

"I'm sorry," he whispered. "I'll tell Q if you want me to."

"No need. It's better off forgotten." Without returning his gaze, I walked back into the living room.

Quinton

The next morning, I woke up early. I needed to walk and get my thoughts together.

When I came back in the house, Imani was up watching TV.

"Couldn't sleep either?" I asked.

"Yeah. I don't know if it's because I'm excited that we're finally going on vacation together or..." she paused.

I took off my sweaty shirt and threw it on the floor. I crawled on the bed over to Imani and said, "You don't have anything to worry about. We've got everything covered."

She leaned her head on my shoulder. I held her close and ran my hand up and down her arm. In an attempt to lighten the mood, I changed the subject. "Don't you owe me something?" I playfully tugged on her pajamas.

"We're in your mother's house, Quinton. Stop! " she said as I tickled her.

"Come on, Imani. You act like you never did it before. You a virgin now?"

"You know I'm hardly a virgin. As many times as I fucked you dry, please! " She rolled her eyes and turned her back to me.

I pulled the cover over us and began to undress her while I caressed her. She played like she was fighting me but I knew she wanted it as bad as I did.

"Q, watch my hair. Watch it," she yelled.

"Shhh, you're going to wake Mama and Pop. Don't fight it, Mani. Take it like a woman."

Pressing my body on top of hers, I held her arms over her head. I used my free hand to play with her while I lined her neck with butterfly kisses. She arched her back inviting me in but I wasn't ready. I wanted to make her moan and grovel. She panted short, heavy breaths as I trailed kisses down to her bush. I parted her legs slowly and licked her inner thighs. With each touch she shuddered.

"Q, stop playing with me," she said, growing impatient.

Ignoring her sexual cry, I used my fingers to part her lips as I sucked on her clit. She rocked and shifted until she could no longer control herself. She cried out in a series of moans and whimpers as her body grew limp.

I crawled back to her side. She turned to face me, trying to catch her breath. "Why did you do that?" she whined as she hid her face under the covers.

"Do what?" I smiled at her embarrassment.

"What if your mother heard me, Q?"

"Then you shouldn't have been mmmming and ahhhing so loud." I pulled the blankets off her head and laughed at her expression.

"Really, that's cool. It's a big joke, right? Let's see how calm you are." She smiled devilishly.

Imani took hold of my rock-hard penis and playfully licked around the head. The touch of her tongue against my shaft caused my toes to curl. She continued to look up at me as she put my throbbing piece of meat into her mouth and slowly bobbed her head. I couldn't look at her anymore. Her seducing eyes and gentle touch were a wicked combination. She let go of my penis and began to suck my balls. One by one she put them in her mouth and played with them. I tried to grab hold of her head but she dodged my grasp. Imani used her mouth to bring me to a point of no return.

"Mani, stop . . . ahhh, shit. Okay, Baby, please . . ." I begged but the more I begged the more she sucked and stroked and sucked and stroked.

My body had reached its boiling point and was about to explode.

"Imani!" I yelled trying to get her to stop before it was too late.

She ignored my warning and took it like a champ. I was in total euphoria. My head spun as I released all that was within me.

Imani stood up and said, "Now who cries like a bitch?" then she mushed my head into the pillow.

"Ain't nobody crying like no bitch! Stop gassing yourself," I said in total denial of the way she turned me from a man into a mouse.

"Stop, Baby. Please, Mani. And who was that?" she bragged.

"Shut the fuck up and move out of my way so I can get in the shower." I laughed as she made muscle man poses. "Are you coming or are you going to stand there looking stupid?"

"I'm coming. You might need my help in there," she joked.

Imani grabbed her towel and bathrobe off the chair and followed me into the bathroom

"Are you ready to relax?" I asked as I started the shower.

"Am I ever? Q, do you ever think about what our lives would have been like if we didn't get back together?" she asked.

"I try not to. I'm just glad no matter what happens between us there was always something or someone to pull us back together."

"Did you tell your mother about the wedding?"

"No, I figured if no one knew, no one could mess it up. Everyone will find out the day of. We'll invite them down to the beach to be our witnesses, and that's it."

"I'm glad we decided to do this. Did Charisse pick up my dress?" she asked.

"Yes, Imani. Don't worry. Everything is going to be fine. Rodney picked up the rings and Charisse has our clothes. This was how we should have done it a long time ago."

"I just wish we could have all our family there." She sighed.

"You almost got your wish. Imani, I promise when everything settles down we'll have a big reception and invite the people who miss this one. At least your mother will be there."

"Yeah, I guess that's a plus," she said.

We showered and talked more about the wedding and our lives after. With me there was really nothing to say. Everything happened for a reason and whatever lay in our future would happen for its reason. No strings attached. No consequences. Just fate.

CHAPTER 24
TROUBLED WATERS

Imani

The soft sands of the Puerto Rican beach swallowed our feet as we walked toward the shore. The kids had played in the water like fish since we had gotten there an hour earlier. Everyone had already checked in by the time we had arrived at the hotel. We all were fortunate to get rooms in the same hotel.

Charisse had left several messages for us. She just wanted to make sure our flight came in all right. We made arrangements to meet up with everyone later. Quinton and I had decided to announce our wedding that night over dinner. What could go wrong in two days? We figured.

Nadine and Anissa's flight was due in any time. Nadine had missed her previous flight. She said she had scheduled a meeting and forgotten all about it with all the drama Omar had caused. She sounded like she wasn't having a good day. This vacation might do everyone some good.

"Have you written your vows?" Quinton asked. He had been reciting his since we left New York.

"I've had my vows written since you first proposed seven years ago. No need to rehearse, it's all from the heart." I patted my chest.

We looked at each other briefly before returning to our conversation.

"Imani, I know I've wasted a lot of time. I was growing up. It took me a long time to be a man. But now, I'm more than a man. I'm your protector, your provider and above all your friend."

"Quinton, you better save some of that for the wedding." I put my arm around his waist to draw him closer.

He followed by putting his arm around my shoulders. "No need. It's from the heart. That's only the beginning of the changes to come," he said.

I was moved by his new impression of love. Quinton was never the man to wear his heart on his sleeve.

Quinton looked away to find the kids.

"Bryan, you bring them here. Y'all are going too far," he shouted.

The kids had begged us to take them swimming before we could even unpack.

"It's about time to start heading back to the hotel. Everybody's probably waiting on us for dinner," I said.

"Yeah, you're right," he said before calling the kids. "Bryan, Jah and Kai, it's time to go in."

We walked into the hotel through the back door. The kids stood amazed as they watched other guests being greeted by women wearing frilly skirts and off-the-shoulder tops repeating, hola and bien vienidos.

Once we got to the room, I pulled out my favorite DKNY sundress. Although I hadn't had a chance to wear it last summer, it instantly became my favorite. Not too dressy but enough for the occasion. It was a strapless, lavender dress with a sheer overlay that reached my ankles. I accessorized with matching stiletto sandals and a lavender clutch. My selection was a perfect choice for the island's stunning atmosphere and tropical weather.

Quinton walked out of the bathroom wearing a pair of tan Ralph Lauren slacks with the matching black Ralph Lauren short-sleeved shirt, a simple selection but he made it look rich as he dressed it with his favorite Rolex and Ferragamos. He looked good in almost anything but that night I seemed to view him in another light. Still, I couldn't shake this feeling. Something was not right.

Our boys were dressed alike in blue short sets with button-down shirts and matching hats. Kai, wanting to be the showstopper, chose her yellow sundress and clear slippers. She called them her Cinderella glass shoes. She wore her yellow sunglasses on top of her head and had let me press her hair before we left so she could wear it loose. I admired my family and myself for a couple of seconds more before we were ready to leave.

The family was meeting in the lobby of the Ritz-Carlton, the hotel where we were staying and would have our ceremony. As we exited the elevator, we were serenaded by the soft sounds of the piano as the pianist played "Close to You." Awaiting us were Shea, Charisse, Rodney, Nadine, James, Mama and my little sister, Anissa. Everyone was wearing his or her evening finest. Even Charisse who had sworn off short skirts and dresses that revealed her knees was wearing a beautiful peach cocktail dress. I placed my hand over my mouth, overcome by emotion.

Everyone cared enough about Quinton and me to travel on short notice and didn't even know yet how much this meant to us. All that was missing were Mia and John.

Every woman was escorted by one of the men to the outside of the hotel where we were greeted by a chauffeur and limo. Quinton hadn't told me about this part of the weekend. I guess it was better off that way. Everyone knew I loved surprises. Nadine and Mama's face lit up as they watched Quinton escort me over to a horse and buggy, just for the two of us. Charisse and Rodney took the kids inside the limo as Quinton assisted me in boarding the carriage.

This was a special treat for me because I had never had a carriage ride anywhere. For all of my twenty-eight years I'd longed for a night like this, and here it was with the only man I had ever loved and with whom I wanted to spend the rest of my life.

Shea in conversation with Nadine followed Charisse and Rodney's lead. Lastly James and Mama entered the limo. Still I had no idea where we were going. This was my first time to this island. Quinton must have done his research.

Minutes later we pulled in front of a restaurant that resembled a castle on the beach. Sparkling lights illuminated the building as rosebushes lead to the entrance. At the door, a man dressed as a knight greeted us carrying a diamond tiara on a red plush pillow. Quinton ushered me to the front of the crowd where he placed the tiara on my head and said, "This is for you, princess."

I was speechless. All of this, for me! After all those years of tears and fears, heartaches and headaches, here was my reward. After placing the tiara upon my head, Quinton bowed as the knight took us to our table.

I was seated at the head of the table with Mama to my left and as per my request Nadine to my right. Kai walked over to my side and whispered, "You look pretty, Mommy."

"Thank you, Baby. You look pretty too," I said, admiring my child's youthful grace and charm.

"Imani, Quinton has definitely outdone himself tonight," Charisse said from across the table.

"Girl, you didn't know about all this. I thought you knew," I said.

"No, girl please! Rodney and Q have been playing secret agent men. All I knew was what you and I had discussed that night. But you deserve it, Mani."

A loud, squeaky sound came over the sound system. Everyone turned to the stage. Quinton stood there with the microphone in his hand.

Quinton

The spotlight was on me. I closed my eyes and exhaled before I began speaking.

"Hey, Baby. How are you feeling? I hope this is to your liking."

A spotlight shone on Imani as she mouthed the word yes.

"I just want to show you how much you mean to me and the kids. To your family and friends. We may not tell you every day but you're definitely a princess. The kids and I would like to thank you for all the years of loving and caring you have given and for the years to come." I paused trying to remember what I had rehearsed.

Slowly I looked around at the crowd of patrons and continued, "Baby, I'm not going to sing a song or recite any poetry. I just wanted to say these words from my heart to yours. Imani, you are the backbone of this family. When times are hard and unbearable, you instill strength and faith in us. Just the other day you asked if I ever thought about where we would be if we weren't together. The truth is you saved me. I'm sure that the streets would have consumed and ultimately killed me if you hadn't kept pressuring me to go back to school, to grow up, to be a man. This man that I am today is because of you. Thank you. I love you." I paused and waited for the crowd to settle down. "Imani and I also have a surprise for our family. Imani and I planned to elope but since you all are here . . . you are invited to our wedding on Sunday." Again, oohs and aahs rose from the crowd.

Family rushed to gather Imani in a collection of hugs. Imani wiped away the tears that had begun to flow down her cheeks. She looked so good tonight. She looked good every day but this evening was different. Her glow displayed her radiant smile and cinnamon complexion. The dress complemented her supple curves as her breasts presented themselves atop the plunging neckline, giving just enough to notice but not enough to be tasteless. Perfect.

Everyone in the restaurant rose as I stepped down from the stage. I
walked toward Imani and blocked out everyone else. Once I reached my lady, I held her tightly and thanked her repeatedly for loving me.

It took several months to put this whole thing together but in the end it was definitely worth it. Just to see the genuine expression of joy that masked her face, I'd do it over and over. Omar's antics may have caused us to rush things but everything turned better than we had anticipated. Our initial plan was to have a private ceremony on the beach. No family, no friends. And although Imani agreed, her face couldn't disguise her unhappiness. It was important for her to have everyone present when we said, "I do." Her dreams had come true.

"That's what I'm talking about," Charisse shouted as the audience applauded.

"You made me proud, Q," Rodney said as he patted my shoulder.

"That's my baby," Mama hollered over the noise. "That's my baby! " After all the excitement died down and we finished eating, Imani and

I escaped to be alone. The kids stayed with Mama and James. We left

Charisse and Rodney in the bar getting drunk out of their minds. Shea and Nadine played cards in the hospitality room with other vacationers.

Back in our room, Imani slipped into something sheer and sexy. We popped open a bottle of Moet and watched the stars as we lay in each other's embrace on the balcony. We recapped the evening's events as we toasted to our new lives.

"Everyone took the wedding news unusually well," Imani said.

"Why do you say unusually? How else were they supposed to take it?" I questioned, confused by her statement.

"I thought they were going to be upset because we didn't include them in our plans."

"Imani, they understood our reason for keeping this a secret for so long. Could they blame us?"

"I guess not." She looked at her watch. "I hope Jada is doing okay."

"Is something wrong?"

"Her pregnancy is killing her. She started losing hair and gained so much weight the doctors had to put her on a diet."

"What are the doctors saying? Isn't that kind of thing normal?"

"Not really but . . ." I placed a finger over her soft lips.

"We'll worry about it tomorrow. She'll be fine. After she has the baby, her body will pop right back." I hope she doesn't ruin this moment, I thought.

We continued to soak in each other's loving vibes until there was a knock at the door. At first we decided to ignore it but we figured it must have been important if the person was coming so late. I picked up my bathrobe and went to the door. Through the peephole I see Rodney and Charisse. What the hell are they still doing up? I thought. I opened the door and let them in, shouting for Imani to cover up as Rodney stepped inside.

"Don't worry, Mani. We're not staying long," Charisse said in a drunken slur.

"Yo, Q. Come here." Rodney motioned for me to join him in the bathroom.

I walked to the bathroom while Charisse went to the balcony to wait with Imani.

"What's up, Rodney?" I asked.

"It's really none of my business, and excuse me if I'm getting personal but do you and Imani still use condoms?"

"Yeah . . . Rodney I know you not thinking about sliding up in Reese! She's a fucking lesbian." I was shocked by the turn of events.

"Shhh, nigga. Yo, if she was a lesbian she's not anymore. I had her on the fucking staircase wet as hell, begging for me to hit her off. Do you got some?" He turned his attention from me to the door and then back to me.

"Hold on. I gotta get them out of my suitcase. You sure you want to do this, Rod?"

"Nigga get me the fuckin' condoms," Rodney demanded.

I left the bathroom and headed toward our luggage, which was by the balcony. I heard Charisse telling Imani how big Rodney's dick was, which was more than I cared to hear.

"Reese, girl. You're drunk. Don't put yourself in this predicament. Let me take you to your room, and tomorrow if you still want him, he'll be here," Imani said to her friend.

"Imani listen." Charisse grabbed Imani's face and looked her square in the eye. "I'm on a fucking island, I'm horny as hell and I want to fuck."

Imani busted out in a boisterous laugh as Reese backed away. "Bitch, you drunk as hell and ain't never had no dick in your life. Once that nigga hit you off you going to begging for more because once you get a taste you never go back. Shit, look at me. I ain't never gonna leave Q. Not only because I love that nigga to death but he knows how to lay it down."

Imani paused then looked through the opening and said, "Right, Baby?"

I was too embarrassed to answer. I just wanted to give Rodney the condoms and get back to our own thang. I took the last two condoms out of Imani's makeup bag and handed them to Charisse as

I pushed her and Rodney out of the room. Whatever happened between them was their business. I wanted no parts of it.

Imani met me back inside. She propped herself up on some pillows and cocked her legs wide open.

"Do you want this?" she asked while she played with her pussy.

"Do I?"

I dropped my robe and hopped onto the bed. I kissed her from head to toe without missing an inch of her butter-soft flesh. In return, she gave me a hot-oil massage as she laid gentle kisses up and down my neck and licked behind my ear, allowing her breasts to briefly graze my skin. She then walked over to the corner with our suitcases and pulled out a small leather bag. She unzipped it and dumped the contents on the bed. There were handcuffs, French ticklers, anal beads, flavored condoms and much, much more.

"Where the hell did you get all this from?" I asked.

"I made a pit stop at the Pink Pussycat Boutique. I thought you might like to use a couple of these things on me. Fulfill some of those fantasies you were telling me about."

She didn't have to say another word. I had Imani bound and gagged within seconds. My insatiable appetite turned me into a wild beast as I changed from position to position. The thought of being in total control sent me into a feeding frenzy, and I didn't know when it would be over.

When daylight came through the balcony windows, we lay opposite each other stretched out across the length of the bed. My head was still spinning from the night before. I tried to bring myself to close the curtains but was too weak. Instead, I decided to wake Imani. Didn't make any sense to spend all our time sleeping.

I took her foot and placed kisses on each toe. She smiled.

"Good morning," I said.

"Hey. How are you feeling over there?" she asked as she propped herself up on a stack of pillows.

"I ain't gonna lie. I'm tired as hell. My body ain't like it used to be. Shit, I felt like I was going to have a heart attack last night after it was all over." I laughed, placing a hand over my heart.

"You're not the only one. My nanee feels like it's about to fall off."

She crawled to the other end of the bed and cuddled next to me.

"So, what's our plans for today?" I said as I licked her inner ear.

"Stop, nasty. I don't know. First I have to see what happened with Reese. You think they went through with it?"

"It's hard to tell with them. Both of them were pretty drunk last night. Why don't you call her room and find out."

I picked up the phone from the nightstand and handed it to her.

She put the receiver to her ear and dialed Charisse's three-digit room extension. She waited several rings but nobody answered.

"She's not there," she replied.

I took the phone and dialed Rodney's room. After three rings, a refreshed voice answered. "Hello."

"Reese? What the hell? Put Rodney on the phone."

They actually did it.

"I can't. He went to get us breakfast. Q, why didn't you introduce me to your friend a long time ago? He is the fucking man." Charisse sounded happy.

"I don't want to hear this shit. Hold on." I passed the phone back to

Imani and then went to the shower.

Imani

"So, girl, what was it like? I can't believe your old ass finally made the switch. What made you change your mind?" I asked.

"Damn, one thing at a time. You acting like people don't do this kind of thing."

In the background Rodney was asking her to whom she was talking. There was a kissing sound before she returned to the phone.

"Anyway, I can't talk right now. Breakfast just came in. What time are you going to the beach?"

I couldn't believe she was going to leave me hanging.

"Q and I are about to get dressed and try to catch up with Mama and the kids. Probably about three. It's almost one now," I said as I turned the clock on the nightstand.

"All right. I have to talk to you later," she said before hanging up.

"Q," I hollered, "let me tell you about our best friends." I laughed before entering the bathroom.

The day turned to night as we continued to absorb the island's delights. The kids played and played until they were too exhausted to move. James and Mama had decided to turn in early. Mama said it was the perfect time to catch up on all those nights of sleep she lost raising Q. Nadine, Shea and Anissa finally showed up. They had spent the day shopping and doing all the wonderful mother-and-daughter things Nadine missed doing with me. Nadine had brought several things that she found in the shopping area for the kids and me. Shea carried Anissa to Mama's room while Nadine, Charisse, Rodney, Q and I went to the bar for drinks.

At first, Q raised a questioning brow when he saw Nadine and Shea together but then he realized Shea was old enough to make his own decisions. It was probably the Puerto Rican love spell that had captured everyone else.

We spent the better part of the evening joking around and reminiscing. Since Q, Rodney and myself attended the same high school we had a lot more to talk about. Rodney started telling everybody about Quinton thinking I was a stalker when we were younger but I didn't remember it being that serious.

The entire evening Rodney and Charisse stood wrapped in each other's arms. It was kind of awkward to see Reese with a man after almost ten years of women but it was good to see them happy. I didn't know how long it was gonna last.

"So Nadine, we haven't heard about you. Tell us about your family. You told me you had a stepson. Where is he now?" I asked.

"That ungrateful bastard. I don't feel like talking about him," She inhaled deeply and exhaled slowly. "He's not worth getting upset."

"Oh, sorry. I didn't mean to upset you," I apologized.

"Ooh. Do y'all hear that? They're finally playing something I can dance to. Come on, Rodney, show me whatcha workin' wit'," Charisse said, imitating the voice of Mystikal as "Shake Ya Ass" poured through the speakers.

"I'm not much of a dancer, Reese," he responded.

"Just do what you were doing last night. I'll handle the rest," she teased.

"Oh, they're crazy," I said as everyone laughed.

Rodney called Q over to join them. Quinton pulled my wrist and lead me onto the dance floor.

The rest of the night was spent partying and drinking until I passed out. I can safely say this was the best vacation I had taken. And the next day would be the icing on the cake. After Q and I got married, my heart would at last be at ease.

CHAPTER 25
THE FINAL GOOD-BYE

Imani

The next morning, I woke up in Charisse's room. Mia had flown in that morning and was getting all the details from Charisse. Kai was running around in her panties, and her hair was standing on top of her head like a wild child.

"Where's Q?" I asked Charisse who was standing in front of my dress.

"Last night was your last night as a single woman. The next time you see your man you will be walking down the aisle to be Mrs. Quinton Banks." Charisse was extremely bubbly.

"My baby girl is getting married. Why weren't you going to tell me?" Mia asked as she wiped the crust out of my eyes.

"I'm sorry, Mia. I just wanted everything to really happen this time. If it didn't, I couldn't blame anyone else but us. You understand, right?"

"Of course I do. I'm so happy for you." She pulled me closer and hugged me with all her might.

As I got a chance to look around the room, I noticed several bouquets of roses. People were walking in and out, moving and rearranging.

"What the hell is going on here?" I exclaimed.

"I know you didn't think I was going to let you have some ole plain Jane wedding."

Nadine came walking over to the bed with a thin square box.

Inside were the most beautiful pearls and matching earrings I had ever seen. Between each pearl were clusters of diamonds. The earrings contained a cluster of diamonds with a teardrop-shaped pearl that hung down. My mouth stood open as Nadine placed the exquisite piece of jewelry around my neck.

"You didn't have to do this. This had to be costly," I said as I ran my fingers over each detailed jewel.

"I know that but I wanted you to have the very best." She placed a tender kiss on my forehead and then backed up to give me a once-over. "Baby, you are not going to go walking down the aisle to the man you love looking like God-knows-what. We need to get you to a spa."

"Nadine, I didn't plan to have a big ole extravagant wedding. We planned it small and simple," I replied.

"Listen, there is nothing small or simple about you," Charisse said, agreeing with Nadine. "You and Q deserve this, Imani. Just sit back and let us handle this."

"I can take care of Kai until you come back. And, Nadine, if you need I'll get Anissa ready before you return," Mia volunteered.

That was it. Everything was settled. All that was left for me to do was shower and allow myself to be pampered, like a true princess should be.

Two hours later I had a manicure, pedicure, facial and a wash and set. In another hour I was scheduled to meet my husband-to-be on the beach where our ceremony would take place. Nadine put out a finger to flag down a taxi to take us back to the hotel. A black Town Car pulled over. We sat inside and give the driver the name and address of the hotel.

After about fifteen minutes, I realized we hadn't reached the hotel, which was about five to ten minutes away.

"Excuse me, I said the Ritz-Carlton. Where are you going?" I asked.

"Shut the fuck up and sit back, bitch! " The partition rolled down, and on the other side was my nightmare. "Omar?" I cried.

"Yeah, bitch. You thought I was going to let you go that easy," he replied in a crazed tone. "Hello, Nadine."

"Omar, what the fuck are you doing? Pull this fucking car over and let her out! She has nothing to do with this," Nadine pleaded.

My heart pounded a thousand times a second as the horror continued. My mother and Omar? The drama became too much for me to bear as I began to hyperventilate.

"Omar, pull over. She can't breathe! " Nadine hollered as she fanned me with a magazine.

"We're almost there. Just wait a fucking minute," he said as he rolled up the partition.

Seconds later the car came to a screeching halt. Omar opened my door and put a gun to my head. "Don't try no shit, bitch. Just get the fuck out and stay quiet." He grabbed my arm and slung me to the ground.

He allowed Nadine to walk freely as he held my arm behind my back and led me to an abandoned shed.

"What do you want from me, Omar? I'm sorry we didn't work out. Please just let me go," I pleaded as he dragged me into the boarded shed.

"Sorry. I'll show you sorry. All I wanted was to be with you. But you never gave me a chance." He paused then looked over to Nadine. "And you, you took my daughter away from me. You told me you loved me. Liar! Like mother, like daughter."

This man had lost his ever-loving mind. Omar had gone over the brink.

"I did love you but you started acting crazy. All you ever cared about was the money. You didn't give two shits about Anissa or me," Nadine said.

"You're wrong. I do love you and I love the girl too. You said we would split the money my father left her. Instead you took it all and left. You grimy, lying bitch," he said as he paced. "And then I find out you signed over all your money to her." He pointed the gun at me.

"Omar, please let her go. She didn't know about any of this. Please. I promise to make it all up to you."

Nadine walked slowly over to him and put her hand on his face.

"You used me. That's why you came back? To use me as your cover?" I cried. "Why didn't you just stay the fuck out of my life?"

"It's not how it sounds. Imani, let me explain," Nadine said.

"Last time I let you explain you conned me into giving you my social security number," I said as I recalled the time she called and asked for the information to buy some savings bonds for the kids. I should have known. I was so excited to have her back in my life I left myself vulnerable.

"Boo-hoo. Fuck all this shit. I'll let you go on two conditions. One, I want my daughter. Two, I want my share of the businesses and investments," Omar bargained.

The greed in Nadine's eyes told me that she was not going to agree.

"Your father left the businesses to me. He knew you weren't capable of keeping them running. And Anissa stays with me. She's not going anywhere near your crazy ass."

"I didn't ask you. I'm telling you what I want. And I'm going to get it or your pride and joy is going to die," Omar warned.

Quinton

It was about that time. Rodney and I walked into the beachside chapel and were greeted by family. John and James were minding the boys while we talked with Charisse and Mia.

Imani occupied my mind as the stars shone brightly and the soft gentle breezes blew mixing the sweet scents of perfumes and flowers. Smooth sounds of the shores played their relaxing song as I contemplated what was about to happen. I sat in the window, looking in amazement over the crowd. The sidewalks were filled with people waiting for that precise moment…Where could she be?

Charisse began to fidget as she looked over the crowd. She tugged lightly on Rodney's jacket and pulled him to the side. I didn't pay it much attention. I figured she was having second thoughts about their relationship. Rodney nervously looked around and then rushed to my side.

"Q, Reese said Imani's not upstairs. No one knows where she is. She left with Nadine hours ago and ain't come back yet."

"No! " I yelled. "This is not fucking happening. I knew Nadine was no fucking good. Where did she go last?"

"She said they were going to a spa," Charisse answered.

"All right. I'm gonna…" My cell phone began to vibrate at my side. I answered the call, hoping it was Imani. In the background were voices. Male and female. Arguing. No…fighting. I checked the number on my

Caller ID. The call was coming from Imani's phone.

"Omar, don't . . ." the female voice screamed. It sounded like Nadine.

Imani

I struggled to gather my emotions as pictures of life passed by. Nana, Justin, Dad. Everything I had ever wanted. Then visions of Quinton flooded my thoughts. People say you never truly appreciate what you have until it's gone. I thought of the many trials and tribulations we had to endure . . . Was this really the end?

I put my head down, not wanting to witness the outcome. After I finished praying, I opened my eyes and realized the green light on my phone was blinking. My phone must have dialed a number when Omar threw me to the floor. Immediately, I started screaming. "Q, he's got me. Anybody please help me. We're on the beach."

"Who are you calling for? Shut the fuck up! Nadine, handle her," Omar said as he put the gun to my temple.

"Mani, please baby. We're going to get out of here. Just wait." Nadine quivered as she spoke.

"Omar, why the fuck did you bring us here? There's nothing Nadine can do from this raggedy-ass shed." I hoped there was someone listening on the other end of the phone.

"She's right, Omar. Take us back to the hotel. I can make a couple of phone calls and have the money transferred to your account by morning," Nadine said.

"What about the girl? Do I get Anissa?" Omar asked.

"What do you want her for? You don't know how to take care of a little girl," Nadine said with attitude.

"I know my father left her a lump sum of money. Why wouldn't he leave his baby girl some security?" Omar said.

"He didn't leave her anything. He knew Anissa wasn't his. I told him everything his last night in the hospital." Nadine huffed.

"Why are you lying to me?" Omar's chest began to heave as he stepped closer to Nadine.

It was obvious she was lying. Her greed was going to be the death of us both. I continued to scream as Omar swung his gun wildly in the air. Suddenly, two shots rang out. He shot two holes in the ceiling. In a desperate attempt to save our lives Nadine lunged at Omar. Nadine struggled to get the gun from Omar as I stood in the corner.

Quinton

Something sounding like gunshots came over the phone as we continued to listen.

Rodney had called the local officials and had them search the beach for a cabin or an old house. One of the officers had remembered an old boathouse on the other end of the beach. We loaded into the jeeps and headed toward the house.

Charisse stayed behind with Mia and the rest of the women while Rodney, James and Shea followed in another car.

When we reached the old shed, sounds of a struggle were coming from the inside. The officials surrounded the house. I began to walk toward the shed but Rodney held me back.

"Let them handle this, Q. We ain't got shit on us," Rodney whispered.

"That's my wife in there. Fuck a gun."

An earth-shattering scream followed by a series of shots came out of the wooden shelter. The officials burst in the door and yelled, "Put your hands up."

Another shot was fired toward the police, and in retaliation, they opened fire.

After the exchange died down, I broke loose from Rodney's hold and ran toward the shed. My heart began to swell. The thought of walking in, finding Imani dead weakened my knees. The officers brought out Omar's bloody body on a stretcher. An ambulance pulled up and paramedics rushed into the house. I stood paralyzed outside waiting for Imani to be brought out next.

The paramedics brought out a woman on another stretcher and my heart shattered. I walked over to view Imani's angelic face one last time.

As I drew nearer, I realized that this woman was too thin and much too fair to be Imani. When I got closer to the body, I knew Nadine was gone.

Two police officers called for me to come inside the shed. My body felt limp. Rodney came and carried me as I leaned on him. Inside the shed, Imani stood tied in the corner. Her head was down and her eyes were closed. Paramedics were checking her vitals while a police officer untied her hands. Blood stained the left side of her shirt. She had been shot. One of the paramedics reached into his bag and took out a small white capsule. He broke it in half and passed it under her nose. Within seconds Imani had come to.

Imani

The pain from to my shoulder had caused me to pass out. As I focused, I cried at the sight of my angel. Q ran over to my side. Rodney walked outside the shed and shouted, "She's alive."

Quinton put his strong arms around me. "Imani, oh, Baby. I'm sorry."

I screamed out in pain, "Quinton, my shoulder." Quickly he released me and continued to apologize.

"What are you sorry for? It wasn't your fault. Nadine. . ." I paused to look around. "Where's Nadine? Q, where's my mother? No! " I broke into a hysterical cry as I realized she was gone—this time for good.

At the station, Q gave the complete history of Omar and Nadine, which he concluded through research and pieces of what I had told him.

Nadine and Omar both were scheming on Omar's father's money. Together they comprised a plan to get hold of all his money and assets. Part of their plan was bearing a child, hence, Anissa. Omar had no idea Nadine was so evil and conniving. Quinton said that after Nadine disappeared Omar had been having me watched and followed. He figured if she ever did show up, the first place would be wherever I was.

Nadine's reappearance had nothing to do with wanting to be a mother, or did it? I realized she put her life on the line for me. She left me all her most valued possessions—both her money and her life. Although her ways

of going about it were misconstrued, I realized it was her way of showing me she did love me and wanted to make up for the past.

EPILOGUE
NINE MONTHS LATER

Quinton

The doorbell rang several times before we answered. I opened the door and a thin Caucasian man dressed in a drab black suit handed me an envelope.

Imani yelled from the living room.

"Who is it?"

"I don't know. He gave me this," I said as I showed her the long envelope.

She stood from her rocking chair and began walking toward me.

"Who's it from?" She asked as she fed our newborn.

"Doesn't say." I opened the envelope to find several sheets of paper. It was the last will and testament of Nadine Allen.

The will stated that she left everything—all her businesses, assets and savings—to her six kids to be divided evenly. Imani would have stood to gain the most since she had already received two hundred and fifty thousand dollars. It was in her account when we came back to New York but no sooner had she discovered the money; she put it in trust funds for Anissa, Kai, Brian and Jahlek.

Life had definitely taken us for an adventurous ride. But I was glad to finally have everything restored to its natural order. All those years of drama could definitely make me appreciate the simpler things in life. Without all the glitz and glamour of the fast life and its popularity, I was still full of love and life. With it, I was completely satisfied.

I decided to give up that life—the street life. I had allowed myself to become consumed by the same influences that had torn my father from his home and ultimately began to pull me from my own. Unlike my father, I had priorities and although it may have taken longer than anticipated, I finally had them in order. There was no chance for me to follow his footsteps. My family was too important and extremely instrumental in my life, to let them go.

An associate of mine sold us his family's five bedroom Colonial house in Allentown, Pennsylvania. When we first visited the house it was boarded up and surrounded by bare trees, shabby rose bushes and patchy grass. However, Imani felt a connection with the old house and since we were desperate to leave New York with our expanding family we bought it and worked diligently to restore its natural beauty.

Our house set on Sumner Avenue, was surrounded by a large yard enclosed in a picket fence for privacy from our neighbors and tall trees to keep our treasure discreet from passerby on the main road. It took us nearly a year to complete but once we were done our home was filled with warmth and comfort. Our new home was a perfect fit for our new family.

As for Imani and me, yes, we were finally married. On Valentine's Day, Imani and I had a very private ceremony in our home. Our kids were our only witnesses. Imani eventually quit her job and decided being a stay- at-home mom wasn't a bad idea.

Imani

Quinton and I have beaten the odds. We made it through the stormy weather and stood united as one.

Life blessed everyone. Once again John and Mia were left to raise Nadine's little girl. Ironically, Anissa was the same age I was when Nadine left. John and Mia's daughter Amber regarded Anissa as a big sister instead of an aunt. Mia tried not to become attached to the little girl at first. She wasn't ready to raise another one of Nadine's children. Mia was concentrating on raising her own. But, as time passed, Mia warmed up to her and opened her house and her heart. John and Mia decided to adopt Anissa, and it was finalized earlier in the month.

Even Reese had found happiness in her new heterosexual relationship with Rodney. They were still a couple and were expecting their own child soon. Reese's ex-fiancée, Myra, didn't act too surprise when Charisse broke off the engagement. Reese said that Myra called and asked if she changed her mind but Reese told her she was happy with Rodney but promised Myra, she'd be the first one to know.

It seemed the Puerto Rican love elixir that flowed brought new heights of passion in everyone.

And after years of sporadic lovemaking sessions, Quinton and I had finally conceived our second child. It had to be the island's love spell.

Unfortunately, Jada lost her baby in labor. Doctors say it may have been from the stress but we knew it was from the constant beatings. Since then, Jada had left Craig and moved into our old house in Queens with Diamond.

Needless to say, life has definitely taught me a lesson or two. For so long I thought that if I could have my mother back, my life would come together. Somehow it seemed as if she was the missing link that kept my life from being complete. But now I know, to be completely satisfied means to accept today for what it is, as it is. The longer I held on to the past, the longer it would take to truly appreciate life, love and all the other blessings that lay ahead.

Quinton was the one to fill that void but I never took time to realize it.

And after all was said and done, my life had come to revolve around my husband and our family, the old—Kai, Jah and Bryan, and the new—our blessings, our new home and our newborn baby-girl.

FROM THE AUTHOR

People wanted to know why I choose the title Completely Satisfied and what it means to me. Through much conversation and interrogation, I have found the phrase to be used casually but its definition is very complex. For me, being completely satisfied is to simply accept today for what it is regardless of where your past may have led. To continue to dwell on history will only build anguish inside, causing inner turmoil and dissatisfaction.

First, we must find inner peace in what we have become, despite life's experiences. Consider our experiences as a lesson learned and find ways to use the knowledge in our future decisions. Second, we must have faith, patience and trust in our evolving relationships, both with family and chosen partners. Last, for complete satisfaction we must live realistically and know that life is not cut out for us; we must pave our own way. Each of these rules I have had to discover through personal experience that has brought me to where I am today, being completely satisfied.

Live life to your own set of rules and make the most of every moment. Life is much too short to wonder about the should haves, could haves, would haves. You'll never be able to move forward if you're always looking back.

Books and Blessings,
Danette Maroney

www.ingramcontent.com/pod-product-compliance
Lightning Source LLC
Chambersburg PA
CBHW061940170626
46813CB00006B/2481